D1522042

FRESH SNOW on BEDFORD FALLS

second chances

G. L. GOODING

ISBN: 978-1-4834-7472-4 (sc)
ISBN: 978-1-4834-7470-0 (hc)
ISBN: 978-1-4834-7471-7 (e)

Library of Congress Control Number: 2017913193

Lulu Publishing Services rev. date: 04/18/2018

For my mother, Velma Gooding, who at 101 is still helping
to make the lives of so many others wonderful.

People find meaning and redemption in the
most unusual human connections.
—Khaled Hosseini

PREFACE

The idea for *Fresh Snow on Bedford Falls* emerged decades after I first saw *It's a Wonderful Life*. This classic film was released the same month I was born, which may have preordained its niche in my life.

For forty-plus years, *IAWL* was a tradition in my household. I would coerce or beg my family to view the picture and watch me cry. One by one, however, the kids escaped to their own lives, leaving me to watch alone.

During one of those solitary viewings, two things I had missed over the years suddenly struck me. First, I noticed that Henry Potter remained embittered and unmoved while everyone else, including the bank examiner, was rejoicing at the end of the movie. Was that intentional or an oversight on the part of the screenwriter?

Second, the show's ending was idealized. Don't get me wrong. The ending was right for the movie; it made me cry every time. But surely there would have been some nasty consequences due to that missing $8,000. What would a more realistic ending have been?

These questions surfaced each year as the credits rolled. They were soon buried, however, under years of work and family responsibilities. Then a marvelous thing happened. I retired and found the time to create answers for these nagging questions.

It may seem odd for someone to research answers to questions generated by a fictional movie. But there I was two years ago doing just that while giving new life to so many beloved characters. The story truly took on a life of its own. Like a sculptor facing a hunk of formless stone, I was unsure what lay within. What ultimately appeared on the pages of *Fresh Snow on Bedford Falls* was quite surprising.

ACKNOWLEDGMENTS

As is the case with anyone writing his or her first book, my experience of writing an acknowledgment was new and daunting. I seriously considered not including this page to save many important people in my life great embarrassment should this work prove to be folly. In the end, however, I decided to acknowledge some folks not so much for their input on this book but for their impact and inspiration on my life.

I want to acknowledge the hardworking and resilient people of the Midwest, where I grew up without much but felt I missed nothing.

To my fifth-grade teacher, the late Miss Lavin, who chose to encourage rather than stifle my imagination, I say thanks. And I owe my enduring joy of writing to another teacher, a nun who taught English at Springfield Junior College, who took interest and time to encourage this undisciplined writer.

I also recognize the valuable writing experience gained in my work and church life. Who says one can't be a creative writer at work? The amateur plays and articles I wrote over forty years certainly taught me much, including the motivation of applause.

This book could not have been completed without the great assistance of many people at Lulu Publications. Their patience, advice, and encouragement were unceasing.

Also, I could not have completed the task without the help of Allan Jones and Marie Selander. Their many hours of editing, proofing, and providing feedback were invaluable.

For all my friends who have been there for me even while wondering whether I'd ever complete this or any other book, this is for you.

Last, this book would not have been completed without the help and support of my wife. Sarah has been my greatest supporter, my harshest critic, and too often an undeserving target of my frustrations.

PROLOGUE

Bedford Falls Gazette

FEBRUARY 11, 1919

Youth Saves Drowing Brother From Frozen Pond

George Bailey is called a hero for rescuing younger brother Harry with the help of friends. The incident occurred on pond owned by the Wainwright family at …

Bedford Falls Gazette

JUNE 10, 1928

Peter Bailey Dead

President of Building and Loan dies suddenly on Saturday. Future of business is in doubt.

Bedford Falls Gazette

SEPTEMBER 11, 1928

George Bailey Named President Of Bailey Building and Loan

After a contentious board meeting, Peter Bailey's son, George agreed to forgo college and take over helm of the B&L. His decision thwarted an effort by Henry Potter to close the business stating …

Bedford Falls Gazette

SOCIETY PAGE MAY 31, 1931

Bailey Weds

New Princeton grad Harry Bailey arrived home with a degree in one hand and a bride, Ruth on his arm. The news took family by surprise. According to brother George, the couple will not be joining the family business, instead choosing research in Rochester where Ruth's father, …

Bedford Falls Gazette

MAY 1, 1932

Run On Bank

The April 28th run on Bedford Falls Bank resulted not only in its closing until Monday, May 9th but a change in ownership. Henry F. Potter assumed control but failed in an attempt to buy up Bailey Building and Loan shares. The B&L's future, however, remains in doubt. The run started …

Bedford Falls Gazette

SOCIETY PAGE MAY 1, 1932

Bailey/Hatch Wed

George Bailey and Mary Hatch wed at the widow Bailey's home on April 28th. The bride and groom delayed their honeymoon due to the banking crisis, which …

Bedford Falls Gazette

DECEMBER 8, 1941

War Declared

Bedford Falls Gazette

DECEMBER 25, 1945

Christmas Eve Miracle Saves Building And Loan

Community's generosity replaced a lost deposit and rescued the Bailey Building and loan last night. Mumbling something about having a guardian angel, George Bailey said the money was just one part of a wonderful and miraculous night. While the Baileys and town celebrated, however, Henry Potter informed this reporter that he would be demanding a full investigation into the missing money. He went on to say …

CHAPTER 1

George Bailey should have been smiling despite the harsh winter wind he was fighting on the walk to work that Thursday after Christmas. It had been just two days since he and his building and loan had faced ruin. But thanks to the generosity of many friends, disaster was avoided, the B&L would open that morning, and he was free.

Trudging up Main Street, he managed a halfhearted smile and wave at Mr. Gower, who was sweeping a dusting of overnight snow from outside the drugstore. The still youthful-looking George was thankful not to encounter anyone else on the street in the bitter cold. He was in no mood for conversation as he approached the familiar stairs to his business.

The holiday had started with plenty of joy and wonder to go around. Indeed, Christmas Eve had seen a nightmare end, with carol singing and the tinkling of glasses and bells. Everyone was ecstatic, believing the crisis had been put to rest. Even George was caught up in the celebration for a while, humbled by all his good fortune.

Then he slowly began to realize that what had happened couldn't truly be over. With each passing day, Bailey fretted more and more. Even depositing the $8,000 donated by the townsfolk to balance the books did little to ease his concern. Sensing that Henry Potter was still conniving to destroy the building and loan given his latest effort to do so had failed added to his uneasiness.

George shunned his usual habit of taking the steps two at a time; he was not eager to face the day. It was still a half hour before the doors officially opened, but as he entered, he found everyone at his or her usual post—Tilly in her chair with headset in place, Eustace at the counter filling the cash drawer, and Uncle Billy visible through his half-open office door.

"Morning, George" came the greeting in unison from his cousins.

George managed a mumbled response as he headed quickly to his office. He heard a loud and joyful "Welcome back" from Uncle Billy's office, but he didn't respond.

As Eustace turned the calendar to December 27, 1945, George paused at his door and told Tilly, "Please hold my calls. I have a lot to catch up on. I'll let you know when I'm available."

"Sure thing, George." Tilly nodded toward the back room. "Fresh coffee is on the stove."

Waving the suggestion off, he entered his office to rehash the matters to be addressed but not knowing exactly what to do about them. There was the issue of the excess money donated to replace the money lost, some $3,000. It had come from many people—some shareholders but most not. Even if he took an $8,000 loan from Sam Wainwright so he had the total donated on hand, there was no way to determine what portion each person had given. He was certain those folks had wanted to rescue him and the building and loan but not provide the institution an unnecessary and undeserved windfall.

Then there was the long-term impact on the reputation of the B&L. Under the cold, gray light of dawn, would all the shareholders—those who had donated and those who had not—recognize what had happened and grow concerned about the security of their money? The books were balanced, but there was still the matter of what had happened to the original deposit. If not resolved, it was possible, perhaps even probable, that faith in the institution would wane and the shareholders might sell their shares, perhaps to Potter. George knew the old man would not rest until he had killed the B&L or died trying.

Then there was the most critical issue of all. The state bank examiner would surely launch an investigation into the disappearance of the money regardless of the fact that it had been replaced. In fact, the authorities would undoubtedly frown on the way the money was restored, especially given the lack of records from that night.

In one respect, he welcomed an investigation, hoping it would lead to the swift discovery of the money and the cause of its disappearance. On the other hand, if the money was never found or the B&L wasn't cleared of blame, the disaster everyone thought had been avoided could still happen.

Bailey felt committed to keeping these disturbing possibilities to himself for the time being. His staff, especially Uncle Billy, and the rest of the family would likely be traumatized when they learned what loomed on the horizon. The longer he could put off informing them while strategizing how best to address each issue, the better.

In his room at the Bedford Falls Hotel, Mark Jerome stared out the window at the town coming to life. The citizenry moved about with purpose in the cold as the first flakes of a new storm came blowing in. The scene brought back pleasant memories of the man's life not long past while he delayed beginning his assignment.

This was his first solo work, and he was nervous. Of course, that was quite silly given the circumstances. This was, after all, only one among an infinite number of ongoing assignments, many more important and difficult than his as a beginner. Beyond a possible delay in his advancement or future opportunities, there was nothing at all to risk for him.

Jerome had been deceased for some two years. In the intervening time, he had slowly adjusted to his new universe and his unique angelic duties. Thorough training had been followed by several successes in assignments paired with his seniors. Joseph had tapped him for this job on the recommendation of his mentor.

As an Angel Third Class, AS3 for short, Jerome would be operating with even greater restrictions than his mentor had faced on recent visits to this same town. In spite of those handicaps, Clarence had made a triumphant return only days earlier from Bedford Falls. With pride, Mr. Oddbody had finally received his hard-earned promotion and wings as an AS1.

The lack of available angelic tools didn't overly concern Jerome. After all, the first part of the assignment seemed right up his alley. In life, he'd been a police detective, which had given him skills that should serve him well. Joseph had been wise to pick this for his first solo effort.

Two other things did concern him, however. First was the fact that the other part of the assignment dealt with redemption and forgiveness, things foreign to him as a detective. His job had been to solve crimes, not pass judgment or manage rehabilitation.

The second concern was the little information he'd been given to work with before leaving. AS3s were expected to operate in the field with few details and discover crucial aspects of any one "case," as Jerome called it, along the way. Apparently, succeeding under such constraints was vital to an angel's learning to bridge the gap between two worlds while resolving earthly problems.

Clarence had told him that these restrictions created the opportunity for new angels to shed any remnants of their earthly lives—bad habits, so to speak—that might negatively impede outcomes. His mentor joked that this practice had worked only marginally on his persistent naïveté and indecisiveness. Jerome thought the whole exercise was wasted on him.

Jerome had never lacked for self-confidence during his forty years on earth; he was sure that once his investigatory talents had solved the matter of the missing $8,000, the rest of the assignment would be finished quickly. His cockiness, impatience, and myopic focus while working cases had often caused him problems. Still, he had clung stubbornly to these habits on earth, feeling they were critical to seeing justice served. This commitment, instilled by his strict policeman father, had driven him since childhood. Being totally honest, Jerome had to admit those qualities had cost him much along the way, ultimately his life.

These conflicting thoughts heightened his anxiety and delayed him from taking the first step. Feelings of uncertainty were new to him. Perhaps this was what his superiors had in mind—trying to get him to address what they saw as his earthly flaws. If that were true, the message seemed to be that he needed to exercise more caution and patience.

Jerome shook his head emphatically at such an unnecessary lesson while gazing once more at the street. Fresh snow had already started to accumulate, a clear sign that he'd waited long enough. He reached for the phone and began focusing on the earthly role he had to play.

It was a near blizzard as George trudged across Main Street and pushed into the hotel lobby. He was initially surprised to get the call so soon from the investigator for the state bank examiner's office. After all, Christmas was hardly over. Then he remembered all the efforts Henry Potter had made that awful night trying to get him arrested. Given the old man's connections, it suddenly made sense.

Stomping snow from his shoes, he looked around for someone he didn't recognize. A man rose from a lobby chair and stepped toward George. Sticking out a meaty hand, he asked, "Mr. Bailey?"

George took his hand unenthusiastically. "Mr. Jerome, I presume?"

"Yes, Mark Jerome. Thank you for meeting me on such short notice."

The two released their grips and headed for the restaurant.

"As I mentioned, I'm a licensed investigator with the New York State Bank Examiner's office. And as such—"

The maître d' interrupted Jerome to say their table was ready.

The two were soon seated at a secluded corner table with a window looking out on a winter wonderland. Menus were distributed, and the two were alone.

Jerome pulled something from his pocket. "Here's my card. As I was about to say, I am deputized by the state examiner's office and the court to function with full authority."

"Like the police?" George asked cautiously.

"Well, I'll be working with the police here, but I also have powers, granted by the SBE's office, much like a district attorney," Jerome said matter-of-factly.

That last statement made George uneasy. "That sounds rather ominous."

"Not intended, Mr. Bailey. Just stating the facts so we understand why I'm here and my authority to conduct an investigation. I have a meeting scheduled with Chief Cook after the New Year. I discovered this morning that he will be on vacation until then."

"I see."

Jerome smiled. "Until that meeting, I'll be doing some background work. Now, shall we order before we get down to business?" I've already eaten, so I'll stick with coffee." George said shaking his head.

Jerome nodded. "Suits me." He waved the waiter over.

The two did just that and sipped coffee and assessed each other in silence. George fixed Jerome as a man near his own age of thirty-eight but much shorter and quite stout. His coal-black hair in need of a comb framed a ruddy complexion and dark brown eyes. His dark suit was a bit dated but of good quality. He wore a white shirt and narrow striped tie. In short, he looked the part of a detective or investigator.

As the waiter poured a refill, the restaurant fell silent with the arrival of two men. During this lull, a gaunt figure maneuvered a wheelchair-bound figure to a table occupied by three obviously nervous men. George frowned deeply, recognizing them all as members of the B&L board.

Jerome's voice drew George back. "Let me guess. That must be Mr. Potter—correct?"

"Yes." George sounded resentful.

"He's been busy these last few days," Jerome said with a slight smile.

George scowled. "I'll bet."

"It seems the man thinks the B&L and you specifically are evil incarnate."

It was George's turn to smile. "Well, whatever we are, he's been trying to kill us for years."

"That sounds like a good place to start," Jerome said. "Please fill me in on events leading up to the recent unpleasantness. I could use the education."

"Aren't you afraid I'll be biased in the telling?"

"If you are, I'll root that out as I go forward. You'll find I'm quite good at my job, Mr. Bailey."

George started then paused. "How far back do you want me to go?"

"Since this conflict with Potter seems to go way back, why don't you start there?"

George nodded and gave Jerome a *Reader's Digest* version of events leading up to the disappearance of the money. He covered everything from the time his father, Peter Bailey, had died and he had taken over the B&L. He remained focused on business matters, glossing over other things such as his marriage and children.

Jerome was most interested in the events surrounding the run on the bank and the near-closure of the B&L, the job offer from Potter, and other battles with the old man at board meetings and the like. George concluded by sharing what he knew about the events of the past Christmas Eve, including a proud reference to his brother's Congressional Medal of Honor.

Putting down his fork, Jerome probed further. "The local papers quoted Mr. Potter as saying you admitted to him that you had lost that eight thousand dollars."

"Oh, right." George leaned in to avoid being overheard. "I can see that would appear to be damning information, but it's not what it appears to be."

"You mean what Mr. Potter said didn't happen?"

"Oh, it did."

Jerome's eyes widened.

Noticing the investigator's look, George hurried on. "I said that to protect my Uncle Billy in case the money wasn't found. After all, as the president of the B&L, I was ultimately responsible for that money."

George was silent as Jerome digested that.

"So what do you think happened to the money?" Jerome asked.

George replied as he chewed. "I'm not sure. It might have been lost, but I doubt it." He paused to wash down the food with coffee. "Either way, lost or stolen, it doesn't bode well for the B&L."

At that moment, Potter and his entourage slowly left the restaurant en masse. Once they were out of earshot, Jerome leaned in and spoke in a low voice. "That's why I'm here—to answer that question and to find that money and the person or persons responsible."

George nodded. "And I know my uncle and I are prime suspects."

"You don't seem overly concerned about that, Mr. Bailey."

"Not about our criminal activity. But unless you find someone else responsible, the B&L is doomed," George said with a frown. "So please be quick about it."

"I understand."

"Good." George shifted gears. "Do you have any other suspects on your list?"

Jerome chuckled. "Other than the entire town?" His smile disappeared. "It would be inappropriate for me to speculate on that at this point." Jerome paused to pay the bill. "I will say that I have neither identified nor eliminated anyone yet."

"Of course. Please excuse my impatience."

"I know the feeling well." Jerome's smile returned. "I suffer the same affliction. I'm eager to get started. To that end, I'd like to talk with your employees."

George nodded. "There's a spare room at the B&L. Will that do?"

"Excellent, Mr. Bailey."

The two men shook on it and moved to the lobby. "I plan to conduct several more interviews before the day is done."

"That's an aggressive schedule," George said as they paused at the hotel entrance to put on their coats. Then he smiled adding, "And that suits me fine. You'll find my staff quite guileless, Mr. Jerome, especially my uncle. Follow me."

George plunged into what was now a full-fledged storm and hurriedly crossed the street with the investigator close behind. Wisps of snow followed both men up the stairs to the Building and Loan office.

CHAPTER 2

The investigator soon understood what George had meant about the Bailey clan. Billy Bailey proved to be among the most trusting people he'd ever met. He was too candid for his own good; he glossed over nothing, took full blame, but for what he couldn't say. At the conclusion of the interview, Jerome felt Billy might not have been all there. What *was* there, however, convinced him that the man might have lost the money but was incapable of stealing it. If it had been stolen, however, Billy, poor "Mr. String Finger," was the perfect patsy.

Eustace and Tilly also proved to be poor suspects. They had alibis and witnesses to their whereabouts all Christmas Eve day and night. The two independently confirmed seeing Billy leave for the bank at noon with money in hand. They also provided the names of three customers present at that time. The investigator made a note to interview them soon.

His interviews at the B&L completed, Jerome thanked them all for their time and headed back into the storm. Pushed along by a strong wind, he scurried across the lanes of traffic past the hotel to the bank entrance.

Once inside the warm interior, he set about arranging interviews with the bank staff. Potter's secretary, Mrs. Taggart, dashed Jerome's hopes of meeting with the old man, however. She said he had left immediately after breakfast at the hotel. The surly woman was vague in the extreme about Potter's whereabouts or expected return.

Unfazed, Jerome borrowed a conference room and began meeting with the staff. That group turned out to be the same crew that had worked Christmas Eve. Still, little of importance was obtained. Many vaguely recalled seeing Billy Bailey that day. Several mentioned the exchange between the two men, but none had been close enough to have heard anything.

It wasn't until Mr. Robinson, the head teller and last interviewee, took a seat in the conference room that Jerome finally got some valuable information. It quickly became obvious to the investigator that Robinson was detail oriented and didn't mind speaking frankly. The head teller also did not seem to be a fan of Mr. Potter.

"I've been here for over twenty-five years, but I doubt the man could pick me out of a lineup," Robinson said.

"Then why do you stay?" Jerome asked.

Robinson shrugged. "Born and raised here, my wife too. Got out of high school and came to work here. Not much else in Bedford Falls for a man of my skills. Soon had a family and—"

"I understand, Mr. Robinson," Jerome said, wishing to move things along. "Now what can you tell me about the events of last Monday?"

Robinson pondered for a moment. He had first spotted Bailey completing a deposit slip at the high counter in the center of the lobby. The next he saw, the man was in front of him at the teller window handing over the slip but no cash. When Robinson pointed this out, Billy acted surprised at first, then confused, and finally panicky. After desperately searching his pockets, Bailey circled the lobby and quickly left.

"You didn't see or hear Mr. Bailey talking to Mr. Potter?"

"No. I didn't even know anything about it until Mr. Daniels came to the window."

"Mr. Daniels?"

Robinson nodded. "Walter Daniels. He owns the theater across the street, the Bijou. He'd been in line behind Billy, who nearly knocked him over as he rushed off."

"You say Daniels had something to say on the matter?"

"Indeed. And Walter Daniels is a man of few words."

Robinson recounted his conversation with the theater owner. Daniels had asked what had been up with Billy. When told, he was surprised since he'd seen Bailey counting out a wad of cash next to him only minutes earlier. Daniels had suggested that Robinson ask Potter about the money since Billy had a run-in with him just before heading to the teller window.

"I was half-listening while counting out Walt's deposit when he called my attention to Potter's office door. I looked in that direction just in time to see the door close."

Jerome's interest was piqued. "What did Daniels say he'd seen?"

"Said Potter and his caretaker were sneaking a look out the door as Bailey frantically searched the lobby. Walt thought the sight quite odd."

"Did you ask why?"

"No time. Walt is always in a hurry. He left without another word."

"Daniels didn't share anything about the, how did you put it, the run-in between Potter and Bailey?"

"He didn't offer anything about that to me, and I didn't ask. I've shared it all, I'm afraid."

"Did anyone else bring up the matter while you were at the window or later in the day?"

Robinson considered the question intently. "No, not that I recall. I left the window shortly after that when Mr. Paul came back from lunch. Except for some discussion later in the day about the missing money, no one had anything insightful to share."

"Thank you, Mr. Robinson. You've been most helpful. Will Daniels be at the theater now?"

"He's always there. I think he lives on popcorn."

The two smiled at the thought as they parted.

After a thoroughly unsatisfactory discussion with Mrs. Taggart, clearly a staunch ally of Potter, Jerome decided his work at the bank was complete. His stomach suddenly sounding like an angry snowplow reminding him that he had skipped breakfast, the investigator chose sustenance over information. Within minutes, he was enjoying the luncheon special at the hotel while staring at the Bijou across the street.

The sun finally won the day as the investigator left the hotel well sated. He again maneuvered his way across Main Street to the Bijou. The female ticket taker warily directed him upstairs to Daniels's office, where there was no answer to his knock.

As Jerome was about to try again, the door flew open and a very large and harried-looking man emerged. "Mr. Daniels? Walter Daniels?" Jerome asked hastily.

Without a pause, the man swept past, replying as he headed for the stairs, "That would be me. And you?"

"My name is Mark Jerome. I'm an investigator from the state bank examiner's office in Albany sent to look into the disappearance of eight thousand dollars from the B&L."

Already halfway to the lobby, Daniels spoke breathlessly. "Ahh, the B&L scandal. What does that have to do with me?"

"Well, I was talking to Mr. Robinson, and—"

Jerome heard Daniels laugh. "I might have known. What did that busybody tell you?"

"He said you were at the bank on Christmas Eve when Billy Bailey was there."

Daniels quickly rushed toward the ticket booth. "Didn't he tell you what I saw?"

Jerome was at a full gallop trying to keep up. "Yes, but there are gaps only you can fill in."

With a frown, Daniels paused at the door of the ticket booth gulping for air. "Very well. But first I have to relieve my wife so she can get home to the kids. Holiday vacation, you know."

Not waiting for a response, Daniels threw the door open. The woman Jerome had briefly talked with earlier exited the booth with an annoyed look. Saying nothing, she grabbed her coat, hat, and scarf from somewhere unseen and was out the door at a run, ignoring her husband's meek, "Sorry, dear."

Finally at a standstill, Jerome asked his questions, and Daniels answered them while handling late arrivals. The general details matched those of Robinson, so the investigator concentrated on the finer points.

Daniels was quite certain that Bailey had been counting enough money that it could have easily been the missing $8,000. He joked that Billy had counted it several times, distracting Daniels from his own deposit. Bailey had finished first and moved off toward the teller window just as Potter entered the bank.

Billy had paused to engage Potter good humoredly, which Potter did not appreciate. Daniels recalled Bailey handing something relatively bulky, a newspaper he thought, to the old man during the exchange. No, the theater owner had not heard any of the conversation, which had been very brief. Billy had done most of the talking while Potter just leered.

Daniels had quickly returned to his own deposit slip and moved to the line at the teller window directly behind Billy. "And you surely know what happened after that."

Jerome shook his head. "Not entirely. Did you hear anything Billy said to the teller?"

"No, not a word."

"Mr. Robinson said you mentioned something about Potter peeking out his office door."

"Oh, that."

Mr. Daniels explained the strange sight in his own words. The old man's door had opened a couple of feet; its creaking had drawn Daniels's attention. He saw Potter and his aide, who was peering over the wheelchair. At first, it had been a comical sight, but it became disconcerting to Daniels, as Potter's expression seemed both sinister and guilt ridden.

"His look made me think something was amiss," Daniels said. "I guess that's why I pointed out what I'd seen to Mr. Robinson. Then I got back to my own business, finished, and rushed back here. I'm always here." He sighed again.

"So that was it?"

"Yup. Haven't talked to anyone about it since," Daniels said with a shrug while moving out of the booth as a woman who looked much like the theater owner's wife rushed through the entrance. "Now if you don't mind, my sister-in-law is here to replace me. I have projectors to deal with."

Daniels rushed up the stairs as the woman entered the booth. Left alone in the empty lobby, Jerome considered his options. It was just mid-afternoon; that left ample time to interview Misters Martini and Gower. Perhaps the impatient investigator might even fit in Mary Bailey.

Hearing a knock, Mary opened the door a crack against the cold wind. "Hello, Mrs. Bailey, my name is Mark Jerome."

"Ahh yes." She sounded suddenly wary. "From the state bank examiner's office." Jerome was surprised until she added. "George called."

"I see," the investigator said with a smile. "Then you know I've been getting some background on the case from many folks in town." Mary nodded, and he continued. "I just finished visiting with Mr. Gower. Saw Mr. Martini as well, wonderful friends of you both. Now if you don't mind, I'd like to spend a few minutes with you."

"Well, it's getting a little late, Mr. Jerome, but I guess so. Won't you come in?" She stood aside as he entered.

"I'm sorry for showing up so late and unannounced especially in such a storm." Jerome stared apologetically at the snow on his coat. "I hope I'm not interrupting anything, the children and all."

"Oh, they're at Ma Bailey's for the day, thank goodness. They've been driving me crazy. Can't wait for school to start again."

Mary waved Jerome toward the living room while reaching for his coat and hat. "Let me have those. Please, take the chair by the fireplace." As he complied, Mary reemphasized her family's concern. "George is anxious for you to complete your work. Time is critical." She sat on the couch and pulled her legs under her. "I'm not sure how I can help you, but I'll do my best."

"I'm sure you will," Jerome said with a nod. "I came to ask you about your husband, his state of mind last week, specifically Christmas Eve day."

"If you're asking me if he was in the mood to steal that eight thousand, the answer is emphatically no." Mary's eyes flashed at such a suggestion. "George was about as happy as a man could be that morning."

In response to Jerome's doubtful look, Mary ran down a list of reasons for that. The war was over, and that had relieved George of many civic duties; Harry was receiving the CME, the B&L was doing better than ever, Potter seemed in hibernation, and it was the holiday season. "When he left for work that morning, he was humming a happy tune."

"Has he always liked his work?"

"Oh, it wasn't what he'd had in mind when he was younger. Designing buildings and bridges around the world was his dream. But something always got in the way. Now, building things is just a hobby." She glanced at the broken models under George's worktable.

"You don't say," Jerome said flatly.

Mary smiled wistfully. "I suppose the children and I were among those *somethings* that got in the way." Mary's face darkened. "Say, are you suggesting George took that money so he could run away and fulfill his dreams?"

"I'm not suggesting anything, Mrs. Bailey."

Mary fought to control her growing anger. "Good, because that would be absurd. Henry Potter is more likely to become a saint before my husband would take a dime that wasn't his."

"I can understand your passionate support for your husband."

Jerome's patronizing tone had Mary on her feet. "Don't take my word. Ask anyone in this town, well, except Potter." Suddenly feeling awkward, Mary sat again. Her anger subsided a bit. "I'm beginning to doubt your ability, Mr. Jerome, if you suspect George."

"What about Uncle Billy?"

Mary was glad for a change of subject. "He's a harmless old man who feels absolutely terrible right now."

Jerome nodded. "Is that because he lost the money?"

"I don't know." Mary flared up again. "I guess he might have, but again, I wasn't there."

"Right." Jerome scribbled something. "If the money was stolen instead of lost, any thoughts who might have taken it?"

"I have just one, and that would be Henry Potter." Mary was unequivocal. "If he didn't do it personally, he knows who did. It's more than likely he hired someone to do it."

"You seem pretty certain about that."

"I am. As I hear it, Potter was there right about the time the money went missing. George was not. Yes, I know, Billy was the last to be seen with it in hand, but—"

"No need to explain. I've already interviewed the B&L and bank employees. Is there anything else you can tell me about that day?"

Mary thought for a moment before shaking her head. "No, not at the moment."

The investigator smiled as he closed his pad. "Then I'll be going. Thank you so much for your hospitality and patience with me."

"I do hope I wasn't too off-putting, Mr. Jerome." She stood and moved toward the front door. "I just get a bit protective when it comes to my husband's character."

"Yes, I can see that."

Mary retrieved the investigator's coat and hat from the rack. "I certainly hope we can count on you being prompt, thorough, and objective going forward."

"I assure you I will be," Jerome said decisively.

Mary opened the door and used it to shield herself from the cold. "If you do that, I'm not worried. Good luck to you for all our sakes."

The two waved casually as the door shut. Mary sighed, deeply relieved that the man was gone. She remained uncertain about the impact of what she had shared. It was clear that the Baileys' future and that of the B&L were in the hands of a stranger.

CHAPTER 3

The last Friday of 1945 had dawned sunny and unusually mild. Drifts from the Thursday storm released rivulets of water across streets and sidewalks. Icicles, some two feet long, dripped methodically from building eaves along the sunny side of the street. Emerging from a solitary breakfast, the investigator found Ernie Bishop's taxi at the curb.

He had learned a lot about Ernie during his interview with him the previous day. This local icon worked seven days a week year round to make ends meet. He wore that fact with pride and a constant smile.

A small cry of surprise came from the cabby at the sudden opening of his back door. He was even more surprised when Jerome told him his destination. The leisurely ride to Potter's estate took all of fifteen minutes. Ernie talked the entire time, mostly about the virtues of George Bailey and the vices of the man the investigator was on his way to see.

The cabbie's monologue ended when they arrived at the rambling estate. Expecting Potter might not be there, Jerome asked Ernie to wait. The investigator rang the doorbell several times without response. Just as he turned to leave, the door opened and a very nervous woman peered out.

After an introduction that included his title, Jerome asked to see Potter. The anxious, middle-aged woman confirmed what he'd feared. Potter was not home and she didn't know when he might return. Not waiting for further conversation, she quickly closed the door in his face. Jerome shrugged at this and returned to the taxi.

"What did Miss Purdy have to say?" Ernie sounded very interested in the answer.

"Is that her name?"

"Yeah, Minnie Purdy, Potter's latest cook. Say, what kind of investigator doesn't even get a name?"

"She didn't give me much of a chance. Said Potter wasn't there and closed the door." Jerome noticed Ernie's doubtful expression. "What?"

"And you believed her?" Ernie asked incredulously.

"Why shouldn't I? His secretary at the bank said the same thing yesterday. You don't believe them?"

"I find it hard to believe when I just saw Latimoore peeking out a window."

"Who?"

"Latimoore, Potter's ghoulish assistant."

"Is he the guy who pushes Potter around in the wheelchair?"

"Yup. He's been doing it for as long as I can remember."

"You say you saw him just now? Where?"

Ernie casually pointed toward a large bank of draped windows. "I saw him clear as day peeking through those curtains. He didn't linger there for long."

"Do you think Latimoore's presence means Potter is here?"

"Yup. If Sterling Latimoore is here, so's Potter. I'll bet your fare on it. That poster boy for the walking dead has been Henry Potter's legs forever. He's the only person allowed to push old moneybags around in that god-awful gothic chariot."

Jerome reached for the door handle. "I'll be back. You don't mind waiting, do you?"

"Wouldn't miss this for the world."

The investigator marched up to the door and this time pounded rather than ringing the bell. The same woman appeared shortly. Miss Purdy feigned confusion over his request to see Mr. Latimoore. Claiming he was not there, she attempted to slam the door again.

Anticipating this, Jerome wedged a foot in the door. At that, Miss Purdy uttered a weak cry and bolted. As the great door swung slowly open, he watched her disappear across a great hall, leaving him standing in the doorway at a loss for what to do next. As he turned to shrug at Ernie, he heard footsteps. A deep voice came from the shadows. "May I help you, sir?"

"Yes you may. Mr. Latimoore, I presume?" Jerome did not wait for a reply; he launched right into a strongly worded introduction emphasizing his legal authority and announcing his purpose. "I am here to see Mr. Henry Potter."

The imposing aide, standing well over six feet in his black boots, shook his head. "Mr. Potter is indisposed at the present. I suggest you call for an appointment."

"If that means he's still in bed, I'll wait. I need to talk to him, and you for that matter, about the missing eight thousand dollars from the B&L."

"Whyever for?" Latimoore asked with raised brows.

"Because both of you at a minimum are material witnesses to the events on Christmas Eve."

After considering that, Latimoore stepped aside and Jerome entered. "Now please inform your *indisposed* employer I'm here."

Latimoore remained motionless, apparently considering the request. "And if he is *unable* to see you, Mr. Jerome?"

"Then I guess I'll have to come back with Chief Cook." Jerome took the chance that the man didn't know the chief was presently unavailable. That paid off.

With a sweep of his arm, Latimoore broke his silence. "Very well sir. Please have a seat and I will deliver your request."

"Wait." Jerome held up his hand, and Latimoore turned back to him. "Perhaps it would be best if I asked you a few questions first since you are a person of interest."

That seemed to rattle Latimoore. "A person of interest?"

"Why yes. As I said a few minutes ago, at the very least, you are a key witness, and at worst ..." He let the sentence drop.

"At worst what?"

"Well, I'm not prepared to go there yet. So let's sit and talk a few minutes, shall we?" Jerome was already moving toward a winged-back chair in the great hall.

Reluctantly, Latimoore joined him. "As you wish."

Facing each other in chairs near a cold fireplace, Jerome asked his questions. He received reluctant and measured replies. The investigator gained as much information from the aide's tone and body language as he did from his words. He claimed to know nothing about the missing money and was indignant at the idea that anyone was avoiding the investigator.

"Well, Mr. Potter's secretary told me he was unavailable, Miss Purdy said he was not at home, and you just said he was indisposed. That sure sounds like stonewalling to me."

Latimoore simply shrugged. "I don't believe that is true, sir."

"Well, if what you say is true, Mr. Potter should be available to see me shortly."

Latimoore stood abruptly. "I will make the inquiry, sir."

"You do that, Mr. Latimoore."

With a perfunctory bob of his head, the unnerved Latimoore headed up the nearest of the two winding staircases. As the tall figure disappeared at the top of the stairs, Jerome sighed in satisfaction and once again took in the splendor of the great room.

Nearly a half hour passed before Latimoore suddenly emerged from a doorway to Jerome's right carrying a tray. The investigator immediately deduced that there had to have been an elevator somewhere. That made perfect sense with a wealthy invalid in the home.

The assistant walked past Jerome without a glance. "Mr. Potter will meet with you in his study." Latimoore continued toward the main entrance. "Please follow me, sir."

The oddly graceful aide reached the front entrance then turned right toward a set of lesser, double doors Jerome hadn't seen before. Latimoore quickly disappeared inside as Jerome followed. Light from a large bank of windows illuminated a spacious yet cozy and toasty-warm study.

A fireplace centered on one wall faced a massive desk. Embers of a recent fire glowed on the grate. The dark wood of the desk matched the dark paneling on the walls. Two leather chairs sat before the desk and looked beyond to a wall of windows with heavy drapes. Paintings hanging on the paneling like those in the great hall looked original and expensive.

Latimoore placed the tray on the desk, stoked the fire, and added wood. Satisfied with the result, he addressed Jerome. "Please take a seat. I will return with Mr. Potter shortly." Then he left.

It was only a few minutes before Latimoore pushed Potter into the room and behind his desk. Jerome stood reflexively and started to speak but stopped when Potter raised his hand dismissively. The aide placed a napkin in the old man's lap and left.

Potter waved Jerome to one of the chairs. "I don't know what to think of your presence, Mr. Jerome is it?" He did not wait for an answer. "I would have thought the facts were clear. Either the Baileys are incompetent or they're thieves."

"Short of confessions, such conclusions usually come after an investigation," Jerome said while placing his coat and hat on the other chair. "That's why I'm here."

"Isn't that a matter for the police?" Potter asked with a sneer.

"Under the present laws of New York, I operate with authority similar to that of the local police. Of course, we will be working in tandem going forward."

Potter's expression softened. He broke into a patronizing smile. "Well then, I'll be more than happy to do my duty as a citizen. What do you wish to know?"

As Potter ate his meal, Jerome conducted his interview. He made sure to avoid giving the impression that Potter or his aide was more than just a material witness. Unlike Latimoore, he did not get as much as a raised eyebrow from Potter when he was questioned about peeking out his office door. After denying the claim, he asked who had said such a thing. To this, Jerome demurred.

As expected, there were no great revelations from the exchange. The investigator was neither surprised nor disappointed. That had not been the primary purpose for his visit. Jerome slowly rose to make his exit. "I shan't keep you any longer at this time. I'll see myself out." He retrieved his coat and hat. "I'm sure we'll be talking again."

The shadowy figure of Latimoore materialized as Jerome left the study. The aide quickly saw him out without uttering a word.

In the back of the cab, the investigator artfully parried Ernie's questions all the way back to town.

After a quick lunch at the hotel, Jerome hurried off into the mild afternoon, hoping to complete a few more interviews before the weekend. He managed to fit in the three B&L customers who confirmed seeing Billy leaving for the bank with the money. He missed Bert Riley, who had been the officer on duty when the money disappeared, so that would have to wait along with a few other marginal sources of information.

CHAPTER 4

The next Monday on the drive to the bank, Latimoore broached the subject of Jerome's visit with Potter. The chauffer realized his boss had dragged him unwillingly into a serious crime when they hadn't returned the $8,000 immediately. Since then, they had continued to collaborate by concealing the crime and related evidence.

Potter had not let the holiday stand in the way of his efforts to destroy the Baileys and the B&L. He called in favors from many powerful sources while maintaining a constant verbal assault through the editorial pages and rumor mill. Latimoore assumed the old man was keeping the damning evidence to somehow use it should his initial efforts fail.

All seemed fine until Jerome arrived. Sensing the investigator was not convinced of the Baileys' guilt and was widening the scope of the investigation, Potter had ordered Latimoore to remove the evidence from the estate and destroy it. Considering that handled, Potter was shocked when Latimoore pulled down a secluded road and turned the engine off.

"What are you doing?" the old man said impatiently. "I have people waiting."

Latimoore turned to the back and spoke impassively. "I think they can wait while we have a little chat. I thought you'd be interested to know that I didn't destroy the evidence as you ordered."

"What? Why? What's the meaning of this?" Potter's surprise quickly turned to anger.

Latimoore's face remained emotionless. "It seemed a pity to waste that eight thousand. I know that amount means nothing to you, but it's a small fortune to me. And when you consider I've received nothing for maintaining my silence and doing the dirty work ..."

Stifling his temper, the old man attempted a weak chuckle. "And what do you think will happen when you start spending it? You'll be caught. And I assure you no one will take your word over mine if you try to implicate me."

"I don't plan on spending it here. I plan on retiring to Florida with the money and taking the rest of the evidence with me."

Potter seemed to relax at that. "Suit yourself. Good riddance to bad rubbish as the saying goes. Once a convict always one it would appear. Never should have been so kindhearted to you for so long."

"Hah! Kindhearted indeed," Latimoore said with venom in his voice. "You've held my time in prison over me for nearly forty years. Expected me to do your dirty work or get fired. You knew no one would hire an ex-con with a bad reference from you. Well, all that's over now. I'm going to retire in comfort. A man can live near a king's life on thirty thousand."

"Thirty thousand?"

Latimoore saw the old man's temporary confusion quickly evaporate.

"That's right. A few more dollars from you, dollars you won't miss I might add, will ensure you never see or hear from me again. Won't see that evidence either."

Potter's face was a crimson red. "You'll never get away—"

"Oh, I think I will." Latimoore nearly grinned. "Without evidence, the investigation will likely conclude that Billy Bailey lost the money. Isn't that what you want?"

Potter mumbled what sounded like agreement.

"And if I'd destroyed the evidence, you'd have been free and clear and I'd still be broke. From my perspective, that just won't do. This way, we both get what we want and stay free."

"But if you ever turned over that evidence, you'd go to jail too," Potter said angrily.

"Perhaps. But you see, my prints aren't on any of the evidence thanks to the gloves I wore whenever I handled it. I guess there's still some larceny in me yet." Latimoore snickered. "Anyway, that evidence is insurance for both of us. I can't use it against you nor can you use it against me without implicating one another."

Much of Potter's heat had faded along with his color. "Ahh yes, I suppose you're right."

"So it will all accompany me to Florida and remain available if needed. Of course, I'll have to linger around here a few weeks to avoid suspicion. We can spread the rumor that I'm retiring for health reasons. Meanwhile, the evidence will be safe with me."

"Undoubtedly," Potter said with a sneer. "You know this is nothing but blackmail!"

"That's rich, Mr. Potter." Latimoore actually croaked a laugh. "Now shall we work out the details so we can get on the road? I believe you have people waiting."

"At least start the car, man. It's freezing in here in case you haven't noticed. Then let's finish this on the way to the office."

With a smile of triumph, Latimoore started the car and headed back to the main road. As he drove, the two settled on a plan that would have the aide headed to Florida a much richer man within the month. As the agreement was struck, however, Latimoore remained uneasy. It was hard to have confidence in an unholy bargain made with the devil.

While still in the car, Potter had already started to plan his revenge against Latimoore. His motive had nothing to do with the money. To him, the amount demanded was a trifle, though parting with a single dollar without profit went against his grain. It was the fact this simpleton was trying to get the better of him that fed his anger. That would just not do.

Potter stewed over the best way to deal with this all the way to the bank. The best way to pin the crime on Latimoore was to use the stolen money and other evidence. The sticking point, of course, was how to locate these items. It was obvious that he could not find them on his own. He would need an accomplice, which would be risky. Still, there was little choice.

After considering several options and rejecting them, he settled on someone. Though not well known by Potter personally, his background was. And he had very great sway over his cooperation both financially and, if necessary, through coercion. Satisfied, he determined to initiate the plan as soon as he returned to the estate and could ensure Latimoore was kept out of the way.

Realizing time was essential, Potter left the bank early. By midafternoon, he was back at his desk in the study ordering Latimoore back to town for papers intentionally left behind. The aide's footsteps had hardly faded when Potter dialed the house phone.

Something had not been right for some time. Changes in Potter's behavior began the day after the conversation in the limousine that cold morning. Potter normally expected the aide to be at his side morning to night. Suddenly, however, Latimoore found he was running daily errands away from the estate, most of which were trivial and bordering on contrivances.

Suspicion soon became paranoia. Besides these dubious tasks, Potter's dismissive ways were gone and replaced with solicitude. The old man's angry outbursts had nearly disappeared. At first, the aide thought the changes were due to the leverage he had gained over him, but then, he started feeling Potter was trying to lull him into a false sense of security.

All his concerns came to a head all too soon when Latimoore was called to the study at a quarter to nine. The old man said he'd once again forgotten important papers at the bank that he needed. That had become a familiar pattern and was out of character for a man who had always demonstrated an innate ability to forget nothing.

That night, warning signals went off in Latimoore's head. Not wanting the old man to sense that, however, he immediately headed to the Rolls. More than ever, the aide was sure Potter was up to something. As he drove through the back gate, his mind was racing; he was trying to think of a way to allay his fears or find out what his boss was plotting.

Reaching the intersection of the rear driveway and main road, Latimoore sat waiting for nonexistent traffic. An intense need to know overcame him. Instead of turning left toward town, he turned off the engine. Stepping out of the limo and into the dim glow of a crescent moon, he shivered, not sure if it was due solely to the bone-chilling cold.

Latimoore felt ridiculous. What did he expect to gain with this folly? Still, he had to stop this madness. If Potter was plotting against him, as he felt intuitively was the case, it was best to know so he could act. He glanced at his watch and headed back toward the main house.

Latimoore hurriedly entered the house though the side door to the garage. Thankfully, the kitchen was empty. He quickly passed through and into the great hall. Halfway across, he heard a muffled voice coming from the study.

Moving cautiously through the darkness, he stopped outside the door. It soon became clear to him that Potter was on the phone. For the next few minutes, Latimoore listened to a one-sided conversation that filled him with dread. His fears were realized.

If what he heard was true, it was clear that part, if not all, of the evidence had been found. From Potter's tone, however, it seemed unlikely. Sensing the conversation was coming to an end, Latimoore headed back to the car, his mind in turmoil.

He needed to confirm what he had heard, but to do so immediately would likely tip off Potter. There would be time for that after he went to the bank and retrieved the requested papers. If they indeed had all the evidence, he would need all the time he could muster to make a run for it. And if they didn't have it all, that would buy him some time to think. What was critical at the moment was to ensure Potter thought his aide was still in the dark.

Stifling panic, Latimoore dashed to the limousine. In what seemed to take forever, he raced to the bank, grabbed the papers, and was on the way back in record time. Nearly smashing into the garage door in his haste, he parked and tried to regain his composure.

There was no way Potter would not have noticed how long he had been gone. Still fighting to remain calm, he rubbed dirt and grease from the garage floor on his clothing. Then with a deep breath, he hastened to the study and knocked. A harsh command to enter confirmed his fears.

Barely through the door, he launched into his excuse. "Sorry to be tardy, sir. A car blocked the road, and the only way to get past it was for me to push—"

"Yes, yes, I see. Just give me the papers. Then go wash up and get back here. I want to get to bed." Potter's tone was venomous and self-assured. Latimoore knew why.

Glancing at the study's fireplace as he left, he wondered if more than wood would soon be burning there. He was back in mere minutes. Desperate to check on the evidence, he was glad Potter was eager to call it a night. After the torturous routine of getting Potter in bed, Latimoore headed to the gatehouse.

Once inside, he rushed to his closet only to find that the box hidden deep in the back of the top shelf was empty. It had contained the newspaper, deposit slip, and envelope. He cursed himself for carelessly assuming it would be safe there from a man in a wheelchair. And he'd been wrong to think that Potter wouldn't risk adding another accomplice.

In desperation, he turned toward his bed. He lifted the left leg at its foot and removed a wadded rag from the bottom. To his great relief, out fell several rolls of bills. Moving to the kitchen with the money, he poured a tumbler full of whiskey and sat down to think. He stayed there motionless until nearly dawn, when he reached his decision.

CHAPTER 5

A brilliant, bitter, and cloudless Monday met Jerome as he headed to the police station. It was only two blocks from the hotel atop the slight hill where the "Welcome to Bedford Falls" sign sat. The chief of police, Adam Cook, had returned from his holiday that morning and agreed to meet him at ten.

A tall, distinguished-looking man strode up to Jerome with a smile and extended hand. "Adam Cook, police chief." His voice was all business.

"Thanks for seeing me on such short notice."

"No problem. Little going on between Christmas and New Year's anyway." The chief waved to his open door. "Follow me." He headed off with Jerome close behind.

Sun cascaded through windows opposite the office door, overpowering the modest space. Beyond the windows was a perfect view down Main Street. A large, neat desk faced the door with one end slid against the wall. The peeling beige walls were covered with plaques and photographs, many of which showed Henry Potter glad-handing the chief.

Cook closed the door and sat while gesturing Jerome to take one of the visitor's chairs wedged in front of the desk. "I got a call from your superior at the SBE office right after you called confirming your authority and requesting we work together."

"Delighted to hear that, Chief Cook," the investigator said with a smile. "I look forward to it."

"Please call me Adam. To be honest, I hadn't given any mind to following up this case so soon." Adams sounded apologetic but moved on quickly. "When did you arrive?"

"I came in on Christmas Day, Chief."

"Really?" the chief asked with a surprised expression "Been hard at it ever since I hear. Why don't you tell me what you've come up with thus far."

"Certainly, Mr.—I mean Adam."

For the next several minutes, the investigator reviewed his activities and then began to share his findings. The chief remained impassive during the account while scribbling a few notes.

At that point, Jerome paused. The chief filled the void. "So, based on what you've gathered, have you come to any conclusions?"

"No conclusions but some theories." When Cook nodded, Jerome continued. "I'll get right to it then. In short, I believe the money was stolen, not lost. If it had been lost or misplaced, it would have turned up by now. From every account, the search after it disappeared was extensive. If the money was lost and someone found it but kept the cash, that would make it a crime just as if it had been stolen in the first place."

The chief nodded with a frown. "Logical but only circumstantial. But, let's accept your premise for the moment. Whom do you think took it?"

The investigator shrugged. "My theories about that are every bit as circumstantial. I think we should focus on what *we* do next in the investigation."

"I agree, but can we cut some corners based on facts you've developed to date?"

"How so?"

"Have you eliminated any potential suspects based on your findings?"

"You'll have to confirm that for yourself, but I believe we can narrow the field of suspects by eliminating George and Billy—"

"You can't be serious!" the chief exclaimed.

"In fact, I don't consider them prime suspects."

Cook raised a brow. "That's quite interesting. What facts support those assertions?"

"Well, for George, it's relatively easy. He had no opportunity to take the money. He had left the B&L before Billy left for the bank with the money. He was visiting with Ernie and your officer Bert Riley at the time Billy arrived at the bank."

"What about George's alleged admission to Potter that he had lost the money? Does he deny that now?"

"Not at all."

"Then how does he explain that?"

"That he wanted to spare his uncle the blame. Besides, the facts I gathered confirm George had no opportunity to take or lose it."

"What about hiring someone to do it?"

"True, but why have the money taken in front of all those people at the bank? Why not just fake a robbery at the B&L? By the way, except for the missing eight thousand, the audit of the B&L showed it was in better financial shape than it has ever been. Why create an unnecessary crisis?"

The chief held up his hands. "Okay, let's move on to Billy for a moment. Surely he's another story."

"I'd agree that Billy would have been the likely culprit if the money had been lost, but several witnesses saw Billy in the bank with the cash."

"And you don't think Billy could have palmed the money so to speak at the bank?"

"Not really, and I don't think you do either," Jerome replied emphatically.

The chief pondered that for a moment and nodded meekly. "It's hard to believe Billy intellectually capable of pulling off something like that."

"You won't get any argument from me on that."

"Still, as sure as we both are on that point, we don't have the facts to back it up."

The investigator was pleased to hear Cook's support of his premise absent hard evidence. "You started with the obvious suspects, the Baileys, before I interrupted. Have you others?"

The investigator presented a relatively short list along with the information he had gathered in support of or against each. It was the last name, Henry Potter, that had Cook's full attention. He was not overly surprised at what Jerome suggested but gravely concerned about conducting a full investigation involving the old man. As if trying to avoid the eventuality, the chief raised an objection. "But surely Potter lacked a motive. That amount of money was meaningless to him."

"On the contrary." Jerome shook his head emphatically. "He had at least two other motives. You surely know he hated the B&L for some reason. This scandal could result in the demise of it once and for all. Hatred is a powerful motive. And total control of the town's financial institution is another. There are plenty of examples of Potter's past efforts in that regard."

"Still, taking on Potter based on such flimsy, circumstantial—"

"Evidence? Flimsy motives? Like the same we have on George and Billy?" Jerome asked with a near smile.

After a pause, the edges of Cook's mouth turned up. He shook his head. "I guess I just didn't like the prospects of confronting the old man about this."

"Without tangible evidence, you surely agree we have no other real choice."

The chief chuckled. "I'm glad you said *we*. I don't like the idea of being in this alone."

The investigator nodded. "And I'll do everything in my power to help you."

"Thanks for that though it may not be enough." Cook's smile faded. "We're dealing with Henry F. Potter here, probably the most powerful man in the state if not the country."

"I realize that, but isn't that irrelevant?" Jerome leaned forward. "It's our duty, and there's more than eight thousand dollars at stake here."

"Of course. It's just a hell of a way to start the New Year. An election year at that."

George sat at his desk that New Year's Eve frowning at the document he held. It contained the names of four shareholders who had already cashed in their B&L shares. The cloud of suspicion hanging over the business was already taking a toll. If the trend continued, their doors would soon be closed, giving Potter his wish.

His reverie was interrupted by a knock at his door. "Come in."

Cousin Tilly swept in wearing an odd expression as she closed the door. "George, you have a visitor."

Checking his calendar, he looked up quizzically. "No appointment here."

"This fellow doesn't have one. And George, you'll never guess who it is."

"I'm not in the mood for guessing games this morning, Tilly." George regretted his tone and softened it a bit. "Why don't you just tell me what's got you all atwitter?"

"You're no fun, George." Her brief frown quickly changed to a smile. "It's Mr. Potter's aide, you know, that Latimoore gent. I didn't even think he could talk. But here he is, wanting to talk with you. And no, I don't know what it's about."

"That *is* strange. I can't say I've ever heard the man speak either. He always seemed more a part of Potter's wheelchair than a person." George began clearing papers off his desk. "This should be interesting. Show him in."

The gaunt figure in his usual black garb entered looking exhausted and anxious as he slunk into the room. Feeling suddenly uneasy, George motioned for him to sit.

"What can I do for you, Mr. Latimoore?" George asked with a forced smile.

"I believe it's something I can do for you, Mr. Bailey, and in doing so prevent an injustice from occurring to us both." His deep and solemn tone matched his dark words.

"That sounds ominous, Mr. Latimoore." George meant it. "Could you be more specific?"

"I am here regarding the missing money."

That got George's full attention.

"I am prepared to assist in resolving this matter, but I must first have your assurance that you will advocate for me going forward once you hear what I have to say."

"Advocate for you?" George couldn't imagine what that meant.

"Yes. Advocate for me with the authorities and against Mr. Potter." Latimoore said, suddenly looking vulnerable.

George leaned forward, challenging his unscheduled guest. "How do you expect me to agree to that without knowing what you have to say?"

Latimoore looked even more uncomfortable. "A fair question. Let me start by saying I have always believed you to be a fair and honest man."

That brought a puzzled chuckle from George. "You don't say. I would never have guessed that was how you felt. Indifferent would be more like it."

"Consider whom I work for, Mr. Bailey. The fact that I came here without his knowledge should speak to the gravity of my circumstances."

"So you say. How do I know he didn't send you?"

"I can understand your being suspicious. But Mr. Potter is currently at the estate probably looking for me." Latimoore swallowed hard. "When he finds I'm gone, I believe that will start events in motion that I'm now trying to mitigate."

"I must say you have me curious." With a wave, George urged his guest to continue. "Since it would appear time is critical from your perspective, let's hear it."

Latimoore told the story of what had happened at the bank on Christmas Eve day and the events that had followed. In the telling, he portrayed himself as an unwilling accomplice while saying nothing about his efforts to blackmail Potter. He wrapped up his story by saying that Potter was likely planning to use the evidence to frame the Baileys and him.

"That's quite a story, Mr. Latimoore. Why should I or anyone else believe you?" George didn't wait for a response. "No one around here knows you at all. You've done a good job of remaining nearly invisible. That will definitely work against you."

"You also know the character of Mr. Potter. You know he's capable of what I just described," Latimoore countered.

"You bet I do," George said ironically. "He probably did what you say and is planning exactly what you're suggesting right now. But he is a rich, powerful man, and you're, well, you're nobody. I would love to see justice done, but Potter isn't someone to be trifled with." George was surprised to see Latimoore's expression lighten.

"I was a *fool* to believe I had him over a barrel when I held all the evidence. That was a big mistake. But Mr. Potter doesn't know everything."

"And pray tell what do you know that he doesn't?"

"Well, first, I know what he's up to, having overheard him. He also doesn't know I am here. He wouldn't expect that. Plus, he thinks I'm not willing to incriminate myself."

"But you are?"

"When the choice is to go down alone or take that bastard with me, damn right I am."

George was shocked at the language and anger coming from the formerly stoic man. "So you're ready to make a confession?" Latimoore nodded. George frowned. "But how do you expect anyone to believe you?"

"Because I still have one piece of evidence," the aide said resignedly. "Potter either assumes I won't part with it or whomever he hired is still looking for it."

"And what is this evidence?" George asked doubtfully.

Latimoore asked his own question in reply. "Are you prepared to advocate for me?"

"I honestly can't say."

Hearing that, the aide stood to leave. George quickly decided he didn't want to lose this opportunity. "Hold on now, Mr. Latimoore. Expecting me to advocate for you while withholding critical information isn't fair. Would you accept such terms from me?"

Latimoore paused, then sat again. He slowly shook his head. "No, I suppose not. I haven't trusted anyone for years. I'm out of practice." He sighed deeply. "But I guess I have no other choice now."

"So show me this evidence and then we'll see about trusting," George said with an encouraging nod.

Latimoore took one last deep breath. "The evidence I have is the eight thousand dollars."

George's mouth gaped. "Where?"

"In a safe place." The aide looked pleadingly. "So will you advocate for me?"

"Once I've seen the money, I'll do my best. If Potter is already putting his plan into action, however, we need to beat him to Chief Cook." George saw fear in his eyes. "Look, where else would I be advocating for you but with the authorities? Now do we go get that money or not?"

As he sipped the coffee that the desk sergeant had just brought in, Jerome glanced at the chief. "What more can I do to help us move this forward?"

Cook smiled unenthusiastically. "You could find the money in Potter's coat pocket. That would be a smoking gun for sure."

"I'm trying to be serious."

"Well, right now, I think I need to be working on some search warrants for the B&L, the bank, the Bailey residences, and—" he sighed, "—the Potter estate. We can bring the information you've collected to the judge and see if it's enough for him to issue them."

"How do you see this working between the SBE office in the person of me and the Bedford Falls Police Department?"

"I'm more than happy to make use of your time and talents," the chief answered. "Most of the local stuff, especially with Potter, however, would be best handled by me."

"Why's that?"

"I just think it would be best if we have one point person, a local." Cook smiled. "Don't worry. There'll be plenty for us all to do. You've done a lot already."

"Thanks." Jerome returned the smile. "I'll expect to be kept busy then."

The chief's phone rang. Not appreciating the interruption, he answered gruffly, "Yes?" Jerome could hear a muffled voice. "How interesting." The chief looked surprised. "Take them to the conference room, sergeant." Putting the receiver down, he gave the investigator a mischievous look. "Two gentlemen wish to meet with me rather urgently."

"Then I best be going." Jerome reached for his briefcase and coat.

"No, don't. Please join me. I think you'll find this quite interesting."

A moment later, the two entered the conference room and saw George Bailey and Sterling Latimoore already seated. The chief enjoyed seeing the astonished look on Jerome's face. The chief waved Jerome to a chair, as he took his own.

"I believe you all know each other." Confirming nods filled the room. "Your arrival at this moment is quite fortuitous. Mr. Jerome and I were just discussing what I assume brought you here. I must say I'm surprised to see the two of you together."

George responded first. "I'd have to agree it's unexpected. Mr. Latimoore here has something to share. I'm here at his request. I promised to see he got a fair hearing."

The comment irritated the chief. "What do you mean by that, George?"

"I didn't mean that the way it came out, Adam," George said contritely.

Cook's irritation quickly faded. "That's okay, George. No offense taken.

"Let's get back to Mr. Latimoore, shall we?"

The room fell silent as all eyes turned to the gaunt figure. He looked more interested in escape than talk. He reached down beside him and brought up a tin box placing it on the table. Without a word, he opened it and dumped out a large, neat bundle of bills. Only then did he speak, his deep bass voice little more than a whisper.

"First, I freely admit to my unwilling part in keeping the whereabouts of this money a secret. I can truthfully say that my actions were motivated by long-standing fear of my employer, Mr. Potter. But I don't expect that will gain me much sympathy.

"As I told Mr. Bailey, I came to him and now you because I believe Mr. Potter has now decided to sacrifice me and the Baileys to save his own skin. In point of fact, it was Mr. Potter who took this money, or should I say kept it."

The others were silent as Latimoore continued. "Given his limitations, Potter has demanded I assist in some distasteful matters over the years. You see, I have a criminal record, which he constantly uses as leverage against me. Up until now, however, what he has asked me to participate in has been within the law if sometimes only barely."

"That's an interesting introduction, Mr. Latimoore." The chief looked skeptical. "Perhaps if you start from the beginning, we can all get on the same page."

Latimoore again described the events of Christmas Eve. He explained how the money had ended up on Mr. Potter's lap and how the old man had made no attempt to return it. He confirmed that the two had peeked out the office door to watch the panicked Uncle Billy searching the bank lobby for the money.

The aide concluded by taking them through events of the week since the crime, starting with Potter's angry response to the community's bailing out the B&L. He told how Potter had directed him to hide the evidence, not destroy it, thinking it might yet be used to sink the B&L. Latimoore made no reference to his attempt at blackmail.

"Then Mr. Jerome arrived and things changed." Latimoore glanced at the investigator.

"How so?" asked Cook.

"Well, Mr. Potter got very nervous and instructed me to destroy the evidence right away." The chief noticed that Latimoore averted his eyes. "His behavior made me uneasy, so I told him I'd done as he wished, but I held onto it instead for insurance."

"That seems to have been fortuitous, seeing as you're here now," Jerome said.

Latimoore shook his head. "I had no intention of being here. At the time, I felt pretty secure. Then over the last few days, I began to feel Potter suspected what I'd done. Last night, my concerns were confirmed. I overheard Potter on the phone talking about, well about everything. From just his side of the conversation, I managed to figure out whomever he was talking to had found where I'd hidden part of the evidence. I'd spread it around, you see, just to be on the safe side. Good thing now in hindsight."

Cook interrupted. "But this unknown person found some of it?"

"Yes. There was the newspaper, deposit slip, and a bank envelope in addition to the money. They were gone from where I'd hidden them in the gatehouse when I checked last night."

"And keeping that much money for yourself must have been tempting," Jerome added.

The gaunt aide shrugged. "I guess you could see it that way."

"Go on, Mr. Latimoore. What happened next?" Cook wanted to move things along.

Latimoore turned to the chief. "There's not much more to tell. After I confirmed what I'd heard, I decided to go to Mr. Bailey. Not much of a plan I know."

The chief shook his head. "How do we know this money is from the B&L?"

"Well, I've never counted it, but I believe you'll find exactly eight thousand here."

"That's a start."

George started to reach for the money.

"Don't touch it." Latimoore commanded.

"Can I at least take a look?" George asked.

Everyone nodded warily before he inspected the top bill at a distance then smiled. "This is the money. Billy always put slips of paper dividing the deposit into equal packets, usually a hundred dollars each. When you pull those apart, I think you'll find the blank B&L deposit slips he always used."

"Thank you, Mr. Bailey," Latimoore said, relaxing a bit. "And I think you'll find the fingerprints on the money interesting. I'm sure you'll find Mr. Potter's prints on the money, Billy Bailey's too, but not mine. You see, I was wearing gloves that day, always do when pushing that wheelchair around."

Jerome picked up Latimoore's train of thought. "And since that day, you've only handled the money with gloves on. But that doesn't prove you weren't an accomplice or worse."

"I know. But I didn't want to damage the evidence that Potter had handled the money."

"Suggesting that would prove Potter was involved," Cook said to complete the thought. "Do you have anything else to add?"

"Only that there's still an outside chance the rest of the evidence hasn't been destroyed. I don't even know if it has been returned to Potter yet. If you act quickly—"

"I understand." The chief stood and moved to the door. "The sooner you put this in writing the better. Then we can consider doing what you suggested. As it stands, however, I must place you under arrest based on what you just shared."

As Latimoore slumped in his seat, Cook opened the door and called for the sergeant. "Ron, join us please and bring a pad and pen, oh, and an evidence bag and fingerprint kit."

"But you will be taking his claims seriously, correct?" George asked.

"His assertions will become part of our ongoing investigation," Cook replied as the sergeant entered. "Brown, I've placed Mr. Latimoore under arrest. Please take his prints and Mr. Bailey's while you're at it."

"What?" George practically shouted. "Me? What about what you just heard?"

The chief took the evidence bag and carefully slid the money into it. "Look, George, we're dealing with Henry Potter. We need to go by the book. Latimoore here made a compelling claim, but we can't skip any steps along the way."

As Cook paused to write something on the bag of money, Jerome interceded. "Adam's right, George."

Cook saw George about to reply and waved them toward the door. "Why don't you take this discussion outside for a moment?"

Jerome led Bailey into the hall and closed the door behind them. As Ron finished fingerprinting Latimoore, the two reentered the interrogation room. "I think George understands now." Bailey nodded weakly. "And I suggest you take my prints as well since I've been nosing around. Just as a precaution, mind you."

"Good idea." The chief felt relieved having that out of the way. "Get it done, Ron."

Once the two sets of prints were taken, Cook directed Ron to stay with Latimoore until the statement was done, then put him in a cell. After that, the sergeant was to call the B&L and bank to tell them he was on the way to take their prints as well. As an afterthought, the chief told the sergeant to keep all this hush-hush. "Nothing on the blotter for now."

As Brown led Latimoore away, Cook, Jerome, and Bailey headed to the lobby. "I need to get this evidence secured," the chief said, holding up the bag of money.

George gave him a stony look. "You talked about practically everyone else. What about Potter?"

"If you give me a chance, I'll be working on doing something about him." Cook held the door open for the two and waved them out. He hoped that would appease George for the time being. Jerome helped him out by pushing Bailey through the door.

"Come on, George. Let me buy you a cup of coffee," the investigator said as he placed an arm around Bailey's shoulder.

"But I didn't get a—"

That was all the chief heard before the door closed. Once in his office with fresh coffee, Cook began organizing the information he had or would need to present to the DA and judge. The chief thought they could provide a compelling case with Latimoore's statement, the investigator's report, and the fingerprint results. Of course, he was making a big assumption that at least one set of prints on the money would be Potter's.

Startled by the phone, the chief grabbed it on the first ring. "What is it? Oh, really?" Cook paused, uncertain for a moment, then made a decision. "Okay, put him through ... Hello, Mr. Potter." The chief smiled. "If you insist, *Henry*. What can I do for you? I'm quite busy. What? As a matter of fact, I'm working on the case right now. Why yes, I've met Mr. Jerome." He shook his head. "No, I don't find him difficult." After a sip of coffee, he replied again. "Is there a purpose for your call, *Henry?"*

As Cook listened with humorous interest, Potter said that he didn't want to add to his burden but that it appeared his aide, Mr. Latimoore, was missing along with his Rolls. He wasn't suggesting a connection with the missing money, but he felt compelled to share that the man had a past. He would share more if the chief came to the estate since he had no driver.

"I'll try to get out there as soon as I can." The chief put him off. "It's turning out to be a busy day. I assume you'll be there all day? If Latimoore shows up, please let me know. I'll get out there as soon as I can, but it might not be today I'm afraid."

Cook hung up and pondered his options. Though he had an invite to the estate, it didn't include permission to search. He decided getting a search warrant was still the priority if Latimoore was telling the truth. The judge might balk at issuing one against Potter, however, based on only the aide's claims and Jerome's findings. But with each passing hour, the odds of finding the other evidence, if it was at the estate, were getting longer.

CHAPTER 6

It was barely eight in the morning when the chief rang the bell beside the huge oak doors of the Potter estate. After waiting several minutes, Cook became annoyed at the delay and started pounding on the door. He hoped Officer Bert Riley standing beside him and the other officers at the bottom of the stairs wouldn't pick up on his anxiety.

Part of the chief's frustration and worry was due to the extra time it had taken him to get the warrant. They had in fact been forced to wait for the fingerprint results before finally securing it. The ominous skies of that morning suggested another storm was on the way. A second one totally unrelated to the weather was likely to occur very shortly.

Miss Purdy finally opened the door, looking terrified. She asked them in. They showed her the search warrant and she went quickly to Mr. Potter's study. Cook and Riley stood uneasily in the foyer listening to a raised voice coming through the half-opened double doors. Then Miss Purdy emerged and beckoned the chief to enter. Cook left her with Bert as he marched off purposefully.

After a loud and rather long exchange, the door flew open again and Mr. Potter rolled out, holding the search warrant and wearing a venomous look. A stranger pushed the old man into the entry hall where he waved him to a stop. The chief, bringing up the rear, was trapped in the doorway.

Potter leaned forward ignoring Officer Riley and attempted to fix his cook with a comforting look. "Miss Purdy, the police are going to be here for a while. Offer them any assistance they need. I'll be gone for a while with Chief Cook." He nodded toward the study. "An officer will be taking everyone's fingerprints."

The woman's legs buckled at hearing this; Bert grabbed her arm as Cook interjected. "This is just a routine procedure, Miss Purdy."

"That's correct, my dear. None of us is accused of anything." Potter glared at the chief. "My lawyer will be calling here soon. I would like you to tell him to meet me at the police station as soon as possible."

When Miss Purdy nodded, Potter addressed the man pushing him with a snarl. "Let's get moving, Crosby."

The startled figure jerked the wheelchair into motion while correcting the old man. "The name's Crosley sir."

Ignoring the trembling aide, Potter launched into a stinging rebuke of the chief for the rough treatment as they crossed the great hall heading for the garage.

Cook turned to Officer Riley. "Potter's buying time by demanding to meet at the station. I'll ride with him. Let the sergeant know I'm on the way. You and the others know what to do here. Get them searching while you start on the fingerprints. When you're done collecting them, get back to the station pronto."

"Right, Chief," Bert said to Cook's back as the chief rushed to catch up with Potter and his new man.

Once in the garage, Cook found Potter impatiently waiting in the back of his old Rolls Royce. Climbing in the front with the aide, the chief watched as the nervous young man cautiously backed the car out of the garage and got on the road. Crosley drove to town as if the chief were giving him a driver's test. His patience worn thin, Cook ordered the aide to pick up the pace in less than kind terms. Once they were up to the speed limit, the rest of the trip was made in silence.

Arriving at the police station, the chief was distressed to see Wade Bradley, editor of the *Bedford Falls Gazette*, exiting the administrative building. He was the last person Cook wanted to see. There was no possible way to get Potter and his wheelchair into the station, however, without Bradley seeing them.

While Potter's new aide pushed the wheelchair up the difficult slope, Chief Cook walked directly up to Bradley, blocking the man's view. "Howdy, Wade. Find anything interesting on this morning's blotter?"

"Not really." Bradley took in the scene. "But this is. Did you just arrive with Mr. Potter? And who's that man with him? Where's Latimoore?"

"Ever the nosy reporter. I'd like to stand and chat, but I don't want to keep Mr. Potter waiting."

"Waiting for what?"

"Oh, we're beginning to investigate where the B&L's money went."

"I heard rumors to that effect. Kind of thought that was a dead issue."

"'Fraid not. I'll be talking to the folks that were around about the time it disappeared." Seeing Potter and the new aide go inside, Cook pushed by the editor. "Now if you'll excuse me."

Bradley called after him, "When can I expect to interview you about this investigation?"

"As soon as I have something, if anything, to report." The chief was gone.

Cook was pretty sure his vague response hadn't satisfied Wade. Glancing out the door, he saw Bradley rushing toward the *Gazette* building and nearly colliding with Dalton Franks, Potter's attorney, hustling in the other direction.

With the attorney arriving soon, the chief barked out orders. The sergeant hustled Mr. Potter to the conference room while the chief quickly introduced himself to the new aide, Mr. Crosley. Without ceremony, Cook led the nervous young man to the break room and instructed him to stay there until someone came for him.

The chief returned to the station's lobby in time to greet Mr. Franks as he entered accompanied by a cold breeze that matched the attorney's expression. The stout, older man had arrived hatless revealing his bald head, a sign of his haste to get there. His suit was rumpled and too small; his tie was askew. Only his cashmere topcoat reflected his true status.

The lawyer's expression did nothing to enhance his appearance. The chief thought Franks could have been a graduate of the Henry Potter School of Charm. He wore a constant scowl, fitting his reputation as an intimidator. The chief and attorney had never gotten along, especially since Cook had defeated Frank's son in the last two elections.

"Dalton," Cook said without warmth.

Franks's reply was just as curt. "Adam. Where's my client?"

Wordlessly, the chief led the way to the interrogation room. Once inside and after the sergeant had left, the chief began. "I've launched an investigation into the money that disappeared from the B&L. Your client called a day ago saying he might have some information to share. Since then, other facts have come to light that I'm now pursuing."

Franks went immediately on the attack. "Information that required my client to be hauled in here in front of the community like some common criminal?"

"We might have avoided all that except your client declined to provide his information or prints at the estate. So we're here now with you present to represent him."

"And why do you need his fingerprints?" Franks demanded.

Cook remained calm. "We've acquired evidence directly connected to the case. We have been collecting prints from staff at the B&L, the bank, and the estate."

Franks was angry. "I don't understand! Why those people? What is this evidence you supposedly have that would justify such a request?"

"We have recovered the missing money," the chief said while watching Potter, who visibly stiffened, causing his wheelchair to creak. "It actually was brought to us by Sterling Latimoore. He claimed Mr. Potter here was responsible for the *theft.*"

A snicker came from the old man as Franks spoke reflexively. "How preposterous! And you believed the man?"

"Didn't say that. I did say that gave us probable cause to get Mr. Potter's fingerprints and search his estate." Cook waved toward the old man. "He has the search warrant."

Franks considered for a moment. "I see." He turned to Potter. "I suggest you let them have the prints. Then we can sort through all this nonsense and end this witch hunt."

"Sounds like good advice to me," the chief said. He could feel the tension building.

Potter rolled forward abruptly. "Good advice, eh? Well, you're not the one being falsely accused by an ungrateful employee whom I rescued from prison years ago. So pardon me if I'm not as enthusiastic as you and my so-called attorney are."

"Now, Mr. Potter, I resent the implication—"

"Stifle yourself, Dalton." The old man wheeled on Franks as Cook fought down a smile. "You're supposed to defend me against such a slanderous accusation for God's sake!"

"I'll just give you two a moment alone." The chief moved to the door. "Then we'll get those prints and have our discussion." Not waiting for a reply, he left the room.

A few minutes later, Cook reentered with the recently returned Bert in tow. He ignored the tension in the room and directed Bert to take Potter's prints. Except for a few innocuous grunts from the old man, the process proceeded quickly, and Officer Riley was soon gone. Taking a seat, the chief began his interrogation.

He started by asking Potter about the information he had mentioned on the phone. The old man quickly pointed a finger at Latimoore, claiming his behavior had been suspicious. Obviously, those suspicions were well founded since the man had possessed the money. It was also obvious the aide was trying to implicate him to somehow mitigate his guilt. Beyond that, the chief got little more. Franks often advised his client not to answer. On those occasions when he did respond, Potter gave ambivalent or evasive responses. Cook expected as much and accepted he was going to get only the fingerprints, his primary objective. But he had to admit it had been enjoyable watching Potter squirm.

With more important things to do, the chief brought the interview to an end. "I think we're finished for now. Thank you for coming in and being so *cooperative*, Mr. Potter. I'll be back in touch with you—"

"Make any contact through me, Adam," Frank said sharply.

The chief couldn't resist a jab at the attorney. "Is that the way you want it, Potter? I mean, you haven't seemed too happy with Dalton today."

The old man hesitated briefly before snarling a curt answer. "Yes, that is my wish."

"Very well. I'll get your new aide, Crosley isn't it?"

"Harrumph."

"Right then." The chief headed for the door then paused. "Oh, Dalton, be sure to inform your client not to leave town without notifying me first being he's now a suspect and all."

Before either man could mount the angry response Cook expected, he was gone. In near record time, Potter was gone as well with the new assistant nervously maneuvering the wheelchair out the station door. The chief watched them while smiling as Franks scurried contritely alongside his client, who seemed to have no interest in the attorney's fawning.

As the entourage disappeared, Cook's smile faded. The efforts of the last day had taken a toll. Once in his office, he retrieved a bottle of aspirin from a drawer. He washed three down with cold coffee while wondering if he needed all this grief at his age.

Being police chief of Bedford Falls was actually a plum job except for the politics. Right after returning from World War I, he joined a force of three. He was a popular hire given his levelheadedness, resourcefulness, and good humor. It didn't hurt that he was an imposing figure at six three. As the town grew, so did Adam's role in the department.

He was approaching forty when a drunk driver killed the previous chief. The mayor and council appointed Adam as acting chief to complete the unexpired term. By the end of those two years, things had gone so well that he ran for the office and won easily. He'd been reelected four times since, the last two contentiously opposed by Dalton Frank's son.

While he was chief, Bedford Falls had doubled in size, as had the force to match the growth. During his tenure, major crime had been rare—one bank robbery, one case of arson, and two murders over twenty years. All had been dealt with promptly to everyone's satisfaction. Routine crime was just enough to keep the staff busy. But the missing money was creating a situation he'd never faced before.

Being caught between the most popular man in town and the most powerful one was disconcerting. He could have easily handled the case if it had been any other pair. Instead, he faced a political minefield. And because of where things seemed to be heading, he feared that Potter, in survival mode, would make everyone's life miserable, especially his.

His wife had been urging him to step down since the last election. Their grandkids, living two hours away, adored grandpa and wanted him around more often. His brother had also been after him to help run the family ski lodge at Lake Placid. At that moment, both options seemed quite appealing especially with a reelection campaign looming.

With a sigh, the chief turned his attention to several files he had been ignoring, other cases that had been put aside to concentrate on the Building and Loan affair. Halfheartedly, he shuffled through each, hardly noticing what he read. With great effort and several rereadings, he whittled down the backlog.

The chief was just setting aside the last of the files when there was a knock at his door. It was an excited Bert Riley waving a sheet of paper. "Got here as quick as I could."

He pointed for Bert to take one of his guest chairs. His head was still pounding. "Have they found anything at the estate?"

"Not yet," Bert said with a frown then grinned. "But they're still at it, and I have fingerprint news."

"I could use some good news." At that moment, Cook was wondering what good news would sound like. "Cut to the chase, Bert."

"Well, based on the money and fingerprints we've compared, Latimoore's story rings true so far. The money was exactly eight thousand, and there were slips of paper dividing each hundred carrying the logo of the B&L."

"George Bailey had said that was what we'd find." The chief waved Bert on.

"We found a lot of Billy's fingerprints on the bills, a few of Eustace's, but none of Tilly's or George's. And Latimoore was right. We didn't find his on any of the money." Bert paused for effect. "But there was one clear set of prints that didn't match any that we had up until today."

"But you have a match now?" The chief suddenly forgot his headache.

Bert smiled. He nodded. "Yup. They belong to Potter."

With a sigh, the chief took the sheet of paper and considered his options. "It looks like it's going to be another fun day ahead for the BFP. Let Mr. Jerome know what you found, would you?"

It was the next afternoon when Potter returned to the station with a much more composed Dalton Franks. Before either could launch into the tirade the chief had anticipated, he struck first. "Can you explain how your fingerprints got on the stolen money, Mr. Potter?"

It was immediately clear to Cook that Potter had been heavily coached since the previous day based on his answer. Contrary to what one might expect from someone confronted with such news, Potter did not hesitate before responding. "I have no clue, but it's not hard to imagine someone with Mr. Latimoore's background managing such a feat."

"You sound quite sure, so you must have some idea how he accomplished that."

"If I did, don't you think I'd tell you? He had many opportunities in the time since the money disappeared. We exchanged money daily for various purchases he made. And he had access to my petty cash fund whenever he wished. So you tell me."

Finding that a dead end, the chief changed directions. "Why would Latimoore claim you had stolen the money and demanded his silence?"

"Again, you tell me," Potter said with a hurt look. "I have employed the man for nearly forty years, took care of him, treated him well—"

"His description of your relationship is quite different."

"He and I have always had a professional, one might call *cool* relationship. We coexisted through the years," Potter said calmly then laughed hollowly. "Oh, and he's always been a bit of a compulsive liar."

"Interesting you'd keep someone on like that."

Potter shrugged. "In hindsight, you might be right given these recent developments."

"If he's not dragging you into this for revenge, why's he pointing the finger at you?"

"Perhaps to deflect attention, get sympathy, mitigate his punishment."

"How so?"

"Well, if a pillar in the community were charged along with him, doesn't that complicate things?"

Begrudgingly, the chief admitted to himself that there was logic in what Potter had suggested. Latimoore was totally defenseless without his claims against the old man. Potter had outlined a strong argument. These thoughts made Cook uneasy.

Franks interrupted Cook's train of thought. "I believe that takes care of the fingerprint issue. What about the search of the estate? Was anything discovered there?"

The chief shook his head resignedly. "No, nothing."

"They were sure at it long enough," Franks said with a confident chuckle. "So you have money that appears to be from the B&L that Latimoore has admitted taking—"

"Money he claims your client took," the chief said to clarify the matter.

"Oh, right, because my client's fingerprints are on it. But they could easily have been planted. And the person making the claim is a known felon. Seems you have no case at all against Mr. Potter here."

"The investigation is far from over," the chief said rather too forcefully. "We'll be talking again, I assure you."

"Of course, and we'll happily cooperate when that time comes." Cynicism coated Franks's response. He stood. "Until then, I think we're done here."

A few minutes later, the chief watched the group exit the station in a much more upbeat mood than they had the day before. Besides the sight being so annoying, Cook was distressed that despite a confession, recovered money, and fingerprint evidence, the facts pointed only at Latimoore with any certainty. With a sigh, Cook headed to his office an unhappy man.

Finding it difficult to concentrate, he grabbed his coat and headed out to a late lunch that stretched deep into the afternoon. Without enthusiasm, he arrived back at his office just as Bert returned from another visit to the estate. With a hopeful wave, Cook beaconed Riley to join him.

"Well, Bert, what have you got? My day has been a bust." The chief dropped heavily into his seat. "I don't suppose you found any of the other evidence?"

"Sorry to say, no. Our guys did a thorough job and left an unhappy staff with lots to rearrange. I got an earful about that this morning from Mr. Franks." His brief smile quickly faded at seeing the chief's scowl. He took a seat and went on. "Speaking of staff, I had no luck finding any of them who had ever seen or heard a stranger calling or visiting with Potter over the last month plus."

"Great."

"But I didn't get to talk to all the staff who had been there between the time the money disappeared and when Latimoore turned himself in, four people to be exact." Bert consulted his notes. "Two were tree pruners, a Bob Cline and an Art Walker. Sergeant Brown interviewed them by phone. They knew nothing and never had direct contact with Mr. Potter."

"And the other two?"

He looked at his notes again. "That would be Roy Black, a gardener, and a maid, Helen James. We're assuming those are their real names."

"And what did you find out about them?"

"Not much except that they're gone."

"Gone?"

"Yup. Seems the last time anyone saw Black was a couple of weeks ago. James left suddenly yesterday."

The chief found that curious. "And no one knows why they left or where they went?"

"Right. No one knows or they aren't saying."

"Does that sound odd to you, leaving so suddenly and without explanation?"

"Not really. Sudden departures seem pretty common at the estate. Either Potter fires staff on the spot or they get fed up with his dictatorial ways and leave without notice. Purdy is a good example. Six months ago, she replaced a cook who walked off after a few weeks. From the looks of her, she's a good candidate to run right now."

A humorless chuckle came from Cook. "I'm not surprised, but let's follow up on Black and James anyway. Their leaving may just be coincidental, but right now, it's about all we have."

"It didn't go well this morning, I take it."

The chief shook his head. "Potter had strong arguments against Latimoore's allegations including his fingerprints being planted on the money."

"Wow." It was Bert's turn to shake his head. "We are in a pickle."

"For sure," Cook said flatly. "And I'm at a loss." His expression turned intense. "I'm going to get Jerome over here and fill him in. Meanwhile let's go over things again."

"You mean—"

"Yes. Interview all the key players again, see if we missed anything." The chief's face brightened. "Let's interview the estate staff at the station. Maybe a change of scenery away from Potter will loosen some tongues."

Bert nodded. "I'll also try to find out more about when and how that gardener and maid left and where they might have gone."

"Good idea." The chief reached for the phone as Bert stood. "You know the longer this remains unsettled, the more likely we'll never know the truth."

Bert nodded again as he opened the door. "At least we have a confession that will send Latimoore to prison."

"But I don't think that will wipe the slate clean for the B&L." Cook began to dial. "I understand from George he's bleeding shareholders already."

"And what if we find out in the end that Billy had lost the money?" Bert asked haltingly.

"Let's not think about that right now."

The chief's attention turned to the phone. "Hello, Chief Cook here. I need to leave a message for Mr. Jerome." He turned to Bert. "Get back to me with anything new."

"I came as soon as I got your message, Adam. Just got back to town from meeting with my superiors about progress on the case," Jerome said breathlessly as he entered the chief's office. "Your note said it was urgent."

The chief gulped down more aspirin, again with cold coffee. "Take a seat and I'll fill you in on the latest."

The investigator grew uneasy at Cook's tone. "That sounds ominous. What's wrong?"

The chief went over the events of the past two days. He started with the results of the money count and fingerprint analysis. Then he moved to the frustrating meetings with Potter, the empty results of the interviews with the estate staff, and the fruitless search of the estate. Cook concluded the summary by covering his meager plans going forward.

"At this point, I feel like I'm at a dead end." Cook smiled weakly. "So I sent for the cavalry."

During the telling, Jerome's apprehensions mingled with

embarrassment. "It seems getting Latimoore to confess so quickly didn't turn out to be the case breaker I'd expected."

"I never thought it would, not with Potter and all his legal beagles." The investigator could see the frustration in Cook's eyes. "And when you add in the fact the man has no motive for the crime, certainly not for stealing such a paltry sum, you see the problem," the chief said.

"Wouldn't everyone in Bedford Falls accept Potter's greed as an adequate motive?" Jerome asked.

"Perhaps, but that won't hold much water in court, especially not one in Albany," the chief responded. "It's true the man has treated the B&L badly over the years, but the same could be said for dozens of other businesses he intimidated."

"But Potter does seem to have a special disdain for George."

"It's been that way for years. Until now, Potter tried to destroy George through harsh but legitimate means. First, his attempt to close the B&L when Peter Bailey died and then take it over during the run on the bank are two examples. I can't see a jury believing he suddenly risked everything by committing petty theft just to ruin the Baileys."

The investigator shook his head as the chief returned to his earlier question. "So does the cavalry have any ideas on where to go from here?"

"Well, you're doing the things I'd be doing in your shoes." Jerome knew his response was weak and tried again. "I guess the only other thing would be to interview Latimoore again, see if he can come up with more information."

"About what?" the chief asked unenthusiastically.

The investigator shrugged. "I really had no specific questions in mind. Maybe ask him about the missing staff or the mystery person on the phone. I don't know."

"I guess if we're re-interviewing everyone else, he certainly should be included though I don't hold out much hope." The chief sighed. "But I'll do that today."

The investigator felt his contribution inadequate for the situation. Void of any other suggestion, he asked, "What part of this would you like me to handle, Adam?"

"How about carrying the good news to George that we have cleared him, Billy, and the B&L? He should be happy with that news since the B&L has been hemorrhaging shareholders lately. I'll call Wade Bradley so he can get that in the paper too."

"All right," Jerome said with a frown as he stood.

"Why the sad face? That should be an easy and pleasant assignment."

The investigator forced a smile. "You're right. But, well, I really need to find a way to end this case sooner than later."

"Pressure from the home office?" the chief asked. "I know about politics."

"In a way. You see, I have other, ah, assignments that are on hold until this one's done."

"Isn't it enough that we have Latimoore and the money?"

Jerome shook his head. "Not really. You see, if Potter walks, that will, well, it'll just make it that much more difficult to successfully complete my other work."

The chief sat back and scratched his head. "I don't understand."

"I'm just rattling on, Adam. Pay me no mind." Jerome sensed he'd said too much and needed to extricate himself. "I'll check in and let you know how it goes with George."

"You do that," the chief replied. "Meanwhile, I'll get those interviews started. I don't want to let Potter off since you seem to really have it in for the old man."

Jerome paused at the threshold. "In a way, I guess you're right." Then he was gone.

CHAPTER 7

Jerome reached several conclusions on his way to lunch with George. One was that his superiors had been right. His eagerness to solve the crime so he could move on to the other phase of his assignment had him putting the cart before the horse. He'd failed to focus on learning enough about the key players in his first job.

He also realized that to have any chance of helping Henry Potter, two things had to occur. The man needed to take a fall from his lofty perch and reach a low that would open him to new possibilities. For that to happen, Jerome would need something monumental to open him to those possibilities.

Solving the crime was now fully in the hands of Chief Cook. He had confidence in Adam, however, and believed he would ultimately bring Potter to justice. To that end, it might be best for him to focus on identifying a viable motive for Potter's actions. Such information could be vital to closing the case sooner, allowing him to move ahead.

Sharing the good news with George at lunch turned out to be the joy he had anticipated. To see the relief in his face at the news was gratifying. There was only a bit of uneasiness over what would ultimately happen in the case.

Over a second cup of coffee, George shared his concern. "I just wish you could have told me that you had ironclad proof Potter was involved. I don't trust the man."

"I don't think you have anything to worry about now," Jerome said dismissively. "Adam will see this through, and I plan on doing some research about the old man that might be helpful."

"I hope you're right, but I have a lot more experience with Potter. He won't go down easily. It wouldn't be beyond him to still lay this off on the B&L somehow."

The investigator chuckled. "You sound a bit paranoid."

George shot back angrily. "Paranoid? Damn straight. I've lived on the edge because of that man for years. And now it appears I have him to thank for nearly ending my life!"

"Whoa, George. I didn't mean to upset you. This was supposed to be a pleasant lunch."

George's anger didn't wane. "Oh, the lunch was pleasant enough. What you just suggested wasn't. I won't rest easy until that man is in the ground."

"You don't mean that," Jerome protested.

A humorless laugh came from across the table. "Think what you will, but I, along with a whole lot of folks in this town, have been wishing him dead for years. If that happened, I'd be the first to dance on his grave."

The investigator was shocked. "I'm surprised to see this side of you, George. To a person, this town thinks you're the epitome of compassion toward all."

"Sometimes that's been an act, Mr. Jerome." The heat had left Bailey's face as he paused to sip his coffee and reflect. "When I got stuck with the B&L after Dad died, I hated Billy for his incompetency. When Harry came back from college married, I hated him too."

"Hated?"

"Well, didn't like them very much." George's lips twitched. "I even resented Mary a time or two."

"What? I don't believe you."

George laughed. "Okay, not Mary." His face turned dark again. "But the years of Potter's torment and torture make it easy for me to hate him."

"I can understand the feeling, but he's—"

"You mean because he's a cripple?" The heat was back. "That's not an excuse. I know guys just back from the war worse off in every way who don't go around punishing everyone else for their plight, especially the Baileys."

Jerome held his hands up in surrender. "True, very true, George.

That's why I'm going to be looking into Potter's past. I intend to find out what makes Henry F. Potter tick, why he is the nasty bastard he is today."

"To what end?" George demanded.

"A good question." Jerome regretted riling Bailey again, but he forged ahead. "First, what I find might provide a plausible motive for his committing such a foolish crime."

George grunted. "If Potter ever goes to trial."

"*When* he does." Jerome paused for effect. "A solid motive may be essential."

"Why isn't closing the B&L and destroying me enough?"

"Because he's tried that many times in the past in legal if not honorable ways. Risking everything by committing this crime would sound ridiculous to a jury and give credence to his adamant denial. And I'm not sure his disability or revenge *was* his primary motive."

This final remark piqued George's curiosity. "What do you mean?"

"I'm not sure what I mean. Hopefully, further research into Potter's background will provide some clues. Meanwhile, my goal is to find a solid motive."

"Sounds like a wild goose chase to me, but have at it." George sighed resignedly.

Jerome smiled. "Thanks for the vote of confidence."

George slid his chair back and stood. "I appreciate your desire to fix things, but what you're suggesting seems like busy work to me, nothing more."

"Regardless, I'll be starting today. Count on me to keep you informed of my progress."

George was unmoved. "I believe you and the chief will be working night and day, but against Potter, that likely won't be enough. Nonetheless, I wish you success."

"Hope is a hollow word without action. And I intend to be very much in action."

They shook hands at the hotel entrance and parted. Jerome watched George move off still projecting anger. The investigator was saddened to have seen the darker side of Bailey. Then he decided it was understandable that someone who days earlier had contemplated suicide thanks to his long-standing adversary might hate that man.

It was early the next day when Chief Cook looked up from his desk at the sound of a knock. "Yes?"

Bert stuck his head into the office. "I finished with re-interviewing the estate staff."

"Already? That was fast." Cook waved him inside.

"Well, for the most part, they seemed more concerned about Potter being upset if they were gone too long than interested in answering my questions."

"That's not unexpected," the chief said peevishly. "So fill me in."

Bert referred to his notes. "Nothing new on any stranger or the crime itself I'm afraid. I had no better luck gathering more on the staff who had left."

The statement depressed Cook even more. He put his head in his hands. Seeing that, Bert explained. "No one was close with either the maid, Miss Angela James, age twenty-two, or Roy Black, the gardener, about thirty. The two apparently kept to themselves. Their histories, families, hometowns, that sort of stuff, were unknown."

"Do you find that odd?" the chief asked.

Bert shrugged. "Maybe not. To check that out, I asked each one for information about his or her current peers. With only a few exceptions, they knew very little about each other."

"Friendly bunch."

"Or an intimidated bunch. They universally feared Potter, and Latimoore too for that matter. They saw the aide as the old man's enforcer."

"Let's move on from what you didn't find out."

Bert nodded. "Everyone with an opinion said the two missing staff had left in the middle of the night, taking all their belongings. We dusted for prints in their rooms and sent what we found to the lab."

"Didn't their leaving so suddenly generate some conversation, some speculation?"

"Nope, nothing."

The chief grew impatient. "Did the maid and gardener even know each other?"

"Can't say. No one said the two were an item. They were seldom seen together except at meal times. Consensus was that James had been there maybe three months and Black a bit longer. I checked Potter's files hoping to find more, but he had no resumes or letters of reference on them, or any of the staff, for that matter."

The chief ran his hands through his hair. "This isn't helping my mood."

"I do have a few items of interest though." Bert checked his notes again. "Miss Purdy and a couple of other staff recalled Black mention a place called something like Springhill, Springfield, or the like, but they didn't know whether it was a town or what."

"I guess that's something." The chief tried to sound positive. "Anything from the train or bus lines?"

"Afraid not. None of the agents recalled seeing anyone matching their descriptions leaving during that time period. For all we know, they could have hitchhiked out of town." Bert closed his pad and gave the chief an apologetic look. "As you see, more dead ends."

"Unfortunately." The chief stood. "I guess it's time to talk with Latimoore again, see if the crumbs you found today might jog his memory."

"Good luck." Bert led his boss into the hall. "Meanwhile, I'll check on those prints from the missing staffs' rooms and"—he paused, smiling weakly—"and I guess wait for your guidance."

"Thanks a lot, Bert. All I need is a bit more pressure." The chief wasn't smiling. "Frankly, we're likely wasting our time on the missing staff, time we don't have."

As cells went, Latimoore's was comfortably large and held a single bed and commode. There were four cells all together along the south side of the brightly painted basement. Light flooded in through small, barred windows and from mesh-covered light fixtures in each cell. Though it was a bit cool down there, plenty of blankets had been provided.

The wide hall in front of the cells was starkly furnished with one table and four chairs. Latimoore and his lawyer had used them once since his arrival. Beyond the table stretching along the entire north wall of the room was a wire-mesh supply and evidence cage. Officers with no interest in conversation accessed it randomly throughout the day.

Latimoore paid little attention to his surroundings or the officers' comings and goings. His mind was consumed with visions of a dank state prison cell. The prospect of doing hard time again was terrifying. Even if his attempt to implicate Potter helped to reduce his sentence, he'd soon be behind cold stone walls that at his age would be the end of him.

He'd been the only person held in the basement since he'd confessed. The only break in his routine of solitude came when officers would deliver food or take him for exercise. So when he saw the chief approaching, he was surprised to find himself eager for conversation and to find out how the investigation was going.

"Hello, Mr. Latimoore," the chief said while taking a key from his pocket and opening the cell. "I'd like to talk to you for a few minutes. Would you like your lawyer present?"

The gaunt prisoner, in jail-issue blue, thought for a moment. "I think not for now."

Cook swung the door open, motioning to a seat at the table. "This shouldn't take long."

"More's the pity. I appreciate the change in the routine." Latimoore slumped into the chair. "I don't suppose you've come with good news, like someone paid my bail?"

Though the question was delivered dryly, it made the chief smile. "You suppose rightly." The chief took a chair. "And I should tell you that Mr. Potter has presented some very compelling arguments refuting your allegations."

"I expected as much." Latimoore's face remained impassive, but his insides churned. "Didn't the evidence confirm my story?"

"Your fingerprints weren't on the money and Potter's were if that's what you mean."

"And what did he have to say about that?"

"Said you could have gotten his prints on it during the course of any workday." The chief leaned in. "He had a whole lot of other points that, well, also made sense."

"So you're here to tell me I'm going to take the fall?" Latimoore asked as his mind returned to memories of prison.

Cook shrugged. "Well, no, I didn't come to say that exactly. But the investigation has stalled, and ..." His voice trailed off.

"I'm doomed."

"I wouldn't go that far." The chief gave him a weak smile. "That's why I'm here. We've been re-interviewing everyone to see if anything was overlooked."

"And?" Latimoore asked hopefully.

"We'll get to that soon enough. First, I want to go over everything with you again from the beginning."

The chief proceeded through events on the day of the crime and the time leading up to Latimoore's confession. Nothing new came from the review. As the questions continued to produce the same answers as before, Latimoore fell deeper into despair. He finally asked the chief to change the subject.

"Okay, let's discuss a couple of the staff at the estate. What can you tell me about Roy Black and Angela James?"

Latimoore found the question almost humorous. "You do know I had practically no contact with any of them except to relay Potter's orders?"

"Yes, but humor me. Right now, it's our only fresh lead."

Latimoore frowned. "Well, they haven't worked there long. Black's gone I think. Very recently though."

"So is Miss James."

"I beg your pardon?" Latimoore was confused.

"They're both gone. You're correct about Black. He left a week or so ago. James has been gone just a day or so."

"Oh, I see." The aide was suddenly interested. "But I don't know much, I'm afraid. I think James was a chambermaid. I know Black was a gardener. But I didn't cross paths with either of them much. And I made a point of avoiding conversation with anyone."

"But you worked on all the garden equipment, right? Didn't you talk to Black then?"

"Not really. He'd bring something that needed fixing, leave it, and I'd do the work."

The chief was incredulous. "Not even a casual word about the weather, his job, cars, places he'd worked, that kind of stuff?"

"I didn't encourage him to hang around." Latimoore was becoming frustrated at having to remind the chief of his propensity for silence. "Not unless I had to."

Cook started to ask another question when Latimoore interrupted. "I do remember Black bringing the garden truck in shortly after the incident, you know, the crime. The carburetor needed an adjustment for the colder weather. It was a simple adjustment, so Black waited. Suddenly, the James girl appeared in the garage and said that Potter wanted to see Black. And I remember I was surprised she addressed him as Roy. I didn't even know his first name at the time, but she did."

"Not proper using the Christian name?"

"Correct, especially at the estate. Plus, I didn't think they even knew each other. But her using his first name and then ..." Latimoore paused.

"Then what?"

"Maybe I'm making this up for my own sake, but to me the two of them seemed a bit too familiar if you get my meaning."

"Like their relationship might go beyond being coworkers?"

Latimoore nodded.

"What makes you conveniently remember that now?" the chief asked.

"I know it sounds contrived, but it's the truth. Miss James pulled Black out of sight around the corner of the garage to talk more privately. I assumed she was sharing something about what Potter wanted. But then I saw them reach out to each other."

Cook looked even more doubtful. "I thought you said they were out of sight."

"They were, but not their shadows. I glanced out the garage door in time to see their shadows touching." Seeing the dubious look on the chief's face, Latimoore explained. "I looked outside because I heard laughter, part of what I meant by them being too familiar."

The chief remained skeptical. "Okay, I'll note that. Anything else about the two?"

Feeling that the chief would become suspicious of anything he said, Latimoore decided to stop trying. "No, I think that's about it, and since you don't seem to—"

Cook interrupted angrily. "There better be more if you expect to help yourself. It won't be long before you'll be going to trial alone, and that won't be pretty."

"Don't you think I know that?" Latimoore shot back. His emotions were spilling over. "You already think I made up that last bit."

The chief's eyes softened. "Okay. I believe you're trying your best." He stood with a sigh. "Maybe we need a change of scenery. How about taking a walk to clear your head?"

The thought of being outside, even in the cold, pleased Latimoore. "I'd like that."

Soon, the two were in topcoats striding along the street headed for the Bedford Falls Bridge and away from prying eyes. The chief waited until they stood looking down at the rushing river before asking, "Would a trip to the estate refresh your memory, say something about Miss James or Black?"

After a pause, Latimoore replied sincerely. "I don't know what that would accomplish. I wouldn't want to waste your time."

"Not a waste if it triggers memories that might open new paths for me to investigate."

"I appreciate your commitment, Chief Cook."

"My commitment is to this case," the chief replied gruffly. "I want to get to the bottom of this mess so justice can be served whether that means sending you to jail alone or with company. Now can we get back to business? Is this fresh air bringing anything back?" Cook shivered against a sudden cold wind as he waited. When Latimoore remained silent with a forlorn look on his face, the chief led him back toward the station.

At the corner across from the administration building, they paused in silence waiting for traffic to pass. It was then that something in the street caught the chief's attention. "Always wanted one of those," the chief said absentmindedly.

"What?" Latimoore looked up from his ruminating.

"I was just saying I've wanted a nineteen thirty-six Ford coupe like that one for years."

"That's a thirty-five, Chief," Latimoore said.

"How can you tell?"

Instead of answering the question, Latimoore grabbed the chief's arm excitedly. "A thirty-six Ford coupe."

"I thought you just said it was a thirty-five."

There was excitement on Latimoore's face the chief had never seen. "I'm not talking about that one. I'm talking about him saying he always wanted a thirty-six coupe."

"Roy Black?"

"Yes. He loved them. He talked about a restored black one he'd seen."

"Now that's progress." Traffic had cleared, and they crossed the street. "Let's get back to the station and explore this further."

Back in the basement, Latimoore recalled that shortly after Black had come to work, he'd started an unwelcomed conversation about wanting a '36 coupe in the worst way. He rattled on without encouragement about a restored one he'd recently seen. The one-sided talk ended with Black laughing at the thought of ever having the money for such a prize.

Beyond this new information, Latimoore produced little else in spite of prodding by the chief. The best he could add was that he thought Black had mentioned traveling if he ever got the car, maybe to Canada or the south, but he wasn't sure.

The chief finally called the interrogation to a halt. "Okay, let's call it a day."

Latimoore felt exhausted. "Good. You've worn me out. I need a rest."

"Of course," the chief said looking apologetic. He escorted Latimoore back to his cell and locked it. "I'll be back later, so keep trying to recall more."

Latimoore watched the chief head for the stairs, feeling appreciative for the man's tireless efforts. As if to affirm this opinion, Cook stopped at the bottom step. "By the way, Mr. Latimoore, do the names Springhill or Springfield mean anything to you?"

Bert was excited as he entered the chief's office. "We got them!"

"They're in custody?" the chief asked with a start.

"Oh, sorry about that, Chief. I meant we know where they are or will soon be and have plans in place to take them in for questioning and maybe more."

Ever since the chief had returned from re-questioning Latimoore, Bert and the other officers had been busy following up on the slim leads that had come from that session. Bit by bit, momentum had started to build and solid information began to flow.

Absent new information regarding the missing maid the focus centered on Roy Black. The first step Bert took was to check used-car dealers and back issues of the *Bedford Falls Gazette* looking for '36 Ford coupes for sale. Bert arbitrarily set a fifty-mile radius and a two-month period as starting points, figuring to expand from there later, if necessary.

During that time, all the dealer sales of black '36 Ford coupes had been made to locals known in the community. Old newspaper ads produced two more possibilities. The first was still on the market; an unknown woman calling herself Angie Willis had bought the second. She had paid cash and driven the car off less than a week earlier.

At the same time he was searching for the coupe, Bert decided to send a sketch of Black to police and sheriffs' departments in towns with the name Springhill and Springfield in New York and all the bordering states. He also sent the fingerprints to the crime labs in the same states, hoping for a response to either inquiry.

Less than two days later, Bert received a call from the Springfield, New York police department. The artist's sketch and prints matched a former resident by the name of Roger Willis. He was a local who had served time for minor crimes during a misspent youth. Upon release some six months earlier, he had dropped out of sight.

Bert asked the authorities to see if Willis had made contact with any family members recently. The next day, an officer called to say the family had received a letter just two days earlier. Roger wrote that he'd come into some unexpected cash and was heading south with a girl to spend the rest of the winter with his cousin in Florida.

"The sheriff's department for Broward County, where Willis's cousin lives, has the residence staked out as we speak," Bert said with finality and a sense of pride.

The chief nodded and smiled broadly. "You and the rest of the team have done a great job and in record time." But his smile faded. "Now we just have to wait and see if they have anything to share that's relevant to our case."

"You don't really think they won't?" Bert was suddenly worried.

"Even if they do, they may be hesitant to share it," the chief said flatly.

The chief's phone rang. He answered. "Yes, Ron? Hold on." He handed the phone to Bert. "Broward County on the line."

It was just past sunrise when the chief, with Bert at his side, knocked at the mansion door. Cook was glad to see Dalton Franks' car in the driveway. The man had obviously taken seriously the hint to be there early. The attorney opened the door looking none too pleased.

"Why Dalton, I see you've finally found a job that fits your talents." The chief immediately regretted the attempt at humor, but only a little.

The attorney colored and replied in a rather threatening voice, "There better be a reason beyond insults to justify dragging me out here at dawn on a Friday morning."

"I assure you there is," Cook said, pushing past Franks with Bert on his heels.

A maid standing nearby stepped up to take their coats, but Cook waved her off. "Thanks anyway, but we won't be here long. You may want to get Mr. Potter's things, however."

Franks' eyes grew large as the chief addressed him. "Is he in the study?"

"Yes." The attorney seemed off balance.

"Let's get this over with, shall we?" Cook waved for the maid to lead the way.

She opened the door and announced the three men, who entered quickly. The door closed behind them. Potter sat at his desk with his new aide standing stonily behind him. As usual, the old man cut to the chase, asking angrily, "Why are you here at this hour?"

The nugget of sympathy the chief had been harboring for the sad figure before him evaporated as he spoke. "In a moment. But I think it best if Mr. Crosley were to leave."

Before Potter could respond, his aide fled the room, slamming the door. As the sound faded, the chief slowly pulled a document from his coat pocket. "Henry F. Potter, I have a warrant for your arrest in conjunction with the theft of eight thousand dollars from the Bailey Building and

Loan on December 24, 1945. In addition, you are being charged with conspiracy, bank fraud, and obstruction of justice."

"These charges are preposterous!" Potter waved his arms wide to encompass all he'd heard. "You have nothing to support these baseless allegations, nothing except that lying thief Latimoore and a meaningless fingerprint."

"Oh, didn't I mention I also have statements from Angela James and Roy Black, a.k.a. Roger Willis?" The chief's words seemed to stun the old man. "They have been most helpful in spite of your bribery and threats." The chief watched Potter sink deep into his chair. "As we speak, they're now keeping Mr. Latimoore company at the jail."

Cook handed the document to Potter, who wordlessly handed it to Franks. The attorney casually glanced at it in silence before pocketing it.

The chief didn't want to drag things out. "Given the purpose of this meeting, perhaps you can now understand why we chose to handle things at this hour."

"I suppose you expect I should thank you?" Potter asked with a snarl.

"I don't suppose anything," the chief shot back. "But I think Mr. Franks would agree that it's in everyone's interest for this to happen with a minimum of fanfare or delay."

Franks nodded and stepped forward to place a hand on Potter's shoulder. "Henry, I see where Mr. Cook is coming from. I suggest we go to town and get the initial unpleasantness over before the town wakes up and gets wind of this."

"I don't care who knows!" Potter shrugged off Franks' hand. "This is just a bunch of trumped-up poppycock, and we all know it!"

Franks' voice crackled with heat. "There is no way at this moment, Henry, that you can avoid the next few hours. I suggest you—we—make the best of it by leaving immediately!"

A few moments later, the study door opened. Everyone entered the foyer. Potter being wheeled by Franks led the way. The maid greeted the old man with his coat, scarf, and hat. Crosley took over from Franks and began helping Potter into his outerwear. Everyone was silent until the old man was ready.

Franks moved to Cook's side and spoke conspiratorially. "I trust we can do this without the usual trappings that accompany such unpleasantness?"

"Potter doesn't make it easy to honor such a request, Mr. Franks," the chief said angrily. Then he softened his tone. "But I have no problem skipping the cuffs as long as you ensure he behaves himself during this morning's proceedings."

"Agreed," Franks replied as the two watched Crosley push Potter off toward the garage.

"And please ride to and from town with him, Dalton. I think that would be best, don't you?" Cook asked rhetorically.

"Yes, although it won't be fun."

"You'll be earning your retainer today for sure."

The two exchanged humorless smiles before the attorney headed after Potter. The maid showed Riley and Cook to the front door.

As they went down the steps, Bert spoke for the first time since they had arrived. "Nineteen forty-six is going to be one interesting year and a very difficult one for Potter."

"As you sow, so shall you reap seems an appropriate sentiment about now, hey Bert?" the chief replied while pulling his coat up against a sudden chill.

CHAPTER 8

As promised, Jerome's investigation into Potter's past started immediately, but he quickly discovered he was extremely handicapped operating as an AS3. In essence, he was functioning as if he were still an earthly detective. His only advantage was the ability to get around more quickly via heavenly transport. But that helped only when he knew where to go.

He had barely gotten started when Potter was arrested. With the Baileys cleared and the crime now solved, the pressure to find a motive in support of Potter's actions at trial diminished. Jerome's focus changed to developing a plan for taking advantage of this turn of events. After all, sending Potter to jail was not his ultimate objective.

He slowly built a picture of Henry's early life gleaned by spending endless hours in courthouses, record rooms, libraries, and newspaper offices across the state. He accomplished that by working backward starting from the present. It was tedious, boring work that produced little in the way of useful information.

According to county records, Potter had bought the Bedford Falls property in 1911. The records gave an Albany address for him at the time. The investigator traveled to Albany and Syracuse in search of more. He discovered Henry Fitzgerald Potter had been born in Syracuse on October 14, 1880. His mother, Rose, had died in childbirth, leaving him to be raised as an only child by his father, Charles, an Irish emigrant.

Jerome found little beyond bits and pieces about the father's growing business and a move to Albany. The investigator turned up no personal information, no clues about what his life had been like during his formative years. When Charles died, he left his son a small, thriving dry goods business and several tracts of land across central New York State.

There was little substantive information about Henry for several years after that. Jerome got the impression that Henry had been rather reclusive even as a young man. Though little was known of him personally, there was much more available about his growing empire.

In early 1912, the veil of anonymity lifted briefly. Newspaper articles at the time announced that the industrialist, Henry Potter was building a new residence near Bedford Falls that would replace his Albany property, which had been destroyed by fire. Then a story appeared mentioning that construction had stopped due to an injury that had confined Potter to a wheelchair.

Subsequent articles were few; they dealt with Potter's businesses rather than the man himself. Jerome was soon immersed in that aspect of Potter's life. Finding the world of business and finance beyond him, the investigator decided his approach was useless without the kind of help he didn't have at his disposal.

After a month of digging, the investigator found he was no closer to discovering the essence of Henry Potter than he had been the day he had started. He was at a dead end much like Chief Cook had been for a time on the criminal case. Seeing few options, Jerome headed back to Bedford Falls to pick Adam's brain for ideas.

"It's been a while, Mark," the chief said as the investigator attempted to cover his frustration with a smile. "Have a seat. I just made a fresh pot of coffee."

Jerome accepted the offer unenthusiastically. "I'd love some, thanks, Adam. Black is fine." He sat his briefcase on the floor and found a chair uttering a deep sigh as he sat.

Cook poured two cups and placed them on the desk. "What brings you back here? Still looking for a motive? You realize it's not really necessary now?"

"I know." Jerome sought the right words. "I just can't seem to let it go."

The chief frowned. "I'd expect other assignments would be keeping you busy enough to take care of that. What have they got you working on now?"

"Not much really. A slow time." Jerome didn't like lying to the man, but he had little choice. "So I'm spending my free time still snooping around Potter's past."

"Suit yourself. We've missed your nosing around, I don't mind telling you." The chief took a swig of his coffee. "So is this purely a social call?"

"Well, since I find myself at a dead end and you have recent experience with such things, I thought I'd seek your counsel." The investigator was relieved to admit that. "I hope you either have some new information or a suggested approach I may have missed."

The chief put down his cup, smiled, opened a drawer, and took out a thick file. "Funny you should ask. I may just have something new for you to explore."

Opening the folder, Cook sorted through papers for a moment before pulling out a single sheet. He slid it across the desk without comment, sat back, and waited.

After a brief glance, Jerome gave the chief an incredulous look. "What's this?"

"A hand-copied version of a marriage license I had Bert make."

The investigator took a longer look at the document and became more curious and excited at what he saw. "Does it say what I think it says?"

"Yes. It's a record of a marriage between our friend Henry and a Lady Abigail Forsyth of Wickersham, whoever that is."

"Where's the original?"

"In Potter's lockbox. He demanded it back, and since it wasn't relevant to the case, I returned it."

Jerome held up his hands, more than a bit confused. "How did you find it in the first place?"

Cook took a sip of coffee and leaned in. "It all started a couple of days after Potter was arrested."

For the next few minutes, Cook explained the chronology of events. Latimoore had requested to see the chief again and asked if any other evidence had been found. Cook had said no, that the assumption was that it had been destroyed. When asked directly, the chief told Latimoore that it was still likely to be Potter's word against his.

When he heard this, the aide asked if Cook was sure the estate had been searched thoroughly, including the hidden safe in the study wall. It turned out it had not been discovered. So with a new warrant in hand, the police returned to the estate and found the safe. After a brief debate with Franks, they got the combination.

"We didn't find any of the missing evidence, just some cash and documents including the marriage license." The chief settled back with his coffee as Jerome's mind whirled.

"Any chance I could see the original?"

"Not likely, but you can ask Potter or Franks."

Jerome nodded. "I'll do that. Meanwhile, is that an accurate depiction? What did the original look like?"

"Old, yellow, stained, a rip or two. I made sure Bert's version was complete. Somehow, I knew you'd be interested in it."

In amazement, the investigator read the document again. "This is ..." He stopped and leaned down to his briefcase, coming up with a jumble of papers. "Hold on a second." After shuffling through the pile, he pulled out several pages then spoke excitedly. "I've found information about Potter buying holdings in England and Ireland. He expanded these holdings slowly, about"—he consulted the facsimile of the marriage license again—"not long before this. Then about the time he started the estate here, he sold them all off. Did you know anything else about his having a wife?"

The chief shook his head. "No, that's it.

"I've looked through tons of archives of all shapes and sizes across this state without a single reference to a Mrs. Potter, not one." Jerome was baffled.

"Maybe they married and divorced in England and Abigail never came here," the chief said. "That would explain no reference over here."

Jerome nodded. "That would explain a lot, but it's just conjecture at this point."

"So now what?"

"First, I need to talk to Potter."

"And if he won't open up?"

"I don't know. Maybe I'll have to do some traveling."

It had been well over a month since Jerome had visited the estate. Just getting the appointment had been most difficult. In the end, Potter would agree to meet only if Dalton Franks was present. The investigator feared that would stifle the conversation, but it was the only way to get time with the man.

Crosley answered the door at nine as Ernie Bishop drove away. Without comment, the aide led the investigator into the study. He was surprised to find Potter sitting alone in his familiar place wrapped in a shawl in spite of a roaring fire. The old man remained silent as the aide directed Jerome to one of the leather chairs before leaving.

"Mr. Franks isn't here yet?" Jerome asked.

Potter spoke without looking at his guest. "He won't be coming."

"That's fine with me," the investigator said with relief.

"I'm so pleased you're pleased."

His host's sarcasm wiped the smile from the investigator's face.

"Now get on with it. Why are you here?"

Ignoring Potter's hostility, Jerome got straight to the point. "I'm here to talk about your wife."

"I have no wife," Potter snapped.

"But you had one once according to the marriage license in your safe."

"That's not your or anyone's business but mine," Potter responded icily. "Taking the document in pursuit of me was an invasion of privacy. I'm considering legal action."

"I have no interest in that, and I'm not here about the case. I've stepped away from that."

"I thought as much. Otherwise, Franks would be here." Potter's voice remained intense. "But if you head down that path, this conversation will be over."

Jerome nodded. "Agreed. My interest at the moment, however, is out of personal interest and curiosity."

Potter's anger eased a few degrees as he took on a confused expression. "I don't understand."

"It's simple, really." Jerome was pleased he could answer Potter honestly. "I have been trying for the past month to find a motive for your actions."

"Really? Why's that?"

"Because I feel that finding a plausible motive would strengthen the prosecution's case." Jerome saw Potter stiffen again. "I just didn't think a jury would buy into your stealing eight thousand when you have millions. It doesn't make any sense. And with Latimoore as the only witness against you, a sound motive seemed critical going forward at the time."

Potter bristled. "I said if you started down that road, this conversation would be over." He started to reach for the button to call for Crosley.

"Hold on." Jerome wanted to assure the old man. "I'm just trying to answer your question."

After a moment of pondering, Potter sat back. "So you were looking for a *plausible* motive. Most people would just chalk it up to the actions of a bitter, old cripple."

"That might explain your ongoing unpleasantness but not a criminal act," Jerome replied. "You'd never committed a real crime before, at least that anyone knows about."

"And so did you find your plausible motive?" Potter asked indifferently.

"I didn't have to. With the testimony of Black and James, the need for that is gone. Ironically, however, I think I have the start of one now."

Potter's eyes narrowed. "You have to be joking. You can't believe that a marriage license somehow motivated my *alleged* criminal activity. Preposterous!"

"Look, Mr. Potter, right now, I'm just curious to know the story behind that document," Jerome said in a pleading tone. "Nothing more."

Potter shook his head. "I see no value in discussing a matter long dead and buried. I can see only negatives."

"Without knowing more, I don't know what value it might have." Jerome saw that Potter remained unmoved. "Look, don't make me pursue this on my own. I have the information off the license to start with, and I'm a very good and tenacious investigator."

Potter thought for some time before replying. "From what I heard about your role in helping create my recent problems, I'd have to agree. But I expect the SBE's office would have none of that."

"Actually, I'm an independent investigator hired just for the case of the missing eight thousand. With things winding down, I've been cut loose. It so happens I have the means to take this on myself, for a while at least, and I intend to do so. I'm kind of obsessed."

Potter waved his arms dismissively. "I find that hard to believe, but suit yourself. You'll do it without my help."

Undaunted, Jerome continued. "Is the story too incriminating, Mr. Potter, or is it just too painful?" The investigator sensed he'd touched a nerve, but he received no answer. "Look, I know from my investigation thus far that there's not a single reference to a Mrs. Potter anywhere in print this side of the Atlantic except for that license." That generated no response either. "I'm wondering when if ever you've shared your story."

The investigator fell silent and waited. The wait was long and broken only by the sound of the wall clock marking Potter's thinking. That went on so long that Jerome was tempted to speak. But he resisted the urge. He felt a breakthrough was near.

Finally, Potter spoke. "I think it would be best if you left, Mr. Jerome."

The investigator was surprised and disappointed. "I don't believe you mean that, Mr. Potter. I saw you just now struggling with the need to share your story. Now, I realize it probably didn't have a happy ending, but—"

"That's not it!" Potter interrupted sharply. "It doesn't have an ending at all, not for me!"

"I don't understand."

"I'd have to tell the story for you to understand what I mean."

"Then do. Maybe I can find the ending you're obviously seeking. I promise to put my skills, resources, and time to that end. One way or another, I'm going to do just that."

A long silence ensued before Potter spoke. "Even if I told you, my story doesn't get very far and leaves much unanswered. But if it will get you out of my hair, I'll consider sharing it. If you promise me two things first."

"What are they?"

"That you will not share what I say with anyone else, and that you will fulfill your commitment to pursue this to its ultimate end as painful as that may be for me."

Jerome frowned as he thought this over. "First, I'll have to share some of it in the course of an investigation. Surely you don't mean I can't do that."

"I mean people like the chief, George Bailey, and the like," Potter replied in a huff. "My story doesn't involve them at all."

"Mr. Potter, I'll agree not to share what you say with those folks, but I can't promise to withhold what I find in my search." Jerome's reply was firm though he feared the impact of his words. "You already have my full commitment to this effort. And if I can, I promise none of this will be used against you in this case."

Potter stared blankly at Jerome then turned his wheelchair toward the windows behind him. Silence filled the room. "Would you still like me to leave so you can have more time to consider?"

The old man held up his hands for Jerome to stay, but he didn't move or speak. Feeling awkward, Jerome settled for gazing out those same windows at the dirty snow and bare trees of a late winter day. He was becoming drowsy from the prolonged wait when Potter's sudden turn startled him.

"Though I hate the thought of reliving that time in my life, it is not as if I don't run it through my mind nearly every day." He paused and smiled weakly. "So I'll share what I know and leave it to you to live up to your promises to find me answers."

He rang for Crosley, who appeared at the door in a few moments. "Bring us some coffee. We'll be here a while." Then he turned again to the window.

The two remained silent until Crosley brought a tray, served the two, and left. Potter cleared his throat. "I suppose you already have a pretty good understanding of my business history."

"Yes, including your slow buildup and rapid divestiture of holdings in England and Ireland. I assume that has some connection to your story."

"You would be right, so I'll get directly to it," Potter said with a sigh. "One of the companies I bought controlling interest in was called Waterston Limited, a farm-implement manufacturer. It fit well with my holdings in the states. I was a healthy young man at the time relishing the challenge of expansion.

"During the first year, as was my habit, I spent a good deal of time in Wickersham, where the company was located. I spent most of my time in the finance department, where I made friends with a young chartered accountant named Matthew Watson. We were single, and we kept each other company during my regular visits."

Jerome watched as Potter paused to take a sip of coffee. When he spoke again, his voice was suddenly upbeat. "Ironically, I had just decided to cut back on my time there when Watson and I headed to the Penny Farthing, the local pub, for a farewell drink and dinner."

CHAPTER 9

She took his breath away. She had incredibly out-of-control auburn hair and emerald eyes, piercing yet playful. Her lithe body gave an instant impression of grace, confidence, energy, and freedom, all traits Henry admired. But it was the first glimpse of her smile and sound of her laugh that stopped him in his tracks and melted his heart. In a word, she left him speechless.

Henry's sudden silence was not lost on his audience in the Penny Farthing Pub that cool November night. His reticence drew the gaze of everyone in the pub; all were wondering what had brought the brash American's ramblings to such an abrupt halt. When the crowd turned to see what had drawn his attention, they fell silent as well.

Three young women stood in the doorway, all save one frozen in embarrassment. Their girlish chatter had distracted them to the point of wandering in the wrong entrance to the combined public house and restaurant. While two of the young women held back and put hands over their reddening faces, the obvious leader of the group continued her contagious giggle.

"Appears we've wandered into the local den of iniquity, girls! We best bid a hasty retreat and keep our virtue."

But instead of following her own advice, the redhead took a bold step forward, her broad smile displaying dazzling teeth between rosy lips.

Her bashful friends made imploring noises and futile attempts to stop her, but she was having too much fun. As her sparkling eyes surveyed the room, her gaze fell on the stunned man staring back at her. At first, the young woman smiled even broader at the sight of his foolish expression. In the end, however, she decided he was in some kind of daze.

While the other girls slipped out the way they had come, she moved theatrically toward the stone-like man as titters broke out in the room. Stopping inches from him, she stood on tiptoes, bringing them eye-to-eye. "Can anyone explain this one here? Be he in a trance?" That brought more snickers from the patrons.

After throwing a casual glance over his shoulder from the bar, Matthew Watson spoke with a mouthful of bangers and mash. "Likely so, lassie, for it would take a trance to stop that Yank from speechmakin'."

The volume of laughter increased.

Still not facing the young woman, Matthew raised a glass of ale. "And we all, especially me, would like to thank ye for the most wicked way you did the deed."

At that, the crowd lost all restraint and cheered.

Only then did Watson turn and catch sight of the girl. His haughty expression fell away. His next words came out as a croak. "Ah, that is, Henry, he's been ramblin' on quite a bit, me lady." He looked around desperately. "Am I right, mates?" Slowly, then with growing gusto, laughter again filled the room as pints were raised.

Henry remained speechless until the noise finally brought him out of his stupor. The girl whom he'd first seen across the room now standing nose to nose with him. This caused him to flinch and slam into Matthew, who spilled his pint over both young men. Though seemingly impossible, the noise level rose even higher.

Back down on her feet, auburn hair flew as the girl turned to leave. "Too bad. Seems he's coming out of it. Guess I better go home and work on me spells." She moved off with a wave then wheeled around at the door and with a wink, said, "Cheers, all!"

"Wait!" Henry's cry brought her up short and promptly silenced the room.

The girl slowly turned from the door, still wearing a smile. "Well, I'll be gob-smacked! He can talk or at least shout a rude bit. Not so much as a by your leave or if you please, just a bawdy demand. And what might make it be worth my *waitin'*, Mr. Henry?"

All eyes shifted to Henry, who had lost his voice again. His lips moved, but only gibberish came out. That got the crowd going again. Laughter and jeers echoed off the walls.

A confident edge returned to the young woman's smile. "Well, if you're a mind to chat me up, best bring it over here. I can't understand a bloody thing you're saying."

Matthew quickly stood and joined Henry, unsure of how his friend might react. He spoke hastily. "Now, me *lady,* we don't want to keep you in this embarrassing situation."

Ignoring him, the young woman spoke to the crowd, continuing her good-natured taunting. "Look, everyone. The Yank's a ventriloquist he is. His lips didn't move a lick while his dummy spoke. Tell me, Mr. Henry, does your dummy here have a name?"

Henry pushed his friend aside and glared at the girl. Laughter in the room faded once more. Jerking a thumb over his shoulder toward his friend Matthew, he found his voice. "This here is Matthew, Matthew Watson. And I can assure you he's no dummy."

Still carrying a grave look, Henry moved purposefully toward the young woman. "And I will have you know, *mee lady,* that I am not the fool you take me for." He paused and leaned in toward the redhead until the two were once again nose to nose. Neither spoke. The tension in the room grew.

Potter glanced at Matthew and gave him a wink before slowly rounding again on the girl. "Though thanks to you, everyone here clearly thinks me one."

With that, Henry lifted his empty glass toward the captivating redhead. "Here's to the woman who showed me up for the fool I was being."

In response, she curtsied again, triggering an involuntary bow from Henry.

The room went wild.

The lass had to yell at Henry over the noise to be heard. "Now I really must join my friends. We were headed for the restaurant next door." She turned again to leave.

"I'm afraid you have the advantage of me, miss, or should I say, *mee lady.*" Henry gently touched her arm. That caused her to stop.

"I don't see how you can say that. You at least heard me called *mee lady,* and I heard you called Henry. I even called you that just a moment ago."

He let his arm fall awkwardly to his side searching for a purpose. "You're right yet again, me lady." His second awkward bow brought a snicker from the redhead. "Let's start again, shall we?" Without waiting for a yes, he held out his hand. "My name is Henry Potter, obviously an American still struggling to understand British customs."

She took his hand. "My name is Abigail Forsyth." She was suddenly nervous. She curtsied reflexively for the third time before releasing his grip.

"And the *me lady* part?"

"Oh, my father is the earl, but I try not to let that get in the way of being normal."

"Normal, as in making me look like an idiot?" His smile let her know he wasn't angry.

"A wanker? Oh no, I wouldn't do that except in fun." Her nervousness rapidly dissipated. "Besides, you did a right good job of that all by yourself."

Henry broke into uncontrollable laughter as Abigail made her escape back out into the night.

Matthew suddenly appeared at Potter's side. "Seems you and Lady Forsyth parted on reasonable terms. I was a bit worried."

"Because I might act badly?" Henry asked, wiping tears of laughter from his eyes.

Matthew gave his friend a reproachful look. "Absolutely. Remember, I've seen you in action at work."

"Bloody right." Henry chuckled. "Listen to me. I'm sounding like a *bloody* redcoat."

"Don't say that too loudly in here." Matthew looked around in concern. "There might be a few customers ready to fight that war over again."

Henry nodded and whispered conspiratorially. "You've got a point. Say, what can you tell me about Abigail, Mat?"

"First, it's only *Abigail* to her father and his circle. To the rest of us, it's me lady or Lady Abigail, and that's quite rarely." There was no humor in Watson's voice.

"Sounds kind of stuffy. Let's get another pint while you fill me in."

The two moved to the bar and placed their orders. Watson continued educating Henry about her ladyship.

"Lady Abigail is one of the Earl of Wickersham's children. The earl, Clive, and wife, Countess Audrey, have three—an older brother and sister, Andrew and Mary. They're about two years apart with Lady Abigail being seventeen—no, that's not right. I believe she turned eighteen last month."

"My, aren't we a plethora of knowledge. Tell me more."

Their beers arrived, but Henry ignored that for the moment. He was far more interested in what Matt was saying.

"Not much more I can tell you since the earl and his family don't mingle with us *commoners*." Matthew gave that last word an haute affect intended as sarcasm.

Henry gave Matt a puzzled look. "Abigail was doing a good bit of mingling just now."

"She does carry the label of rebel in the earldom." Watson was beginning to lose interest in the topic. "The earl, a member of the House of Lords, spends a good deal of time in London. Andrew is at university. The rest of the family hang around at the estate or travel in a very tight clique of titled gentry."

"Sounds like a right proper lot." Henry rediscovered the recently arrived pints and took a sip while sliding the other to Watson. "Cheers, old man."

Mat raised his glass and drank deeply. "Actually, Lady Audrey and Viscount Andrew, that's what the brother's called being the oldest son of the earl, those two are aces. Sister Mary seems the stiff one. Ah, but Abigail is the best of the best if a bit cheeky."

Henry lifted his glass in agreement. "I'll say, and she's quite, what's the British expression for beautiful?"

"Beautiful *is* used over here too, but the unsophisticated would call her a stunner." He leaned in covertly. "And she is more than a bit of all right in that department."

"Well, she is truly stunning in any language." Potter's attention was suddenly drawn to a door in the pub that led to the adjoining restaurant. "Say, are you hungry?"

Beer nearly came out his friend's nose at the question. "Are you potty or something? I just finished a huge plate of bangers and mash."

Henry ignored Matt. "I'm suddenly famished. How about joining me in the restaurant?"

"I won't bore you with the details of our courtship," Potter said. "Would you pour?" As Jerome did the honors, the old man went on. "I'm afraid I was quite naïve in that area, a bit of a bull in a china shop, which was a mistake I'm afraid."

"How so?" the investigator asked as he sat back with his own refill.

"Well, that brings me to the earl." Potter's earlier enthusiasm for the telling faded. "By early 1904, Abigail and I had fallen in love in spite of the clandestine nature of our romance."

Potter then proceeded at length to outline the couple's rocky road to the altar. In the weeks that followed their first meeting, they were together at every opportunity. This was not easily done. The press of his business plus the scrutiny of her father and staff at the estate were complicating factors. Still, they saw each other often enough to fall ever deeper in love.

Because of the circumstances, their romance had not followed the traditional English courting customs. Besides bypassing the requirement of seeking the parents' permission to court, the closest things to chaperones were Abigail's two friends, Emily and Florence. Still, Henry worked hard to avoid putting Abigail in any compromising situations.

Their time together was further impacted by Henry's need to deal with business matters in the states. With each separation, Henry found it harder to leave and returned more quickly each time. After yet another tearful goodbye, Henry vowed not to leave Abigail again.

During one of his visits to America, a letter from Abigail arrived saying she was on the way with her family to Paris for several weeks over Christmas. The earl had announced these plans at the last minute, which made her suspicious that he knew something of the young lovers' relationship. Concerned about this possibility, Henry headed back to Wickersham.

When his ship arrived a few weeks after the start of the New Year, Henry was distressed to find that Abigail had not yet returned. More worrisome was news from the estate that the earl and Abigail's brother had arrived back without the women. Apparently, the ladies were traveling beyond Paris with no specific time set for their return.

After waiting impatiently for several more weeks, the press of business once again required Potter's return to New York. He left behind a message with Watson for Abigail. In it, he promised to return as soon as he had heard from Matthew that she was on the way back to Wickersham.

Nearly a month later, a letter from Watson arrived in Albany containing ominous news. Abigail had returned but was gravely ill. She had apparently contracted an undiagnosed ailment that had been compounded by extreme seasickness and vertigo on the ship home. The combination had nearly proved fatal.

Henry dropped everything and headed for Wickersham. The letter he sent to Abigail via Matthew had her up and about, nearly fully recovered, even before his arrival. She was doing so well that her family agreed to hold a ball in celebration of her recovery. Invitations to prominent members of the community, including Henry, went out just as he returned.

The celebratory party for Abigail was the first formal event at which Henry and she were seen together. Though Henry felt, at the time, Abigail and he had hidden their feelings well that night, the next day, things began to change. The earl began to restrict Abigail's movements and to require someone of his choice to accompany her at all times.

A few weeks later when Abigail asked her father to invite Henry for dinner, the request was flatly refused. The earl told her that Mr. Potter was not of their class and certainly no gentleman. When she shared details of her heated conversation with her father at their next clandestine meeting, Henry told her about the earl's men investigating his business and him. It was clear they had been found out.

In spite of that, Henry remained confident that he would ultimately win her father over. Abigail was rightfully doubtful. Over her objections, Henry suggested they keep their distance until he could slowly reestablish his credibility and reputation in the eyes of the earl. The two parted with him knowing Abigail didn't share his optimism of ultimate success.

Potter sighed deeply and sat back for a moment. "She was right, I'm afraid."

"Would you like a warm-up?" Jerome reached for the carafe, but the old man waved him toward the water pitcher instead. After filling a glass and sliding it across the desk, the investigator encouraged his host. "This sounds like the content of a romance novel. At least I know you get your woman in the end."

"But it didn't happen quickly or easily," Potter replied. He continued the story.

After weeks that stretched into months of following his strategy, their circumstances had not improved. In fact, they had gotten worse. Over time, the earl, through his minions, managed to keep the couple totally apart, and he intercepted all written communication between them. In time, Abigail became a virtual prisoner, and unknown to Henry, fell ill again.

"Our salvation came indirectly from my friendship with Watson." Potter's dark expression brightened a bit.

Jerome waved the old man on. "How so?"

Henry had turned to Matthew for help. The young accountant's soon-to-be fiancée, Florence Foyle, was one of the two girls with Abigail the night Henry had met her at the Penny Farthing. Further, she was one of the few people allowed to visit Abigail unescorted. Most important, the earl's treatment of Abigail had made Florence his enemy eager to help her friend escape her prison.

After each visit, Florence would meet with Henry and Matthew and fill them in on Abigail's fragile state and the situation within the walls of the estate. All too often, the news was troubling, especially as it related to Abigail's health issues. A slow decline continued over the intervening months until Henry felt there would soon be no way to save her.

When she visited Abigail, Florence usually came with gifts, flowers, books, hair combs, and the like. She would hand them over to be searched with a smile. They never yielded anything. Meanwhile, she concealed letters from and to Henry in her clothing. This two-way correspondence became a desperate lifeline between the lovers.

These messages and verbal updates on Henry's efforts to reach her helped keep Abby's spirits from total collapse. While surreptitiously reading and rereading his letters, she reveled in his commitment to her. Each new letter also positively affected her heath. The effect, however, was always short lived.

News carried by Florence that the earl would soon be taking Abigail to a warmer clime to recover brought things to a head. Over the next few weeks, plans were made and communicated to Abigail through Florence. Surprisingly, when she heard the details, her health improved dramatically, and that enabled the drama to play out.

It was an unusually warm, moonless spring night in the English countryside. All was as silent as it was black. A clandestine rendezvous on such a night was a blessing and a curse. There was little chance of being seen but also of seeing. Fortunately, the location was familiar to all.

"They should have been here by now."

It was impossible to tell from where this voice had come.

"Patience, my friend" came a second whisper that barely carried over the rustling of leaves in the breeze. "We told them to be careful and take their time. They're doing just that."

"I wish I shared you confidence, but until—Wait. Did you hear that?"

"Yes."

Ghostly shapes that quickly faded again into the darkness confirmed the sound heard in the distance. Then all fell quiet again. It seemed an eternity until once again movement could be seen at the edge of the woods. More-distinct shapes soon could be seen crossing the meadow, disturbing the solid wall of blackness.

The sound of those approaching cut the silence, and moments later, two faintly iridescent figures in white emerged into a clearing. This sight brought two dark-clad forms out of the trees whispering excited words of relief.

"Thank God, Abby! I'd almost given up hope." Even though uttered as softly as possible, Henry's words startled the women, who could not restrain a brief croak of alarm. The sound echoed through the empty night, freezing everyone.

Then with a soft laugh, Abigail rushed to her lover's arms. "Oh, Henry, it's been so long, far too long."

"That will all be behind us soon." They exchanged a long-anticipated kiss as Florence and Matthew embraced as well. The couples were temporarily consumed with each other. Then the four joined in impromptu revelry performed in mime.

Henry regained his composure and worked to calm the others. "Hold on. It's too soon to celebrate. Let's not risk failure when we're this close to success. There's a long, hard carriage ride ahead. I hope you're feeling up to it, my dear."

"Do I have a choice?" Abigail's tone was playful. "Of course I'm up to it, silly. Without you, I'm doomed. With you, I feel invincible."

"Good." Henry turned to Matthew and Florence. "Are you two sure you want to be a party to this? You know it will put you in a terrible position with the earl."

"Nonsense. What are friends for?" Florence's whisper was nearly blown away by a sudden gust of wind.

"Well said, Florie." Matthew said as Henry could just see the two embracing again.

Watson turned to him. "Our efforts don't come without a price, however."

Henry got the gaggle moving as he sought clarification. "I should have figured as much coming from an accountant. Okay, what will we owe?"

"Returning the favor this summer."

Matthew's words generated low giggles from the girls as they hurried off.

"What a wonderful price to pay," Abigail responded breathlessly as they exited the woods near the coach.

"We're running late. The vicar of Nottingdale expects us by midday. We might just make it if we fly like this wind." Henry followed the last of the party inside as a gust blew the carriage door closed behind him.

Matthew rapped the roof of the coach as Henry yelled, "Get us to Nottingdale before noon, driver, and there'll be an extra quid in it for you."

With that encouragement, the driver cracked the whip and the horses leaped forward. The jerk caused Henry to fall unceremoniously at the feet of the others. They all laughed joyously while being tossed about.

At eleven forty-five, Henry parted with the extra pound and escorted the wedding party into the tiny Nottingdale village church.

Jerome exhaled vociferously. "And I assume the marriage actually took place, no last-minute intervention by the earl."

"Indeed, it went off exactly as planned," Potter said with an air of satisfaction. "By that night, my wife and I were settling into an inn on the west coast of Wales. We returned two weeks later and settled into a rental home in Wickersham. To say our reception upon our return was interesting would be an understatement."

"And so began the not-living-happily-ever-after part of your story, right?"

Potter shrugged. "Well, for a while, all that stuff—the earl's alternating verbal assaults and stony silence—didn't bother us. We were in love."

For the next half hour, Potter covered the years following the marriage. The couple had immediately started building a new home, which was completed a year later. While the earl ignored his daughter and tried to make Henry's life miserable, Abigail tried to reconnect with her mother and brother. She managed occasional meetings with them when her father was in London, but they were too infrequent to be satisfying.

Henry was content with just Abigail alone, but she was not. The earl attempted unsuccessfully to undermine Potter's business and construction of the new home, while Abigail's efforts to win over her father continually failed. These factors contributed to a slow escalation of tension between the couple.

Shortly after moving into their new house, Abigail became pregnant. She gave birth to a son, William, in the spring of 1907. This event pulled the couple together and opened the doors of the estate for a time at the insistence of her mother. However, the earl continued to boycott interactions with his daughter even with the child on the scene, and Henry was never welcomed.

And so the stalemate continued and slowly wore down Abigail and Henry. Finally, the acrimony began to affect her health. She fell deathly ill again, and it took her a year to recover. That was the last straw for Henry, who began planning to move the family to America. Doctors told them, however, that Abigail's frail health and vertigo would not allow her to survive the voyage.

"This drove me over the edge," Potter said matter-of-factly. "It may surprise you, but I once had a pretty good sense of humor. That disappeared as my temper grew. I felt trapped and took it out of everyone, especially Abigail. Saddest of all, I began to escape more often to the states."

"How did that affect her?"

Potter got the impression Jerome already knew the answer. He grunted. "She got sick again, so I stayed put for a while. Besides her general health improving, Abigail presented me with a second son, Charles. That was in late 1910. You would think that would have helped, but it really didn't. The earl kept up the pressure.

"So at my insistence, Abigail and I met with an endless stream of doctors seeking a treatment that would allow Abigail to make the journey to America." Potter's voice began to tremble. "With each failure, I grew more angry and distant. I actually started blaming her. What a fool. Abigail, on the other hand, never wavered in her love for me. In the end, I'm ashamed to admit I ran away." Potter flashed back to the terrible decision and was filled with self-loathing. "And my actions gave the earl what he wanted—me gone and the chance to get his daughter back and under his control once again."

CHAPTER 10

Andrew Forsyth, Abigail's brother, entered the drawing room at his mother's request unsure of the reason. The atmosphere at the estate over the previous few months had grown increasingly tense and acrimonious. On several occasions, he had scurried off to escape being caught in the middle of the latest parental row.

The fights were always about Abigail, her health, or getting her and the children back to the estate since Potter was gone. That morning, Andrew had risen to the news that the earl had left early for London; that meant peace in the household for at least a few days. At breakfast, the butler, Stephens, said his mother wanted to see him in the drawing room when he had finished.

He found his mother pouring tea for two. "Good day, Mother. You wanted to see me?"

"Indeed. Join me in a cup?"

"Perhaps in a moment," Andrew said suddenly uneasy. "Is there something wrong?"

"Oh, do sit down, Andy. You're making me nervous."

"I can't help it with all the goings-on around here. It's like I'm watching a war without guns, you and Abby on one side, Mary and Dad on the other, and me in the middle."

"I've noticed your distinct lack of bravery during it all," the countess replied snippily.

"Thanks so much, Mother." Andrew felt the sting of judgment in her words.

The stately woman rolled her eyes. "Oh, posh. Please sit and have some tea." The young man continued to pace the study instead. With a sigh, she went on. "I called you here because I have some quite disturbing news."

Andrew forgot himself for a moment. "Is it about Abigail?"

"In part. You see, Dr. Smyth stopped by the estate yesterday after seeing Abigail and told your father and me that if she didn't improve soon, he feared the worst."

Andrew moved quickly to his mother's side and took her hand as he sat on the couch. "That's horrible news. What did Father say?"

"The usual, I'm afraid." The countess frowned. "He was more committed than ever to getting your sister back to the estate."

"As if her being here worked so well before," Andrew said sarcastically. "She nearly died before Henry took her away."

"True, but that is not the only reason I sent for you."

"What else then?"

She fixed him with a look Andrew felt was somewhere between pity and contempt. "Part of Abigail's decline has been because of Henry's failure to write in spite of her regular stream of correspondence to him."

"Yes, and that surprises me," Andrew said angrily. "I didn't believe my brother-in-law could be so callous."

"He wasn't."

"I beg your pardon?"

Her expression turned conspiratorial. "I was surprised too. So I wrote Henry several weeks ago. Dropped the letter in the village post myself." Andrew sat dumbfounded as his mother continued. "And he wrote back to say he'd been sending letters to Abigail almost every day. Further, he indicated not a single letter from Abigail had arrived. As soon as I found this out, I intuitively knew who was behind this."

"Father." Andrew's response was not a question.

The countess snarled her response. "With the help of that vile Mr. Bates."

"Anthony Bates, but of course. I always thought that man was evil." Andrew stood his voice rising indignantly.

"I confirmed all this by borrowing Stephens's keys and going through your father's desk. I found both sets of letters hidden in a bottom drawer, each opened and obviously read."

"That is abominable and I daresay criminal." Fear suddenly gripped Andrew as he looked around quickly. "But Bates. He's around here someplace."

"What if he is? It's too late," the countess replied angrily. "Henry will be here soon, and when the Potter family is together again, I will be there with them. No more will I allow Abigail, her husband, or children to suffer at the hands of your father or that bastard Bates. And I expect you to be there with me."

"Oh, I'd love to, Mother—you know I would," Andrew said unenthusiastically, "but Father would have my head, or worse, send me to god-awful India."

"I do wish you would stand up to him as your sister does."

His mother's sad look filled him with shame.

"Abigail inherited the backbone in the family, I'm afraid," Andrew said, attempting a smile. "I got the glib sense of humor, cowardliness, and taste for brandy. I'll just take your word about the letters."

Andrew considered having a drink but then thought better of it. "Did you tell Abigail?"

"No, I didn't, not then. Her health was so fragile that I feared the news might be too much. I decided to wait until I wrote Henry again, filling him in on the earl's evil deeds and imploring him to return immediately."

"And?"

"He's coming," the countess said triumphantly. "His cable said he would be on his way as soon as possible."

"What? He's not left already?" Andrew asked indignantly.

She shook her head. "Ironically, he too has been ill, probably due to the stress of this terrible ordeal. Anyway, whatever he has is contagious and prevents his traveling for another few weeks or so. I learned this from his letter that arrived a day ago. After reading it, I sent a message to Abigail saying I had good news to deliver in person."

"We should go right away," Andrew said eagerly, feeling a sense of joy for the first time in a long time.

"I agree and am ready. Have been for some time. Will you ring for Stephens?"

As he stepped toward the pull cord, Andrew thought he spotted the butler passing in the main hall. "There Stephens goes now. I'll have him order up the carriage."

He stepped in the hall just in time to see the door to the adjacent study closing. In a few long strides, Andrew entered the room. "Oh, Stephens, would you—" He stopped, seeing it was Anthony Bates crossing the room toward the earl's desk. "Oh, I beg your pardon." Andrew began to leave but stopped. "What business do you have in here, Mr. Bates?"

With a casual smirk, Bates replied dismissively, "Why, taking care of estate business while the earl is away, sir. Is there something I can do for you?"

"No, that won't be necessary." Andrew felt heat rise in him as he turned and left. The anger was soon replaced with anxiety. He headed back to tell his mother that Bates might have overheard their conversation.

Just then, Stephens came into the hall from the kitchen. "May I be of some assistance, sir?"

"Yes, Stephens. Would you have the carriage brought around to the front? The countess and I will be going ..." Andrew paused, thinking of Bates in the room nearby. "We'll be going out for a ride."

"Very good, sir." The butler nodded and turned to leave as Andrew moved to the drawing room door. He stopped when Stephens spoke again. "Oh, sir?"

"Yes, Stephens?"

"I was just wondering if you saw Mr. Bates, sir. He was asking after you, actually, you and the countess a short time ago. I told him I hadn't seen either of you but suggested he check the drawing room and the study."

"Yes I saw him, Stephens. Thank you. Now let's have that coach, shall we?"

A sense of foreboding once again overtook Andrew as he returned to his mother.

Potter's pause lingered as he contemplated his cowardly departure. Jerome decided a change in subjects might help. "I'd sure like to know a bit more about this character Bates." This worked, as the old man came to life.

"Ah, Anthony Bates, yet another evil man to rival the earl." Potter's anger was palpable. "Mr. Bates was the earl's right-hand man—resident bully more like it. And he was a thorn in my side for years."

"What exactly was his role?" Jerome asked taking a disinterested bite from his plate.

Potter continued to ignore his meal, as he replied. "He oversaw security including hiring and firing. Over time, he took on more and more duties. And he did all the dirty work for the earl."

"Dirty work? That sounds ominous."

"It should." Potter's face darkened. "When he started making my life miserable on behalf of the earl, I looked into the man. It wasn't hard to get people to talk about Bates."

Potter summarized what he'd learned. When young, Bates had hired on as a constable in Wickersham. For years, he used his position to threaten everyone, good or bad. He welcomed bribes whether to overlook a crime, imprison an innocent, or worse. His closet overflowed with skeletons. He was a very bad man.

Years before Potter arrived, Bates had run into some trouble and had left town abruptly. A gang leader had been stabbed to death. Most locals were convinced Bates had been hired to do the job by a rival ring. Certainly that's what the victim's gang thought. Suddenly a marked man, Bates had disappeared only to show up years later at the earl's side.

"Sounds like a very nasty but resourceful sort." Jerome looked troubled. "But surely, the earl reined him in?"

"You would think so, but alas, that wasn't the case." Potter sounded casual, but his expression showed deep resentment toward the earl and Bates. "For sure I should have been more wary of what Bates might do with or without the earl's permission."

The earl had left London before dawn in response to the note delivered the night before. It was nearing midday after a torturous ride over rutted back roads when he reached the rendezvous point, a run-down tavern in an obscure crossroad village. The earl was not the least bit happy at this inconvenience, especially having to meet a man he detested.

After instructing his driver to wait outside the tavern, the earl entered. The change from sunlight to near darkness forced him to wait at the entrance while his eyes adjusted. When they had, he saw only a bartender, barmaid, and a single customer at the bar. It was a bit early for the lunch crowd.

Then a figure emerged from a far corner and waved the earl over to a table shrouded in shadows. The lord self-consciously crossed the length of the room, passing the only source of heat in the establishment, a huge stone fireplace. Satisfied with the level of privacy afforded by the secluded location, the earl took a seat with his back to the dark room. He skipped the pleasantries. "This better be good, Mr. Bates. And why all the secrecy?"

Glaring from under the brim of his well-worn hat, the dour figure took a sip from a half-empty pint before responding. "I was concerned that I might be followed."

"By whom?" the earl asked incredulously.

Bates hesitated briefly. "Your son for one. I think he knew I had overheard the conversation between him and the countess."

"The subject of your note?" Bates nodded. "Get to it then."

"As you wish, my lord." Bates didn't try to hide his sarcasm. "The day I sent the note, I overheard your wife tell Andrew that Henry Potter was only weeks away from returning to Wickersham permanently. Further, her ladyship indicated she was committed to supporting the Potters' reconciliation to the fullest, regardless of your objections."

The earl snorted. "That's preposterous. My wife would never challenge me like that." But his assured tone was edged with doubt.

"Believe that if you wish," Bates said with a shrug. "But I would suggest that you are now dealing with a mother no longer willing to watch her daughter slowly die, a grandmother choosing to be with her grandchildren, and, begging your pardon my lord, but a wife who is no longer going to tolerate your tyrannical behavior."

The earl's voice rose. "How dare you, you insolent swine! I should fire you right here and—"

Bates interrupted calmly. "I am simply sharing what I heard directly from the countess, my lord. You see, she knows about the stolen posts."

The earl was stunned. His bravado vanished. After considering Bates's claim for some time, he remained disbelieving. "But how?"

"I missed the how part of the conversation, but I didn't miss her angry response." Bates drained his glass. "Believe me when I say the countess will not be moved. Do with me what you want, but facts are facts. You will soon face a Henry Potter bolstered by a new and formidable ally, Lady Audrey."

Feeling a mixture of fury and foreboding, the earl could not form a response for some time. When he did speak, it was with renewed anger. "So if all this is true, a fait accompli, why did you drag me all the way to this place?"

"That depends."

"On what?"

Bates looked around furtively. "I think it would be a good idea if we ordered something. We're drawing too much attention from the bar." He waved toward a barmaid as the earl stifled an objection. After the order was placed, Bates continued. "Now as to your question, it seems you still have a small window of opportunity to address this matter."

"I don't understand," the earl said, feeling frustrated at apparently losing control of what he had thought was well in hand.

Bates waited as two beers were delivered before responding. "For reasons that are not important, I know Potter doesn't leave for England for at least two weeks. That leaves enough time to do something to stop what otherwise could be the inevitable."

The earl pushed his pint aside without taking a drink. "How?"

"That, your lordship, is the question." Bates said, draining half his beer in one gulp. "What are you willing to do to ensure your son-in-law doesn't return?"

CHAPTER 11

Henry arose from a fitful night without prompting in the Waldorf Astoria well before the appointed hour. In spite of limited rest, he was energized like a schoolboy off on an adventure. He rose and filled the time before dressing, fantasizing, and scheming about the future.

He had been thinking a great deal about getting his family to the states as soon as possible. That would not be easy given Abigail's health. The first step would be to ensure her full recovery from the recent relapse. With her rapid improvement whenever he was present, Henry was confident recover.

While Abby gained strength, travel plans would be made that minimized the impact of her vertigo and seasickness. The newer, more stable ocean liners would help. Crossings were faster and less uncomfortable for everyone. The plan also included hiring the best medical specialist to travel with them all the way to Bedford Falls.

Henry had also acquired some new drugs from top physicians in New York just the day before. He hoped all this would give Abby the courage to make the trip. When all was in place, Henry was confident she would survive the trip. If she did become ill on the way, however, she would have the finest care and then a lifetime to recover.

After a quick bath and shave, Henry put on a brand-new tweed traveling suit ideal for shipboard life. He had several of them in his suitcases along with gifts for the boys and a very special necklace for his beloved Abby.

At six-thirty, he checked out and requested his bags be brought down while he ate breakfast. Henry settled for coffee, juice, and dry toast. There would be plenty of food on the *Adriatic*. As he paid, he saw his bags come off the elevator. It was just after seven. A slowly brightening haze hung on the streets, signaling the approaching dawn.

A quick inventory showed all his belongings piled neatly near the bell captain's station. Henry turned to ask if there was a carriage waiting for him when a very large smartly dressed coach driver approached him.

"Beggin' your pardon, sir. Would you be needing a carriage this fine morning?" the man asked deferentially, his hat in hand.

Henry saw a smile emerge from within a heavy beard beneath a tangle of thick, black hair. Potter's first impression was that the man's impeccable if tight-fitting uniform seemed incongruent with his grooming. The man's meek demeanor also belied his bulk. He stood six inches taller than Henry and weighed perhaps twice as much.

"Yes I would. Are you the driver whom the hotel—"

"I'm your man, sir," the driver butted in. Sensing his rudeness, the driver dropped his head for a moment. "Sorry, sir. I just figured you was likely in kind of a hurry and I didn't want anything to hold you up."

Henry waved off the apology. "I'm not in that much of a hurry, but I appreciate your concern." He pointed out his bags near the bell station. "Those are mine over there."

"My pleasure, Mr. Potter. If you wait here, I'll assist you up in a moment."

Henry laughed as he moved outside. "I think I can get in the back of your carriage on my own."

"Suit yourself. I'll be up top in a flash, Mr. Potter sir." The hulking figure easily collected all the bags at once and moved to the rear of the coach.

Henry stepped to the bell captain and placed a coin in his hand while thanking him for finding a cab. The man looked quizzically at the coin then up at Potter. With a shrug and a smile, the captain pocketed the coin and wished the departing guest a good day.

As Henry moved back to the coach, he saw the driver struggling to get his luggage in the spacious rear trunk of the coach. Henry chuckled at the sight then stepped easily into the chaise. He settled on the plush seat and glance out the window at a lingering fog. The air felt quite chilly after the warmth of the hotel. A shiver coursed through him.

His attention was drawn to the motion of the carriage. Apparently, the loading process was continuing. Henry felt it was absurd that a man of the driver's size would have such difficulty. He was about to complain when the driver popped into view at the carriage window.

"I'd suggest shutting these here flaps, Mr. Potter, against the cold and the, well, the less-than-savory sights and smells on the way to the dock."

Though he hadn't considered the other factors, Henry did find the chill unpleasant. His excitement had him burning energy at a rapid rate. For a moment, he wished he'd eaten a bigger breakfast. "Right you are, ahh ... I don't believe I caught your name."

"That's 'cause I didn't throw it, sir." The man laughed heartily at his own joke. "It's Dikens. Not like the writer. No *c* in my name."

"Well, Dikens, I'll take your advice and have those flaps down."

"I'll get right to it, Mr. Potter." The seemingly gentle giant tipped his top hat to Henry before closing a flap and fumbling with the clasp that held the covering to the coach. Then he shuffled to the other side and repeated the process more quickly. Henry glanced over his shoulder and saw the small window above his head was already closed tightly. The inside of the coach was already feeling warmer if a bit coffin like.

The carriage leaned noticeably as the hulking driver climbed aboard. A check of his watch confirmed they had plenty of time to reach the docks. At the crack of a whip and a window-shattering shout, they were off into the swirling wisps of a stubbornly drab November day.

Henry settled back for what he recalled was no more than a half-hour journey. At that hour, it might even be less though you never knew about traffic in New York. He remembered the route was either straight down Lexington or Park Avenue to Fourteenth Street. A hard right turn onto Fourteenth, and it was straight out to pier 54.

The ride proceeded relatively smoothly considering the condition of the streets. The carriage was sturdy with soft springs to absorb all but the worst potholes. Henry dozed briefly and lost track of the time. Jarred awake, he reached for his pocket watch again, seeing it was approaching seven thirty. He was a bit surprised they hadn't reached Fourteenth Street.

Henry tried to get a look out the slit between the canvas cover and the window frame without success. The cover was doing its job very well.

From the angle of the light, he could see they were still headed south. Then a moment later, they began to make a turn in the wrong direction.

As the coach negotiated the tight bend to the left and straightened again, the sounds of the city grew more intense. It seemed as if they had traded the wide thoroughfare for a crowded industrial or commercial street. The noise continued to grow. There was no longer anything familiar about this routine trip to pier 54.

He began banging intently on the roof of the carriage with his fist. "Mr. Dikens, where are you going? Mr. Dikens?"

There was no reply.

"Mr. Dikens, can you hear me?" Henry shouted.

Beyond the dissonance of the surroundings, the only reply was clattering hooves and the creaking suspension of the carriage as it traversed the roadway's rough surface. He banged and yelled again but still received no response.

Then the carriage began to gain speed, leaving much of the crowded street noise behind. There was no doubt that his third attempt to raise Mr. Dikens had to have been heard, but still there was no response from the driver.

Henry was now truly alarmed. He grabbed the door handle, but the door wouldn't open. It was either locked or barred shut. The same was true on the other side. While he was trying to understand what was happening, the sounds of the city changed yet again as the carriage made a hard right turn. Then the horses slowed to a canter.

New sounds were accompanied by the distinct smells of salt air and decaying fish. It was the docks. Henry relaxed, thinking he'd been delivered to his ship though by a very strange route. Mr. Dikens was going to get a large piece of his mind and a very small tip. His relief evaporated quickly, however, as the coach didn't stop.

It continued slowly. The muffled sound of machinery reached Henry's ears. The sound grew steadily louder until the cacophony drowned out everything. It was a steam-driven crane, the kind used to load ships. In desperation, Henry added his unheard shouts to the disharmony playing out just beyond his reach. Not surprisingly, no one answered.

The racket soon faded and was replaced by cries of seagulls, barks of seals, and distant ship horns. The pace of the carriage picked up again briefly. Then Dikens's voice cut through the stillness commanding the horses to halt. The carriage rocked dramatically as the driver climbed down. Henry began to shout at the man again but got no response.

Then there was the sound of twisting metal and creaking wood. Moments later, Dikens was back aboard and turning the horses and coach sharply to the right then slowly forward. From a symphony of echoes, Henry sensed they were moving into a large, empty space. The slit of light around the canvas covered windows faded to black.

With a shout from Dikens, the team halted and the echoes died. The coach tilted once more as the driver got down and moved off. Moments later, the screech of iron and wood returned, punctuated shortly by an earthshaking boom. The rasping sound of heavy chain followed before all went silent. Then he heard footsteps headed his way.

Trying to remain calm, Henry called out, "Hello, Mr. Dikens. Could you or your friend please let me out? It's gotten quite stuffy in here." There was no response, just the footsteps approaching the rear of the carriage. Dikens and whoever was with him began unloading Henry's luggage.

Although both angry and frightened at being waylaid, his focus remained on getting to the ship. With that in mind, Henry changed his tack. "Mr. Dikens, if it's valuables you're after, I have my purse with me. This doesn't have to become any more distasteful than it already is. I'll just hand over the money and you can be off."

At this, whispering began, low at first then growing into a loud and heated argument. "There's plenty in here for you all. Just let me out and it's yours."

There was a much more strident exchange this time. Henry caught only a word or two but not enough to understand what was causing such a strong disagreement.

"I won't miss the money and don't have time to raise a fuss either. You see, I need to be onboard a ship bound for England shortly. In a few hours, I will be out of your way."

Frustratingly, no response came. Then suddenly someone stepped quickly to the coach and tugged on the door. Loud, unintelligible swearing and what sounded like a struggle followed. Then Henry heard two gunshots in rapid succession. Once the echoes had died, all Henry could hear was heavy breathing and a feeble groan.

After a long silence, Henry heard Dikens' voice. It was thin and vacant. "Ahh, why'd ya have to do that, Sam?"

An ominous voice whispered. "'Cause he saw you, stupid. Besides, it leaves more for me." Another shot rang out. Silence followed.

Henry panicked. All thought of getting to the ship vanished. A man with a gun, someone not afraid to use it, had apparently just shot Dikens and probably killed him. Henry was sure they were in a secluded place because there was no response to the gunfire. If this Sam wanted his money, there was nothing to stop him. And then Henry would be dead as well.

Looking around desperately, he saw no avenue of escape, no weapon with which to fight back, no way to save his life except bribery. Could that work? At least there was only one man with which to bargain. Perhaps offering more than he had in his wallet would be enticing enough. It was doubtful, but at the moment, it seemed his only option.

As his mind raced, the stranger moved. Instead of approaching the coach, however, the man headed toward the horses. The muffled clanking of harnesses was followed by the echoing *clip-clop* of hoofs. The horses were being moved but not far. They stopped and shuffled about nervously. The jingling of harnesses gave Henry the impression that the team was being hitched again. Of course, using a separate getaway vehicle made sense.

Once this fellow was done harnessing the team, he would likely be coming for the purse Henry had cavalierly bragged about, and from a killer's point of view, the only good witness was a dead one. This sent shivers down Henry's spine and launched another frantic search for a means of escape or defense.

As he groped around the pitch-black space, Henry's hand hit the edge of the seat across from him, causing it to move slightly. Lifting the edge, he discovered a hinged storage space. With renewed hope, he probed inside. All he found however was a generous supply of warm blankets for the comfort of passengers.

Sitting back dejectedly, Henry worked to control his ragged breathing and listened to what was going on outside. It took a while to determine that the killer was now moving the luggage to the other carriage. It was taking whomever it was several trips.

Then from nearby came grunts and labored breathing accompanied by scraping sounds and staggering footsteps. Henry wondered what the murderer could possibly be doing. Then it hit him. This Sam character couldn't leave Dikens behind. The dead man's identity would lead the police right to him. Dikens' size accounted for the extreme effort.

Apparently, the murderer was saving Henry for last. That made sense too. One more shot and then the killer could be off free and clear. That thought spurred Henry into action yet again.

It occurred to him that the seat beneath him might also conceal a storage space, hopefully one containing something other than blankets. There indeed was another nearly coffin-like box beneath the rear seat. After lifting the lid and groping inside, however, he found only a half-empty can of axle grease with a stick protruding from the container.

Frustrated, Henry set it aside. As he started to close the lid, he noticed dim light coming up through the bottom. Looking more closely, he saw a rectangular bead of light around the entire space. Leaning in and probing again, his hand struck a leather strap attached to the bottom. Pulling on the strap, the rectangle came inward and pale light flooded the cavity.

At first, Henry thought it was an escape hatch. On closer scrutiny, however, he realized it was too small for that purpose. Most likely, it was a used for maintenance on the rear axle, which lay just below the opening. It was covered with a thick layer of grease. The driver could apply extra lubricant while on duty without getting his uniform dirty.

Henry heard footsteps approaching again. Apparently, the killer had dealt with his late partner and was ready for the final act. A quick "Give me your money," one well-placed shot, and the assailant would be off while Henry lay dead. The time for coming up with a plan had run out.

The assailant was nothing if not cautious. Instead of simply opening the door, the man he knew as Sam detached one side of the canvas covering the window. He spoke in a disingenuous tone of conciliation. "Mr. Potter, don't be afraid. I'll just have that purse you mentioned and then be on my way. If you cooperate, I see no reason to harm you."

There was no response from inside the carriage.

"Now don't be causin' me no trouble, Mr. Potter. Just slide over where I can see ya and hand it out nice and easy like."

There was still no response or movement.

The killer hastily removed the last strap holding the canvas, and as the cover fell away, he took a quick step back and to the right, pistol at the ready. Straining to see inside, he saw nothing move. Moving to his left, he peered in again but did not see Henry on either seat.

Sam made a poor attempt at sounding calm. "Playing games with me will do no good, Potter. Remember, I have the gun."

Silence.

Rage and fear apparently overcame the last vestiges of the man's caution and self-control. Sounds of frustration accompanied scratching at the door, which flew open moments later.

"Think you're clever, hey," a venomous voice shouted. "Think I'll just step in there and you'll let me have it. Well think again."

A shot rang out followed by a primal scream as Sam leaped inside, swinging his gun wildly about and hitting nothing. In the near total darkness, light from the partially open rear storage box caught his eye. He reached down and opened the lid causing the axle grease can propping it up to fall inside. A dim rectangular shaft of light illuminated Sam's shocked and panicked expression.

Henry held his breath, hoping the man would assume he had somehow escaped through the narrow opening at the bottom. Taking the bait, Sam raised the lid full open and leaned awkwardly into the space trying to confirm his fears. At that instant, the lid of the other seat flew open and Potter emerged, shoving the man as hard as he could.

A glancing blow sent the off-balance killer into the space beneath the seat. In near total darkness again, the killer thrashed about, kicking Henry with his legs that protruded from between the lid and front edge of the box. While Henry was thinking what to do next, a bullet pierced the front of the seat and barely missed Henry.

Potter groped for the edge of the lid and slammed it down violently on the killer's exposed legs. There was a sharp crack followed by a scream. Adrenaline pumping, Henry prepared to smash the lid down again when another shot that whistled by his ear and out through the top of the carriage.

Potter slammed the lid on the man's legs again with a thud, eliciting another cry along with a string of epithets. Seeing no merit in remaining a target in a confined space, Henry leaped out the door. He landed hard but regained his balance and found himself in a large warehouse. A few windows at the top of twenty-foot-high brick walls were fighting a losing battle against the darkness. Barely visible was a second coach some twenty yards away with the horses nervously crow-hopping about in full harness.

This far-less-opulent vehicle faced the exit to the warehouse. A quick glance in that direction revealed the bright outline of large carriage doors. These were closed and secured in some fashion. Light shone through dozens of small holes in the wood.

Hearing movement from the carriage behind him, Henry dashed toward the doors some seventy feet away. Once there, he found a massive chain wrapped around two sturdy iron handles. A new and imposing lock held everything securely in place. He realized he was still trapped, just in a much bigger cage. He had the advantage of movement, however, while his adversary's leg was injured badly, he hoped.

The thought of the killer had Henry peering back into the darkness from which he had come. He saw a muzzle flash and heard a thud. Wood splintered a few feet away. Diving to his right, Henry looked back to see that he'd been standing in front of the crack between the doors, making him an easy target.

Henry crab-crawled to the wall next to the doors and searched along it hoping to find another exit. Some twenty yards later, he reached a corner. A noise drew his attention back to the carriages.

As he rested in the deep shadows, Henry assessed what he could see. Thanks to scant light coming through and around the doors and high windows, he could make out the dim outline of both coaches and the skittish horses. Where he lay was in near total darkness. Glancing up, he made out the edge of a second level that shielded him from the light of the high windows.

Henry rose to a crouch and began to creep along the second wall void of light. He soon found himself bumping into and slipping around remnants of packing crates and neglected machinery. With each encounter, he expected to hear the report of the gun.

He was soon within a few yards of the second coach and horses. He remained perfectly still as his eyes scanned for any other movement. There was none. Henry realized his escape depended on finding the man and getting the key to the lock.

It was then that the murderer came into view. Obviously in pain, he was dragging himself slowly onto the coach seat. A sorrowful groan echoed through the huge but empty warehouse as the man sat down awkwardly.

Glancing in Henry's general direction, the killer spoke through gritted teeth. "Seems I'm out a practice, Potter. I'm really a better shot than I've shown thus far, laddie." He chuckled. "I really need to tie up loose ends, you know, throw you in with the fishies along with Dikens back there." He waved his pistol casually behind him, keeping his eyes where he thought Henry might be. "I'd luv your bulgin' purse too. But the cash I've already got is more than adequate. Makes this here gimpy leg almost worth it."

As he listened, it struck Henry that first Dikens and now Sam had called him by name. And the killer had mentioned a payment he'd already received. It became sickeningly clear that this wasn't meant to be a robbery. It was supposed to be a murder. The robbery was just a cover for the real motive. Someone had hired these thugs to eliminate him.

The killer's voice drew Henry back. "I guess you're not going to speak up let alone step out here where I can get a clear shot."

At a distance, Henry thought he saw a sinister smile crease the killer's face as he waved the gun about.

"And so I'll just take my chances with the law. Once I get this leg fixed, maybe I'll take an ocean cruise like the one you're missing." A stab of pain cut Sam's laugh short.

As the murderer rubbed his aching leg, Henry broke his silence. "How do you know my name?"

The startled man stood with difficulty and pointed his gun vaguely in the direction of the voice. Easing the weapon down, he snarled a response. "Wouldn't ya like to know?"

"As a matter of fact, yes." Henry's words echoed off the warehouse walls as he shifted his location a few precautionary yards.

"Then why don't you come a little closer and I'll tell ya."

A hollow laugh came from the darkness. "I'm no fool, Sam. Not like Dikens."

"You think he was a fool, hey?" The criminal wanted desperately for Henry to keep talking on the off chance he could get a clear shot.

"For trusting *you*, absolutely."

Sam chuckled again. "True, true." A sound behind him prompted the murderer to turn abruptly, in pain and collapsing onto the seat. In pain, he snarled in Henry's direction. "Nice try, Potter, but that don't scare me much."

"But me knowing your first name and Dikens' too should. I can describe you and your dead pal pretty well. I have influence in this city. I could get a pretty good manhunt going for the likes of you in no time."

"Since you won't come out and face me like a man, I guess I'll just be takin' my chances. Once I leave and lock you in here, I'll be long gone."

"How do you hope to manage that lock with a bum leg?" Henry almost regretted asking the question, suddenly figuring that the man would have to kill him to accomplish that without fear of an ambush.

Sam leaned down into the well of the wagon and lifted up a shotgun. "I got this here to take care of the lock on this side." He propped it up in easy reach. He leaned to retrieve something else. "And I got these spare locks for the outside."

"You're a resourceful killer, I'll say that." Henry shifted again, wanting nothing to do with the shotgun. "But before you go, wouldn't you like a last chance at my bulging purse?"

"What do you have in mind, a fight to the finish, winner take all? That wouldn't be fair what with me nursin' this bad leg. Then again, I do have these here guns."

"True. But I figure you're going to get away and I'm going to live. So I'm feeling much better than I did a short while ago. And I know my legs feel better than yours."

"Very funny, Potter," the killer said without humor. "But what's your point?"

"The point is I have this money and plenty more where that came from." Henry moved deeper into the shadows, sensing Sam was trying to target him by his voice. "What I don't have is the information about who hired you. I'd gladly make a trade."

Henry could see that Sam was giving the idea careful consideration. The man smiled at a spot several yards to Henry's left.

"Okay. You got a deal. Toss me the money and then I'll tell you."

"How about I toss you half, you talk, and then I'll toss the rest."

Sam shook his head. "Two problems with that. What are you going to toss it in? You've got only your wallet. And how will I know you'll throw the second half?"

"Good points," Henry replied. "But I have about two thousand dollars here. If I stiff you with the second half, you're still a much richer man." He actually had only half that in cash. "After I toss the wallet with half the money to you, you can toss it back empty."

Sam gave that plenty of thought. "Okay. Step out here so I can see where you're tossing it from."

Henry laughed heartily and kept moving in the shadows. "That's a good one. I'm not stepping into the light with you armed to the teeth."

"So we have a stalemate again."

"Not if you agree to put the pistol in the well there and the shotgun on the top of the carriage out of easy reach. Then I'd consider stepping out long enough to toss it to you."

Though the men didn't trust each other, the money was too tempting and the information too important for them not to agree.

The first exchange went without a hitch. Once Sam counted the thousand, he flung the wallet back into the darkness toward Potter and started talking. It didn't take him long to confirm what Henry had suspected.

"Now I've lived up to my part of the bargain," the killer said righteously. "You gonna welsh on the last part?"

"No, Sam." Henry said once again moving toward the dim light. "Here it comes." Henry flung his empty wallet high over the murderer's head. As Sam automatically reached up to grab it, Henry rushed in and spooked the horses then headed for the killer. The horses jerked forward just enough to send Sam sprawling onto the roof of the carriage. He cried out in pain as he struggled to regain his balance.

Henry reached the top of the coach as Sam righted himself. Both instinctively glanced to the shotgun on the coach roof and to the well, where the pistol lay. Neither was within easy reach without undue risk. But feeling he had the advantage over the injured killer, Henry lunged at the man only to see the blackjack in his hand too late.

As he lifted his new weapon to strike, Sam stepped onto his injured leg and nearly fell. At the same time, Henry's foot tangled momentarily in the reins lying at the bottom of the driver's well, causing him to miss the blackjack and having to settle for a hunk of the killer's coat sleeve.

With his left hand, the killer grabbed the lapel of Henry's coat. Using his intended victim's momentum, Sam accelerated Henry past him. The only thing left to Potter was his hold on Sam's coat. Trying to break free of this grip, the killer pivoted further to his left on his good leg, deftly avoiding Henry's careening body. In the same motion, the criminal applied a glancing blow with the blackjack to the side of Henry's head.

Desperately holding onto Sam's coat, Henry wavered on the verge of falling to the rock-hard dirt floor a dozen feet below. To avoid following Henry to the ground the killer yanked back hard on his coat sleeve. It came free.

Simultaneously, both men began to fall. In order to break free, the killer was forced to place his weight once again on his damaged leg. Unable to take more abuse, the limb collapsed, throwing him off balance and backward over the front of the coach. The murderer landed directly beneath the flashing hooves of the four terrified horses.

An instant later, Henry hit the floor headfirst with a sickening thud. He never felt the impact. The blow from the blackjack had already rendered him unconscious. He lay unmoving with limbs askew in a billowing cloud of long-dormant dust.

CHAPTER 12

"So that's how you ended up in that chair?" Jerome said flatly. "That explains a lot."

The investigator's comment brought Potter out of his reverie. "What? Oh, well, I don't know what you mean by that. If you're saying I'll get some kind of sympathy out of this, that's not why I told you. I'll stick with my attorneys in court."

"What happened then? How'd you get out of that warehouse?" Jerome asked.

Reminded of the reason behind his confinement, Potter suddenly felt the room close in. "I'm calling an end to this, Mr. Jerome. I have other things to do and frankly am tired of dredging up the past, especially the sad parts."

"I understand, Mr. Potter," Jerome said but paused to make sure Potter would not change his mind. When it appeared he wouldn't, Jerome stood. "Do you think we could meet again and finish the story?"

That angered Potter. "I said I was done! You'll have to be satisfied with what you've learned already, more than I intended to share, I might add."

Jerome held his hands up in surrender. "I'm sorry to upset you. You've been more than generous. I'll just have to fill in the rest myself."

"The rest?" Potter asked incredulously.

"The aftermath of your injury," the investigator explained while shifting from one foot to the other. "Of course your time in Bedford Falls is well documented. So it's just that period between the kidnap attempt—when was that anyway?"

"January of nineteen twelve." Potter answered reflexively then scowled. "Clever, Mr. Jerome. Now will you leave?"

"I wasn't purposely baiting you," Jerome said with an embarrassed smile. "But I'm not sure if I can proceed without knowing a bit more, like what happened to you and Abigail after the accident."

Potter reached to ring for Crosley but realized what Jerome had said was true. He laughed weakly at his folly and sighed. "Sit back down, Mr. Jerome, and let's get this done."

"What?" Jerome looked surprised and pleased. "Oh, very well. Whatever you say."

As Jerome settled again, Potter began in a rush. He and the bodies were found the next day thanks to the ungodly racket made by the starving, thirsty, and panicked horses. He spent the next two months in a coma. He awoke to paraplegia and amnesia. The police used his ship ticket and travel papers to find Henry's solicitor in Albany, who came to his aid. Since the man didn't know about Abigail, he made no attempt to contact her.

Potter paused at this point and tried to explain why he'd kept his marriage secret but fell short. He mumbled something about his nature of being very private in business, and apparently, the habit extended into his personal life. His family being in England seemed to make it logical and easy at the time. In truth, it left Abigail hanging another two months while his memory slowly returned.

When he finally got the news about Abigail's condition, construction on the new estate outside Bedford Falls immediately stopped and the workers released. He wired the countess telling her he would be on the way to England as soon as he recovered from a case of scarlet fever. A few days later, he headed to New York. As far as the few people he'd informed in Albany knew, he was leaving permanently. Next to no one knew him in Bedford Falls.

The investigator shook his head. "And those in Wickersham were clueless as to why you never showed up."

"Since I was essentially incommunicado, that was true stateside, but not for those in England." Potter saw a confused look on Jerome's face.

"As I found out much later, the earl informed Abigail and the countess that I was near death and wouldn't survive let alone return to England."

"How did he explain knowing that?"

Potter gave the investigator a knowing smile. "It seems Mr. Bates happened on this dire news while on assignment in the states. Convenient, eh?"

"Ah, *now* I understand why you suggested the earl hadn't reined in Bates," Jerome said disgustedly. "Bates arranged for the kidnapping and botched murder while in New York. And there is only one person who could have sanctioned that."

"That was what that murderer Sam told me, at least the part about Bates," Potter said with some satisfaction. "I have to admit, I didn't believe her father would go that far. Bates, yes, but not the earl."

"When did you find out about what the earl told Abigail?"

Potter thought for a moment. "In May or June nineteen twelve. I went to a convalescent hospital in Albany, where I immediately came down with pneumonia and nearly died. Then very slowly, my physical health improved though my memory lagged.

"It was late summer when I began to recall things in volume, one of which was Bedford Falls. Details including the name didn't emerge for perhaps another month. When it did, I was still too ill to travel, so I sent my attorney there. He returned with the contents of the post office box.

"It contained a single letter from Abigail. In it, I learned what the earl had claimed. She was frantic to know the truth," Potter said despairingly. "The letter also said regardless of that truth, she was coming. She would not raise the boys anywhere near the earl. This surprised me greatly given her fragile health, especially since she never arrived."

"Did she outline her plan for getting here?"

"No. The earl had more or less imprisoned her again, so she was keeping the details secret from everyone and trusting nobody. She was paranoid of her father and Bates. The only other thing the letter disclosed was her intent to see me by spring if I was alive. I read that letter at least nine months after its writing. She never came."

"That was the only letter from your wife. What about the countess or any others?"

Potter rubbed his chin. "There were a couple of cables from Matthew Watson about what was going on, but since he was quite removed from the situation, they were obviously quite vague. Then there were the letters from the countess. They began shortly after the date of the one from Abigail. Mostly, they centered on whether Abigail and the boys were with me and why there was no communication from either of us. Each letter was more frantic."

"And all that time you were incapacitated and Abigail nowhere to be found?"

"I explained that to the countess when I was finally able. In her next letter, I learned that Abigail's health had declined to the point that she moved back to the estate. She was there when the earl broke the news about my condition. Shortly after that, in spite of her medical issues, Abigail and the boys disappeared one night without a trace.

"When she also shared that the earl had conducted his own investigation first, which delayed involvement of Scotland Yard, I immediately started my own search. I hired private investigators in England and here. But by then, the trail was cold."

"How long did you search?"

"For years." There was anguish in Potter's voice. "At first, it was a full-time effort, but it slowly subsided. I think it came to a near halt when I learned that the countess had died. Some say she committed suicide."

"When was that?"

"A year or so after the disappearances. After she was gone, there was only Andrew and, well, he was never too keen on crossing his father." Potter sighed sadly. "So my last link to that past life, Abigail and the boys, seemed to be gone until now."

"I can imagine how hard that period must have been," Jerome said softly. "Discovering this all after what you'd already been through must have been devastating."

Potter laughed hollowly. "And it justifies my behavior over the years? Even an alleged crime?" His expression turned dark. "I'll admit coming close to ending it all several times during that period. I would have if not for the hope of finding my family. That kept me going until, well, right up until today I guess."

Potter had a thought that made him smile again.

"What's so funny?" Jerome asked incredulously.

Potter's look hardened. "Not funny, just ironic. There was one good piece of news I learned from the countess. One of her letters included the fact that my nemesis, that Bates, had also disappeared at about the same time as Abigail. And to my knowledge, he has never been heard from again either."

Jerome left Potter in a state of near exhaustion after completing a journey through a life few had known anything about. The investigator felt he'd gleaned all that the old man had to offer up to the disappearance of his family. The daunting task remained to solve a mystery over thirty years old that had baffled so many skilled professionals.

He decided the place to start was Albany since Abigail would have been headed to the convalescent hospital where Henry was. After weeks of searching death certificates, property deeds, and other individual records plus newspaper archives produced nothing, he expanded the scope finally, going all the way to New York City. Still, he found nothing.

It became clear no records existed; that most likely meant Abigail had never reached the states. That left England as the last hope. The first step he took in that direction was to send cables addressed to two individuals often mentioned by Potter while telling his story. Though he could not be sure, there was a good chance both were alive and living in Wickersham.

He was delighted to receive responses from both men. Mathew Watson, now managing director of the company previously owned by Potter and quite curious to learn what had happened to his former boss. And it turned out that the current earl was none other than Andrew Forsyth, Abigail's brother.

There was no way to achieve the desired results via letter or cable. So the investigator made haste for England and the village of Wickersham. Once there, Jerome conducted a thorough review of General Registry Office records and newspaper archives. Armed with information of the events following Abigail's disappearance, the investigator headed to Matthew Watson's office.

After sharing the news of Potter's current circumstances with

Matthew, Jerome probed what the man knew about Abigail's disappearance. It wasn't much. At that time, the earl had isolated his daughter at the estate, keeping everyone away. Most thought it was to preserve her health. It was weeks later that the news she was gone reached the town.

The only piece of new information Matthew provided was about Abigail's maid and the boys' nanny. It seems she had disappeared shortly before the family went missing. No, she had never been found. He couldn't recall her name, but his wife, Florence, supplied the name Elizabeth Crandall. As for Bates, the Watsons knew little about him and even less about his vanishing.

Next, Jerome stopped at the home of Emily Cox, the woman Watson suggested might know more about the maid. Cox had been a close friend of Abigail and had grown up playing with Elizabeth Crandall. Elizabeth was about the same age as Abigail and had been with her ladyship for years. Emily had heard only that she'd been fired but knew nothing about the circumstances.

Emily had no clue where either woman had gone. She did know, however, that at least one of Miss Crandall's parents was alive and lived in a small hamlet a few kilometers outside Wickersham. The investigator added the Crandalls to his short list of follow-up contacts.

As for Bates, she bristled at the memory of a man she'd first met when he was a constable. She recalled him as a man disliked and often hated by the community. He was every bit as evil as the earl and a perfect partner to assist his lordship in harassing Abigail and Henry. The cause of his disappearance was a mystery but very welcomed by all.

Bidding Emily Cox good day, the investigator headed to the estate. Jerome had already gathered a great deal of information on the present earl. The investigator felt that the tragedies in this man's life, short of being crippled, could have rivaled Potter's. He was more than curious to see how Andrew had weathered his own storms.

Andrew was the last Forsyth left from that time; the others had died or disappeared. He'd lost a wife, raised two apparently ungrateful children on his own, and watched his estate go nearly bankrupt along the way. At the time of the investigator's arrival, the earl was struggling to retain ownership of the estate while holding onto his dignity.

Leaving the cab, Jerome moved up the great stone steps of an estate that had seen better days. Expecting to see the butler as the massive doors opened, instead the investigator was greeted by someone he assumed to be the earl. The man was smiling broadly as he extended his hand. "You must be Mr. Jerome."

"That would be me." The hand was taken and smile returned. "Thank you for making time for this visit, your lordship."

"Oh, don't mention it. I'm delighted for the company." As the earl spoke, the investigator saw that the man looked less than robust. Though tall, his posture was stooped, placing them eye to bloodshot eye. His pale, almost translucent skin contrasted sharply with his ruddy face. *This is a man who drinks,* thought Jerome.

"Please come in." The earl held the door open.

As the two passed, Jerome noted the earl's dress, which spoke volumes about his circumstances. Once expensive but currently threadbare and dated, the suit hung on a too-lean frame. But even with those imperfections, the Fifteenth Earl of Wickersham's demeanor conveyed an image of one born to the aristocracy.

The earl led Jerome into the main hall. "I apologize for the appearance of the place. I'm afraid we've been putting off some needed refurbishing due to a shortfall in our finances. Father is likely spinning in his grave."

The earl uttered a small chuckle at the thought while moving toward a large drawing room. "We're a bit short staffed as well. My butler, Stephens, is in the kitchen."

"You don't mean *the* Stephens, your father's butler?"

"None other." The earl's smile turned to a more thoughtful expression. "My my, Mr. Jerome, it would appear you've done your homework."

"Well, yes, but I didn't expect to have the chance to visit with you and Stephens."

The earl nodded knowingly. "I expect he knows as much as I do about the events surrounding my sister's disappearance. Would you like him to join us?"

"That would be most gracious, my lord," Jerome said and meant it.

The earl looked around before whispering conspiratorially, "I tell you what—why don't you call me Andrew. My earldom isn't too impressive these days, and, after all, it is nineteen forty-six."

"As you wish, my lord."

"Andrew, remember." The earl admonished Jerome as a portly, bald man entered the room carrying a tray. "Here's Stephens now. Stephens, this is Mr. Jerome, the investigator I mentioned. It seems he'd like to visit with us about Abigail."

"Very good, my lord," was his response, but Jerome sensed a slight displeasure in the man.

"Put the tray on the table, pour some tea all round, then sit," the earl said rather emphatically.

"Oh, sir, I would really rather—"

His lordship interrupted with a wave. "Now I know this makes you uncomfortable, but this could take a while, and you can't stand the whole time."

The butler gave his master a hard look before responding, "As you wish, my lord."

As the tea was poured, the earl added, "And I've asked Mr. Jerome here to call me Andrew." Stephens' brow went up but he said nothing. "So don't think the man impertinent."

After distributing the tea in general silence, the butler sat on the couch across from the other two men. Jerome considered his obvious discomfort almost humorous.

"As my cables indicated, I'm here on behalf of your brother-in-law, Henry, though to be honest, he isn't a fan of me." The investigator smiled wryly. "But that's not important. I promised him to try to solve the mystery of what happened to his wife and sons."

Andrew choked off a laugh. "That is one tall order. Do you have any idea how many others tried that but failed?"

"Indeed I am, and frankly, I've made little headway so far." Saying that left Jerome feeling more than a little inadequate and wanting badly to move on. "But a commitment is a commitment. So shall we start with what you know about Abigail's disappearance?"

"That won't take long, I'm afraid," the earl said with a frown. "I was on the continent when that happened—had been for almost a month. I can say things weren't very good when I left. Tensions were high between everyone, and Abby spent most of her time sick in bed."

"You left before news of Henry's accident?"

"No, after."

The earl explained what happened next. He'd delayed leaving to console his sister. Soon, however, she insisted he go, saying at least one of them should be happy. Over the next month or so, he received several cables from her and his mother. The correspondence from the countess was always filled with concern for his sister, while, oddly, Abigail's conveyed her determination to be with Henry again.

Then the cables from the women suddenly stopped. It was fully two weeks after Abigail had actually vanished with the boys that he received the news from his sister, Mary. Andrew read the cable in disbelief recalling how deathly ill Abby had been the last time he'd seen her. What she hoped to gain by running off in that condition was beyond his comprehension.

"She was landlocked, you see. With her recurring illnesses, ocean travel was out of the question," the earl explained as he poured his own refill, much to Stephens' chagrin.

Andrew had wired back his intention to return immediately but received a cable from the earl commanding he stay out of the way until notified otherwise. That notification came many weeks later. Arriving home, he found a failed search, his sister Mary sent away, Bates gone, a father raging, and his mother near madness.

Within days, Andrew had alienated his father yet again by suggesting his mother needed more-professional help than Dr. Smyth could provide. In response to the suggestion, the earl sent Andrew to join Mary and her husband in Scotland. They remained there until the fall. By then, it seemed his father had moved on as a perfunctory search effort continued.

"And that's all I can tell you," the earl concluded. "Stephens here was at the estate before, during, and after the disappearance. I'm sure he has a lot to share."

The investigator saw immediately that the butler was not eager to open up. "There is nothing to fear, Mr. Stephens. This is a private matter and will stay that way. You won't be betraying anyone or anything."

The butler's continued hesitance prompted the earl to step in again.

"For God's sake, Stephens, Father has been dead for over twenty-five years. In fact, except for me, there is no one this side of the pond and above the ground who would give a damn."

This seemed to do the trick. "Very well, my lord. I shall do my best."

"And that's all I ask," Jerome said reassuringly. "Let's start with what you remember about the period leading up to the disappearance."

The butler seemed comfortable with that topic and began from when Abigail had reluctantly moved back to the estate. It had not gone well. The earl and his daughter rarely spoke, which created a deeper rift between the countess and her husband. Lady Abigail's depression immediately deepened, and several physical maladies had her withdrawing.

Though the countess tried her best to make things work, her youngest did not respond positively. The earl's apparent lack of interest in his grandsons didn't help. Though there was plenty of staff to care for them, he found the children loud, disruptive, and undisciplined. Stephens said he thought this was a byproduct of the earl's hatred for Mr. Potter.

Then a thought long dormant stuck Stephens. The first month after Abigail returned, her health began to fail as it had so often. Soon, her mother seemed to be joining in the decline. Then slowly, subtly, the butler and other staff began to notice improvement in the women.

When asked for specifics, Stephens said Lady Abigail cried less, smiled occasionally, and seemed healthier. At first, the butler thought these changes were a sign of adjusting to her new circumstances. Later, however, he wasn't so sure. Under closer scrutiny, Stephens noticed both women reverting to an image of despair in the presence of the earl.

As weeks passed, Stephens saw that the women's behavior in front of the staff every day and their demeanor at family gatherings contrasted dramatically. It was as if Lady Abigail and her mother were playing a game with the earl and his minions. That anomaly ended, however, when the shocking news about Mr. Potter's accident arrived.

Stephens vividly recalled being in the study when the earl informed Lady Abigail and the countess of Henry's dire condition. Bates had been there as well and produced a letter from a doctor in Albany detailing a carriage mishap along with the resulting paralysis and coma. The letter closed with the prognosis that there was no hope.

"And Lady Abigail took the news hard, of course," Jerome said. His statement was met with a surprising response.

"Well, at first she and the countess were both devastated."

"She didn't stay that way?" the investigator asked incredulously.

"I'm not exactly sure, sir. Let me try to explain."

After the first few days, Abigail's anguish transitioned to anger and then to something a bit more contradictory. On the surface, she was totally dysfunctional, looked awful, took meals frequently in her room, and with few exceptions talked only to her mother and Elizabeth, her maid.

Within two weeks of hearing the news, Abigail had nearly withdrawn completely into her suite, taking the boys with her. Seeing the impatient looks on the faces of the earl and Jerome, Stephens began to add the layers of contrasting behavior that had confused him at the time.

With her family, Lady Abigail appeared to be in decline. Stephens and a few other staff, however, occasionally saw evidence to the contrary. When unaware, she sometimes exhibited behavior inconsistent with the image the family saw. At the time, the staff assumed that was just Abigail having a rare good day.

Stephens also recalled that the maid and nanny, Miss Crandall, also behaved oddly at times. Crandall's demeanor, which generally mirrored her ladyship's, was not maudlin in the least. Her upbeat, almost frenetic mood was accompanied by frequent absences to run errands for Lady Abigail. The purpose for the errands was never shared.

"That's why I was surprised when I awoke one morning to the news that Miss Crandall was gone, fired by Lady Abigail." Stephens sounded puzzled by that, even years later. "She did so without consulting me, which was quite unusual. I was responsible for all staff—hiring, firing, and the like, you see."

Jerome sought clarification. "You were *never* directed to fire someone?"

"A few times, but in those cases, it was always at the earl's direction," Stephens said. "That's why I brashly asked her ladyship the reason. She said she'd caught Miss Crandall stealing valuables from her room. But that just didn't make sense to me."

The investigator pressed for more. "How so?"

The butler didn't hesitate. "Miss Crandall wasn't the type to steal. Plus, she had been more like a sister to Lady Abigail and an aunt to the boys than staff. Most of all, however, was how unemotional Lady Abigail was while sharing this news with me."

"Could she have been in shock from all the recent events and learning about her husband?"

The butler considered that for a while and shrugged. "Quite possibly. Still, even in that case, I would have expected her to be much more distraught or to have consulted with me first."

Seeking a connection between this event and the disappearance, Jerome asked, "How long after that did Lady Abigail vanish?"

Stephens thought at length again. "About a fortnight."

Jerome nodded. "And did anything else of interest happen during that period?"

"Nothing as striking as what I just described, sir. I guess the only other thing I recall is Lady Abigail's further decline and near-total seclusion after Miss Crandall left."

"How did that affect the household?"

"The earl just became more sullen and withdrawn, and the countess was near a nervous breakdown," Stephens replied. "I kept the staff busy, so they had no time to react."

"Who took over for Elizabeth?"

"I don't believe anyone did full time. She refused entry to everyone except her mother and the doctor. Various maids delivered food and tended to her basic needs."

Stephens put down his still-full cup of cold tea. "When I would ask how Lady Abigail was doing, the maids had little to share. She remained in bed giving few if any directions."

"Is there anything else you can think of that might be helpful in my search, Stephens?"

The butler paused before tentatively shaking his head. "Not at the moment. Perhaps given more time ..." His voice trailed off.

Jerome smiled and nodded. "That's fine, Stephens. You've been of immeasurable help already. Do stay with us in case something the earl says triggers a memory for you."

"Yes, do Stephens," the earl added.

"As you wish, sirs." The butler sat back uneasily, still wearing an impassive expression.

Turning to the earl, the investigator pursued a new subject. "One thing I've been struggling with since the beginning is why the earl hated Henry enough to destroy the man and his own daughter in the process."

"Besides my father's general hatefulness, he had more than one reason to want Henry out of the picture." The earl stood and moved to the large window looking out on the unkempt grounds. "He also had selfish reasons to seek revenge against his daughter, and I was here to see that unfolding."

Andrew related the events that coincided with Henry's arrival. For many months, the earl, his father, had been seeking to make a match between Abigail and the Duke of Cromwell's son. Much to his sister's chagrin, the earl was pushing relentlessly for an engagement and quickly.

The reason for the earl's obsession was simple—money. The money that had come his way with his marriage to the countess had saved the estate from his poor management while giving her a title. But after the dowry had run dry, the estate was again on the brink of bankruptcy.

The daughter Mary was already wed into a titled family but no better off financially. The earl's money problems were so well known in royal circles that the prospects of marrying off Andrew at present were nonexistent, even if an available female showed interest. That left his youngest daughter as his last hope.

Fortunately, Lord Abercrombie thought the earl's lovely redheaded daughter was ideally suited for his son, Alexander. Unfortunately, Lady Abigail could not stand the young man and wanted no part of a marriage to him. It was easy to understand why; the chubby, pimply-faced teen was known by all to be an immature, insufferable ass.

Blind to or simply not caring for his daughter's feelings, the earl decided to hold a grand ball in honor of Lord Abercrombie and his son. At a minimum, he saw this as a major step in bringing the young couple together. As the date of the gala approached, both fathers put even greater pressure on their children—one to propose and the other to accept.

At the ball, Abigail was radiant with happiness not for what was coming as her father thought. So when Alexander asked for a waltz late in the evening, she was too preoccupied with thoughts of Henry to decline.

Andrew paused and turned to the butler. "Stephens, would you get us some light refreshment? All this recollecting has given me an appetite and a fresh thirst."

Stephens stood quite nimbly for one of his age and size. "But of course, my lord. More tea, or would you prefer coffee this time?"

"I believe coffee. Do make enough for three."

"Very good sir."

Stephens left the room as Andrew continued. "I was about to say that poor Alexander tended toward the anxious and impulsive."

To Abigail's relief, the waltz finally came to an end. All her toes still seemed to work in spite of Alexander having spent most of the dance stepping on them. With a smile carrying no warmth for the duke's son, and curtsied weakly. She quickly turned to leave, but Alexander stopped her with a croaked "Wait."

Abigail was perplexed and a bit shocked to see the young man dropping to his knee. "What on earth are you doing, Alexander?" she asked quite annoyed.

Oblivious to her comment and the crowd around them, who watched the proceedings with growing interest, the young man nearly lost his balance as his voice cracked again. "Lady Abigail, my love for you is without end. Will you marry me?"

At first, Abigail assumed she had not heard Alexander correctly, but she resisted the urge to ask him to repeat what he'd said. The room fell deathly silent as the words slowly registered. When they had completely, Abigail's shock turned to incredulity. In the moment, all she managed was a weak laugh and the reply, "You must be joking."

Wavering at her feet, Alexander didn't know what to say; he simply gave her an awkward grin. The pregnant silence lasted for several more seconds before it was broken by Abigail's hysterical laughter. She immediately tried to stop it but cackled only louder.

"I'm sorry, Alexander. I don't mean to be rude, but really, you can't be serious." Abigail suddenly felt a hundred pairs of eyes on her. "I mean, I don't know what gave you the idea—" She thankfully caught herself, realizing she was about to make things even worse.

Turning a deep red that nearly matched his coat, Alexander struggled to his feet as he found his voice. "But your father—"

It was his turn to stop abruptly.

"What about my father?" Abigail's face turned from humor to anger in an instant. "What does he have to do with, with this absurdity?"

"I didn't mean to suggest he had anything to do with this. It was my own idea."

"Then why mention him?" Abigail demanded.

Alexander's eyes scanned the room as if looking for a fast way out. "I, ah, I just sensed he would approve from his treatment of me and comments that reached me."

"Oh, I have little doubt he'd approve of our marriage," she snarled in response, ignoring Alexander's obvious distress. "But he's not the one you're asking. And why would you possibly think I'd say yes?"

Alexander fumbled for words. He was suddenly aware of the crowd staring at the two. "Well, ah, I just thought we seemed to be so compatible, so well suited, so—"

"You thought? You *thought*? Did you think it might have been a good idea to ask me how I felt first before embarrassing yourself like this?" With great effort, she brought herself under control. "I'm sorry, Alexander. But I think you know my answer. Now if you'll excuse me."

Abigail stomped off, just catching a glimpse of Alexander still standing mouth agape in the middle of the hall. In a few minutes, she was locked in her room pacing as she waited for her father's inevitable arrival. She didn't have to wait long.

Abigail let him pound some of his anger out on her locked door before finally opening it calmly and stepping aside as the earl charged past. "Do you know what you have done?" he screamed.

Fighting her normal fear of the man, she responded with incredible control. "I turned down a proposal, maybe not very artfully, but you'd have to agree it was a bit unexpected."

"I don't have to agree with anything." The earl paced the room, huffing like a runaway steam engine. "You not only turned down a wonderful man—"

Abigail chortled. "Boy, you mean."

The earl ignored her sarcasm. "You did it in such a way that I will never be able to rebuild a relationship with the duke."

Coolly moving to a chair, she continued speaking in a calm voice. "And I know what that means, Father. I'm not ignorant of your circumstances, but don't expect me to go along with you shipping me off to the highest bidder."

"How dare you suggest such a thing!" In one large stride, the earl stuck his face inches from Abigail's. "Alexander is a fine young man, and his family has one of the most respected peerages in England. And it is not without precedent for marriages to be arranged for the mutual benefit of all."

"All except me." Abigail felt her control begin to wane. "I will not be forced into marriage with anyone I do not love."

"What do you know of love?" the earl spat back.

"Maybe I don't know what love is, but I certainly know what it isn't." She headed to the bathroom and slammed the door.

During Andrew's summary, Stephens returned carrying a tray with coffee, cups, and a plate of small sandwiches. As the earl concluded and Stephens placed the food before the two, Jerome spoke with a chuckle. "I would have loved to be a fly on the wall for that argument."

"Indeed. After that, a war of wills raged on between Father and Abigail. Apparently during this time, Henry was busy sweeping my sister off her feet. You got the details from Henry directly."

"Do either of you know how the earl found out about Henry and Abigail?"

Andrew shrugged. "I don't think it was too long after the blowup. Do you remember, Stephens?"

"It was perhaps a month later. A letter came from the duke claiming that Abigail had rejected Alexander because she had started an illicit relationship with an American by the name of Henry Potter." Stephens suddenly looked regretful. "I'm ashamed to say, Lady Abigail was never told of this note. Nor was the countess. I was sworn to secrecy."

Andrew reacted hotly. "Good God, man! You've kept that secret all these years?"

"I am sorry, my lord." Stephens dropped his head. "But you see, it wasn't long after that things came out in other ways making the information superfluous. And until Mr. Jerome asked today, I'd forgotten all about it."

Andrew quickly softened. "Completely understandable, my good man. Don't give it another thought."

The investigator chimed in. "That's right, Stephens." He gave the man a weak smile. "Besides, that bit of information explained why Henry and Abigail never quite understood what had happened. No wonder your father hated Potter. And that's when your father launched his vendetta against Henry and your sister."

Andrew scowled deeply. "Suffice it to say you don't want to raise the ire of an evil man. Ironically, Henry's wealth would have saved my father, but rage, anger, and pride blinded him. He put all his energy into keeping Abigail and Henry apart, and when that failed, he tried to destroy their marriage. In the end, he destroyed so many others."

"That could qualify as an understatement," Jerome said with a wry smile. "And what about this Anthony Bates? What role did he play in this?"

If possible, Andrew's expression turned even darker. "He was at my father's side through the whole fiasco." He turned to Stephens. "Would you agree with that opinion, Stephens?"

The old man nodded.

"It was Bates who traveled to America in search of Henry," the earl continued. "He oversaw all the efforts to keep Abigail and Henry apart and to make their lives miserable once married. He produced the doctor's letter about Henry's accident. After Abigail disappeared, it was he who coordinated the manhunt until he vanished as well."

"That happened not long after Abigail disappeared, correct?"

Andrew shrugged. "I wouldn't know. I wasn't here."

Stephens answered the question. "Within a week or so. There was no clue what happened to him either. Most thought Bates had left immediately after the earl fired him for Lady Abigail's escape. But I personally saw him in his room days after the initial uproar."

"What was he doing?" Jerome asked.

"Nothing. He was ill, had been since returning to the estate from an assignment for the earl the very night of Lady Abigail's disappearance."

"Didn't they search for him?" Jerome asked.

Stephens shook his head. "Not really, what with the focus on finding Lady Abigail and the boys. Besides, everyone assumed Bates was off searching on his own and didn't care much."

"Do either of you know anything else about his whereabouts?" Seeing shakes of their heads, he returned to the subject of her ladyship. "Is there anything either of you can add regarding Abigail's disappearance?"

Stephens was first to respond. "Only that things were chaotic for months." He turned to the earl. "You missed most of that, my lord."

"Thankfully, though my poor mother suffered tremendously. She was near madness when I returned for that short time before being sent to Scotland. My father had isolated her from everything going on. Only he and the doctor saw her regularly."

"So she was unaware of the search?"

"I don't know," the earl replied.

"Most definitely she knew nothing of it, my lord," said Stephens emphatically. "Staff was not allowed to share anything with her, especially newspapers. The earl treated her the same way he'd treated Lady Abigail, like a prisoner."

"And do you have any insight to share about the search itself?" Jerome asked Stephens.

"No sir. All of that was handled very secretively until the police got involved." The butler paused. "I was interviewed much like this by the police but was then left alone. I knew better than to discuss the subject with anyone, especially the earl."

"Understandable given the state he was in."

"Indeed," Andrew said. "By the time I left to join Mary in Scotland,

I wasn't sure who was crazier, Father or Mother. Come to think of it, I believe they were equally so."

Jerome's requests for anything more yielded nothing, so he wound down the interview. As he and the earl shook hands, his host had a final thought. "I don't know what good they might do, but I do believe William's and Charles' birth certificates are still here." He turned to Stephens. "Could you find them?"

"I believe I know where they might be, my lord," Stephens said and was quickly gone.

While they waited, the earl added, "If you haven't talked to Doctor Smyth, I'd suggest you do so."

"Why so?" the investigator asked as he jotted down the name.

"He's been our family doctor since I—all we children were young."

Jerome was surprised to hear this. "And he's still around?"

"Yes and still practicing. He was a young physician when he took over for old Dr. Walters," the earl said with a smile. "He cared for Abigail when she first became ill, and he delivered both boys. His signature is on the certificates Stephens is looking for. He knows us all well."

"I see," Jerome said as Stephens returned with a packet of papers. He handed them to the earl, who in turn handed them to the investigator after a cursory look. "I hope these prove helpful in some way."

"I hope so too," Jerome said.

Then after yet another handshake with Andrew and a nod to Stephens, Jerome was gone.

CHAPTER 13

Abigail's bags were gone, carried off by Elizabeth. All she was left with were the necessary clothing for the boys and her disguise. She would have only a small valise with last-minute items to carry, along with Charles.

As she waited nervously for the appointed hour, memories of the events leading up to that moment flooded her mind. Ever since Henry had arrived what seemed a lifetime ago, battle lines had been drawn. Indeed, to Abigail, it felt like a war. She had once found freedom with Henry only to be imprisoned again in a place that offered no comfort, just pain.

William and Charles had been staying in her room for some time supposedly to boost their ailing mother's spirits. There was plenty of room for them in her spacious suite. The children had finally fallen asleep that night with difficulty, likely from sensing their mother's tension. After struggling with them by herself, Abigail sorely missed Elizabeth's help.

The plan for escape complete, Abigail put things in motion early that afternoon by intentionally triggering another argument with her father. She called the earl a liar and received the desired response. At the height of the heated exchange, Abigail collapsed and was assisted to her room by Stephens and a maid. The doctor was called.

Once the doctor had left and she was in bed, Abigail directed Stephens to tell her family that she would be unable to attend a dinner party scheduled for that evening at the estate. She would dine with the boys in her room. Under no circumstances was she to be disturbed.

Preparations for escape had started immediately after hearing that Henry was injured. Since that information had come from Bates and her father, she was immediately leery of their claims and the content of the American doctor's letter. Still, the fact that Henry had not arrived was proof enough he needed her. She felt no choice but to make the attempt.

Alone in her room, Abigail had spent every waking hour planning. Every plan she devised, however, ran up against the same problems—her health, time to get away before being discovered, and traveling undetected with two children.

The one thing that she could work on while she struggled for answers was her mental and physical health. Success in whatever plan she devised would depend in great part on her condition. She improved in that respect to the point that her mother remarked on how pleased she was at lunch a few weeks later. "It is so nice to see some color back in your cheeks, Abigail. Do you see that, Clive?"

The earl looked up from his meal and grunted. "It's about time. I hope that means she's putting memories of that dreadful man and the past behind her."

"That will never happen, Father. And those two boys are a constant reminder of the life I lost." Abigail left the table in tears.

Later that night while sneaking to the kitchen for a supplemental snack, Abby heard her father's voice coming from the study. She stepped quietly behind the partially open door and listened intently. "It seems Lady Abigail has turned the corner."

The deep and sinister voice of Bates replied, "That is good news, my lord."

"Yes indeed. But it raises a concern that she may soon be well enough to leave."

"And go where, sir? What with her husband as good as dead?"

Abigail was shocked to hear the two men laugh. She resisted the strong temptation to barge in and confront them.

"She could demand to go back to her home for one," the earl said. "So I don't want to take any chances. As long as she continues to get better, I want her watched more closely."

"Very well, my lord. I will report back on what I've put in place."

"You do that, Bates. If she ever escapes, it will be your head."

Her father's tone made Abigail shiver in the warm hallway.

Hearing movement toward the door, Abigail ducked out of sight. Once Bates passed, she headed to her room contemplating the obvious—no plan to escape had any chance of success unless everyone in the household believed she was too ill to even try.

Overnight, her family saw a dramatic downturn in Abigail's condition. She began coming to meals appearing weak and feverish. Her appetite disappeared, and she even vomited on occasion. Her loosely hanging clothes framed a ghostly face. The doctor made regular visits but found no reason for the relapse.

As family and staff slowly became convinced Abigail's life was slipping away, the other pieces of her plan took shape. In the end, the plan would have made her father proud under other circumstances. As good as it was, however, it had only a marginal chance of success. Thankfully, she finally had an idea of how to deal with the boys.

Another full month passed as finishing touches on the plan were made. As the date of execution drew near, Abigail's anxieties increased exponentially. No plan was perfect, and she was up against those with almost limitless resources. So each element was scrutinized repeatedly. Each review resulted in small improvements that in turn produced greater anxiety.

During this period, Abby's health improved dramatically, contrary to what others saw. The ruse started with clothes sizes too large burgled from trunks in the attic. These were altered by Elizabeth to be unrecognizable by the other women. Heavy perfume masked the mustiness, and the sickeningly sweet smell added to the effect. The result was the appearance of Abigail's steady decline.

To complete the image, Abigail went to great lengths to appear ghostlike. Before leaving her room, which she did less and less often, she would turn her face ghoulish with white powers and dark eye shadow. Without lip color, she looked ready for the grave.

The last part of the illusion came at mealtimes. When she occasionally ventured down to dine with the family, Abigail picked at the food, eating little. Within a few weeks, she nearly stopped coming down completely. Instead, meals were delivered to her room. These too were returned nearly untouched. In secret, Abby was gorging on food slipped to her by Elizabeth.

Abigail had elicited Elizabeth Crandall's support early on in her scheme. The maid's loyalty was unquestionable from the day she arrived as little more than a child to be the lady's maid to a new bride. The two young women, girls really, bonded quickly and shared confidences like sisters. She was a godsend for Abigail during the long periods of estrangement from her family.

Elizabeth had remained at Abigail's side during all her emotional and physical ups and downs over the years. She grew into an exceptional maid and then nanny for the two boys. When Henry left the last time for America, Elizabeth was a strong, capable, right hand who supported Abigail during those dark times.

In the more relaxed atmosphere of an American-run English household, Elizabeth had the freedom to go about the town running errands or enjoying her time off. Though Abigail greatly relied on Elizabeth's skills, they also talked regularly about the future. Those conversations often occurred when Henry was away and the boys were asleep.

Increasingly, their talks turned to the life in America Abigail longed to experience but could not have because of her health. It wasn't long before Elizabeth was drawn in by visions of life there. She began to see immigrating there as the best way to break the cycle of life as a maid and open doors to other opportunities.

These ideas were temporarily sidetracked when Elizabeth met a young Welsh mechanic named Jack Evans. He was passing through on his way to London to seek employment in the fledgling auto industry. These plans were soon derailed by love. Instead of leaving Wickersham, Jack found a modest job repairing farm implements and began courting Elizabeth in earnest.

Over the months, their love deepened. Even as it did, Elizabeth intuitively saw little future for them given their circumstances. His job barely paid for his own needs let alone a wife. And no married staff was allowed to work at the estate. She was so sure things wouldn't work out that she didn't even introduce Jack to her parents. Much to Jack's displeasure, Elizabeth resisted her feelings and told no one about him.

Her resistance waned when Elizabeth told Jack about Lady Abigail's plans to travel to America and take her along. Instead of objecting to the idea, Jack was enthusiastic. He saw the opportunity for a prosperous future together in the states. Though he lacked the funds, Evans began working on a plan to join Elizabeth if that day ever came.

Excited at their prospects, Elizabeth told Abigail about Jack, their love, and their plans. Her ladyship greeted this news most enthusiastically. The three began to meet casually in the village over tea. When asked, Elizabeth told her friends that he was her distant cousin. Jack and Abigail liked each other immediately. From then on, the three endlessly discussed overcoming the challenges keeping their dreams of America at bay.

The meetings and planning came to a sudden end with Henry's abrupt and angry departure. Abigail went into a tailspin of sickness and despair, resulting in a move back to the estate. Her subsequent confinement along with the news of Henry's accident dashed all hopes of America. What had seemed a growing probability had become seemingly impossible.

Then, mere weeks after the news of Henry's accident, Lady Abigail shared her dramatic plan to escape and join her ailing husband. To execute this plan, however, she needed Elizabeth and Jack's help. Breathlessly, Abigail shared what they would be asked to do and what their reward would be if they agreed. As Abigail explained her plan, Elizabeth's thoughts ranged from shock and amazement to curiosity then excitement. At the end of her proposal, Abigail asked Elizabeth what she thought.

Though enthusiastic, the maid had grave doubts the plan could work because of her ladyship's poor health. When Abigail explained her plans for dealing with that issue, however, Elizabeth's resistance melted. If Jack were agreeable as well, they would gladly help. But if he wasn't, she could not go. Their love was now too strong for them to be separated.

A few days later, Elizabeth and Jack rendezvoused at their usual location, the empty church. Holding hands, she shared Abigail's plan, their roles, and the potential to achieving their dreams. Jack had questions, some of which Elizabeth could not answer. He also had ideas to improve the plan. A week later, with questions answered and plans changed, all were in agreement. The plan was launched.

Jack was in charge of arranging all travel and lodging after the escape. He was also to purchase and store new clothing and other necessary supplies. Besides managing the plan, Abigail worked to convince the household she was a dying woman while at the same time growing stronger. Elizabeth assisted Abigail in her masquerade as seamstress, food scrounger, and go-between with Jack.

To fund the plan, Abigail relied on a substantial sum from the Potter bank account she had brought with her when she moved back to the estate. At the time, she didn't know exactly what had possessed her to do so. Now, however, it seemed to have been quite prescient. The money was secreted away in a compartment in her desk until Elizabeth had transferred much of it to Jack.

Beyond these clearly defined assignments were other critical issues not so easily resolved. Chief among these was William. Unlike Charles, he would likely be unpredictable and restless at his age. He was a gregarious boy with a large vocabulary and a tendency to use it. Abigail's plan had them on the road and at times in public for days.

Though they would try to minimize the need, Abigail felt the boy had to understand the seriousness of the situation so he would obey instructions from any of them immediately and without question. Trying to make the escape and journey just a game alone seemed too risky. Somehow, William had to embrace his role at an age when all most children wanted to do was play.

This effort proved more difficult than anticipated and created great angst. The two women repeatedly told William they were going to find his father, but they needed to travel in secret because bad men would be trying to stop them. William was excited at the thought of seeing his father but didn't understand why bad people would want to stop them.

Seeing his mother looking so sick at some times, and so well at others further confused William. To address that, Abigail said she was acting and it was part of the secret plan. He seemed to accept that. She worked on getting him used to pretending to be Elizabeth's and Jack's son, Will. He never seemed to grasp or accept the idea, so Abigail abandoned the effort and continued without success trying to help him understand about bad people.

Then one evening, William saw Bates verbally assault his mother in the hallway outside her room. Later, he asked her if the bad men who would chase them would be like bates. When she said yes and they would try to keep him from his father, William said defiantly that his name was now Will and he would be a good little actor from then on.

Less than a week later, Elizabeth left to meet Jack, who had written he was returning that day from London. Since the plan had been set in motion, they had continued to meet clandestinely at the local Methodist church. For the next few hours, Abigail waited anxiously for her return.

When Elizabeth finally tapped at her door near midnight, her face was aglow with excitement. Abigail had a hard time calming her down before she could speak. Finally, the two settled on the bed, and Elizabeth shared the news from Jack.

He had immediately headed to London, purchased all the items for the escape, and stored them in his rented room. Then he focused on the complex travel plans. To ensure the plan's feasibility, Jack traveled each route and checked every detail. After a few adjustments, which Elizabeth shared with Abigail, the arrangements were completed.

While still in London, Jack made rounds of the medical community per Abigail's request. His task was to obtain the latest information on treatments or remedies for seasickness and vertigo. Elizabeth was sad to report there was little in the way of encouraging news. Jack had bought some suggested medications, but none of them was a panacea.

Jack had returned to Wickersham with everything packed in the new suitcases he had purchased. Except for what Abigail planned to take in her case and valise, the rest would be waiting outside the estate. After Elizabeth shared the status of preparations in the estate with Jack, they agreed all that remained was Abigail's blessing.

Wishing to be certain, Abigail and Elizabeth went over the entire plan one more time. At the conclusion of the review, Abigail agreed that the preparations were complete and just in time for the new moon. It seemed luck was on their side. After sharing an excited hug, the two went to bed with little hope of sleeping.

The next day, Abigail fired Elizabeth. From her bedroom window, she watched Elizabeth depart carrying baggage filled with items for use in the escape. Abigail suddenly became apprehensive. Even with all the careful preparation, there was no margin for error during the arduous journey to come. And each day offered opportunities for their plan to fail, none more critical than in the first three hours.

Looking at the mantel clock yet again, Abigail was frustrated to see the hands had hardly moved. As if to mock her, the clock softly struck the half hour. Seven thirty had arrived, well past time for the game to begin. Abigail's prayer to hear more than the ticking of the clock went unanswered.

Abby had ensured there would be no interruption after seven. As the maid removed her uneaten dinner, she rang for Stephens. When he arrived, she told him that under no circumstances was she to be disturbed again that night and would ring for assistance when ready in the morning. Stephens was barely out the door when Abigail began changing into traveling clothes.

Glancing into the dressing table mirror, Abigail saw an almost unrecognizable reflection. Her face was disguised to look like an older women. Her mouth twitched at the image she saw. A dowdy tweed skirt and jacket fastened tightly around her artificially padded body completed the disguise.

Abigail began again to practice the stooped gait she intended to use once outside the estate as part of her transformation. She soon found herself back at the mantel just in time to see the minute hand click over to seven thirty-six. Panic started to set in.

It had been gratifying to see security slackened over the last several weeks. She assumed that was because her father and Bates had totally accepted her portrayal of a dying daughter. Still, there were one or two guards constantly roaming the grounds. Thankfully, Bates was off on business that night, making the timing as good as it would get. So, she was mystified at the delay in Elizabeth's arrival.

These thoughts took her to seven thirty-nine. If things didn't start soon, the next phase of the plan could not be achieved. And if that happened, the whole escape would be—

A soft knock at the door stopped her fretting. Elizabeth stepped into the room without invitation. She shrugged an apologetic look but wasted no time in explanation. She crossed to the nearest bed and with some difficulty swept up William. The boy stirred briefly but remained asleep in his traveling clothes.

Abigail gently gathered Charles, exposing the dress he wore. They struggled to put coats on the children without waking them. They then moved to the door. Opening it slightly, Abby stuck her head through and saw that the hall was dark, silent, and empty. Distant voices drifted up the main staircase from those in the dining room.

With a nod, Elizabeth exited and headed immediately for the backstairs. Abigail pulled the door nearly shut then paused to toss the note she'd almost forgotten back into the room while balancing Charles on her shoulder. After ensuring the door was latched tightly, she picked up her valise and swiftly disappeared into the darkness.

Gingerly descending two long flights with the children, the women arrived downstairs adjacent to the kitchen. It bustled with activity; the staff was preparing the next course for the dinner guests upstairs. Their timing was good; Stephens and the footmen were upstairs serving a course at that moment.

Making a hard right with their cargo held tightly to their chests, they made the dash down the long corridor toward the back door. Abby knew the door was unlocked as that was how Elizabeth had gained access. It usually remained unlocked until late, especially when there was an event in the house.

As Abby reached for the knob, the door suddenly opened and a footman came in heading toward the kitchen. Reflexively, her free arm swept Elizabeth in among the layer of overcoats, hats, and scarves hanging from pegs next to the entrance. As Abigail joined her hidden in wool, the footman passed by and entered the kitchen at a rush.

His arrival brought a loud rebuke from the cook. "Where have you been, Thomas? The others are all upstairs doin' your duties *again*. Stephens will not be pleased."

"Sorry, Mrs. Baker," a squeaky voice replied. "I just needed to—"

"No time for that now. Here, take this wine upstairs and be quick about it."

Moments later, the women watched from their cocoon of coats as the young man headed upstairs with a bottle in each hand.

Sighing with relief, Abby reached for the handle only to have the door fly open once more. The women instinctively threw out their free hands to stop the slab of heavy oak mere inches from ramming into the boys. With hearts pounding loudly enough to give them away, the two watched as a large figure entered and slammed the door with his back to them.

One of Bates' security staff, a burly man named Dobbs, strode purposefully to the kitchen, speaking at just below a shout. "Blimey, it's nippy out there. Thought me replacement would never show."

The harsh sound had William stirring in Elizabeth's arms. Thankfully, he remained silent as the guard continued. "Smells mighty good in here." As the man disappeared into the kitchen, the women heard the cook tell Dobbs to keep his bloody fingers off the roast.

Not waiting to hear more, they snuck out the door and closed it silently behind them. They paused long enough to sigh in relief before Abby stepped off toward the main gate. As she did so, Elizabeth grabbed her arm. "Jack said to wait here, ma'am. He'll give a signal when it's clear."

As if to confirm this, they saw a light appear outside the gate. It briefly moved up and down before going out. "That's the sign. Let's go, my lady."

The two headed down the gravel drive making far too much noise for a clandestine escape. At that moment, however, they heard shouting coming from outside the walls of the estate. That got them moving even faster as they stepped off the gravel and into the lawn, silencing their footfalls. The shouts had faded by the time they reached the gate.

Elizabeth arrived first with Abby right behind. Both were panting heavily from exertion and fear. Usually locked, the gate was cracked open to allow for quick passage of the guest coaches. This allowed the women, in a single step, to escape the estate and be free.

No sooner had Abby slipped from her prison than a third figure approached. The trio looked at each other's uncommon attire with some amusement. While Abigail was the image of a dowdy, middle-aged woman, Elizabeth and Jack were dressed in fine traveling suits. The two looked every bit the part of the aristocracy.

After a moment's scrutiny accompanied by approving whispers, Jack painstakingly pulled the gate shut soundlessly and affixed the lock.

Seeing this, Abby smiled at him speaking softly. "Was that you making the noise along the wall?"

"A diversion," he whispered as he took William from Elizabeth's arms. "Enough talk. We're behind schedule." Jack turned and headed off toward the village. Elizabeth took Charles from his mother, picked up the valise, and rushed to catch up. Free of any load, Abby quickly followed, reveling in her newfound freedom.

Jack led them in single file along the edge of the road, looking back from time to time checking if they were being followed. The plan had called for them to travel on foot for more than a half hour to the village's outskirts. Except for those in the public houses, everyone had already turned in for the night. They made the journey without encountering anyone.

The three came to an exhausted stop across from their objective, having made up some of their lost time. They stood in an alley next to a darkened storefront with an excellent view across the wide street. At the moment, it was empty.

Without speaking, Jack handed William to Abigail and moved off behind the nearby building. He returned moments later with several suitcases he had deposited earlier that evening. He placed them beside the women, who stood hidden in deep shadows. With a confident nod, Jack stepped into the street and strode resolutely across to the train station. The clock above the entrance read eight forty.

While they waited, Elizabeth whispered an apology to Abigail in her best titled-lady accent. "I am sorry for being late. Jack and I slipped through the gate behind the last carriage and hid in the bushes nearby. The guard we saw at the back door was—"

"Dobbs?"

"That's the one. He was manning the gate and was so close I thought he surely would hear my heavy breathing. Not more than five feet away he was."

Elizabeth noticed Abby was struggling to hold William. "Here, me lady. I mean Margaret. Take Charles for a bit. I'll handle that load." The exchange made, Elizabeth continued. "Then we waited like you said for seven o'clock and dinner to start."

She paused as the door to the station opened. An elderly couple exited and turned up the street away from them. Once they disappeared, Elizabeth continued. "We no sooner started for the house when the bloody guard Dobbs appeared making rounds. We just managed to hide against the carriage buildin' in time."

Abigail was only half listening. The three had managed to arrive at the station with time to spare, making Elizabeth's explanation superfluous. What was beginning to worry her was why Jack hadn't returned. Buying tickets shouldn't take that long.

Elizabeth plunged ahead with the story out of sheer nervousness. "After the lout moved on, we headed to the house. Once inside, I had to wait for the first course—"

Abby stopped her with a loud whisper. "That's enough, *Agnes*." Abby used Elizabeth's alias. "I understand. No harm done. But where is that man of yours?"

A figure appeared from around a corner a block away. Shadows made recognition impossible. The person slowly angled across the street toward the station, finally passing under a street lamp. It was a constable. The two women slunk deeper into the shadows and held their breath as the policeman entered the depot.

"That's not good," Abigail unintentionally said aloud.

"Now my Jack is a very smart fellow, ma'am. I expect he won't create no—any problems."

"I'm sure you're right," Abby said unconvincingly while anxiously watching the station clock pass 8:50. Abigail nervously readjusted Charles on her hip as she voiced her growing concern. "If Jack isn't out that door in the next five minutes—"

Before she finished, the bobby exited the station and glanced up and down the deserted street. At that moment, Charles started to whimper. Abigail froze, staring across the wide gap at the officer. Still hidden by shadows, Elizabeth slowly reached out and flipped the edge of the blanket over the restless boy's head to muffle the noise. That seemed to satisfy Charles. He once again fell silent.

But in response to the vague sound, the bobby cocked an ear searching for its location. His eyes scanned the buildings across the street from him. Abigail wanted to slink deeper into the shadows but feared the policeman might see or sense the movement. So she remained stark still as Elizabeth did the same.

After what seemed an eternity, the bobby stepped off the curb toward the women. His course was uncertain; he veered one way and then the other. The general route, however, was bringing him ever closer to the alley where the women stood.

Suddenly, the station door opened drawing the bobby's attention. Abby and Elizabeth expected to see Jack, but instead, an obviously drunk man staggered into the street. When the man finally recognized the constable through his alcohol stupor, he attempted an about-face. His balance was poor, however, and he fell clumsily to the pavement.

Soon, the bobby had assisted the man up and was escorting the unsteady and vocal prisoner off toward the center of town. Silence returned as the women sighed with relief. They shared nervous giggles while peering at the station's clock once again. It read nine o'clock, ten minutes before the train was due. A distant whistle punctuated that fact.

With a sense of foreboding, Abby turned to Elizabeth. "We can't wait for Jack any long—"

As if clairvoyant, Jack emerged from the station and rapidly crossed the empty street to his anxious companions. In the dim light of the nearest street lamp, the women saw his smile and uttered sighs of relief again.

Jack immediately handed Abigail a ticket as he explained what had happened. "Sorry it took so long. An older couple in front of me occupied the only agent forever with their questions about tomorrow's train schedule."

Abigail interrupted Jack unceremoniously. "We don't have time for this now. I heard the train whistle just a moment ago."

Jack gave Abby a reassuring look. "I know. I heard it too. But remember, we want the train to get here and unload its passengers before making our move."

Abigail nodded and mumbled an apology. With a dismissive wave, Jack continued. "I know you saw that bobby come in." The women nodded. "He put me a bit off my game. Seems he had come in to use the gents' in a hurry. So I hunched down at the window getting my tickets, and as I finished, he came out of the WC."

A train whistle blew again. Before Abby could protest, Jack held up a hand. "One more whistle and we'll go. The goal is for as few locals as possible to see us leave. So we wait."

Abby fought her anxiety as Elizabeth squeezed her arm. Appearing unflappable, Jack continued his story. "The constable was focused on a man sleeping on one of the benches. So I slipped out to the platform and waited until the policeman left. Then I went back in."

"Did you see the bobby heading our way?" Elizabeth asked.

"I sure did. I was a wee bit concerned."

"Thank God that drunk wandered out when he did," Abby said with a sigh that mingled tension with fatigue.

"God and me." Jack's smile grew. The women's expression moved from confusion to understanding. "Mind you, I don't think he liked being disturbed."

"I should have known." Abby attempted a clumsy hug with Charles in her arms. "Elizabeth said you were a smart man, and she obviously knew what she was talking—"

A loud whistle was accompanied by the sound of a steam engine. Elizabeth thrust William into Jack's arms and pulled Charles roughly from Abby's grasp. She leaned down and grabbed one of the suitcases. Abigail grabbed another while Jack lifted the large one and adjusted the comatose William on his shoulder.

The train's whistle called out again, this time as if it were on the street next to them. The rasp of metal on rails, the hissing of steam, and clanging of a bell signaled the train's arrival. Like some kind of a dying beast, the train lurched to a stop, exhaling one last steamy breath before falling silent.

Shortly, the doors flew open and a small group of arriving passengers burst out and disappeared in all directions. Once the street emptied, Jack turned to the others. "All clear. We have five minutes to board. No time to waste."

Elizabeth and Jack emerged ghostlike into the dimly lit street while Abigail remained behind as planned. Fighting the urge to move, she waited for Jack and Elizabeth to reach the depot entrance. To calm herself, she concentrated on her upcoming performance as a middle-aged woman with a slow, labored gait.

As Jack and Elizabeth reached the station entrance, they bumped into a man trying to exit. By that time, Abigail had begun crossing the street at a slow and steady pace, headed for a wooden walkway beside the station that led to the platform. Halfway across the street, she glanced at the entrance. Illuminated in the light from the station door stood the man who had collided with Jack, Anthony Bates.

At the sight of Bates, Abigail stumbled and nearly fell on the uneven cobbles. Regaining her footing, she willed her eyes away from the entrance. Forcing an even slower, feeble walk, she finally reached the building's protective shadows. Leaning against the depot wall, she ventured a quick glance around its corner.

A familiar carriage had just pulled up, and Bates laboriously climbed aboard. The driver whipped the horses into a quick trot before the door had even closed. All too quickly, the coach raced by a few yards from where Abigail stood staring in its direction. She thought she saw someone staring back.

Whirling around, she took a few quick steps toward the platform before remembering her role. She slowed and forced herself not to look back again. She hoped Bates had not noticed her panicked movement. If he had, all could be lost. Recognizing nothing could be done about that now, she continued and emerged onto the platform in a tremble.

The train consisted of six coaches, three for first-class and three for second-class passengers. Abigail saw Jack and Elizabeth struggling to get the children and luggage into a first-class compartment. They were the only other passengers on the platform. As she turned back to the second-class berths, the conductor's voice rang out, "All onboard!"

Abigail needed to get across the wide platform and into a coach as quickly as possible while remaining in character. The conductor impatiently watched the primly dressed, plump figure move slowly to the train. As the woman finally reached the nearest carriage door, the agent turned and waved his flag, signaling all was clear to leave.

Head pounding, Abigail tossed the valise on a seat in the empty compartment and slammed the door as the train jerked forward. This threw her awkwardly onto the bench seat, which was thankfully well padded. Struggling to sit up, she glanced out the window expecting to see Bates racing toward her. Happily, she saw an empty platform.

Once the station and village lights faded, the estate came into view glowing dimly on a distant rise. Thoughts of her mother and the hurt she was inflicting on her plus the brother and friends she had left behind had her nearly in tears. Envisioning far-off reunions helped ease the pain a bit. Feelings of hatred toward her father took care of the rest.

Drained by emotion and bone tired, Abigail fell into a restless sleep, interrupted shortly by the conductor's arrival to collect her ticket. She asked him to wake her at a specific time. Once the conductor was gone, she went quickly back to sleep.

CHAPTER 14

"Mr. Bates! Mr. Bates!" A hulking figure shook the nearly comatose former constable, totally ignoring his condition. "You best get up, sir, right now."

Swimming up from the depths of an illness-induced sleep, he forced his eyes open. "Wha ... Dob ... Dobbs? Bloody hell! Can't you see I'm sick? Leave me alone."

As Bates shoved his head into a pillow, Dobbs explained breathlessly. "But she's gone!"

Bates gave no indication he understood, so Dobbs tried again. "Lady Abigail is gone. The boys too. The earl is demanding to see you."

In his diminished state, Bates began to believe it was some kind of nightmare. Only the relentless and painful poking and prodding by his assistant said otherwise. "What is it? You say what?"

"I'm to have you downstairs in his presence immediately or there will be hell to pay for both of us," Dobbs said, dragging Bates to his feet. The chief of security still wore his clothes from the night before, having been too ill to remove them. Forcing Bates into his crumpled suit coat, Dobbs pushed the stumbling figure out the door toward the stairs.

The earl's enraged voice echoed through the house as the men reached the main floor. If not so deathly ill, Bates might have been anxious about what was to come. As it was, he could barely stand.

Bates had arrived at the station the evening before feeling awful. He had vomited on the train and barely avoided the same on the coach ride to the estate. Thankfully, a dinner party was in progress when he arrived, giving him an excuse for not reporting to the earl. Instead, he staggered upstairs and fell into bed, where Dobbs had found him minutes earlier.

The sight of the disheveled Bates in the doorway of the study brought a brief halt to the earl's tirade. Dobbs stated the obvious. "Here he is, me lord. He seems quite ill."

"Is that so?" The earl bit off the words. "Well, if he thinks he's sick now, wait until I get through with him."

Reflexively, Dobbs shoved his boss into the room and stepped back. Bates could not muster any response. He sagged onto one of the couches like a ragdoll as the earl launched into him. "Between last evening and noon today, my daughter and grandchildren vanished from the estate! I hold you personally responsible."

Bates tried again to respond, but no sound came out. The earl didn't seem to notice as his rant continued. "You set up the guard system here. What good was that? And where were you while this disaster was unfolding?" There was no pause for a reply. "Oh, that's right. You were off setting up a network to be used if just such an event happened. An event I might add you suggested would never happen. Well, you were wrong, just as you were about Henry Potter's impending death."

The earl paused to take a breath before shouting, "What do you have to say for yourself?"

Bates looked up vacantly opening his mouth to speak but vomited instead on the earl's fine Persian rug. Then he slumped back on the couch, apparently unconscious.

"Get that man out of here!" the earl shouted at Dobbs, who rushed forward and began dragging Bates from the room. "And see what you can get out of him about this new network of his. Then once you do, inform him he's fired and send him packing."

Meanwhile, the train ride north had gone well. Abigail had slept until roused by the conductor right on schedule. Within an hour, she stepped out on the platform of a station well short of the destination on her ticket. She greeted the day dressed and looking like Lady Abigail.

As planned, Elizabeth, Jack, and the boys had remained on the train.

They would detrain for the night a few stops up the line. Abigail would join them later.

She was soon eating breakfast in a small restaurant less than a block from the station. She made a point of asking the proprietor when the next train for Glasgow left and repeatedly looked at her watch nervously. If asked, the man was likely to recall a redhead of such fine breeding. She walked back to the station and changed clothes again in the loo. Then Abigail purchased a first-class ticket to Glasgow for the nine o'clock train that morning and boarded with the crowd.

At the second stop two hours later, Abigail exited into the hustle and bustle of a large city. Crossing the main street and entered an elegant hotel, she registered, paid cash, and carried her valise up to her room. A short time later, an attractive woman in her late thirties in a tailored suit left the room and exited the hotel carrying the same valise.

The disguised Abby took a circuitous route before arriving at an even nicer hotel very near the one she had just left. At the desk, she inquired about guests, the Hightowers, who were expecting her. A call to the room confirmed that indeed a Mrs. Grosvenor had an appointment.

Leaving her luggage at the desk, the clerk had a bellman take her up to the Hightowers' suite. A short time later, Mr. Hightower came down to the desk. He secured an adjoining room for his children's new nanny and took her luggage up personally, declining assistance.

Theorizing that representatives of the earl were already searching major ports, Abby's plan had them staying in this city for two days. It was inland where they were not known and hundreds of miles from their final destination in England. They remained in their rooms for the duration of the stay except for daily walks with the children in a nearby park.

The boys proved easier to deal with than Abigail had expected. William was living up to his promise and seemed to be having a great adventure. Charles mainly slept. It was the three adults who remained on edge, constantly watchful, anticipating discovery at any time. What sleep they got was fitful.

Coming to, Bates had no idea how long he'd been unconscious. He was in his bed dressed in his nightshirt. How it had gotten on him he didn't know. The last he vaguely remembered was hearing the earl fire him and tell Dobbs to throw him out. Yet he was still at the estate and still feeling miserable.

He tried to rise but was too weak. He fell back on his sweat-soaked bed. Before he could drift off again, however, he heard footsteps, and a shadow fell over him. "About time." It was Dobbs, and he didn't seem the least bit happy.

The room's stale, hot air drove Dobbs to throw open the drapes, followed by the sash. The sound was like an explosion in Bates' aching head. As he wallowed in the bedclothes, Dobbs poured a glass of water from a pitcher and thrust it at him.

Bates drank while Dobbs took a seat in the one available chair. He spoke in a whisper. "I've been waitin' for you to come around for two days."

That shocked Bates.

"You don't know what I've been through tryin' to keep you hidden."

That struck Bates as odd. He wanted to know more but could only muster a "Why?"

"'Cause the earl is expecting me to take over finding Lady Abigail," Dobbs said as he shifted uneasily in his seat. "He's already threatening to fire me next if I don't produce."

"So tell me ..." After a pause for breath, Bates managed to complete his sentence. " ... what's been happening?"

Dobbs eagerly launched into an in-depth review of events over the past three days. The countess had discovered Lady Abigail gone at noon. A note she found said that she was sorry for deserting her mother, hoped to reunite one day, and loved her. There was not a word for the earl, which spoke volumes.

With Bates unconscious, there was no way to contact the nationwide network the then head of security had just completed establishing. The earl hastily appointed Dobbs as the new head of security but kept Bates around, hoping to obtain the information sooner or later. Dobbs's first suggestion to call the police was flatly rejected by the earl. He preferred to conduct his own investigation.

So Dobbs began by searching Lady Abigail's room and discovered several items hidden in her desk, including three letters from Henry Potter each hinting at possible rendezvous points in Europe, where he hoped she could get to given her poor health. He promised to travel to the one they had secretly selected once physically able.

After reading the letters, the earl immediately ordered men to all points of departure referenced in them. He also offered a £1,000 reward for information that led to finding his daughter and grandchildren. This proved a mistake, as the estate was soon flooded with alleged sightings, each requiring follow-up.

It was at this point that the earl ordered Bates removed from the estate even though he was still unconscious. Instead, Dobbs had left him in his room. With the help of one intimidated maid, he provided minimal care for the next two days. This was not an act of sympathy. Dobbs said he kept him round because he needed Bates' skills to find Abigail.

When he heard this, Bates managed a brief laugh that was quickly cut off by a coughing jag. After another drink had settled him, he asked, "Where are the letters?"

"In the earl's study."

"Bring them to me."

Dobb flared angrily. "Need I remind you who is head of security now?"

"Need I remind you who has the information about the network? Since I've been fired, there's no incentive for me to share that with you. And what if the earl were to learn I was still here?" That speech exhausted Bates, who fell back on his pillow gasping.

After a pause, Dobbs gave his former boss a halfhearted smile. "I see your point. I'll bring the letters as soon as I can."

"Has there been any progress?" Bates' head was beginning to throb.

"There's been no progress, and the earl's on the warpath again. He has us running around wastin' time chasin' worthless lead after worthless lead from those greedy folks after the thousand pounds."

With a feeble nod, Bates whispered, "Did you find anything else when you searched Lady Abigail's room?"

"Well, all Lady Abigail's and her boys' belongings, or at least everything the staff could recall, were still there. So were her ladyship's toiletries," Dobbs said with a blush.

Bates nodded. "Not surprising. She would undoubtedly have disguised herself and the boys before attempting such a bold move. But how did she get the clothing?" Bates asked, not actually expecting an answer from the likes of Dobbs.

"I wondered that myself," the new head of security said a bit defensively. "Anyway, the only other things I found were a sheet of Lady Abigail's stationery covered in odd scribbles along with a map."

Hearing that, Bates struggled up on his elbows. "Tell me more about those items. Can you get them to me as well, please?" Bates asked patronizingly.

"They're with the letters in the earl's office, so I suppose I can get them to you for a look-see. While I'm taking care of that, why don't you give me the names of your contacts around the country?"

"Won't the earl be suspicious where you got the information?"

"Not if you write it down and I claim to have found it hidden in your desk here." Dobbs nodded toward the small secretary in the corner. "It might even get him off my back."

"You're smarter than I give you credit for, Dobbs," Bates said genuinely. "I'll make a list for you to share while you get those items for my review."

Dobbs stood to leave. "I don't know the earl's plans for the day. If he doesn't go out, it could take a while."

"Do make it happen, Dobbs," Bates said sharply. "*We* don't have much time."

Early on the third day after the escape, the fugitives headed back to the train station and were lost among a throng of travelers. Boarding at eight thirty, the five traveled together in a private, first-class compartment. The atmosphere inside was almost euphoric as the adults reveled in their good fortune thus far while the children basked in their newfound freedom.

Abby felt that their success to that point was due in part to the items she had intentionally left behind. She'd hoped the fictional letters from Henry, a sheet of codes, and the map would confuse, delay, and misdirect pursuers. So far, that part of the plan seemed to be working every bit as well as the other elements they had painstakingly designed.

The train ride north had been part of the deception. At the first stop she made, Abigail had intentionally dressed and looked like herself. She surmised that if she were recognized there, men would be rushed to Scotland or west to Wales, meaning fewer pursuers looking in the right places. That would increase their chances of reaching their final destination.

Still, Abigail was wary, realizing that the earl and Bates would not be fooled long by her deceptions. She expected the manhunt would soon be redirected and the effort redoubled in more-logical ways. In recognition of this possibility, Abigail's plan had them heading for that morning's train and their final stop in England.

A long day's journey in the private compartment brought the smell of the sea wafting into the car. The outline of a city and harbor that soon appeared contrasted starkly with the setting sun. Night had fallen as the train entered the station.

Just before arriving, the women transformed again. Abigail became a plump, jolly nanny of fifty or so complete with a gray wig and the nondescript, flowered hat she'd worn on the night of the escape. William found that confusing at first, but he laughed at his mum's new look. Charles was far too young to care.

The boys also morphed. William was dressed at the station to blend with other proper boys his age. Charles, however, was transformed into a toddler girl complete with pink bonnet and dress. That had William laughing again until he was reminded how important it was for him to play the part of Will. With a stern nod, he focused again on getting to his father.

Jack and Elizabeth remained in their aristocratic attire. Disguising them further seemed unnecessary. It was Abby and the boys being sought, less likely Elizabeth. And Jack was unknown to everyone in pursuit. That was a real blessing for the escapees as he could move about at will to make final arrangements and keep an eye out for pursuers.

The crowd jamming the platform waiting to board more than matched the many passengers exiting the train. This sight delighted Abigail. The mass of people and growing darkness made it easy for them to remain obscure. Even William's frightened whimpering and Charles' crying went unnoticed in the pandemonium.

They moved quickly out of the station to the street and hailed an enclosed carriage for the short ride to the hotel. A suite and connecting room had been reserved under yet another set of assumed names. Shortly, they were resting in their rooms, the day having gone flawlessly.

While Jack and Elizabeth took dinner in the hotel restaurant, Abby and the boys shared a meal in the room. The waiter would long remember the verbose and jolly nanny who made it difficult for him to do his job. The poor man was so distracted that he could not tell how many children there were let alone if they were boys or girls.

Though things had gone remarkably well, the constant tension was beginning to wear on the adults. The children had apparently picked up on that and were becoming more restless and difficult to handle. Abigail began to think her plan was taking a bit too long. With additional days yet to wait, could they all survive the strain?

It was after noon when Dobbs returned with a tray of food and pockets full of documents. By then, Bates was beginning to feel human again and his mind was working at nearly full power. After shooing Dobbs away, the former constable chose to chew on the documents rather than the food.

He started with the letters from Henry. They made no attempt to hide the fact that they were including many rendezvous points and possible points of disembarkation to hide their actual plans. There were a dozen locations in Europe reachable by short boat trips from at least two dozen ports. It was a clever scheme.

For a moment, he considered how wrong he'd been about the fate of the man in America. It had been a shock to learn Potter had not died, though he would likely live with significant limitations. To read he would be able to travel to Europe had Bates shaking his head in disbelief. He had no time to dwell on that, however.

Bates switched his attention to the sheet of stationery that contained what looked like code of some sort. An hour's scrutiny yielded nothing, however, so he shifted to the well-worn map of the UK. It appeared to him that every port city in England, Wales, and Scotland had been circled and then some had been crossed off.

He compared the map first to the stationery with little success. He soon found that the ports crossed off the map corresponded to the ports referenced in the letters. It took the rest of the night and the next morning to connect the letters, map, and writing on the stationery.

Abigail had used code to first identify the port cities on the map and in the letter. She had also added dates and times of ship departures to rendezvous ports in Europe. All the dates fell around the time of her disappearance.

He sat back exhausted from the effort but pleased with what he had learned. When Dobbs returned, they would discuss what to do with the information. It was not as simple as passing it on to the earl. They needed a plan to win their way back into his favor.

As he waited, however, he began to feel uneasy about what he'd just discovered from the three sources. He went back over it again but came to the same conclusion. Still, he had no explanation for his disquiet. Then it struck him. Could it be that this information had been purposefully left to mislead him?

Someone clever enough to plan such a successful escape would not have left letters behind accidentally. Those letters had produced exactly what Lady Abigail must have intended—chaos and diversion. His admiration for his young adversary grew.

On the first day at their new location, Jack left very early. His first stop was the ticket office for the steamship line. He'd made reservations and sent payment via cable weeks earlier. It was time to pick up the tickets and the required personal information forms. These would be completed at the hotel and brought to the ship at boarding time.

The documents would reflect that Jack and Elizabeth would be traveling as Mr. Jack Hightower, a wealthy industrialist from Edinburgh, and his wife, Agnes, the daughter of a viscount named Herbert. Their children, Wilbur and Charlotte would be accompanied by their nanny, Miss Margaret Grosvenor.

Along with these aliases, a litany of additional data was required, ranging from age and sex to the last home and destination addresses and more. Jack smiled at the thought of the fun they would have that night making up things. With tickets and papers in hand, he moved on to his last and from his perspective the most important stop of all.

Arriving at the suite an hour later, Jack ushered in two guests. They found Elizabeth lying in bed looking deathly pale. Standing near a side door was a forlorn-looking, middle-aged woman near tears.

Stepping to the bed, Jack leaned down and whispered to Elizabeth, "Darling, I brought the minister and his secretary as a second witness. Are you sure you're up to this?"

Her eyes fluttered open. "Oh yes, dear, if it's the last thing I do."

With that, a brief wedding ceremony ensued. By the end, all were in tears as Jack produced a surprisingly large diamond ring from his pocket. Elizabeth nearly fainted for real at the sight of it. Once all parties signed the marriage certificate, Jack gave the vicar a handsome sum and hurried the two on their way.

Once alone, the three could not contain their laughter. Feeding off each other's giddiness, the revelry went on until it was brought to a halt by crying from the adjoining room. While Abby took care of the boys, Elizabeth climbed from the bed fully dressed as Jack headed downstairs for some refreshments.

On this penultimate night before their voyage, the three ordered room service and celebrated until all hours. Their happiness was tinged with sadness at what they were leaving behind. As they headed to bed, they agreed that the promise of new beginnings mitigated the pain of their losses. And the first of those new beginnings would occur that very night with a change in the sleeping arrangements, much to the delight of the newlyweds.

When Dobbs returned in the afternoon, he found Bates neatly dressed and waiting with a complete list of the network he had put together. He explained the results of his review of the documents and handed over another list, this one of the ports where Abigail was most likely headed. He neglected to share his hunch about what the real purpose of the documents was, however.

The new head of security was impressed and pleased. Thanking his former boss, Dobbs rushed off to return the papers and find the earl. He seemed confident this information would put him back in the earl's good graces.

Using crude copies of the documents, Bates continued ruminating them. He felt Lady Abigail's goal had been to confuse them and spread their resources thin. That might be all there was to it. Still, that seemed too simple. He kept asking himself what he was missing in the documents, what was there that he just didn't see.

Frustrated with his lack of progress, he began exploring something else that puzzled him. Clearly, her ladyship and the boys could not have avoid detection so long without help. But who had helped them? And even with help, it would be nearly impossible to keep a woman, a sick one at that, and two children hidden that long.

Finding no logical answers, Bates made a note to suggest Dobbs have people check all the doctors and medical facilities on the way to each of the possible ports. A woman as sick as Lady Abigail was supposed to be surely would have sought medical assistance by then.

Late that night, Dobbs returned to say the earl had made contacts with the men on Bates' list and the key ports were under heightened surveillance. There had also been a sighting of someone answering Lady Abigail's description headed to Glasgow by train. Efforts were redoubled in that region. When Bates made the suggestion about checking medical facilities, Dobbs left immediately to follow up on the idea. Still weak from his illness, Bates slept.

He awoke the next morning with an appetite for the first time in days. Over a generous breakfast delivered by Dobbs, he listened to yet another empty report. After a bit of annoying small talk, Bates shooed the needy man off and turned again to the mysteries he felt were hidden somewhere in the three documents.

After another frustrating hour poring over the pages he had nearly memorized, Bates tossed them on the desk and went to the window. Staring at the main entrance to the estate, he tried to visualize Lady Abigail and the boys disappearing through the iron gate. The thought brought him back to the issue of who had helped her.

Though no individuals came to mind, it struck him that whatever help she got to get out of the estate would have been wasted unless assistance had continued on the outside. Dragging two small children alone undetected wherever she was headed would have been impossible, especially given her fragile health.

As he considered that, Bates absentmindedly watched a group of staff enter the grounds carrying bundles. As they approached the mansion, two footmen broke away from two women. Then one man called out to the women, who stopped. He rushed over and handed a bundle to one of the women before rejoining the other man.

Starting to turn from the window, Bates suddenly paused and looked upon the scene again. Something about it struck him as relevant to his ongoing ruminations. Slowly, the implication registered, and he began to see a solution to the mystery. In frustration, he cursed. Clearly, the illness and fever had clouded his thinking.

Not only had Abigail disguised all their appearances but most likely they were not traveling alone. To further the ruse, someone or ones could be traveling separately, each with a child. That would help explain everything, at least as it related to them remaining undetected for so long.

If that were true, not that many could be involved he expected, as a greater number would have made it too hard to maintain secrecy. His guess was no more than two or three, but whom? He quickly eliminated family members. Andrew was in Europe, the countess was bedridden, and Mary was her father's ally. That left only someone on staff or from the village.

Then Bates recalled the maid Lady Abigail had fired, something he had thought odd at the time. To his knowledge, no other staff had left since then. Perhaps the firing was part of the plan. It certainly would have allowed the maid to help without being missed. She likely could be one accomplice. But could two women, one ill, pull off such a disappearing act?

Bates abruptly ended this line of thought, realizing he was wasting time trying to validate his theory and identify potential allies of Lady Abigail. Intuitively, he felt that was how she had managed to evade discovery. It was closing in on four full days since the disappearance; that meant she was likely already on a boat to Europe.

CHAPTER 15

Abigail turned back from the window of the seaside hotel in response to a gentle knock from the adjoining suite. Crossing the room casually, she opened the connecting door to find Elizabeth already dressed for bed. "My goodness, is it that late?"

"Oh, no, me lady. It's not quite seven." She smiled sheepishly. "I just came to make sure you and the boys were settled. Our last day, and they seem to be catching our excitement."

Abigail grinned as she urged the maid inside her room. "Don't worry, Elizabeth, I mean *Mrs. Hightower.* I won't be disturbin' you *any* tonight, I promise."

"Thank you, Margaret." Elizabeth used Abby's alias with a wink. "Jack was a little anxious about that if you get my meanin'." She blushed and dropped her eyes.

"Indeed I do. I trust you'll keep the noise down, Mrs. Hightower." Abigail continued poking fun.

"Oh, we won't be botherin' you!" A deeper crimson crossed the newlywed's face.

"I was more concerned about waking the neighbors," Abigail said.

Elizabeth giggled. "Oh, me lady—I mean Margaret. Don't be embarrassin' me so. And don't say anythin' of the kind round Jack. He'd die on the spot."

The women convulsed with restrained laughter.

"And would you do me one favor?" Elizabeth asked seriously. "Would you please call me by my real married name just once?"

"Of course, Mrs. Evans." Abigail leaned in and hugged Elizabeth.

"Soon enough, you'll be called that all the time." Releasing her friend, Abby gently urged her toward the door. "Now go on. The boys will be fine, and I've got packin' to do."

Elizabeth started to curtsy then caught herself as Abby shook her head. "Now *Lady Agnes,* it would not be doin' us any good tomorrow if your ladyship went about bowin' to her maid now, would it?"

"Sorry, ma'am, I mean Abby." Even in the half-dark, Elizabeth's blushing face was apparent. "I mean Mrs. Grosvenor. Oh, I'll never get the hang of this!"

"You better. Now try to spend part of the night *sleepin'*."

They shared a last chuckle as the door closed.

With a broad grin still gracing her face, Abigail drifted over to her boys. William seemed content playing with a tin boat. Charles was busy doing what he did best, sleeping. Moving to her bed, she reached for clothing and started folding them. As she toiled, she glanced at her heavy coat draped atop the side chair reminding her of the adventure to come in just one more day.

The breakthrough for Bates came in midafternoon. He felt certain he had identified Lady Abigail's final destination. And it turned out not to be from anything he had found in the letters or stationery or on the map. In fact, the importance of those documents turned out to be in what was missing from them all.

Dobbs had just left after delivering lunch and a dismal report on the continued failure to find her ladyship. After retrieving the hidden copies, Bates picked at his meal, trying to ignore the papers mocking him from the desktop. It was then he saw the newspaper on the tray. Preferring it to another attempt at the documents, he opened the paper.

Knowing there would be no news of her ladyship's disappearance since the police had not yet been notified, Bates nearly ignored the front page. Then a small-bordered article at the bottom of the page caught his eye. After a quick perusal, he read it again more slowly. With renewed interest, he took yet another look at the three documents.

Back and forth he went through the letters, the sheet of stationery, and the map. It seemed so obvious now. How could he have *missed* something so blatantly *missing*? He marveled at the simplicity of Lady Abigail's strategy. It was a testimony to artful misdirection played against entrenched assumptions. It had been elegantly constructed.

Bates was now certain Lady Abigail had left these clues specifically for *him*, assuming he would lead the search. She could not have anticipated his illness and fall from grace. But what she hoped would happen was indeed taking place. The combination of his sickness and the incompetence of Dobbs and the earl was giving her plan every chance of success.

But Bates suddenly felt uncertain about his conclusion. To be feasible, Lady Abigail could not have been the sickly figure she had seemed. Then again, he'd seen her vomit once, as he had so recently, and she was nearly bedridden full-time when he left on his last assignment.

Still, given her success at avoiding capture, she surely was capable of such a convincing act. Just the effort of hiding and moving about should have put her in the ground if she had indeed been as sick as she had seemed. In that case, her body should have shown up by now. No, that was the answer. The mystery was solved. He was sure of it.

A knock at the door startled Bates out of his triumphant mood. "Come in."

Dobbs entered looking forlorn. "I just left the earl, who wants to hang me. There's not been a single positive report, no sightings or clues from any of the ports all day. I think he's about to call Scotland Yard. Unless we come up with something soon, we're both out of here. Thank God he's gone for the afternoon."

Bates chuckled at the reference to "we." "I'm sure you're right." He paused, contemplating whether to share his theory. He chose not to. "Look—I've got nothing, and my staying only makes things worse for you. It's time I took my leave," the former constable said earnestly. "I can be gone within the hour."

Dobbs went suddenly pale. "I, ah, I guess that's a good idea. Where will you head?"

"No idea. Probably London." Bates was already gathering his belongings.

"I have a cousin there with a place you can stay," Dobbs said. "Then when you find work, you can let me know if you need help. I have a feeling I'll be lookin' for work soon."

Bates started to decline the offer but changed his mind. "I appreciate that. Give me the address, and if I do head that way, I'll look him up." He watched Dobbs scribble a note.

Dobbs handed over the paper and extended a hand. "Good luck. Maybe we'll be seeing each other again."

Bates restrained a laugh and took Dobbs' hand. "Yeah, sure, the same to ya."

The hulking figure shuffled off as Bates finished packing. He grinned at the possibility of winning his way back into the earl's good graces on his own. It was a long shot but the only one he had.

Less than a half hour later, he slipped out the main gate as Dobbs watched from a window. Though still weak, Bates hurried to the station as other eyes watched his retreat with interest.

It was their last evening on English soil, and Abigail was going stir crazy. Packing was hopeless. The adults' tenseness and the children's fussiness had made for an extremely stressful day. It felt like time had stopped with the sun stuck on the horizon.

After picking at a shared meal and putting the restless children to bed, claustrophobia overcame her. An incredible need for fresh air took hold and spurred her into action. Ignoring the packing, she grabbed her shawl and hat. After checking on the sleeping boys, she tapped on the adjoining door before entering.

As she cracked the door open slowly, she saw Elizabeth hastily tying her robe and heading for the bathroom while Jack lay on the bed attempting innocence without success. "Oh, I do apologize." Abigail stammered.

Jack forced a smile. "Do you need something, my ..." He smiled. "Mrs. Grosvenor?"

"I must get out of here. After five days cooped up waiting, I'm about to scream." She nodded at her room. "I'll just leave this door open so you can—"

Jack stood unsmiling. "Are you sure you want to do that?"

Abigail nodded.

"Then wait a second, and I'll go with ya'." Jack reached for his coat.

Abby grabbed his sleeve. "That would be a bad idea. A man of your position should not be escorting his nanny. Besides, no one will recognize me under all these clothes. I promise not to wander far. A couple of blocks in each direction, and I'll be back."

"I don't know." Jack gave Abby a grave look. "We're so close to being out of here."

Abigail raised her hand. "I could have been halfway back by now. Besides, when you returned from dinner, you said there was nary a criminal or policeman in sight."

Jack said nothing, but his frown remained.

"I promise to keep a wary eye and waddle back here as fast as a fifty-year-old nanny can move if I see anything suspicious." Abby's smile disarmed him. She moved to the door and exited.

Minutes later, Abigail was already two blocks down the main street before remembering her promise to Jack. She had seen no one suspicious, but a promise was a promise. She compromised and decided to go one more block before heading back. At the next corner, she found a side street nearly as busy as the one she was on.

Abigail plunged into the crowd confident she was safe among the throng. Walking at a leisurely pace while window-shopping soon brought her to the end of the block. Looking in the direction of the hotel, she frowned. This new street was dark and nearly deserted. She turned back along the same path she had just taken.

Only then did Abigail realize she'd abandoned her plump, matronly gait. A good dose of self-recrimination soon replaced her brief sense of alarm. But changing her behavior at that point might draw more attention. Besides, she hadn't seen anyone looking her way. With a sigh, Abigail retraced her steps at a slightly brisker pace.

Abby felt a bit like a fish swimming upstream, as the majority of pedestrians were headed in the opposite direction. As a supposedly older woman, it would not do for her to aggressively push her way through, so she contented herself with moving toward the main street in fits and starts.

Halfway along the side street, Abigail was forced against a wall next to an alley as a large group of loud and boisterous youth passed. As they came abreast of her, she felt a strong grip on her arm and was pulled into the alley so quickly that no one on the street noticed. A hand suddenly covered her mouth, stifling her attempt to scream.

As she was pulled deeper into the alley, Abigail became terrified. Was she about to be robbed or raped? Why had someone decided to pick on a middle-aged woman of no means? It made no sense.

All became clear to her, however, when she heard a familiar voice whispering in her ear. "Nice to see you again, my lady. Your father *will* be pleased."

CHAPTER 16

Incredibly, his timing was nearly perfect. Arriving at the station, Bates headed for a fashionable restaurant on the corner for a late dinner. He sat at a window facing the main street lined with fine hotels. He was fatigued from the remnants of his illness and the trip; thoughts of a good night's sleep grew more appealing by the minute.

Bates just picked at his meal, on edge about whether his huge gamble would pay off. Even if this place was right, he could still have been too late. Failure would mean more to him than a lost job. He'd need a new safe place to hide from his relentless enemies. Because of them, the trip had been risky. He had even briefly considered making his own escape to America.

Giving up on the food, Bates paid the bill, rose languidly, and moved slowly out of the restaurant. The main street was a jumble of activity and noise with people everywhere. Yawning and stretching in the cool night air, his gaze fell again on the brightly lit hotels across the street. Their lights beckoned him like a moth to a flame.

Glancing both ways, Bates picked his way across the cobbled street. Checking his bearings at midpoint, he glimpsed a figure exiting a hotel twenty yards away. Something about the plump, gray-haired matron pricked his memory. The large hat festooned with a garish flower was somehow familiar.

Nothing in her appearance suggested Lady Abigail, but she was all that had been on his mind these days. It seemed beyond all reason that he would be rewarded for his deductive skills so soon. That was too implausible. Still, he willed it to be true. As he stood watching, motionless in the street, the woman spoke briefly to the doorman before heading down the street away from him.

A shout of alarm from a man atop a wagon came just in time for Bates to avoid being run down. Snapped out of his trance, he made his way to the far pavement and looked again for the woman. If not for the flowered hat, he would have lost her in the crowd. He took off at a trot after the gaudy poppy bouncing on that hat.

Getting closer, Bates noted the woman's gait did not fit her age. His mind flashed on the night he had arrived in Wickersham feeling near death. While waiting for the carriage, he had glimpsed an older woman crossing the street toward the side of the station. He briefly thought it odd that she would be out alone so late. Bates' last image of that woman was the outlandish flower on her hat.

Had Bates known then that Abigail was already gone or, he had not been so ill, seeing the older woman might have garnered more of his attention. In spite of the vagueness of the memory, however, the ridiculous hat was more than a coincidence. The woman had to be Abigail.

Bates watched her turn down a side street a few yards ahead. Slowing to a brisk walk, he followed. Shops ran only a block deep off the main street. His target weaved in and out of the crowd thick on the sidewalk, glancing casually into brightly lit storefronts. Bates mimicked her pace until reaching an alley halfway down the block.

Melting into the shadows, he stealthily watched the woman's progress. At the end of the block, she hesitated, turned, and headed back toward the main street. Bates sank deeper into the darkness. In that instant, he decided to take her right then if she gave him the chance. She did.

With his hand clamped over Abigail's mouth, Bates dragged her deep into the darkness. The noise of the street masked her muffled cries. The alley widened several buildings beyond the alley's entrance in. Windows on three sides cast shafts of light, randomly cutting the darkness. Sounds from inside these buildings told Bates they were public houses filled with rowdy Monday crowds.

Bates pushed the stunned woman hard against a shadowed wall. Her breath escaped in a rush as Abigail's knees buckled. Releasing his grip with one hand, he caught the sagging figure and propped her more gently against the bricks. In one swift motion, Bates removed the flowered hat. As he did so, a thick gray wig and fake glasses fell to the ground.

His hand back over her mouth, Bates addressed his captive once again. "Now I'm sure it's you, my lady. And *I'm* the one that found you."

He relaxed his grip slightly and uttered a guttural laugh. In that instant, Abigail pushed by him and rushed up the alley screaming at the top of her lungs. Reflexively, Bates threw a fist blindly in her direction, striking the side of her head. Her screaming ceased as momentum carried her headlong into the nearest building.

She dropped like a sack of grain and lay motionless. Bates stared down in horror, thinking her dead. Stepping quickly to her side, he bent down and placed his fingers on her neck. After a few seconds, he uttered a sigh of relief. At least she was breathing. How badly her ladyship had been hurt he couldn't tell.

Grabbing her arms, the ex-constable dragged Abigail deeper into the sparsely illuminated alcove. He found a shadowed corner and propped her limp body against a clapboard wall. Suddenly sweating in the cold, Bates hovered over the body, considering what to do next.

Several scenarios raced through his mind. He rejected each in turn. Seeking help to move her would only complicate matters, while moving her alone was bound to draw attention. She likely needed medical attention, which would bring lots of uncomfortable questions. And leaving her alone to search for a hansom risked his returning to find her gone.

The only viable alternative was to wait and hope she came to and was ambulatory. Even if she could walk, there was the question of where to take her. As he considered the matter, Lady Abigail moaned. Leaning in to check her pulse again, he heard a soft footfall. He started to turn just as something stuck him hard on the temple. His world went black.

Mere seconds after Abigail had left, Jack emerged from the hotel. When Elizabeth had exited the bathroom in the suite and found out what her mistress was doing, she was furious. Throwing his coat at her husband, she shoved him out the door, demanding he not return without her ladyship.

Glancing in both directions, Jack saw no sight of Abigail. The street was too packed to see much of anything. As he pondered what to do, the doorman appeared at his side.

"May I help you, sir?"

"Did you see a woman leave here just a few moments ago?" Jack asked calmly.

The man looked incredulous and bowed slightly before speaking. "Sir, many people have entered and left in the past few minutes. Can you describe her?"

Jack held a hand at shoulder height. "She's about this tall, heavyset, in a tweed outfit, gray hair, glasses, and hat with a single flower."

The doorman nodded. "Ahh yes. She headed that direction." He pointed to the right.

With a brief thank you, Jack stepped off briskly. He reached the first corner not having seen a trace of her ladyship. Remembering her promise to go only a few blocks, he crossed the street and continued along the main thoroughfare. He thought he glimpsed her inside a store filled with toys. Perhaps she had stopped to buy the boys something.

It took a minute to discover Abigail was not there. Returning to the street, he hurried on to the next corner with growing concern. Jack was disappointed not to see her returning. Realizing they could have passed each other, he considered returning to the hotel, but the thought of facing Elizabeth empty-handed held no appeal.

Assuming Abigail would return to this corner on the way back, Jack waited there, constantly jostled by a sea of humanity. When she didn't appear after several minutes, he turned up the busy street to his right. Jack passed by more stores crammed with shoppers. Deciding against searching each of them, he stood on the sidewalk scanning the crowd.

Seeing nothing, Jack continued on, passing an alley halfway up the block. Pausing at the end of the block. In the deafening noise, anything short of a gunshot would have gone unnoticed. Cries for help would have been futile. Declining to think such thoughts, he crossed the street and headed back to the main road, growing desperate.

At midblock, Jack paused and slowly made a full turn, scrutinizing the street from end to end. There was no plump woman, no garish hat in sight. As he turned to leave, however, his eyes glimpsed two burly men standing in the alley entrance across the street like guards. They had not been there when he passed earlier. Thinking that odd, Jack headed toward them.

Bates began to regain consciousness to find his hands and feet bound tightly. An oily rag was stuffed in his mouth and tied on with strips of cloth. He tried to focus in the darkness without success but sensed more than knew that he was still in the alley.

There was a slight movement at his side accompanied by the creak of wood and leather and the clank of chain. The nervous nicker of a horse confirmed for Bates that a wagon stood nearby. He struggled momentarily at his bonds but realized there was no escaping them. The captor had become the captive.

Bates felt breath near his ear accompanied by the smell of stale beer and cigarettes. "Know who this is, boy-o? Oh, look how his eyes be buggin' out now. I guess he does, mates." Soft laughter came out of the darkness. "Yes sir, this be you're ol' pal Peter at your service. It's been a long time."

Though it was hopeless, Bates again strained at his fetters and uttered a muffled cry. That brought more snickering from several directions. He stopped the futile struggling, exhausted from the effort. Stark fear remained.

"We thought ya'd never wand'r 'way from your safe little hidin' place bein' the coward ya are and all, boy-o. Right nice of you to come to our neck of the woods. We been folla'in' ya since ya left Wickersham this afternoon. Train can't compete with the telegraph, ya know, boy-o. Ya got careless in your old age.

"And what were ya up to with that lady over there, boy-o? Seems a bit old fer ya, sport. Could ya be snatchin' her purse? Strange indeed what with ya bein' a former man'a the law. Ahh well, makes no never mind to us. She got ya here, and that's all that matters."

Bates's eyes had adjusted to the pale light. He saw the man stooping over him gesture toward the half-hidden body across the alley. "It's a wonder she's still alive. Ya'll be wishin' ya were in that state in a bit yourself, boy-o, rather than dead, I means."

One of the other men stepped forward. "Come on, Pete. We've already been here too long. We'll have more time for conversin' with Mr. Bates later."

"Aye, right ya are." Low laughter from the darkness returned. The thug named Pete stood with some difficulty and stepped away. "Ya'll be gettin' a whole lot of reminders about our old mate Sammy before this night's over."

Another voice came from out of the darkness. "Yeah, before we feeds him to the fishies."

That brought such loud guffaws that Pete had to hush them.

Once the group quieted, Pete continued. "That's right, mate. And no one will be the wiser. Now one of youse, clip him again and let's get outta here."

"But what about her?" a voice asked from the darkness.

Bates saw Pete glance toward Abigail. "None 'a our business. Besides, I think she's dead." He leered at his captive. "Time to go night-night, Mr. Bates."

A figure stepped over him. The last thing Bates saw was the dark silhouette of an arm coming down.

Their nondescript black clothes and watch caps pulled low over their ears and eyes gave the impression in Jack's mind that the two might be up to something. The fact that they did not move or flinch at his approach indicated to him that they had no intention of stepping aside. To test his theory, Jack tipped his hat and attempted to pass.

A large, muscular arm casually stretched out and barred his passage. "No one's allowed down there right now, mate."

Jack's indignant reply was nearly lost in the den of passersby. "And why not?"

"'Cause I says so." For emphasis, the extended arm swept Jack back into the crowd, where he collided with several pedestrians and received harsh looks in response.

More than a little interested at that point, Jack pushed forward again and protested loudly in hopes of drawing the attention of others on the street. "I must protest, sir! I have business down that alley and demand to pass."

Before the first man could respond again, the other slid in front of Jack, trying to mollify him. "Sorry about my friend here, mate. He never got no learnin' about manners."

"You're right about that." Jack smiled coldly. "Now if you'll just let me pass, I'll—"

The second man, who was only slightly less imposing than the other, held his hand up casually to stop Jack. "My friend was right about that part, sir. Ya can't go down there just yet."

"And why is that?"

"Ahh, because we have a group down that way loadin' some valuable merchandise that needs protectin'. If I was to let ya wander down there unannounced like, there'd be a good chance of ya gettin' hurt."

"That does sound like something mighty valuable." Jack stepped sideways, trying to see into the darkness without success.

The man continued his explanation. "Besides, they, our pals that is, got a wagon with two horses, mean 'uns at that, blockin' most 'a the alley. Ya'd no be gettin' through there until that wagon's gone."

Shifting his stare from the alley to the speaker, Jack was unconvinced. "I don't see anything down there. How can they be loading something without a light?"

Without missing a beat, the man replied. "'Cause we's wouldn't want anyone to see us breakin' the law now, would we?"

Jack's expression changed from incredulous to shocked. The look brought a broad smile to the two men. The smaller one began to laugh. "I be pullin' your leg, jocko. They just put their torches out a minute ago, which means we'll be on our way soon."

In confirmation, a low whistle barely audible above the street noise came out of the darkness. The larger man poked his friend and winked at Jack. "See, mate? He wasn't lyin'. Now if you'll step aside, that wagon will be comin' through and we'll be gone."

The larger man turned and left without waiting for a reply while his associate held his ground and spoke in a conciliatory tone. "Sorry for the holdup, mate. As soon as I see the wagon come into view, I'll be jumpin' onboard and the alley'll be all yours."

Jack started to reply when two horses appeared out of the gloom. As the horses continued out of the alley, the black-clad man next to him swung agilely up on the wagon. The horses slowly passed Jack followed by a flatbed wagon with a half dozen men sitting on or standing around a large crate.

Once the alley was vacated, Jack headed into the blackness. He moved slowly along in the darkness, groping in doorways and behind containers along the passage. Halfway down, the light coming from windows illuminated a small alcove. The sound of revelry came from behind the glass.

Stepping into the space, Jack glanced through one of the windows and saw a raucous party underway. Through another, he came face to face with diners who looked more annoyed than surprised to see him. Partially blinded by the bright lights inside, Jack made his way toward a door to one of the buildings.

That's when he stumbled over something. Regaining his balance, Jack dropped to his knees and groped for what he had fallen over. He quickly realized it was a body. Fearing the worst, he dragged what turned out to be the unconscious Lady Abigail into the dim light. There was blood on her face and swelling with bruises near her temple.

Much to Jack's relief, Abigail stirred. "Lady Abigail, it's me. Can you hear me?" She said nothing but moved her head slowly from side to side, moaning. "Lady Abigail, it's me, Jack," he said again in the hopes she'd respond to his name. She didn't. "Me lady, can you hear me?"

Her eyes rolled up to him, but they were vacant, unfocused. She began to shake uncontrollably. Jack took his suit coat off and covered her. A moment later, Abigail vomited, thankfully only on the ground. Once her retching stopped, Jack moved her as gently as possible away from the mess to a nearby backdoor. He saw her wig, hat, and glasses in a shaft of light and collected them.

Returning to Abigail, Jack placed the items awkwardly on her head, adjusting them the best he could. Satisfied her disguise was more or less in place, he wedged her in a corner then tried the door. It opened. He disappeared inside.

A few minutes later, Jack emerged holding a cold cloth and a cup of hot tea. Behind him came a man wearing a concerned look. "She sure does look like she had too much. But I don't remember her being in my place tonight."

Jack snapped at the man. "I didn't say she got this way at your establishment. I found her at your back door. I think she was trying to get inside."

"Oh, I see. Do you know her?" There was apparently no end to the barkeep's curiosity.

"Unfortunately yes. It's me mum. We just got off the train today, and look at her." He feigned disgust and shook his head. "Now would you get that cab I asked you for and tell them to pull down the alley?" Jack reached in his pocket. Without bothering to look, he pulled off several notes and handed them to the man. "Take this for your trouble and make it quick."

The man looked down at the money, did a double take, and smiled. Without another word, he abruptly disappeared inside as Jack turned his attention to Abigail. It was hard to assess her condition in the dimness, but at least she had stopped shaking and seemed semiconscious. "Can you hear me now, my lady?"

Once again, her response consisted of an effort to move her head in his direction. "Help's on the way, ma'am. Will be here very soon," Jack muttered.

"What did you ..." Abigail's words came out more a moan than a question.

Startled, Jack looked down to see Abigail's glazed eyes trying to focus on him. "What did you say, my lady?"

With great effort, she tried again. "I said what did ... you say?"

Jack almost laughed at the absurdity of the exchange and the relief he felt at hearing her voice. "Oh, it was nothing. I just was saying I hoped help would arrive soon."

"I ... I hope so too."

She slumped against Jack's shoulder and drifted off.

After a torturous wait, a horse and carriage entered the alley led by the lantern-carrying man from the bar. With the help of the others, Jack placed Abigail in the hansom cab and covered her in layers of blankets.

Climbing up with the driver, Jack plied the man with cash and strong words to reach the hotel service entrance in all haste.

A short time later, Elizabeth opened the door of the suite to Jack's hushed plea and gasped. "Oh, my god. My la—"

Jack cut her shocked reaction short. "My dear, *Mrs. Grosvenor* has had a terrible accident. Let's get her to bed, shall we?"

"What? Oh yes." She rushed to the bed and threw back the covers.

After the dead weight was awkwardly placed in the bed, Jack ushered the driver quickly to the door. "Here's another quid for your trouble." He pushed the man out and turned to see Elizabeth stripping the clothing from Abigail and checking for broken bones. Jack calmed his nerves with a glass of brandy while averting his eyes.

For the next half hour, the couple tended to Abigail. As they did, Elizabeth berated Jack for allowing her ladyship to go out alone. Once his wife calmed down, Jack explained how he had found her unconscious in the alley with no clue as to what had happened.

Beyond her head injuries, Abigail seemed in good condition. Her pulse was strong, and her breathing was steady though ragged. Given the state of her face, however, those other factors gave them little comfort. The blood from a superficial scalp wound was easily addressed, but her facial swelling, bruises, and most of all her unconsciousness were beyond their capabilities to address.

"We need a doctor," Elizabeth said tensely.

Jack shook his head. "Lady Abigail would have none of that. If we got the doctor, the jig would very likely be up. She'd never forgive us."

"Then what do you suggest, sit here and watch her die?" Elizabeth asked angrily.

"Of course not," Jack said defensively as he began pacing the room. "Her pulse and breathing are steady right now, and she seems to be resting reasonably well. So I suggest we wait for a while and see if she comes to or gets worse."

"How much worse does she have to be, Jack?" Elizabeth said anxiously following him around the room. "She's unconscious and looks a fright."

"I don't know what worse would look like. I'm no doctor."

"Exactly my point."

Jack took his wife by the shoulders. "Look. If there's no change for the better by midnight, or if she shows the least sign of worsening, I'll get the hotel doctor."

"You promise?" Elizabeth asked imploringly.

"I not only promise, I'll also let you be the judge of when I should go." Jack felt his wife relax.

Elizabeth gave him a hug and moved back to the bedside. "Good, but I'll need something to keep me busy while we wait or I'll go crazy."

"Let's be optimistic," Jack said. "I think Abigail still has a lot to pack, and we need to finish ourselves. That should fill the"—he glanced at his watch—"the next three hours. I'll take the first watch."

Nodding in agreement, the two checked on Abigail and found her state unchanged. Elizabeth quietly entered the adjoining suite while Jack poured another glass of brandy and settled into the chair next to the bed. He was surprised to find himself shaking.

In the other room, Elizabeth turned on a lamp, which illuminated a bed covered in clothing and two boys sleeping soundly nearby. Glad for the distraction, Elizabeth began folding clothes absentmindedly while wondering what the next three hours would bring.

CHAPTER 17

Jack was nodding off in the chair less than two hours later when he nearly fell to the floor at the sound of Abigail's voice. "Could I have some water, please?"

She said this clearly while trying to lift her head. A shooting pain sent her back to the pillow with a groan. "My head feels like it's falling off."

Jack's face showed relief as he rose and went quickly to the door of the adjoining room. He waved to Elizabeth, who joined him while still holding a partially folded blouse. "She's awake," Jack whispered unnecessarily as his wife rushed by him.

"Thank God!" Elizabeth exclaimed, dropping to her knees by the bed and taking her ladyship's hand. "We were so worried."

"I can see that." Abigail's attempt at a smile fell short. "How did I get here?"

"I brought you back," Jack said as he joined Elizabeth. "You couldn't have been in that alley for long, but you were unconscious when I found you. You awoke there briefly a couple of times, but you've been out now for several hours straight."

"About that water … " Abigail said.

"Sorry, my lady." He rushed to the table and poured a glass from a pitcher. Starting back, he paused by the first aid supplies. "I expect you might like some aspirin."

"Yes. My head is splitting."

Jack handed her two tablets and gently lifted her head. After taking the pills, Abigail finished off the entire glass of water. "I'd like some more. I feel parched."

While Jack complied, Elizabeth felt her ladyship's forehead. "You don't seem to have a fever. That's good. But your face ..."

"What about my face?" Abigail asked, a bit alarmed.

Jack returned and handed her the glass. "It's bruised and quite swollen, like you'd been hit. I encountered a gang of nefarious-looking men just before I found you. They might have done this. Do you remember?"

Abigail shook her head and immediately regretted the movement. "My mind's a blank at the moment."

Elizabeth patted her hand. "That's not important. What we need to talk about is what to do next."

"Do you think you are up to that?" Jack asked.

"Do I have a choice?" her ladyship asked in reply.

After a pause, Elizabeth answered. "Well, since we are only hours away from when we were to leave for the ship, I guess not."

"Then let's get started. From the looks on your faces, you seem to have doubts about those plans."

So, the three discussed—more like argued—over what to do given Lady Abigail's delicate condition. Though adamant that she would board the ship the next day no matter what, Jack and Elizabeth felt that could have dire consequences. At the argument's zenith, Jack even suggested the attempt could kill her.

Abigail scoffed at this and said she'd rather die in the attempt than return to the estate. Jack suggested taking another ship after she had fully recovered. Concern that waiting would give the earl time to find them plus the nearly depleted state of the group's money nixed that idea.

Elizabeth's threat to stay behind failed to change Abigail's mind. She just said that once on board, there would be plenty of help available to take care of her and the boys. And she would have six days on the ship to recover. Besides, she was convinced that neither of her friends would abandon her at that point.

The argument continued while they ate leftovers from their earlier dinner. Elizabeth pointed out how little Abigail ate and that she looked deathly ill from the effort. Once again, Abigail minimized her condition, saying it was less than a mile to the ship, and a luxurious stateroom waited aboard.

"And I promise to stay there for the rest of the voyage," Abigail concluded. "That will give me time to recuperate plus keep me out of sight. I'll be worried about being discovered until we land in New York. I guess I'm a little paranoid about that."

Jack looked askance. "Doesn't that imply your plan wasn't as good as you thought?"

"In fact it wasn't, Jack." The queer tone of Abigail's voice matched the look on her face. "I just remembered a bit of what happened tonight. It wasn't those thugs whom you saw. It was Bates." Seeing their looks of disbelief, she continued. "It's true. I know my head's a bit addled, but I'm certain of that much."

"But he wasn't there when I arrived," Jack said incredulously. "Where did he go?"

Abigail shrugged and winced again. "You may recall I was unconscious at the time. Someone, maybe you, must have scared him off."

"Maybe those men I mentioned had something to do with that," Jack said. "And if Bates is here, most likely others are also and looking for us right now. I guess it isn't unreasonable to expect one or more might get on our ship."

Abigail nodded without a grimace. "All the more reason to leave sooner than later."

That brought the debate to an end. They were committed to leaving in the morning. While Elizabeth and Jack quietly finished the packing and laid out clothes for the next day, Abigail drifted between awareness and unconsciousness. Even she had grave doubts about making the short journey to the ship.

But thanks to the efficiency of her companions, everything was ready before midnight. They could board anytime between eight in the morning and five the next evening, so Abigail could sleep in and hopefully be able to make the trip. Over her objections, the newlyweds slept in the room with the boys so as not to disturb Abigail.

It was nearly ten the next morning when Abigail finally stirred. Her eyes slowly came into focus. She was shocked to see a strange woman standing over her. At first, she was confused. Then she became frightened.

Was this one of her father's people? She'd always assumed they would be men, but ...

These thoughts were interrupted by a familiar voice. "Oh, me lady, I didn't mean to frighten you. It's me, Elizabeth."

Instant relief was replaced by a pounding in her head. Abigail tried to speak, but her mouth was so dry that she could only croak. With a second effort, she managed, "Water. Aspirin."

Two hands magically appeared holding a glass and two pills. "Here you are, me lady." Jack's concerned face came into view as she downed the medicine and water in a few gulps. She didn't have to ask for more as Jack was already there with another glass.

It was several minutes before Abigail was composed enough to engage in conversation. The first order of business was to discuss how she felt. Though claiming to feel quite well, she saw legitimate doubt in her companions' eyes. She waved that off with a reminder that they had agreed they would board the ship regardless.

It was then that Elizabeth shared the reason she was dressed the way she was. During the night, she had gotten the idea that it would be much easier for Lady Abigail to make the trip as the invalid wife of Mr. Hightower than as a nanny caring for two children. So, the maid now wore the clothes of Margaret, the nanny.

After a breakfast in the room, Elizabeth helped Abigail dress. The process required much time. Undaunted, Abigail urged them on with a faux smile, suggesting the sooner she was on board the better. Over her objections, Jack insisted they would need assistance if they were to succeed.

At half past eleven, Jack left the suite to check out and arrange for transportation. Twenty minutes later, he arrived at the door with a wheelchair and two burly men. Soon they had transported Abigail with her head wrapped to hide her face to the back entrance of the hotel.

In spite of all the help, Abigail was exhausted and looked pallid as she settled into the backseat of the carriage. A few moments later, a stocky woman joined her with two children in tow. With the handsome husband of the invalid onboard, they were off to the ship. It was a short but rough mile to the pier, each bump an agony for Abigail.

Activity swirled around the ship as excited passengers and their families milled about. Abigail stayed in the coach while Jack obtained the assistance of the bursar to arrange getting his injured wife onboard. Soon, crew arrived and carried Abigail up the steep gangway to a waiting wheelchair. While on the way to their staterooms, she fainted.

Lady Abigail awoke in a large bed, not realizing where she was. Slowly, the gentle movement of the room let her know she was aboard the ship. The motion also brought a wave of nausea that thankfully passed. As her eyes focused, she saw Jack leaning over her, placing a cold cloth on her forehead. She saw concern on his face.

Seeing her eyes open, he smiled. "Welcome back, me lady."

She must have looked disoriented.

"We are in your suite, and Elizabeth has taken the boys out for a stroll so you could rest."

With effort, Abigail scanned the room. It was as luxurious as the hotel they'd just left. There was ample parlor space for privacy and plenty of fresh air pouring through numerous portholes. Everything was made for comfort except the constant roll of the ship.

Another wave of nausea swept over her as Jack removed the cool cloth. "There, there now, me lady. Just lay back and close your eyes. The doctor said—"

Abigail's eyes grew large. "No!"

"Don't worry. We kept our stories straight. As far as he's concerned, you're my wife." That confused Abigail. "Because of your injury, you and Elizabeth changed roles at least in order to get on board, remember?" Jack patted her hand reassuringly. "Now that we're aboard, we can relax. You won't need to wear that crazy outfit again. I'm sorry you missed the departure. It was grand—music playing, people cheering, and a few crying. Oh, and the whistles! But you slept though it all. We've been at sea now for a couple of hours.

"Besides, the doctors—do you know there's a slew of them aboard? They evidently have facilities that would rival the best hospitals in London. Can you believe that?"

Abby moved her head minutely as Jack continued. "Anyway, the doctor left some medicine. I think it's just more aspirin and something for seasickness. I'd mentioned your afflictions. Anyway, he will be back to check on you occasionally now that we're at sea."

That fact suddenly sank in, and she was overcome with relief. They were at sea. They were free. But her weak smile was quickly replaced by a look of discomfort as the ship rolled slightly over a modest swell.

Jack reached for a nearby basin and wrung out the cloth. "I guess that news is both good and bad for you."

Abigail couldn't manage a smile, but she found her voice, weak as it was. "Not bad news, Jack, all good."

He mopped her brow gently and smiled his agreement. "You did it, my lady. We're all on our way to America together."

Abigail squeezed his hand before lying back. Her color drained in response to another roll of the ship. Jack shook out a pill from the envelope the doctor had left. "He said to give you one of these when you woke."

When the pill stayed down, her ladyship soon drifted toward sleep again. Jack stood. "I'll let you rest and see that the others don't disturb you." Stepping toward the window, he paused. "Would you like me to send a wireless message to Mr. Potter?"

Abigail's head lolled from side to side. "No, Jack. Wait … Be sure my father … No one on board."

"I understand. We have six days at sea. Plenty of time for cables."

Abigail nodded weakly. Whatever the doctor had given her was working fast. She couldn't keep her eyes open. Through the haze and discomfort, she managed a faint smile aimed at no one. There was joy in her heart knowing the plan had succeeded and she would be reunited with Henry in a few days, a few rough days.

CHAPTER 18

It was a short walk from the train to the hamlet of Larkford. After an inquiry at the post office, Mr. Jerome walked a few blocks to a small row cottage on a narrow lane. Even without an address, there was no mistaking the place. The picket fence fronting the whitewashed house contrasted dramatically with the bright-blue door. Window boxes filled with early spring flowers flanked the door of the tenth house on the left.

Jerome pushed through and covered the short distance to the front door in three strides. Taking a deep breath, he knocked sharply. After a second knock, he heard footsteps inside. The door opened revealing an elderly man wearing a somber expression. "Yes? Something I can do for you?"

"Would you be Mr. Crandall, Mr. Harold Crandall?" Jerome asked in a most cordial tone while assessing the man. The investigator concluded that he would have been quite tall if not bent with age. The man's thinness rivaled that of Latimoore's.

"Might say that I am, might not." The gaunt figure stepped out to block the doorway before continuing. "Who's askin' and why?" The unfriendly greeting was mitigated somewhat by the softness of the man's eyes.

"My name is Jerome. Mark Jerome. I am a private investigator from the United States looking into the disappearance of Lady Abigail of Wickersham thirty-plus years ago."

Harold's expression darkened. He closed the door a few inches as if to shield him from what might come. "And what does that have to do with me, my family?"

"I think you have a pretty good idea, sir." Jerome stepped closer but dropped his voice to a whisper. "I don't want to make this difficult for you and the missus, but in the course of my investigation, your daughter's name has come up repeatedly."

"So you say. Makes no never mind to us. Our daughter's dead."

"You know that for a fact?" the investigator asked abruptly.

"Don't be impertinent, sir." Harold attempted to close the door but was stopped by Jerome's strong right arm. Harold's voice registered his alarm. "Say! Let go of the door or—"

He was interrupted by a frail female voice from inside. "Harold, love, who is it?"

Harold turned away from the door. "Just a stranger looking for directions."

As the elderly man turned back, Jerome gently pushed the door open a few inches and raised his voice. "Mrs. Crandall, I'm here to talk about Elizabeth. I need your help."

The door slammed shut. The investigator knocked again several times without a response. Raised voices came briefly from inside, followed by silence. Unsure of what to do next, Jerome waited. As he hoped, it wasn't long before the door opened again.

This time, a short, thin, and unhealthy-looking woman stood in front of a glaring Harold. "Do you know something about my Elizabeth? Do you know what happened to her?"

"Your husband said she was dead, Mrs. Crandall," Jerome replied.

The woman's reedy voice was filled with emotion. "He said that because she's been gone for well over thirty years without a single word. She wouldn't have done that if she were alive."

"Oh, I see." The investigator was relieved to hear that. "I'm afraid I don't have any firm evidence regarding your daughter as yet." Her sad expression at hearing this prompted him to add, "But I intend to solve the mystery with your help."

This brought the woman's head up. Her eyes brightened. She was about to speak when her husband gently pulled her aside and stepped forward. "We've been through this too many times only to be disappointed. Can't you see my Mavis isn't well? Please go."

It was Mavis's turn to push forward, giving her husband a harsh look. "I don't want to go to my grave not knowin'. I'll risk more disappointment. I can't hurt more." She opened the door wide and stepped back bumping Harold aside. "A cup of tea, Mr. ...?"

"Jerome, ma'am. Mark Jerome." He stepped inside, removing his hat and coat and hanging them on a rack near the door. Mavis directed him to a small living room. He took the seat offered as Harold begrudgingly plopped into a well-worn rocker near a dying fire.

"Please call me Mavis. We don't see many Americans in Larkford," she said while moving to a tiny kitchen a few steps away. Once the kettle was on, she returned carrying a plate of biscuits. "Won't you tell us how you ended up on our doorstep?"

Jerome did. He started with the events in Bedford Falls and concluded with his conversations that day with Emily Cox and the present earl. His summary was interrupted only for the pouring of tea and consumption of a biscuit to be polite. Mavis had been most attentive while Harold conveyed total disdain.

At the conclusion, Harold snorted. "An interesting story, Mr. Jerome, but it contains nothing new from my way of thinkin'."

"That may be true, Harold, but I believe Mr. Jerome came here to get information as much as to share it," Mavis said as she poured more tea for everyone. "My husband is the weak one. He's too often endured the dredging up of these memories to no good end."

"I can understand that, but if I am to have any success, I need to find out if Lady Abigail and Elizabeth's disappearances were connected," Jerome said, looking at Harold, who ignored him. "My intuition tells me they are." Harold remained silent as Jerome sighed in frustration. "Look, I know I'm asking a lot of you, but if I succeed, you'll get your answers."

Harold rocked forward abruptly. "I already know the critical answer. I believe she is dead."

"True or not, don't you want to know what happened?" Jerome asked the older man.

Mavis answered for him. "I do, and so does Harold if he were to be honest."

"Then a possible lead from you two might be the breakthrough I need."

The room fell silent as the Crandalls stared at each other. As Harold's gaze dropped to the anemic fire, Mavis turned and nodded to Jerome. She rose and went to the mantel and retrieved a battered tin box. Opening it tenderly, she withdrew a folded piece of paper.

As she turned back, Harold grabbed her hand and looked imploringly into his wife's eyes. "Don't, Mavis. Don't put us through this again." His voice was soft and full of pain. Mavis just squeezed his hand and took her seat.

Mavis reverently handed the paper to Jerome. "We found this in that very box."

Jerome took the papers and slowly unfolded a letter consisting of three pages on tissue-thin paper. Jerome's eyes widened when he read the date and salutation. He looked from Mavis to Harold with an expression seeming to say, *This is what I was talking about.* He read it.

> April 1, 1912
> Dearest mum and dad,
>
> I'm sorry for writing instead of talking to you. I hope this will help explain a bit about what has happened in your absence. Just exactly how mysterious things still are as you read this letter I can't say. I hope it turns out that this is just a humorous addition to other letters from me that you'll find waiting for you upon your return. If future correspondence is delayed, however, I'll try to share as much as I can right now.
>
> You know I have always wanted a better life. Blame yourselves for creating such ideas. My life at the estate was good but not good enough for my liking. Until now, however, that seemed the best I could expect. For reasons I cannot fully share right now, a new future for me has unexpectedly presented itself.
>
> By the time you read this, I should be well on the way to my final destination. The location, which is far away, I'm afraid, must remain a secret for now. I will not be

traveling alone as a special someone has recently entered my life. Don't worry. You raised me a proper lady, and I will not shame you. So I go expecting to find a well-paid job, a better education, and a life partner! I promise to give you all the details in the first letter I write from my new home.

Things may be all aflutter when you get back. Then again, if our plan works, all will have been revealed by then. I request, however, if things are still unclear that you not share this letter with anyone, even the police. Instead, wait to hear from me.

I know this all sounds too mysterious, and I apologize for any anxiety my adventure may cause. I trust when all is made known, you two will feel the same joy for me that I now feel in my heart.

I will close now although I hate to let go. I will be traveling on my birthday, a great gift for my twenty-fifth. The strength of character the two of you have instilled will guide me every day. Because of you and your love, I face what may come with the confidence to prevail over all save that which only God controls.

With undying love and adoration,
Elizabeth

Jerome had difficulty coming up with words to describe his reaction to such a moving letter. When he did speak, he addressed Harold. "I can see why the mystery and promise in this letter would sour when Elizabeth was never heard from again."

Harold was silent. Mavis replied, "Thank you for your understanding. I've never let go of hope. If you present even a small chance of bringing closure, I want to help."

Jerome smiled his thanks and held the letter up. "First, is it fair to say that you knew none of this before reading the letter?" Mavis nodded. "And beyond what you got from the letter came from the authorities and press?" Both nodded.

"And they were no help." Mavis sounded bitter. "When weeks passed without another letter, we finally took the letter to the police. They were surprised to find another person missing."

"You must mean in addition to her ladyship and Bates," Jerome said.

Mavis frowned. "That's right. And with the earl's influence, my daughter and that Bates fellow got short shrift."

"By the time that hubbub died down over Lady Abigail, so had any interest in a missing girl of no means," Harold added bitterly.

"Did you seek other help when the authorities failed you?"

"We didn't have money to hire anybody," Harold said apologetically. "Like Mavis said, our little Lizzy took second fiddle to the gentry. Don't get me wrong. Those boys and their mum needed to be found too. But still …"

"Did Elizabeth ever talk about moving away either alone or with someone?"

The couple considered that for a moment before Harold spoke. "She did mention America."

"That's right," Mavis said. "Apparently, Lady Abigail had suggested she might try to reach America and take Lizzy with her. But her ladyship's health and Potter's leaving, well that put an end to that dream."

Harold nodded. "That's right. She was quite disappointed, but by the time of that letter, she seemed to have gotten over the idea."

"So when you read this letter, you had no idea where or with whom she was going?"

Harold scowled. "Not as far as any *special* someone if that's what you mean. We never laid eyes on any special someone."

Mavis frowned at her husband and addressed Jerome. "You see, once he gets back into this, Harold can't let go of things any better than I can. Anyway, we have no answers to that question."

"Just like with Lady Abigail and the boys." Harold's voice had softened. "All the earl's money and manpower found out no more than we did about Elizabeth."

Jerome moved on. "What do you know about her being fired?"

"Nothing," Harold said flatly. "We'd headed up north for our annual trip to help my brother and his wife on their farm. Did tillin', plantin', and birthin' every spring back then. Stayed over a month. All this with Elizabeth happened while we were gone."

Mavis sighed. "We heard about it when we got back and started our search. They said she was fired for stealin', but that couldn't be true. Her letter mentioned none of it."

"Given all she didn't tell us before leaving, however, made it hard to refute." Harold stoked the fire again. "We didn't dwell on that at the time, figuring she'd explain when she surfaced."

"I'm curious what you two knew about what was going on at the estate at that time."

"Beyond the fact that Mr. Potter had gone to America—" Mavis said before Harold interrupted her.

"Abandoned his family, more like it."

Mavis ignored the snarky remark. "We knew Abigail had moved back to the estate for health reasons. Elizabeth shared that things were not good between the earl and his daughter. Then just before we left to go north, we heard about Mr. Potter being injured. More tea, Mr. Jerome? I'll be happy to brew a fresh pot," Mavis said.

"No thank you, ma'am. Unless you two have anything else to share, I think I'll get out of your hair."

"I don't think we helped you much," Harold said apologetically. "After our discussion, do you still think the disappearances are linked?"

"Most definitely. There are too many coincidences to be otherwise," Jerome said confidently. "The timing of the disappearance, your daughter acting out of character, her letter hinting at faraway places, new opportunities, a bright future—"

"Does that mean you think she's still alive?" Mavis asked hopefully.

Jerome frowned. "I think that would be a long shot. The way you describe her, there's no way she wouldn't have been in contact with you, I'm sorry to say."

"Then I guess we'll have to be satisfied with what you find out for us." Harold stood as he spoke. "After we've had to revisit this tragedy again, you owe us that much."

"I'm committed to that end, Mr. Crandall." Jerome stood. "I won't rest until I do."

“That’s a mighty big promise,” Mavis said, “but we started with lookin’ and then moved to hopin’. Now, we’ll settle for knowin’ before we’re gone.”

The investigator extended his hand and gripped Harold’s. “I hear you both loud and clear.” He went for his hat and coat. “If you think of anything else, I’ll be at the hotel in Wickersham for another day or two.” Jerome had a final thought. Turning from the early evening cold, he spoke quickly. “I’m sorry to keep you, but your daughter’s letter mentioned traveling on her birthday. What day was that?”

Mavis’s face looked even sadder if that was possible. “Her birthday was April tenth.” Her voice cracked. “She’d be almost sixty now.”

Harold took her hand. “We’ve lived too long, my dear.”

CHAPTER 19

"How's she doing tonight?" Jack's voice expressed real concern.

Elizabeth shook her head. She had dark circles under her eyes. "I'd like to say she's a wee bit better, but I don't want to jinx things."

"When Bates hit her in the head, it seemed to have brought back the vertigo," he said with a sigh. "Up until yesterday, I thought we were going to lose her."

Jack and Elizabeth were seated on a tufted couch in the opulent and thankfully empty sitting room adjoining their stateroom. Though they had been at sea for four days, it was the first time the two had been able to use the space. Lady Abigail and the children had demanded constant attention. Now, miraculously, all three were sleeping.

They would have preferred sitting on the private promenade, but the weather had turned cold; it had dropped throughout the day to the thirties. The sitting room, however, was delightfully warm, and the subtle roll of the ship had the couple dozing. Occasionally, the sound of revelers from the grand ballroom reached their ears.

The two sighed over the fun they were missing but couldn't complain about traveling in such style to their new life. As an alternative, they happily sipped the brandy delivered moments earlier by the porter. For the next hour, they alternated between checking on the others and snuggling together in the luxury of the elegantly appointed room.

The sea that night had been dead calm, allowing Lady Abigail to fall into a deep sleep after a meager meal. Taking advantage of the brief respite, Jack and Elizabeth took the children on a brisk walk around the promenade. The crisp air worked its magic; they put the boys down for the night early and had stolen some time alone.

After four full days and nights of caring for Lady Abigail and the boys, a full night's sleep was something Jack and Elizabeth needed badly. It finally looked like this might be the night. It was early, however, so they savored their drinks and held their breath.

"Lady Abigail is sleeping more soundly than she has all week," Elizabeth said with a smile as she returned from the latest check. The still-new bride relaxed into her husband's arms.

"I don't need to ask about the boys, right?"

Elizabeth nodded, and they both uttered contended sighs.

The couple snuggled deeper into the sofa. It had been their longest time alone since their wedding night less than a week earlier. Being in each other's arms was a gift far beyond that of their luxurious surroundings and the liquor.

Jack pulled Liz to him and squeezed her hand. She looked deep into his eyes. Thinking he knew exactly what she wanted, Jack prepared to kiss her. Instead, she shared a thought. "I think Lady Abigail may have turned a corner."

Jack broke into a startled laugh at the disparity between his thought and Elizabeth's. She sat up abruptly and scowled at him. "Did I say something funny?"

Jack pulled her back to him while shaking his head. "No, not at all. It's just that I wasn't thinking about Abigail's health at the moment."

She slowly grasped his meaning and gave him a peck that soon became something more. Breaking the embrace, she blushed.

While catching his breath, Jack acknowledged his wife's comment. "It would be great if her ladyship was on the mend. Do you think she'd be up to a conversation when she wakes?"

"Maybe. Why?"

"Because we reach port in less than two days, and she has never sent a message to Henry notifying him of our pending arrival."

"But she still seems concerned about being discovered," Elizabeth said.

"That's her illness talking. I'm convinced the earl has no one on board.

I've visited the wireless room daily checking on wires to or from my 'old friend,' the earl. Both operators have kindly checked, and the answer has always been no."

"How clever you are." Elizabeth smiled and squeezed his hand. "So I'm convinced too."

"Glad to hear it." Jack returned his wife's smile. "So it's clearly time to let Henry know we're coming. He may be too ill to come and needs time to arrange for someone to meet us. Either way, he'll need time to prepare."

"Quite right," Elizabeth said with a wink. "I'm so lucky to have married such an intelligent man."

"Don't forget handsome." Jack mockingly puffed out his chest and beamed.

Elizabeth shook her head and stifled a laugh before whispering, "That goes without saying."

Then suddenly she looked about the room furtively. "Do you hear that?"

Jack stiffened and strained to listen for what had drawn her attention. After a moment, a puzzled look crossed his face. "I don't hear anything."

"Me either." She giggled. "No retching, no boys stirring, all silence, all alone."

Jack sunk farther into the couch. "Ahh, you're right. At last a chance to take it easy."

Elizabeth slowly stood. "That wasn't what I had in mind. There'll be time for that in a few days." She stood and held out her hand to help Jack to his feet.

At a remarkable speed, the recently married couple slipped into their stateroom. The door closed every so quietly to avoid any chance of ruining the moment.

Elizabeth and Jack had unintentionally fallen asleep and awakened with a start. How long had it been since they last checked on Abigail and the boys? Grabbing his watch, Jack saw it was nearly eleven o'clock. The two dressed quickly and freshened up before heading to Abigail's stateroom.

They slowly opened the door. Light from the passageway shone on

William and Charles sleeping soundly. When the light fell on Abigail's face, however, they saw that her eyes were open. For a terrifying moment, Jack and Elizabeth thought she had died. Then she blinked and spoke to them quite strongly.

"I was beginning to wonder what had happened to you two." The slightest smile worked at the corners of her mouth. Then it faded as if the exertion was too much.

"Oh, Lady Abigail! We were ... I was ..."

Elizabeth's stuttering attempt at an apology had her mistress laughing before a wave of nausea overcame her. A moment later, it had passed, and a slightly healthier color returned to her cheeks.

"It's good to see you looking a bit better." Jack's words lacked conviction. "But don't get carried away. We need you to concentrate on walking off this ship in less than two days."

"I'd like nothing better." Abigail licked her lips. "Do we have any water? I'm parched."

Elizabeth reached for the nearby pitcher and tumbler. She quickly brought a glass to Abby, who took a nice, long drink. Elizabeth and Jack waited nervously to see if it would stay down. It did.

"I feel a bit hungry," she said, which made her friends smile as they rushed around the room looking for something edible. Elizabeth found a leftover dinner roll hidden in the folds of William's blanket. It was unchewed, so the maid brought it to the bedside.

As Abigail took a tentative bite, Jack pulled up a chair to her bedside. "Lady Abigail, there's something we need to discuss."

Abigail swallowed and said, "I know what it is. Time to send a wireless to Henry."

Jack smiled. He was pleased to hear that as well as see she was able to keep the bite of roll down.

"Thank you, my lady." Jack stood and moved to the table for paper and pen. "Write what you want sent. There shouldn't be a crowd in the wireless room at this hour."

Abigail looked at Elizabeth. "Why don't you send a cable to your parents too?"

"Oh, me lady, that would be wonderful." The maid moved to the desk and sat to write her own message.

"What about you, Jack?" Abigail asked.

Jack shrugged. "No one to send it to." He smiled at her. "This is my family now."

Her ladyship smiled at this while consuming another bite. She tried to sit up without success. Dropping back on the bed, she waved in the direction of the paper and pen. "I can't manage that myself. Let me dictate the message."

"Good idea, Mrs. *Potter.*" Jack emphasized the name as he handed the paper and pen to his wife. "You do it, Elizabeth. You know my handwriting is atrocious."

Elizabeth nodded. "Just let me finish this."

In another minute, her note was complete and she was ready to transcribe Abigail's brief message. Once done, Elizabeth handed the two sheets to Jack.

He checked his watch. "My goodness, it's after eleven thirty already." Without further hesitation, he went out the door.

Jack headed to the wireless room. Their B deck staterooms were just aft of the forward grand staircase. The Marconi Room was two levels up on the Boat Deck a short distance forward of the same staircase on the way to the bridge. At a walk, the trip took two or three minutes, but Jack was in a hurry and took the stairs two at a time.

He had just started his ascent when the ship slowed slightly and leaned hard to starboard. The sudden movement unceremoniously threw Jack on his arse. He ended up seated on the bottom step of the second flight of stairs leading to A Deck. The ship steadied as he wondered what the blazes had just happened. Then, remembering his mission, he shrugged off the incident and continued on his way.

He turned right at the top of the stairs onto A Deck and headed back toward the next flight up the grand staircase. As he did so, Jack noticed a group of men standing in a starboard lounge peering quizzically out the large windows in silence. Giving the men little attention, Jack swung around the banister onto the first tread of the staircase.

As he did so, the ship began to tremble. The motion was gentler than the first incident, much as if the ship was bumping against a dock. The trembling continued, however, accompanied by an odd rasping sound like heavy fabric slowly being torn. At the same time, Jack heard gasps coming from the men he had just passed in the lounge.

Having a firm grip on the rail, Jack maintained his balance. He paused for a moment considering a return to the men but decided against it and headed up to the Boat Deck. By the time he arrived at the next level, the rasping sound had stopped and all seemed normal again.

Jack made a sharp left through double doors into the crew section of the ship. As he entered the wide passageway, two officers hurried past him headed to the bridge with concerned looks on their faces. Ignoring them, he turned left into the narrow passage leading to the Marconi Room.

When just steps from the wireless room another member of the crew rushed past Jack from the other direction. The sailor jostled him without apology and hastily disappeared into the main passage. He seemed to be heading in the same direction the officers had gone.

Reflexively, Jack followed the crewmen, hoping to find out what was so urgent. Though the main passage was just steps away, Jack found it empty. Picking up his pace, he reached a passage a few paces toward the bow. At its end, a door leading outside was just closing.

He rushed quickly down the hall and out into the frigid night only to find an empty deck and the echo of footsteps in the dark headed to the stern. Glancing toward the water, he found his view blocked by a large lifeboat swaying slightly from its davits.

With a shiver, Jack headed back into the welcome warmth of the interior. In the main passage, he encountered a steady stream of sailors and officers heading in all directions. He was swept along in a sea of anxious faces before being deposited at the hall leading to the Marconi Room. In seconds he entered the room.

The operator turned at the sound of the door opening. His headset was half on. He held a ship's phone to his free ear. He gave Jack a distracted wave while listening intently. Jack waited for the one-sided conversation to end, sensing it was a ship's officer on the line; the operator's responses were too clipped and deferential for it to be anyone else.

With an "Aye aye, sir," the operator hung up and looked distractedly at Jack. "Sorry to keep you waitin'."

There was more than a slight edge in the young man's voice.

Jack held up the notes. "Quite all right. I have cables here I want—"

"Perhaps a bit later, sir." The young man interrupted sharply. "There is something my superiors have requested I attend to right away. Perhaps in an hour or two if you don't mind."

"But it's already near midnight!"

"I understand that sir, but I have me orders you see. We're scheduled to open at eight tomorrow if you don't wish to wait."

"Very well. I'll be back in an hour."

"Thank you, sir." The operator ushered Jack out with a constrained sense of urgency.

As Jack considered his options in the main hall, a loud knock drew his attention down the passage he'd just left. Standing before the door adjacent to the Marconi Room was the wireless operator, raising his hand to knock again.

"Harold? Harold? I'm goin' a need you. We have a—" Seeing Jack staring at him, the man paused. "There may be something that requires both of our attention. Do ya hear me?" A muffled reply from inside filtered through the vent in the door. Satisfied, the operator quickly returned to the Marconi Room.

His curiosity piqued, Jack drifted back down the short passage. Then the door that the operator had been pounding on opened suddenly nearly hitting Jack. A disheveled young man entered the passage clad only in pants and undershirt. He stumbled hastily through the wireless room door.

Jack stepped to the entrance in time to hear the new arrival speak. "What's up, Mr. Phillips?"

"Seems we hit something," the other operator stated rather matter-of-factly.

"We? You mean the ship?" the other man asked.

"Yes, Harold" came an annoyed response.

"What did it hit?" Harold asked still sounding half-asleep.

"Come on, mate. I'll give you a hint. It was one of those big white things we've been gettin' wireless messages about all evenin'."

"A bloody iceberg!" Harold's tone changed from confused to concerned. "How bad is it?"

"Don't know," the unruffled first operator said. "They're checkin' it out now. Just remember, Harold, this here is the *Titanic,* the *unsinkable Titanic.*"

"That was what some bloody magazine called it. There ain't no such thing as an unsinkable ship." Harold sounded more than a little worried.

"That's why I got you up?"

"You mean in case we ain't unsinkable?"

"Exactly right, mate. Nothing gets past you."

"You're still makin' awful light o' this. You really don't think it might be possible that we're sinkin'?" Harold's voice registered his concern.

"Ain't sayin' we is, ain't sayin' we ain't. Hey, close that door will ya? Don't need anyone hearin' about this till the capn' give the order. In the meantime, I plan on keepin' me life vest nice and—"

The rest of the operator's comment was lost behind the closing door, but Jack had heard enough. He took off at a run. Flying down the two flights to A Deck, he again saw men seated in the starboard lounge engaged in relaxed conversation. Ignoring the incongruity, he rushed down to B Deck. Stumbling off the last step, he charged down the passage and into Abigail's stateroom. His arrival elicited muffled screams from the women.

"Jack! You scared me to death!" Elizabeth said sharply while checking on the boys. She was glad to find they had remained asleep.

"Something has happened to the ship." His breathless words came out awkwardly.

Elizabeth's face turned ashen. "What do you mean *something* happened?"

"Didn't you feel the ship change direction or hear the strange noise a few minutes ago?"

"Well yes." With some effort, Lady Abigail raised up onto her elbows, looking alarmed. "We were just talking about that when you arrived. Tell us what you know."

"The wireless man said we'd hit an iceberg."

That brought gasps from the women.

Elizabeth moved from the boys to a chair next to Abigail. She spoke, taking her ladyship's hand. "Are we going to—" The mere thought cut her question short.

Sensing the need to calm them, Jack quoted the wireless operator. "Remember, the *Titanic* is supposed to be unsinkable. So this will likely be just a nuisance."

"I certainly hope you're right. I can feel us slowing down though." Abigail said lying back.

Elizabeth was still focused on sinking. "Should we be doing anything just in case?"

Jack took his wife's hand and felt tension in her grip. "In case of what?"

"The worst. I mean that we sink." Elizabeth trembled at the thought.

Jack uttered a halfhearted laugh. "Now isn't that impossible for an unsinkable ship?" Seeing his humor did not satisfy them, he continued. "Tell you what. Why don't you gather up all the life vests while I go and learn exactly what happened and what we need to do."

The women seemed to relax a bit at that suggestion.

After giving his wife a quick kiss, Jack left the women to their duties and fears. He desperately hoped that what he feared was unfounded. Intuitively, he knew better.

The B Deck corridor was empty as Jack headed back to the grand staircase. He was greeted by loud voices drifting from above. Taking the stairs up to A Deck in great leaps, he found the men in the lounge area now milling about uneasily. Jack stopped.

"Excuse me, gentlemen, but have you heard anything about what's happened?"

A rather tall, tuxedoed man in his fifties spoke for the group. "No sir. Ever since feeling and hearing something, we've been trying to get answers from the crew passing by. Most didn't stop. Those that did mumbled they knew nothing. Damn frustrating."

A second man added, "Bloody rude if you ask me."

Jack ignored the man and made a suggestion. "I'm headed to the boat deck to inquire. Anyone like to join me?" Two men stepped forward. "Good. The rest of you might want to head to your cabins to wait for instructions. This may be nothing serious, but we should—"

A voice sounding frightened cut in. “I say, sir. What do you mean serious?”

“I’m just suggesting we be prudent and get some answers so we can be prepared.”

“For what?” Someone pushed forward, anxiety in his question.

“I don’t know for sure. That’s why I’m headed up there.” Jack looked up toward the Boat Deck. “We’ll likely laugh about this tomorrow, but in case …” Jack let his sentence drop and turned toward the stairs, followed by the two volunteers, as the others scattered.

Jack passed crowds of confused but unconcerned passengers on the way up the grand staircase with his two companions close behind. On the Boat Deck, the threesome emerged into bitter cold on the starboard side at lifeboat station 7. There they saw crewmen already at work. Still other crew rushed by headed toward other stations.

With growing disbelief and fear, Jack nudged the well-dressed man next to him and gestured along the deck. “I don’t know what you think, but I’d say it doesn’t look good.”

The other man glanced both ways. “Bloody hell.”

The two men who had been with him turned and rushed back inside. Instead of heading back to the women, Jack headed for the bridge. As he passed the last lifeboat station, he collided with a high-ranking officer rushing in the opposite direction. Running to catch the man, Jack yelled, “I say, sir, are we sinking?”

Instead of responding, the white-clad figure continued down the boat deck shouting orders. “Put your shoulders into it, men!” He ran to the next boat. “Be ready to swing it down on my order!”

At the next station, the officer addressed a sailor. “Mr. Jones, what’s the trouble there?”

“The cable’s jammed sir, frozen solid, sir” came the terse reply.

After a quick check, the officer moved on, shouting over his shoulder, “Get a hand spike or wrench and get that bloody thing working.”

All the time, Jack was desperately trying to get the man’s attention. Stopping amidships, the officer bellowed a message for all to hear. “As passengers arrive, make sure women and children go first. Captain’s orders. Pass it on.” The officer turned at the next corner, heading to the port side.

Jack had seen and heard enough. The ship was going down, and it wasn't going to take long. He quickly entered the doors amidships leading to the familiar grand staircase and saw the space suddenly crammed with passengers and crew. He pushed through the crowd only to find the stairs clogged with bewildered and anxious passengers. He was trapped.

CHAPTER 20

It took an eternity for Jack to fight through the rapidly growing throng to the B Deck. Back at the suites, he found Elizabeth calmly sitting next to the bed stroking Lady Abigail's hand. A glance told him the boys were dressed warmly while still dozing in their beds. He was shocked at Abigail's appearance. Hiding his reaction, Jack immediately started updating the women. "The news isn't good."

They heard a steward rapping on cabin doors to wake passengers. Jack nodded at the life vests. "Good. You've found them."

"Is that your way of telling us they'll be needed?" Elizabeth asked tremulously.

Jack realized this was no time to be cavalier. "I'm afraid so, dear. They're preparing lifeboats for launching as we speak." He tried to convey optimism. "It's lucky I heard about this earlier than most. As soon as we get the boys in their life jackets, we can all be among the first to the boats."

Elizabeth looked to Abigail and whispered to Jack, "I'm afraid Lady Abigail had a very difficult time getting dressed. Seems she's had a bit of a setback, the vertigo and all."

Jack went to check the mummy-like figure on the bed as Elizabeth woke the boys and wrestled them awkwardly into life jackets, saying, "I've gathered extra blankets to take."

"Good idea," Jack said while waiting to assist Abigail up, but she didn't move. "Can you walk, my lady?"

"Not far, and not on my own I'm afraid." The few words sapped her strength.

"Just rest, my lady." Jack turned to his wife and whispered, "Abigail cannot get to the boat deck on her own."

"Then take her first, Jack," Elizabeth implored. "I'll wait here with the boys."

"No, Elizabeth," Jack said emphatically. "We'll lose our slim head start doing that. As passengers learn the truth, I predict wholesale panic. If that happens, we'll never get these boys to a boat. And you'd agree, they're our first priority. Once you three are safely in a boat, I'll bring Lady Abigail. We need to go now!"

Jack picked up William and nodded for Elizabeth to take Charles. "Once on the Boat Deck, I'll come straight back and get Lady Abigail."

Jack saw Elizabeth frown, but she made no further protest. She quickly picked up the toddler and extra blankets. Before opening the door, Jack said to Abigail, "Rest here, my lady. I'll get your boys and Elizabeth safely to the boats then return for you, I promise."

Abigail waved weakly. Jack led them into a crowded passageway. He told Elizabeth over the noise, "Shout if you need help or have to stop. And for God's sake stay as close behind me as you can."

Then they were off. Jack did not stand on politeness as he pushed his way toward the grand staircase. Over a den of anguished cries and angry shouts, he heard the stewards calmly requesting everyone to get their life jackets and proceed to the Boat Deck. It was clear to Jack that few were listening.

When blocked, Jack pushed through unapologetically. He urged others headed in the right direction, thus improving the pace. Still, it took far too long for his liking to reach the staircase. Once there, the reason for the delay was clear. Passengers clogged both sides of the stairs, some heading up and others down. No one was moving.

Jack heard the sound of music above the noise. It was the gentle strains of a waltz. Somewhere, an orchestra was playing. He doubted what he was hearing at first, but the music soon became more audible as other passengers noticed it too. To his pleasant surprise, Jack saw the people calming down.

The calm was short lived, however, as the *Titanic*'s massive steam whistle gave forth a mighty blast. Any doubt in the minds of the passengers around him that the ship would sink was gone. In an instant, the crowd was once again in frenzy.

Suddenly, Jack was pushed aside by a pair of very large crewmen. Once the two reach the stairs, they began the seemingly impossible task of organizing the flow of people. Forced back, Jack bumped awkwardly into Elizabeth, nearly causing her to drop Charles.

"Make way!" Jack yelled loudly. "We have children being crushed here." His plea went unnoticed. Jack swept Elizabeth and the boys toward the first-class lounge on the starboard side. As soon as Elizabeth was seated on a sofa, Jack placed William on the arm next to her. They were momentarily safe but no closer to the boats.

As they caught their breath, the mighty whistle blew again, drowning out the orchestra. From where he stood, he could see the hallway to the elevators nearby was as packed as the staircase. There was subtle ebb and flow between the two locations as passengers frantically debated their choices.

Jack's voice sounded eerily calm to Elizabeth. "Stay here. I'm going to check things and be right back." She nodded and returned to soothing William and Charles.

Jack took a few steps toward the confusion, trying to recall in his mind's eye the layout of the ship. The primary means of moving between decks were the two grand staircases, one aft and the one near him. The elevators just beyond the forward staircase were most often the second choice for travel between decks because they were rather slow.

Jack saw that the crewmen were making steady progress in getting traffic moving on the stairs. Both men yelled for passengers on the landings to use other stairways. Most paid no attention, couldn't hear, or as Jack believed, didn't know where the other stairways were. He did, but the problem was getting to them.

The hallway that led past the grand staircase and elevators to the stairs at the bow of the ship was jammed. Looking aft, Jack saw a similar logjam a hundred yards away at the other grand staircase. In between, more passengers were emerging from staterooms and joining the bedlam. With a sinking feeling, Jack saw no avenue of escape.

Wrestling with what to do, he noticed for the first time a slight slant of the deck toward the bow. No one else seemed to notice it, however; they were preoccupied with the regular and frequent blowing of the ship's whistle, which heightened the panic.

Without a plan, Jack started back to Elizabeth. He glimpsed movement. The two crewmen had gained the upper hand. A garbled yell rose from the landing followed by a sudden surge up the stairs. Many abandoned the wait for the lifts and pushed toward the stairs. That created a small gap along the wall of the passage leading to the bow.

Instantly, Jack rushed to the sofa, grabbed William, and told Elizabeth, "Follow me now!" just as the ship's whistle blew again. He headed off.

Using his bulk and motivation, Jack burrowed through the tiny space, to the dismay of many agitated passengers heading the other way. Luckily, the gauntlet lasted fewer than twenty paces. Breaking free into a nearly vacant passageway, Jack maneuvered them around a few disoriented souls and headed toward the bow.

Bursting through a door at the end of the passage, they emerged onto a broad, enclosed promenade. A blast of cold air and the sound of the ship's horn greeted them. The passage ran perpendicular across the bow, ending at matching bulkheads. Without pausing, Jack headed to the right and then turned right again at the bulkhead, where he found the stairs he sought. Falling in line behind a small group ascending the stairs, the couple paused to comfort the tearful boys.

These external stairs went directly up to the next two decks. In less than a minute, the four were on the Boat Deck. Once there, officers and stewards directed them to waiting lifeboats. At boat 7, they were ordered to stand against the wall. From there, they watched crewmembers work feverishly to prepare the thirty-foot vessel for launching.

The sight generated no panic among the initial gathering of passengers; they stood in silence listening to the continuing orchestra music or talking in hushed tones. The chaos two decks below had morphed into eerie politeness and calm. Once they were free of the bedlam, Jack's doubts again surfaced about the seriousness of the situation in spite of the activity going on before them.

Just as the ship's whistle sounded again, a young officer addressed the gathering crowd, sounding more as if he were announcing a shuffleboard tournament. "Not to worry, folks. The boats will be down shortly." He gently moved the group back. "Let's make way for the crew to do their work now."

As he spoke, more passengers filled the Boat Deck. Once there, the new arrivals too fell silent in harmony with those who had preceded them. The contrast between the noise and activity of the crew and the stillness of the passengers was stark. The whistle blew. The orchestra played on.

Seeing the growing throng, Jack turned to Elizabeth. "I need to get her ladyship up here right away. You and the boys get on this boat when it's ready. If we don't get back to join you, we'll get on another and rendezvous out there." He waved into the blackness.

"No! Don't leave us, Jack!" Elizabeth grabbed his arm.

Jack wrenched free and sat William before her. "You know we can't leave without Lady Abigail. So stop delaying me and we'll all get off this ship alive."

Elizabeth watched Jack disappear inside and fought the urge to chase after him. An overwhelming sense of foreboding settled on her as the ship's whistle blew so loudly close by that she nearly fainted. Before she could regain what little composure that remained, there was the sound of an odd thud followed moments later by the flash of a flare.

The sights and sounds intensified Elizabeth's growing terror. The children were becoming more restless. William tugged insistently at her leg, sobbing softly while Charles howled. Their displeasure didn't bother her nearly as much as the sight of lifeboat 7 descending while Jack and Abigail were nowhere to be seen.

Her husband had been gone only minutes, but to Elizabeth it had been an eternity. Before Jack was even out of sight, she had decided not to get on a lifeboat unless everyone was aboard. Her commitment to that desire was being challenged as lifeboat 7 settled at deck level.

First Officer Murdoch, a familiar figure to most of the first-class passengers, appeared. After a quick glance at the boat, he turned to the crowd. "We're ready to load, starting with women and children." No one moved.

Murdoch looked incredulous. He addressed several crewmen. "You there, form a cordon two paces deep. Spread these passengers along the deck and see the same is done aft as well." With a crisp salute, the men went into action.

Turning back to the group waiting behind the deck crew, Murdoch repeated the familiar order. "Remember, women and children first. Please step forward."

Again, no passenger moved, seemingly mesmerized by the gap between the deck and swaying boat though it was tiny. Seeing that, Murdoch scanned the crowd until he found a woman holding a baby. "Would you like to be first, ma'am? We'd like to launch this boat soon so we can move on to others." The women stood fast. "Come on, madam. We must get started."

The women leaned tentatively forward and spoke in a loud voice. "Do we really need to do this?"

"If you wish to save your baby, yes you do." That response delivered strongly got the young mother moving. Soon, she and the baby had been assisted safely into the boat.

Murdoch turned to an elderly woman who seemed to be alone. "Madam, may we assist you into the boat?"

"Why thank you, sir." The woman seemed genuinely glad to be moving even if it was toward a swaying lifeboat many stories above a frigid ocean.

Once she was aboard, Murdoch encouraged others. "See how easy that was? Who's next?" A husband and wife stepped forward, but Murdock stopped the man. "I'm sorry sir, you'll have to wait. Women and children first—captain's orders."

The wife responded angrily, "This is my new husband, and I'll not be separated from him when that boat is nearly empty. You can't seem to find people willing to board, yet here we stand."

Murdoch considered for a moment. "You're absolutely right, madam." He turned to the crew on boat 7. "Until women and children step forward, we'll take all comers. And we will launch"—he looked at his gold watch on its fob—"in five minutes. So step forward now, folks, or go to the back of the line." But even that admonishment produced tepid results.

While that was going on, Elizabeth was too conflicted to move at first.

She slipped deeper into the crowd despite the many people around her who were encouraging her to board. Recalling Jack's admonishment that the children were their priority, she was filled with guilt and struggled to find a middle ground.

Then she saw with some relief three other lifeboats descending farther forward. She made an instant decision to move on to one of them, buying time for Jack to arrive with Abigail. She also vowed to herself to get the children on board one of the next boats.

That settled, Elizabeth adjusted Charles on her shoulder and guided the frightened William toward the bow and her target, boat 3. It was then that she noticed the steepening slope of the deck accompanied by a slight list to the left. The increased angle and crowded walkway hampered her progress and brought her to the edge of exhaustion.

"Here, madam, let me help you on board. Boat 5 is ready." An officer took her arm.

"Oh, thank you, but I'm headed for boat 3, where my husband and maid are meeting us. Could you help me get there?"

Elizabeth and the boys were soon among passengers waiting for lifeboat 3. Those milling about her had finally grasped the gravity of the situation. Their agitation was not helping her cope with all her swirling emotions. Only the sight of Jack could help with that.

Her eyes scanned the deck once again to no avail. Breathing rapidly, heart bounding, Elizabeth was rapidly reaching the end of her rope. William was trying frantically to join his wailing brother being nearly smothered in her arms. Her emotional turmoil, not the bitter cold, had her shaking uncontrollably while at the same time she was drenched in sweat.

Where the hell are you, Jack? She cried out in silence. *Where are you?*

Jack had darted through the nearby doors and headed again for the great stairs expecting a crowd. He wasn't disappointed. This time, however, passengers were moving in a more orderly fashion, thus allowing him to reach their suite on deck B much more quickly.

Entering the room, he was surprised to see the bed empty. Looking around frantically in the dimness, his eyes settled on a heap on the floor near the bathroom. Jack rushed over and grabbed Abigail's wrist. He felt a weak and reedy pulse. Lifting her to the bed, he assessed her condition.

It was soon obvious that he would have to carry her the entire way. That would be difficult given the way Elizabeth had put extra layers on to protect the fragile woman from the harsh weather, a good plan if she had been mobile. Since she wasn't, her extra clothing added weight and restricted his ability to quickly transport her.

He removed the outer layers beneath her overcoat as gently as possible. The process was painfully slow. At last, she was in her coat again. He put a wool cap on her head. If she needed more clothing at the boat, he'd give his coat to her.

As he carried Abigail out of the stateroom, Jack glanced at the large wall clock. It read 12:50. Out in the hall, he again heard the orchestra playing. The song had ominously changed from a waltz to "Nearer, My God, to Thee." The music was drowned out by a blast of the ship's horn as he set off down the deserted passageway.

Soon at the grand staircase yet again, Jack took the stairs two at a time all the way to the Boat Deck, hardly noticing his load. Once there, he encountered many passengers milling about and peering through the windows onto the exposed deck. Ignoring them, Jack rushed across the space and out to where he had left Elizabeth. Boat 7 was gone.

Tremendously relieved that Elizabeth and the boys were safe, Jack turned his full attention to Abigail. Toward the bow, boat 5 was descending as passengers still on deck strained forward to exchange goodbyes. The crowd blocked Jack's view farther forward, so he looked to the stern. Lifeboat 9 was gone, but number 11 was still loading.

Weaving through the crowd, Jack glanced out into the blackness, hoping to glimpse the boat carrying Elizabeth and the boys she loved like sons. Intellectually, he knew the effort was folly, but emotionally, he ached for the connection. When he tripped on a cable nearly dropping Abigail, however, he refocused on the job at hand.

Quickly arriving at station 11, Jack immediately observed two things. First, the tilt of the deck had become far more pronounced. Second, the demeanor of the crowd had changed dramatically and not for the better. His prediction of panic was coming true.

Just as he arrived behind the wall of passengers waiting to board, a pistol went off somewhere on the boat deck. Jack whirled around, nearly dropping Abigail again, but it was impossible to determine from where the sound had come. Turning back, Jack saw the anxious crowd was aggressively pushing toward the waiting lifeboat.

Jack heard the voice of First Officer Murdoch clear and sharp above all others. "We must have order to get this boat away as quickly as possible. I am asking one last time for all women and children to come forward." A middle-aged woman approached Murdock on her husband's arm. "Please hurry, madam."

The woman looked forlornly at her companion. "But Alfred, I don't want to leave you."

"Don't worry, my love. I'll be on a later boat." He gave his wife a gentle kiss and pushed her toward Murdoch. His voice sounded like someone leaving for work rather than saying goodbye perhaps forever. "I'll see you soon, Ruth."

Tearfully, the woman entered the boat as her husband disappeared into the crowd.

The sight wrenched Jack's heart as he imagined Elizabeth and the boys alone on the lifeboat not knowing his fate or that of Lady Abigail. Then he remembered that he'd failed to kiss Elizabeth before leaving her earlier. The thought filled him with anguish; he feared it might have been his last chance to hold her and convey his undying love.

"Last call for women and children for boat nine!" Murdoch announced loudly.

These words brought Jack out of his stupor, and he shouted at Murdoch, "I have a woman who needs help to board. Make way!"

Jack rushed forward as the crowd parted. Seeing the woman's condition, Murdoch took her in his arms. His look confirmed what he already knew. She was near death. Without further hesitation, Murdoch turned to the boat. "We have a special need here. Mr. Gage, come here immediately."

A huge crewman was quickly at Murdoch's side. "Gage, find a comfortable place for this one. Make sure someone attends her." He gave the hulking man a hard look. "I'm not sure she'll …" He let the thought drop. "Just make sure she's attended to."

"Aye aye, sir." Gage took Abigail from Mr. Murdoch's arms as if she were a bag of feathers. With neither concern nor assistance, he stepped off the deck and onto the boat as some in the crowd gasped. He laid her gently beside the middle-aged woman, who rested Abigail's head in her lap.

It was then Jack remembered his topcoat. Taking it off, he stepped forward only to be stopped by Mr. Murdoch. "Women and children, sir."

"I don't intend to board. I just want to get this coat to Lady … to the lady."

Murdoch took it and gave Jack an approving nod. "Certainly sir. Now please step back."

As Jack complied, a junior officer yelled to him, "The name, sir."

Jack was confused. "What?"

"Her name, sir. I need it for the list of those on this boat." The man raised a piece of paper to explain his request.

"Oh, right. Her name is …" Jack paused, uncertain what to say. For some reason, all that came to him was "Margaret Grosvenor."

The cry went out one last time. "Women and children for boat eleven step forward." When no one came, Murdoch gave the order, "Lower away!"

Lifeboat 11 began its descent as Murdoch headed toward the bow. Passengers onboard and those in the lifeboat stared at each other transfixed; the silence was broken only by the relentless whistle, strains of a hymn, and an occasional sob. Eyes met and hands came up on both sides of the railing bidding farewells.

As the boat dropped from sight, a flare bursting above them illuminated faces showing despair, fear, and resignation. It was the first Jack had seen. He wondered how many had been launched before. As he pondered that, the *Titanic*'s whistle blew again. As it died away, the soothing sound of the orchestra returned.

Joining the migration following Mr. Murdoch to the port side, Jack noticed the ship was listing significantly in that direction. The angle of the deck toward the bow was also becoming acute. At this rate and given the number still onboard, he thought his chances of survival were slim.

Nearly mad with anxiety and doubt, Elizabeth saw boat 3 nearly full and waiting. It was the moment of truth. The boys needed to be on that boat, but could she do that? Go with them and leave Jack and their mother behind? Could she honor her commitment?

Shouts for her to come forward came from the crew and passengers already onboard. In an instant, she made her choice. Stepping up, she scanned the boat until she found a likely candidate. She pushed William toward the officer in charge. "See that young woman over there?" He nodded as Elizabeth struggled with what she was about to do one last time. "Please give him to her."

Once this was accomplished, the officer turned to assist Elizabeth and the baby into the boat, but Elizabeth pulled back, shaking her head. "No. I'm supposed to wait for the"—she paused—"for the boys' mother and my husband. They should be here shortly."

"But you should get in here with the boys right now, ma'am," the officer implored. "We're not going to wait. I have orders to launch immediately."

Elizabeth handed Charles to the officer. "I understand, but I must wait. Please find someone to care for the baby until we're reunited."

A female voice came from behind the officer. An older woman leaned forward. "I'll take care of him, ma'am. I have grandchildren of my own. He'll be fine with me."

Reluctantly, the officer handed Charles to the woman. He turned to Elizabeth. "Now come on, ma'am, don't be foolish. Those young-uns need ya." As if to confirm that, William let out a wail and tried to wiggle free.

"No, just go." Tears began to run down her cheeks. "I'll be close behind." She sobbed while taking another step back and turning away, unable to bear the thought of what she'd just done

As she stumbled to the wall of the boat deck, a voice came from behind her. "Mrs. Hightower!" For a moment, she forgot the part she'd been playing for a moment. Finally realizing this, she turned to find Mr. English, one of the B deck stewards, approaching. "Mrs. Hightower! Where's your family?"

Elizabeth said nothing; she just looked over her shoulder and pointed to the boat.

Mr. English was confused. “I see the children, but why aren’t you with them?”

“I’m waiting for Jack and …” Elizabeth suddenly couldn’t remember what to call Abigail.

As she tried to think, an officer behind her shouted, “Lower away, men.” Shocked at hearing this, Elizabeth turned to see boat 3 make its first jerk toward the sea below. She froze.

Mr. English hesitated then rushed forward protesting on her behalf as the boat dropped from sight. “Stop! This woman needs to be on board with her children!”

The crewman manning one pulley lowering the boat shook his head. “Too late, Mr. English. Can’t bring her back up with all those folks in it. Best get her on the next boat.”

Mr. English rejoined Elizabeth as she stared into the void left by boat 3. Only the sound of the ropes spooling through the squeaky pulleys remained. In tortured silence, she slowly moved to the rail while the steward attempted to shield her from the cold.

“I have to see the boat pull away. I have to know they’re safe,” Elizabeth whispered, still agonizing over what she had done.

“Of course, ma’am.” The steward’s voice was amazingly calm given the circumstances. “Then after that, we need to get you to the next available boat.”

Elizabeth looked up from the blackness and spoke with a detached smile. “Thank you, Mr. English. But if you don’t mind, I’d like to find my husband after I see the boys off.” Her eyes returned to the nearly invisible waters below.

The crew lowering boat 3 was having difficulty with the ropes that were quite stiff from the cold. Every few yards, the cables caught; it took valuable time to wrestle them free. Occasionally, one side caught while the other continued playing out. When that happened, cries could be heard from below as one end of the boat dropped several feet.

Though out of sight, Elizabeth was horrified by the sounds. She envisioned the boys being tossed into the sea and going to their deaths alone. Why had she been so selfish, abandoning them when they need their nanny? With each near disaster, her guilt grew, and Mr. English had to restrain her from leaping into the abyss.

At last, a voice bellowed up from below, "On the water!" Hearing that, Elizabeth collapsed into Mr. English's arms. Tears of relief joined those of anguish. The voice from below came again. "We've got a jam down here. Going to need to cut free."

Elizabeth's heart began to race again. "Don't worry, Mrs. Hightower. They should remedy that quick enough."

"Ropes away!" came a shout from below as if validating the steward's promise.

The crew immediately began to stow the ropes and pulleys, wasted effort under the circumstances. As the cry "Boat three away" came from below, a nearby sailor let out a cry of his own. "Look out below!" Seconds later, a crashing sound came out of the darkness. The crewmen handling the davits for boat 3 leaned over and looked down anxiously as shouts of alarm rose from the sea.

"What happened?" the steward asked anxiously as Elizabeth stood stunned at his side.

"Lost a pulley," was the terse reply.

At that moment, a shot echoed through the crisp night air, drawing everyone's attention. Sensing it had come from the port side, the officer launching boat 3 sent a man to investigate. The crew returned to their work, and once done, they headed for boat 1. Elizabeth and English were left wondering what had happened on board and on the water.

Then a brief glint in the water caught Elizabeth's eye. She tugged at the steward's sleeve. The two squinted into the darkness at a boat being rowed away. "They are off, Mrs. Hightower," English proclaimed. "Now let's find your husband, shall we?"

As he guided her toward a door and the warmth of the inner ship, there was another thud followed by a flash. A flare lit the surroundings like the sun. The two glanced out and saw several of the lifeboats already joining up a good distance away.

"See, ma'am? Them boys are out there right now waiting for you," English said confidently. "Now let's try to get the rest of the family out to them."

The young steward led her down a narrow passageway to the main hall. While heading toward the lounge by the grand staircase, they passed the hall leading to the Marconi Room. The *tap-tap-tap* of Morse code was clearly audible, the only sound in the eerily empty passage.

Finding her a seat in the lounge, Mr. English spoke to her urgently. "Now you rest here, Mrs. Hightower, and I'll find your husband." He pulled a well-worn watch from the breast pocket of his still immaculate uniform coat. "See, it's one thirty-seven by my watch. You stay here and keep an eye out for him. I should be back in less than ten minutes."

Elizabeth nodded weakly. "But is there time for all this?"

"I'm sure several lifeboats are yet to be launched, but we do need to be quick about it. So stay here nice and warm and I'll be back with him before you know it."

Elizabeth grabbed his arm. "But shouldn't you be takin' care of yourself?"

"The Lord will take care 'a me, Mrs. Hightower. Meanwhile, keep my watch so you'll know when to expect me back."

Not waiting for a response, Mr. English headed quickly out onto the port side. Elizabeth settled back, checking his watch that read 1:40 just as the ship's horn blew and another flare exploded illuminating the room. That happened again at 1:45 and 1:50. In between, she heard music. Except for a few crewmen rushing by, no one came for her.

Horrified at the thought of hearing the horn and seeing another flare, the hysterical Elizabeth headed for the portside doors. Before she reached them, however, Mr. English came rushing in gasping for breath.

Elizabeth grabbed him roughly and screamed, "Where have you been? Where's Jack?"

"I'm sorry, Mrs. Hightower. I couldn't find him. I was hoping he was here. Better yet, I hoped to find you gone. Anyway, the ship is going down fast and most of the boats are gone. I must get you aboard the last of them, ma'am. I think the best bet is this way."

They started in that direction just as the horn sounded and another flare exploded. This brought Elizabeth to a halt at the top of the grand staircase. English tugged at her arm urging her on. "Come on, Mrs. Hightower. We have to go!"

Pulling free, she looked down the stairs. "Maybe they're still in the suite."

"I find that hard to believe, ma'am. They surely made their way up here by now."

"But you don't understand! Lady Abigail was quite ill."

"Lady who?" English was beginning to think Mrs. Hightower was hallucinating.

"Her lady—" Seeing his confusion, Elizabeth tried again. "Mrs. Grosvenor's been quite ill the whole trip. Jack went to get her after we brought the boys up to the Boat Deck."

"But that was long ago, Mrs. Hightower." Mr. English tugged at her sleeve again. "I need to get you on a boat now!"

Elizabeth pulled free again, not paying attention to the steward's desperate words. "But he could still be down there struggling to help her."

English glanced around weighing the chances. "Look, Mrs. Hightower, I'll go down and check if you promise to head for the boats right now. You have very little time."

"I'll not go without him, without them, without you. I'll wait here."

With no time to argue, English grunted and launched himself down the grand staircase. Elizabeth gripped the banister against the pronounced list of the ship and waited. The steward had not been gone long before she heard footsteps.

English spoke before he even reached the top. "There is already too much water for me to get there, Mrs. Hightower. They must be on a boat. Now let's go!" He grabbed Elizabeth at the landing, and they stumbled downhill to the doors leading to the port side.

As they clumsily exited onto the precariously steep deck, English lost his grip and Elizabeth began to slide toward the railing. Halfway across the highly polished deck of the dying ship, an arm reached out and caught her by a coat sleeve. Gasping for breath, she looked up into the eyes of her husband.

Jack pulled Elizabeth up and looked at her in horror. Ignoring the look, she threw her arms around his neck and kissed him long and hard. "I love you," she said breathlessly.

Jack's expression changed to deep sadness then resignation. "But we're going to—"

Elizabeth put a finger to his lips. "I know, dear. We'll do it together."

The watch Mr. English had given her swung gently across Jack's back. The time was 2:06 a.m.

CHAPTER 21

After a productive visit with Dr. Smyth, who willingly shared the boys' medical records found after a lengthy search, Jerome felt he'd exhausted the sources in Wickersham. He was no closer to discovering how Abigail had escaped or where she had gone. The former was far less important than the latter at that point. If he didn't answer that question, he would fail.

Rather than rushing back to America, Jerome decided he ought first to spend some time in London. There, he would review records at Scotland Yard and in the newspapers of that time about the disappearance. With matters in Bedford Falls less critical, he decided to take earthly transportation and practice patience while reviewing and organizing his findings. Perhaps he had overlooked something important.

The train he took was a local. A middle-class couple and their two children soon joined him in the carriage along with an old, stoop-shouldered man with a floppy hat and cane. As the family settled across from him and the old gentleman found a corner on his side, he introduced himself. "Hello, my name's Jerome. Welcome aboard."

"Ahh, a Yank," the father said with a smile. "My name is Harvey, Alex Harvey. This is my wife, Hazel. These two are Theodore and Peter, ages six and four."

"And I'm Albert Hume," the old man added rather solemnly.

"Fine lads you have there," Jerome said to the Harveys. "And yes, I am from the states."

"What brings you to Britain if I may ask?" Hazel's eyes shone with interest.

"I came looking for information in Wickersham about an acquaintance of mine."

"And did you find what you were looking for?" Alex asked as he casually pulled his bickering sons apart. "Settle down, you two. Can't you see we're talkin' here?" He nodded for Jerome to continue.

"More or less." Jerome's reply was intentionally vague; he deftly changed the subject. "Where are you all headed?"

Albert Hume was a long retired workman from upcountry. He had moved to the village that the train had just left to be near his children after being widowed. He was headed to the funeral of a longtime friend who had lived the last few years outside London.

"I've been makin' this kind of trip a lot these days," Albert said matter-of-factly. "Me wife's been gone now seven years. And I've lost a half dozen close mates since then." He cracked a sly smile. "Havin' a higher casualty rate now than when we were in the war together, World War I that is. Was called the war to end all wars back then."

Mr. Harvey snorted. "Somebody shoulda told Hitler that. I was in the last one and luckily didn't get a scratch in three years of service. Airplane mechanic." Jerome and Mr. Hume gave him understanding nods. "Hazel took the boys to the country to avoid the bombs. Really young they was then. We lived in Liverpool when the war started."

Albert perked up. "I worked there most of me life, 'cept for *my* war that is. Built ships from nineteen hundred until I retired in thirty-seven to take care of Doris. All those years with me workin' in the bad air and she's the one who got consumption." A look of sadness crossed his face. "She died in time for me to move down here and miss the bombs too."

"You were lucky, sir," Mr. Harvey said gravely. "Did you know Liverpool was second only to London in the number of bombs that fell during the Blitz? We were lucky too what with Hazel's parents able to take her and the boys in down this way at the time. I escaped by workin' at an airbase repairin' Spitfires durin' the Battle of Britain as it's called now."

Albert's face showed admiration. "I bet you didn't miss out on *all* the fun."

"No, but I don't like talkin' about it, about any of it." Alex's face turned dark. "Right after the war, me, Hazel, and the boys headed back to Liverpool, but there was nothin' left of our old neighborhood. The city was in ruins."

"I must have gone there about the same time out of curiosity. Wished I hadn't." Albert's gloomy expression mirrored Alex's. "I saw the same thing, turned around, and left."

Jerome tried to lighten the conversation by changing the subject again. "You must have great stories about shipbuilding, Mr. Hume."

"I bet you're right, Mr. Jerome," Alex said turning to his oldest. "Teddy, Mr. Hume here used to build ships."

Teddy turned from the train window; his eyes grew large. Seeing that, Alex asked, "Will you tell us about some of the ships you built?"

"Mainly I worked on ocean liners." Hume sounded pleased to talk about his career. "It was the golden age for those ships when I started. I worked on some famous ones."

"Which ones?" Theodore asked eagerly.

"Let's see, there was the *Baltic* and *Adriatic,* sister ships I worked on in my early years. They were small compared to the ones that came later. Among the bigger ones were the *Olympic* and *Britannic*. They weighed in at over forty-five thousand tons."

"What ship line did you work for, Mr. Hume?" Jerome asked.

"I worked for several over the years, but mainly the White Star Line."

"Isn't that the line that built the *Titanic*?" Alex asked.

Albert's reply was subdued. "Aye, it was."

"Did you work on the *Titanic,* Albert?" Mr. Harvey asked.

Albert gave a pensive sigh. "Yes, afraid so. I worked in Belfast for the first dozen or so years before I got married. I was foreman of a crew that laid the keel in '09."

"I see you're still greatly affected by that experience," Jerome said.

Albert nodded somberly. "A lot of us still are. The whole country mourned for years." His expression suddenly brightened. "Ahh, but the day she sailed from Belfast for Southampton, she was a magnificent sight. I rode on her that shakedown cruise just before its first and last voyage."

"That must have been something," Hazel said dreamily.

"Maybe for the first hour. After that, it was back to work." Albert's words surprised her. "Me and my men spent the rest of the cruise doin' the biddin' of the officers down below. Only saw the main deck gettin' on and off."

"Good thing you did get off in Southampton," Alex pointed out.

Hume chuckled without humor. "You're right about that. It turned out to be a backhanded birthday present to me."

"How so?" Jerome asked casually.

"Well, the ship sailed for America on my birthday," Albert replied. "At the time, I was disappointed. Days later, I felt differently."

"I wasn't even born yet," Hazel said.

"I sometimes forget how long ago it was," Hume said gravely. "I turned thirty-six that day and was stuck on a train headed to Liverpool when she left port."

Hazel pressed for the date. "Don't keep me in suspense, Mr. Hume. What day was it?"

"Oh, right, ma'am," Albert said apologetically. "It was the tenth of April. The *Titanic* left Southampton that day in nineteen twelve. Went down four days later."

It took a few moments for what Jerome had heard to register, and it took a little longer for him to make the connection. *Wasn't that Elizabeth Crandall's birthday too?* He quickly confirmed that from his notes. That couldn't be just a coincidence. Was it possible that Lady Abigail risked her own life to reach Henry in America? Clearly she had not remained in England. If she had, the fate of the *Titanic* could perhaps explain everything.

Smiling to himself, he knew what he'd be digging for at Scotland Yard. He suddenly couldn't wait to get to London. The earl had not brought Scotland Yard into the case until April 12, however, a week after the disappearances and two days after the *Titanic* had sailed. Up until then, the search had not included Southampton.

Records and articles at the Yard clearly indicated the earl had relied on the information discovered in his daughter's room. The letter, list, and map convinced him that her health would have severely limited travel options, so he had concentrated his resources at UK ports with ships heading to Europe. Once involved, the police expanded the search, but the trail was cold.

From that information, it was not a great leap for Jerome to theorize that by the time Scotland Yard checked on ships headed for America, Lady Abigail and the boys had already sailed. If true and they were never seen again, the ship had to have been the *Titanic*. Based on that assumption, Jerome headed for Liverpool and White Star's headquarters. If proof of his theory existed, it was likely buried somewhere in the shipbuilders' records of the disaster.

Arriving in Liverpool and heading for 30 James Street, however, his optimism waned. Why should he expect to find proof when so many others had failed who had actually been present during the events?

Even if Abigail and the others had been on board, however, the likelihood of their going unidentified seemed remote. The conditions required to produce such a result would have to have been extraordinary, going well beyond disguises and aliases. That might have gotten them from the estate to the ship. But then what?

That was the focus of Jerome's research for a full week. It took only a few minutes to eliminate the obvious; no passengers named Forsyth, Wickersham, or Crandall were aboard in any class. He found that the vast majority of women and children in all classes had survived. Of those lost, most bodies had not been recovered.

Assuming for the moment that Abigail had traveled in first class, Jerome started with that list. The manifest included surnames and Christian names, genders, ages, addresses, occupations, and the cabin numbers. Columns had been added after the disaster noting whether the passenger had survived. If not, a number noted the order in which any one body was recovered; the notation NR stood for not recovered.

Jerome was surprised to find that of all the female passengers in first class, only seven had perished. Of those seven, only one body had not been recovered. It didn't take long to narrow the possibilities. Almost immediately he focused on two names:

Hightower, Agnes, Mrs., F, 26, Scotland, Edinburgh, wife, B55, D, NR.
Hightower, Jack, Mr., M, 29, Scotland, Edinburgh, Financier, B55, D, NR.

The ages were about right for Elizabeth Crandall or Lady Abigail. The male could have been the mystery man hinted at in Elizabeth's letter to her parents. The next entries seemed to confirm that he was onto something.

Hightower, Wilbur, M, 15, Scotland, Edinburgh, child, B53. D, NR.

Hightower, Charlotte, F, Infant, Scotland, Edinburgh, child, B53, D, NR.

Jerome felt his heart sink. Wilbur was listed as fifteen at the time, and the second child was listed as a female infant. If the information was true, the children couldn't have been William and Charles. Furthermore, even if they were by some chance the Potter boys mislabeled intentionally, they were listed as dead and never recovered.

Disheartened, the investigator continued wanting to at least confirm his theory about what had happened to Abigail and the boys. If he was right, there should be a second woman, either Abigail or Elizabeth under another alias. He found a woman he thought might have been her on the list just above Agnes Hightower.

Grosvenor, Margaret, Mrs. F, 51, USA, Albany, NY, nanny, B53, deceased, #127.

The age was wrong, and the nationality American, but this discovery gave him renewed hope. With Albany, New York listed as her home and being in the suite with the Hightower children had to be more than a coincidence. Aliases, disguises, and falsified entries on the manifest could easily explain all the other discrepancies.

The more he thought about it, the more convinced he became that this was the solution to the mystery of Lady Abigail's disappearance. The irony of this conclusion, however, was that everyone was listed as deceased. Still, he wanted to be more certain of his dramatic deductions before carrying this news to Henry.

Taking what he'd discovered to the curator of the archives, he confirmed that the personal information on the ledger had come from the passengers themselves and that the details wouldn't have been heavily scrutinized. Boarding the *Titanic* in 1912 was quite casually managed. All that was required was minimal biographical information and a ticket. There was no such thing as a passport at the time.

Regarding the process of identification after the disaster, the curator acknowledged it had been chaotic and created in the moment. Hundreds had been involved in both New York and Liverpool. The demand for information from families, authorities, and the media was more than intense.

Dealing with survivors was relatively easy. Coming off the rescue vessels, they were checked against a copy of the ship's manifest provided by an officer of the *Titanic* on one of the lifeboats. The victims were much harder to address in part because so many had been lost.

Besides the search for bodies at sea, the challenge of identifying those lost was complicated by the fact that many bodies initially recovered were immediately buried at sea. Of the 333 bodies recovered, mostly third-class passengers or crewmembers, 209 were taken directly to Nova Scotia. Of those, only 59 were claimed while the rest were buried there.

Given that background, Jerome asked the curator what the possibility was of someone noted as lost on the records actually surviving, specifically the Hightowers or Mrs. Grosvenor. The curator was confident that was not the case especially regarding the adults. He was a bit less certain when it came to the children.

The Hightower children were the only first-class children reported as deceased and not found. Another fifty-six children in the other classes had lost their lives; all others had survived. In addition, however, four initially unidentified boys arrived in New York aboard the *Carpathia*.

At that stage, they were listed as unidentified awaiting someone to come forward. The curator shared the story of two boys being reunited fairly quickly with their mother in England. Her husband had kidnapped them and boarded under aliases. The four-year-old provided his mother's name, and the woman recognized them from the picture in the paper.

The other two, both boys, were a different story. At first, it was thought they were the Hightower children. Doubts soon arose, however, when the manifest indicated that one of their children was a girl. The ages listed also didn't correspond remotely to the records. Since none of the stewards who had served on B deck had survived, no one could challenge the entries.

A woman in the lifeboat with the two also claimed she'd seen the other boys in steerage during the voyage. When it was suggested that she'd seen the two recently reunited with their mother, she was adamant they were not the same children. And Jerome agreed. The ages and genders of the two unidentified boys matched the Potter children exactly.

Though he was greatly encouraged to hear this, the investigator was baffled as to why William Potter had not spoken up as the other boy had. The curator did not recall, so they headed back to the archives. They soon discovered the answer. The older boy had been struck in the head by a pulley during the launch of the lifeboat. He arrived at pier 54 on the *Carpathia* in a coma and near death.

A dismal day rose over the Hudson as a stretcher reached the bottom of the *Carpathia*'s gangway. It bore the first survivor from the disaster. An officer urgently scanned the packed dock until he saw a canvas-covered wagon with a red cross on its side. Turning to the litter bearers, he said, "Follow me and be quick about it!"

Rushing ahead, the officer confronted a white-clad figure casually smoking a cigarette next to the enclosed wagon. "Are you a doctor?"

Caught off guard, the young man uttered a less-than-intelligent reply: "Do you need one?"

"What do you think, you fool?" The angry retort was accompanied by the arrival of the stretcher.

Failing to stop fast enough, the litter bearers collided with the backside of the ship's officer and nearly dropped their cargo. This was the last straw for the harried man. "Bloody hell! If you drop that boy, I will personally have you both up on charges."

The seaman froze at attention as the officer turned to the ambulance attendant. "Now, about that doc—" He stopped in midsentence as the orderly disappeared around the back of the wagon. Moments later, he returned with a tall, young man in a cheap suit.

"I brought you the doctor, sir," the attendant said before scurrying aside.

"Quite" came the terse reply from the intensely focused officer. Turning to the physician, he spoke quickly. "I am Medical Officer Blackmarr of the *Carpathia*."

The young man extended his hand, which went unshaken. "I'm Doctor Long from Saint Vincent Asylum. How can I help you?"

"We will be bringing those needing medical attention off first. I took the liberty of triaging them during our time at sea."

"Very good, Dr. Blackmarr. Are there many?"

Blackmarr shook his head. "Plenty in shock and suffering from hypothermia. Otherwise, not many other injuries and none as serious as this boy."

Dr. Long leaned down in the dim morning light to check on the youth. "We have more than adequate resources to take care of the other issues you described. What can you tell me about the boy?"

"Head trauma. He has been slowly deteriorating. Pulse weak, respiration marginal, and his temperature spiked to a hundred and three during the night. It was a hundred and one just minutes ago. I suggest getting him in the wagon and to the hospital."

Dr. Long nodded and waved the stretcher to the ambulance. He turned to his orderly. "O'Toole, help them get the boy strapped down, and be gentle about it."

As he watched the aide responded gingerly, Dr. Long addressed Blackmarr again. "We'll leave as soon as he's secure."

"I believe that you should wait to take one more victim with you." Blackmarr's request required no additional explanation as another officer arrived carrying a toddler.

"Of course, the other unidentified child. He has no injuries, right?"

"That's correct," Blackmarr said. "He gets quite agitated if separated from the other boy however." Seeing the child asleep in the officer's arms, he added. "Except of course when he's sleeping."

This elicited a brief smile from the men. Dr. Long took the child. "Okay, O'Toole, let's get these two back to the hospital quickly."

Blackmarr gently grabbed Long's arm. "Could I accompany you?"

"Of course. Climb aboard."

Long moved to the back of the ambulance as Blackmarr spoke to the other officer. "You're in charge, Holland. I'll return to the ship by eighteen hundred hours if not sooner."

The other officer saluted. "Very good sir."

Blackmarr joined Long and the boys in the back of the ambulance, and they were off. The pace over the potholes and cobbles was torturously slow. All the doctors could do was check vital signs and pray to arrive soon. The boy was not looking good.

The trip of less than a mile to St. Vincent's Hospital took the better part of a half hour. Not only was the condition of the streets abysmal, but they were also crowded with workers headed to factories. Even at the cautious pace, O'Toole kept, the pavement and the wagon's poor suspension collaborated to jar everyone on board relentlessly.

As soon as the ambulance pulled up to the entrance of St. Vincent's, emergency room staff rushed forward. A crowd of reporters and gawkers descended, thoughtlessly getting in the way. A lone police officer tried unsuccessfully to keep them back.

Dr. Long jumped down, joined the officer, and spoke angrily to the mob. "Get back or I'll have you all arrested!" Space immediately appeared around the ambulance. Long called to a nurse standing at the door, "Jones, go tell them to prepare for surgery immediately and get someone over here to take care of this infant."

The flurry of activity had the boys quickly inside the main door and headed in different directions. The chaos had woken the toddler, who let everyone know he was not pleased. As the boys disappeared through doors at opposite ends of the main hallway, Long and Blackmarr conferred in the ER waiting room.

"It's amazing he made it this far, doctor. I commend you," Long told Blackmarr. "But I think he is hemorrhaging."

"Subdural hematoma? I agree." Blackmarr's tone conveyed the gravity of the situation.

Long nodded. "We'll get him to the OR right away. Fortunately, this sad-looking facility is home to the best brain doctor in the city, Doctor Isaac Shulman."

"He better be or that boy won't have much chance," Blackmarr said as the two moved off toward the operating room.

From articles in the *New York Times*, Jerome discovered that the boy's life hung in the balance as he remained in a coma. Meanwhile, the toddler, still traumatized, was kept isolated from prying eyes in the orphanage attached to the hospital. Thus, little new information and no photos of the boys appeared in print for nearly two months.

Two things stuck the investigator in these articles. First, the White Star Lines, press, and police had received no creditable claim for the boys. Each lead had been investigated and found wanting. Second and perhaps more revealing was the fact that there was no record of anyone inquiring about the Hightowers. He found the same was true about Mrs. Grosvenor; there was no evidence of anyone in America inquiring about her even when the name appeared on the list of victims. Further, Mrs. Grosvenor's body had remained unclaimed in Nova Scotia. Her grave marker there bore her name and the number 127.

The investigator considered a trip to Edinburgh but decided against it. Instead, he sent a telegram to the office of records in the city asking for a list of all Hightowers residing in or around the city at that time. He sent a similar inquiry to Albany. While he waited for a response, he continued his research. Within days, he received the responses he had expected—no one by those names could be found, and the addresses were fictitious.

As he continued through the clippings and other correspondence, thankfully filed chronologically, news about the tragedy and specifically about the boys came less frequently. He finally came across pictures of them, the older still swabbed in bandages and the younger being uncooperative and looking more like a girl with long curls.

These photos and stories produced no better results at the time. By summer, there was only a trickle of news. The last front-page article, a single column, appeared in August stating that the boys remained at the orphanage. After that, the two became back-page news. With each passing month and a world war on the horizon, they were slowly forgotten.

Only one thing prevented Jerome from being certain he'd solved the mystery based on what he had unearthed. It seemed illogical that the earl and his hired professionals would not have explored the possibility that the unidentified boys from the *Titanic* were his grandsons. With the help of the curator, he endeavored to explain this incongruity.

They quickly confirmed there was not a single verified sighting of Lady Abigail, her children, or Elizabeth after their disappearances.

Whether that was due to a well-designed plan, Bates' absence, the delay in police involvement, or the initial belief that Abigail was too sick to travel, allowed enough time to reach the *Titanic*. But that explained only how they could have gotten on board, not why the earl hadn't considered asking about the boys from the ship. Jerome and the curator were stumped. Nothing in the police records, news articles, other correspondence, or the investigators' interviews explained that fact.

Jerome recalled that the present earl, Andrew had stated that his mother had suffered a breakdown after the disappearance. He'd also said his father had withheld all news from her during that period. Since Andrew did not return from Europe until weeks later and his sister was in Scotland already, they were not around to make the connection.

Over time, however, Jerome and the curator began to focus on the earl's significant character flaws. These included extreme callousness especially toward his daughter, grandchildren, and wife. His was a vengeful nature, which contributed to Abigail's near death, the attempt on Potter's life, and more. As they talked, it became easier to believe how the missing boys had been overlooked intentionally rather than through incompetence.

Overnight, his daughter and grandchildren had disappeared. Why hadn't he contacted the police immediately instead of conducting his own failed search first? Why not join forces? The only reasons Jerome and the curator could agree upon were the earl's self-centeredness, ego, pride, and paranoia. All these traits pointed to him purposefully ignoring that potential truth.

It was relatively easy to see the earl's overwhelming desire to avoid headlines pointing to his failure as a father. Imagining a headline in the *Times* such as "Earl's Daughter Found after Escaping," or worse yet, "Missing Earl's Daughter, Grandsons, Die on *Titanic*" would surely have distorted his thinking.

Losing his daughter and grandchildren anonymously might well have been preferable to a mind as sick as his apparently was. When these boys showed up in the news, it took little imagination to think the earl would rather let them stay unclaimed than suffer the embarrassment and ridicule associated with the truth. No one will ever know what actually happened—whether he knew or the idea was suggested to him but rejected. Whatever the case, he had done nothing.

Jerome and the curator wanted to believe such behavior was beyond even the earl. In the end, however, the investigator decided the information he'd gathered on the all-consuming malevolence of the man made such a horrific choice entirely possible.

Whatever remaining doubts Jerome had evaporated with the curator's final remark. "You know, I just thought of a very simple confirmation of your theory."

An exhausted investigator gave his host a dubious smile. "I'll bite. I can use all the help I can get at this point."

"Don't laugh," the curator said hesitantly, "but this could be a mystery today for only one of two reasons. Either no one was clever as you, or someone solved it and chose not to share their findings. And who might have solved it but decided to withhold the truth?"

Jerome considered this thoughtfully. He smiled while shaking his head. "You know, as convoluted as that came across, I think you're right. Any police agency, investigator, reporter, or company representative would have shouted such a finding from the rooftops. Yet no one did, meaning no one solved the mystery."

"Except perhaps the earl."

At that point, the investigator was convinced beyond a reasonable doubt. He hoped his efforts to track down the boys would provide the final proof for his conclusion. He quickly thanked the curator and his staff.

Before returning to the states, he sent telegrams to Mr. Watson, the Crandall's, and the earl in Wickersham informing them of his findings. Then he sent two more cables, one to Chief Cook and the other to George Bailey. Within the day, he was on his way to New York to dredge up back-page news on William and Charles.

CHAPTER 22

Jerome went directly to St. Vincent's Hospital and Orphan Asylum in lower Manhattan. He was surprised to find someone who had been there when the boys arrived. The current mother superior had been a new nun in the spring of 1912. Her first assignment was to care for the two boys at St. Vincent. She shared tender memories of that experience.

They had arrived as nameless refugees of the disaster. The staff had given the two temporary names, as was often done with children left at the doorstep. The older boy, who was severely injured, had ironically been christened Will. The toddler was called Happy or Hap for short.

The two endured much in the early months. William came out of his coma nearly a month after arriving. The first thing he saw was a very young boy he didn't recognize. The toddler blinked in surprise then uttered a cry of delight that brought nurses running. Annoyed by the noise and bright lights, William promptly went back to sleep.

Sometime later, he awoke again to adults fussing over him and calling him Will. He had no idea why they were calling him that, but when he tried to recall his name, he couldn't. Nor could he understand where he was or how he had gotten there. William was suddenly terrified. It took a doctor and nurse some time to settle him down.

His anxiety only increased when he discovered his voice was gone. One of the doctors who visited regularly told him about hitting his head and explained he was getting better. That did little to ease his fears, however, as the man gave him no idea when if ever he would speak again or remember things.

After emerging totally from the coma a few weeks later, his fears remained. Even the repeated visits by the ever-energetic Hap did nothing to raise his spirits. It wasn't until a young woman dressed in black, a nun called Sister Angelica, started visiting regularly that his anxieties began to subside.

Besides total memory loss and ongoing confusion, William had several physical issues. His eyes wandered, limbs twitched, and legs randomly gave way. He remained in the critical care area several more weeks before going to a room filled with other patients. After what seemed a lifetime to William, he was moved into the orphanage.

Though he tried every day during that time to speak, his mouth would just not work. At best, he managed a wordless yell of frustration. To let someone know he was hungry or thirsty, he would simply point to his mouth.

He paid little heed to Hap and became easily irritated with the little one's constant attention. He would often pretend to be asleep until Hap left. The toddler, however, never stopped coming around. Sister Angelina's visits were the best part of his day. Her smile and gentle voice soothed him, and her constant encouragement kept him trying to talk.

The arrival of summer saw interest in the boys wane as news of the Olympics in Stockholm and a looming Balkan war were generating the headlines. Updates were still issued regularly by St. Vincent's but were often ignored. Inquiries fell to one or two a week, mostly about possible adoption. Given Will and Hap's continuing issues, such requests were put aside.

By that time, William had accepted the name Will, having recalled no other. Physically, he was better, almost back to normal. His speech, however, was painfully delayed. Frustration over that grew daily and was sometimes manifested in incoherent outbursts and the throwing of handy objects.

Then one day, Will decided he'd had enough of Hap and in frustration hurled the nearest thing at the child, hoping he would leave. As it happened, he'd thrown his favorite gift from Sister Angelina, a picture book. He immediately regretted his action.

As he watched, Hap started to leave with the book in hand. Will yelled, "Stop!" Hap continued around the corner earning another command from Will. "That … that's mine! Bring it back!" After a moment, a wide-eyed Hap poked his head around the corner of the door smiling broadly.

Realizing what had just happened, Will collapsed on his bed laughing joyously. Soon, he was talking incessantly and exhibiting a broad vocabulary and exceptional mastery of language for one so young. Sister Angelina told him he sounded just like a New York boy. He didn't understand why she and others smiled whenever that was mentioned.

After this breakthrough, Will happily joined the other orphans in the dormitory. He welcomed the camaraderie, which eased his fears and anxiety. Hap remained his constant companion. When Will needed time alone, Sister Angelica would take the little pest away. Will hardly noticed that the sister was spending less and less time with him.

Though Will felt normal in most ways, he still could not recall anything from the past. His memory started the day he opened his eyes and saw Hap's face. Since that moment, nothing else had surfaced in spite of constant prodding and encouragement from the doctors, nurses, and Sister Angelica.

As things grew more normal, Will worked on developing new friendships among the boys and girls in the orphanage. Each day, he built new memories with these friends. Each day, he had less interest in a past that refused to visit him. By September, he was just another orphan. His interests focused mainly on the present with little thought for the future.

The story that the mother superior told Jerome had ended with the morning the boys joined a hundred others on an orphan train in early October. She stayed behind, and the records of what had happened were sealed. She did identify the organization that sponsored the orphan trains over the years. The destiny of the children on that specific train, however, was sacrosanct.

After an overnight storm, the predawn in early October was hot and humid, making sleep difficult. As Will slept, matrons entered the dormitory and shook all the children awake. They urged the children to dress quickly and head for the cafeteria. Yawning as he pulled on his pants Will saw Hap, who could sleep through anything, tangled in his blankets.

Will finished dressing then roused his little friend. They were among the last to arrive for breakfast and nearly missed the meal. After using the facilities, the boys and girls were herded onto the cathedral steps. The morning sun was peeking over the factory roofs, illuminating a line of lorries and teams of great dray horses on the damp street below.

As Will and a matron held Hap's hands, Fr. O'Malley exited the church accompanied by a middle-aged couple. Without preamble, the priest announced to the children that they were bound for bright new futures aboard what he called an orphan train. The term was foreign to Will and apparently to most others from their expressions.

Once the priest had introduced a Mrs. Monroe, who represented the organization responsible for the train, O'Malley prayed, made the sign of the cross, and disappeared into the cathedral. As Will's eyes followed the priest's retreat, he glimpsed a tearful Sister Angelica standing at the entrance. Then she was gone as well.

At that moment, Will realized what it all meant. The thought had him squeezing his little friend's hand until Hap yelped in pain. Loosening his grip, Will struggled to grasp the loss of one so dear and his unknown future without her. His chest began to ache as tears filled his eyes. He fought them back, not wanting to frighten Hap, who seemed oblivious.

Will stood in silent agony as Hap looked around excitedly. Among all the boys and girls, his little friend seemed one of the youngest. Most were much older than Will; some were teens. As everyone watched, the woman and a well-dressed man with her descended the steps and spoke to another tall man. Will thought this second man looked as frightened as he himself felt.

The couple and the nervous man then walked to each lorry, checked inside, and spoke briefly to the drivers and attendants. That seemed to take forever. Sweat began to roll down Will's face, as Hap began to fidget. The sun, now fully up, created steam off the wet street, adding to everyone's discomfort.

Stepping under parasols, the couple watched as children began boarding the lorries. Will and Hap, still accompanied by a matron, were among the last called. The woman released Hap's hand as they approached the last lorry. Suddenly frightened, Hap stopped at the lorry steps. Will nearly ran him over before coming to an abrupt halt. A young attendant reached down and lifted the toddler aboard, speaking to him reassuringly.

Before Will could board, however, he heard an angry voice from behind. "Get movin', kid." Accompanying the order was a rough push onto the steps. Will's feet shot out behind him, catching the huge attendant in a most delicate location. The man dropped to his knees, crying out in pain.

Will scrambled to his feet and hurried inside the lorry, taking the first empty seat and hunching down out of sight. He wasn't fast enough, however. The angry man leaped up the stairs and looked up and down the aisle until he found his target. He swung mightily, striking the side of Will's head and driving him to the floor.

Shouts and scuffling reached Will's ears before he fell into blackness. Coming to briefly, he didn't recognize where he was or how he'd gotten there. Voices around him spoke gibberish, as one small boy kept repeating the word *will* without ever saying what he was going to do. A sharp pain shot through his head, and he lost consciousness again.

Periodically, Will came around to the sounds of what was happening about him. Most often, he found the same man leaning over him looking concerned while checking him over. He heard a girl's voice nearby, but she never came into his view. Other adults came by from time to time and gazed upon him with the same concerned looks.

The periods of consciousness came more frequently and lasted longer. At first, his ability to comprehend what was going on failed him completely. He heard names like Anderson, Wake something, James or Jamison, Hap, and even Alice. These names, however, were imbedded in conversations that made little sense to him.

A whistle blowing brought Will back from a lengthy bout of unconsciousness. The first thing he noticed was movement and the sounds of a train. He was suddenly nauseous and fought hard to keep from vomiting. As he wretched, a female voice came from a seat across from him.

"Mr. Jamison, he's awake." Her loud voice pushed him over the edge. He expelled what little there was in his stomach. "And bring a bucket."

As Will regained his seat, a tall, lanky man in a white smock arrived at his side, looked away, and called out, "Mr. Clarke, he's come to. No, Hap, go back to sleep."

Will's eyes rolled listlessly up toward the other seat; he was having trouble focusing on anything. Once they did, he saw a mass of auburn hair framing the freckled face of a skinny girl. She wore an ill-fitting dress covered in an outlandish flower print. Her big eyes stared back at him over a concerned grin.

"Hi. I'm Alice. I'm eleven," she said and waited for a response. When none came, she said, "Me and Hap have been watchin' after you for nearly a full day along with Mr. Jamison here." She looked up. "Oh, and you too, Mr. Clarke."

As Will attempted to look in the direction Alice was glancing, a sharp pain shot through his head and he cried out. "Take it easy, son," one of the men said reaching to clean up the mess on the floor. "Mr. Clarke, hand me that rag."

Everyone fussed over him for a minute while he had a drink and took a pill. They settled him again on the bench seat across from Alice with blankets under and over him and one serving as a pillow. A small boy he didn't recognize put a cool cloth on his forehead.

"You 'wake," the child said with a weak smile. "You better?"

The tall man gently took the toddler by his shoulders steering him away. "Not right now, Hap. He's awake but still not feeling well. I promise to let you visit longer soon."

"Me stay," the boy they called Hap said firmly and pulled away from the man, rushing back to Will's side. "He my friend."

Again, he was ushered away. "We know, Hap, but Will needs to rest. He'll get better sooner if we let him rest. Then you can play, okay?" Not waiting for an answer, the taller man said, "Mr. Clarke, could you take over here?"

"Sure thing." A large figure stepped forward and swept Hap away as he kept saying, "Later, later."

The rhythmic clatter of the train replaced the voices and made Will's eyes heavy again. He saw Alice start to say something then think better of it. She sat back staring at him. Despite his persistent headache, he was soon asleep again.

A sudden jerk brought Will back to consciousness. Still disoriented, he was relieved to see Alice smiling down at him. "Had to stop for another train. Just started up again. How are you feeling?"

He was surprised to find his head not hurting nearly as much as it had when he'd last been awake. With effort, he sat up, managing the task without becoming nauseous. "I ... I'm better I think. How long was I asleep?"

"This time?" the girl asked. He nodded though cautiously. "Only a little while. Long enough for most of the others to settle down for the night. But it's early yet."

"Can you tell me where I am? And what's your name again?" Will asked tentatively.

Alice looked perturbed at his question. "I'm *Alice*, and we're on the orphan train. You should know that. We got on it together in New York at the orphanage."

"Orphanage?" Will asked.

"Yes, Saint Vincent's," Alice said with a frown. "When you first came to the orphanage, you couldn't remember nothing either. Can't you remember any of your time at Saint Vincent's?" He shook his head slowly. "Then what I heard must have been true?"

"What?"

"That you got beat up by one of the people supposed to be helpin' us along the way."

"Beat up? Why?"

"No idea. I just heard Mr. Jamison and Mr. Clarke talkin' about it." Alice paused. "Are you up to my tellin' all I know?"

"Yes, but let me get comfortable first. I'm not feeling so good again." Will lay back and pulled the blanket up around him then nodded for her to continue.

With enthusiasm, Alice began. While still in New York at St. Vincent's orphanage, a brute named Anderson had hit Will hard. She had not seen the incident. Mr. Jamison had carried the boy onto the train and placed him on the bench across from Alice, where he'd lain for more than a day.

Will was suddenly frightened. "What happened to the man, Andrews?"

"Anderson, and don't worry. He got thrown off the train." Alice smiled reassuringly. “Jamison and Clarke wondered why he wasn’t left off right away in New York instead of stayin’ on board. They stopped wonderin’ when they found out that Anderson was related to a guy named Wakefield who’s managin’ the train, somethin’ like that.”

“Stop.” Will said cringing. “I can’t understand what you’re saying. And my head’s starting to ache again.”

“But don’t you want to hear about the big fight?”

“A fight?” Will sat up forgetting his headache.

“Yup. And I saw that firsthand.”

Alice described Anderson boarding their coach at the last stop. He’d apparently been on one of the other train cars. Right in front of her, he confronted Mr. Clarke and Mr. Jamison. He threatened to kill them both and Will too before Wakefield, the guy in charge, put an end to it.

“That was the last anyone saw of Mr. Anderson.” Alice gave Will a doubtful look. “You don’t remember the man at all?”

“No, not at all,” Will said apologetically.

“Well, he was an ugly brute, big as a house.” Alice held her arms wide. “I’m surprised he didn’t kill you with those fists of his.”

“But he’s left the train?” Will asked anxiously, not sure he’d heard rightly.

“Yup. But he didn’t leave willingly. During the night in the station—we stayed there all night—police came and searched for him. Didn’t find him, but they stuck around until we left this mornin’. And that wasn’t the only fight yesterday.”

“Another fight?”

“More like an argument. I heard it all. Happened right there.” She nodded toward the aisle next to where they sat.

Alice shared what had happened after Anderson had been sent packing. Jamison had wanted to take Will to a hospital in Philadelphia. He said Will should never have gotten on the train.

Mr. Wakefield said he was the boss, and felt the boy would be fine. There was no need to leave him and at least one person as an escort behind. After Wakefield left, Mr. Clarke suggested the manager didn’t want the people in New York to know about what Anderson had done. If they found out, he’d likely lose his job too.

"So you came along with the rest of us, those that didn't get took."

"Took?"

"Yeah. A bunch of us got took by families back in Phil'depia. Then we moved on to a place called Harrisburg. I can say that," she said with a smile. "More got took there. You know, 'dopted." Alice sounded frustrated. "That is the reason we're all on this here train. Don't you 'mem ... Oh, that's right. You don't 'member nothin'."

"Why didn't you go?" Will asked. "And that other little kid?"

Alice glanced down the coach. "Oh, Hap and me got held back to be with you. Mr. Jamison demanded that as part of the deal for you stayin' on the train. Somethin' about you needin' familiar faces when you woke up." She laughed. "A lot of good that did you. But now with you awake, I expect we'll be joining the others at the next stop tomorrow."

"And who is this Hap?" Will asked.

Alice looked surprised. "Why, he's the little boy who's been by your side ever since you came to Saint Vincent's. You arrived together from some boat that sank. He treats you like a brother. Won't let you out of his sight and throws fits when they separate you two. And you don't know him?"

Will shook his head feeling empty. "No I don't. In fact I don't remember anything before I woke up and found you staring at me."

"Oh my goodness! How awful." Alice gave him a piteous look. "That must be awful."

"What must be awful?" Mr. Jamison's voice made both children jump. "Oh, sorry to scare you two. I see our patient is awake again."

"Seems for good this time," Alice replied then frowned. "But he can't remember nothin'."

"Anything, Alice."

"Oh, right. He can't remember *anything*," she said sheepishly.

Jamison turned to the boy. "Is that so?"

Will nodded.

"I'm sorry to hear your memory is gone again."

"Again?" Will was incredulous.

"From what I've been told, you arrived at Saint Vincent's with amnesia."

"Am ... what?" Alice asked.

Jamison gave her a warm smile. "Amnesia, loss of memory."

"Oh."

The aide looked at Will quizzically. "What *do* you remember?"

"Waking up across from Alice is all."

"Nothing about Saint Vincent's or before that?"

Will shook his head sadly.

"Let's hope your memory comes back soon. How are you feeling otherwise?"

"Better. Headache's gone. And I'm hungry."

"That's good news. I think Mr. Clarke has a basket of food left from our last stop. Let me get it."

Will was soon digging into leftover fried chicken, bread, and apples as Alice and Jamison watched. Once he'd eaten his fill and drank copious amounts of water, Will made a successful if shaky trip to the facilities at the other end of the coach. The return trip seemed a bit easier.

"It looks like you're indeed much better. Ahh, the resiliency of youth," Jamison said with a yawn. "But you should get more rest. We don't want you to relapse."

Will frowned and shook his head. "But all I've been doing is sleeping. Now I'm not the least bit tired."

"Me either," Alice said.

Jamison threw up his hands, chuckling softly. "Okay, I get it. You two can stay back here and chat until you get tired again." His yawn returned. "I'll just settle in this empty section over here." He nodded at an empty space usually used for luggage across from the two children. "If you need anything, just holler."

"Thanks, Mr. Jamison." Alice waved him off. "And we'll be nice and quiet."

The train streaked on through the low mountains of Pennsylvania as the two chatted quietly accompanied by occasional train whistles, the singing of the rails, and the *clickety-clack* at crossings. The car was dark except for a dim lantern illuminating the facilities at the far end of the coach, where Mr. Clarke sat. All but the two of them were asleep.

Alice suggested a game of twenty questions to see how Will's brain was doing. He reluctantly agreed. They went through numerous rounds before Will started to get bored. Alice solved the latest riddle with a whisper and a smile. "A snake."

He nodded disinterestedly.

"And I did it in only five questions."

"Don't be such a smart aleck." The boy pouted. "Let's do something else."

Alice got to her feet. "I know. Let's get some air. It has to be cooler out on the landing than it is in here. I'm about to melt."

Will jumped at the idea. "Let's." The boy was up in a flash ready to go as he saw Alice glance toward the rear of the coach. At that moment, the back door started to open.

Alice clamped a hand clumsily over Will's mouth while pushing him up on the bench. They flattened against the full partition that stood behind the last seat of the coach. Shocked into silence, the boy stood confused and motionless. Next to him on the bench, Alice whispered, "Anderson."

Will was terrified and started to shake. A quick jerk from Alice made him stiffen. They both pressed harder against the partition that concealed them as Anderson moved slowly down the short corridor.

Emerging from the darkness, Anderson was illuminated by passing lights outside the train. In his hand glinted the blade of a knife. His massive figure paused less than three feet from Will and Alice. Fortunately at that moment, he was looking the other direction. Then the coach went dark except for the dim light far down the aisle. They saw Anderson standing still apparently waiting for something.

When lights from outside again illuminated the car, Will saw Anderson raising the knife over Mr. Jamison. In that instant, Alice swung something at the man's hand, causing him to drop the knife. It fell silently on one of the blankets strewn about the floor. Turning in surprise, Anderson lost his balance and started to fall.

Alice gave the off-balance giant a shove, grabbed Will's hand, and dashed for the back door of the coach. Once on the narrow platform, they looked back though the glass in the door and saw Anderson slowly rising and then rushing for the door. As Will stood unable to move, he felt a tug on his arm and a whispered command: "Climb!"

He looked at where Alice was pointing and saw a metal ladder heading through a hole up to the roof of the coach. With a hard push, she got him climbing with her hand on his heels. At the top, Alice gave him another shove onto the top and scrambled up.

As she was about to join Will, a meaty hand grabbed her ankle and yanked. Will watched in terror as Alice disappeared from view. Scooting toward the opening, he peeked over the edge in time to see her twist free and fall at the edge of the platform. With a roar audible above the wind, the huge man raised his boot to push her off the train.

Will impulsively swung down on the ladder and kicked the man, catching him in the chest. Off balance, Anderson stumbled backward. Will's momentum caused him to lose his grip and fall onto the platform, his breath escaping with a whoosh. As he gasped for air, Anderson's boot struck his head; the glancing blow plunged him once more into darkness.

The sun pouring through the train window struck the boy right in the eyes. Alice watched his face contort and his eyes open. "Welcome back."

He did not respond.

"How do you feel?" She smiled at him weakly. "Seems we ask you that a lot."

The only response was Will's eyes closing again, so she shrugged and went on. "We're alone right now. Everyone else is inside getting looked over if you know what I mean."

It was clear in his face that he didn't.

"You sure cause a lot of trouble for a little guy." Her smile returned. "You should have seen the ruckus over you this morning."

That got a flicker of his eyelids.

"When Jamison told Wakefield about your relapse, well, things went straight downhill from there."

Alice was becoming frustrated by Will's lack of response. "Don't you want to know what happened?"

The boy rolled over, letting her know he didn't.

"That's the thanks I get for saving your life."

That got Will to turn back over, but instead of asking what she meant, he simply said, "Water."

With a harrumph, she got up and poured a glass from the pitcher Jamison had left behind. Turning back, she thrust it out to Will, spilling a good portion on the boy. "Here." Her angry tone quickly wilted in the heat. "I guess we ended up saving each other."

Finishing the water, Will held out the glass to her.

"You want more?"

He nodded, and she sighed. "If I get you more, can I tell the story? You're the only one I can share it with." She took his blank stare as approval. After giving him a second glass and glancing around to ensure they were truly alone, she told him what had happened.

After Will had saved her from being booted off the train by Anderson, the thug had knocked him silly, as she put it. Then he'd leaned against the back rail of the coach and raised his boot high to give Will what surely would have been a deadly kick.

At that moment, the train passed over a crossing and gave the train car a good shake. Anderson hung there over Will trying to retain his balance when Alice charged forward, attempting to stop him. She'd grabbed his raised boot and pushed with all her might. The next thing she knew, Anderson was gone.

She paused at that point to see Will's reaction. To her, it seemed he had not even been listening. "Did you hear what I just said? Anderson fell off the train and is likely dead."

"Who's Anderson?" Will said in all sincerity.

Alice didn't know what to think. "Are you kidding me? The guy who nearly killed you twice! And—" She came to a sudden halt. "Your head! He hit it again. You have that amne … amnesia stuff again, right?" She snorted. "Why am I asking you that? Then I don't have to tell you how I got you back in here and hid the fact that anything happened, well, except for your relapsin'." She blew out a big breath as she contemplated this latest revelation. "And here I was worried you'd give me away. You know, blab that Anderson had been here and attacked us."

Will looked puzzled, then lay back down and closed his eyes. She sighed in relief. "I guess I told you more than I needed to already. Consider the subject closed."

After Will was clearly asleep again, Alice walked the coach checking to see if the others were returning. Seeing no sign of them, she strolled back to her seat. Though stuffy, the train was not too uncomfortable for sleep. She had not gotten much the night before and was soon nodding off.

Just before sleep overtook her, however, Alice looked down and spoke with sadness to her unhearing friend. "I wonder if you'll ever remember Hap. He'll sure remember you. He didn't like one bit bein' hauled off today." She sighed deeply. "I expect he won't be back. And what will happen to us?" She laughed. "You probably won't remember that either."

But when the children not selected returned to the train, Hap was with them. Mr. Clarke brought him aboard and watched him race to Will's side. By the time the slow-moving aide made the trip to the other end of the coach, he found Will slowly waking up and rubbing his eyes. Alice had been shocked upright by the toddler's loud arrival.

"Hap! You didn't get picked?" The girl was surprised. "I was sure you would be."

Clarke shook his head. "He might have been had he not cried nearly the whole time and yelled for this one here. I spent half the time outside with him in this heat."

Although looking at Will, Clarke addressed his question to Alice. "How is he doing?"

"Well, he's awake, but that's about it," she said with a frown. "He can't seem to focus. And guess what?"

"What."

"His memory's gone again."

"Good grief." Clarke grew uneasy. "When Jamison hears that, I can see the sparks flying."

As the train jerked into motion, Clarke looked around for his partner but saw only Wakefield walking up the aisle. When he arrived, Clarke peered over the man's shoulder. "Where's Jamison?"

"On his way back to New York, or at least he will be soon."

At first, Clarke was shocked at hearing this. Then he became angry. "Why's that?"

Wakefield replied matter-of-factly, "Because we didn't need him anymore what with so many of the children already gone."

Clarke's anger grew. "And without him there's no one to stand up for this boy here."

Wakefield bristled. "Ease off, Mr. Clarke. You could be next." After the two stared each other down, Wakefield asked, "How is the lad anyway?"

"His memory's gone again, and he can't seem to focus, as if you really cared," Alice said, likely saving his job, Clarke thought.

"That's enough, young lady," Wakefield said angrily. "Let's just cool off."

"As if that's possible in this heat," Clarke said testily.

Wakefield ignored his insubordination. "Then let's make sure that all the children are hydrated and urged to rest."

"Water!" Hap exclaimed, giving the manager time to move off to safer territory.

By the time everyone had been tended to, things had settled down as the train raced on toward Youngstown. At that station, the train had to sit in the scorching midday sun, so Wakefield decided everyone would go to the church where the adoption process was to take place. Wakefield assured Clarke that Will was going only to protect his health and not to take part. Clarke was sure the man wanted Will there to keep Hap calm so the toddler would be selected.

Alice told Clarke repeatedly on the way to the church that she was keen on participating. Wearing a smile guaranteed to dazzle, the girl wondered aloud who might smile back. The aide saw that her excitement contrasted dramatically with Hap's look of dread and Will's total apathy.

Once all the children arrived in the cool basement and were well fed, potential parents circulated through the room assessing the *merchandise*. Shortly, the adults were escorted upstairs and the children taken to seats in the basement. Most could not sit still and were soon up again playing quietly under the supervision of a bevy of volunteers.

Mr. Clarke had taken the passive Will to the farthest corner of the room, where they watched Hap waddle around trying to play tag with several of the older boys. Every few minutes, the toddler drifted over and checked on his friend, sometimes bringing a bit of food, which Will ignored.

After an hour of near chaos in the basement, volunteers came downstairs and started taking boys and girls back up. Clarke was not surprised that Alice was one of the first girls called. She grabbed her possessions and pranced off, waving in their direction. She received a slight wave from Will, which Clarke took as a sign the boy was improving.

Perhaps an hour later, Alice came bounding downstairs, her bag of belongings swinging wildly at her side. She rushed across the room directly to Will.

"I have a new home, Will!" Her joy was lost on the silent Will.

Clarke filled the void. "That's wonderful news, Alice." He felt truly happy for her.

She glanced his way. "Thanks, Mr. Clarke." She turned back to Will. "And guess what? The lady, my new mommy, has red hair and freckles like me. The daddy is a quiet one, but I can see in his eyes he likes me a lot. My real mom said you can tell about people from their eyes."

As she spoke, Alice dug in her burlap bag of belongings, finally pulling something out as she finished her thought. "I hope she's right."

"What's that?" Clarke asked with interest.

Alice's face turned melancholy. "It's a purse. My mommy gave it to me. It was hers."

"What's inside?"

Alice's face brightened. "Nothin' yet."

The odd response intrigued Clarke. "You sound awful happy about having nothing in your purse."

"I've been carrying it that way since I came to the orphanage," Alice explained keeping her smile. "Momma said I should keep it that way on account of savin' it to put thin's I'd get from my new family if'n I ever got one. And now it looks like I'll be fillin' it soon."

"That's nice," Will said. "You can explain more about it later." It was obvious that the boy didn't understand what was happening.

Alice seemed to play along with Will's lack of understanding. "Maybe

I can, but just in case ..." She pulled Will from his chair and gave him a big hug, which startled him. She turned to Mr. Clarke. "Take good care of him."

With a lump in his throat, Clarke watched her rush to the volunteer waiting by the stairs. Her smile was back as she turned once more and waved excitedly. Clarke poked Will, and they waved back as Alice disappeared up the stairs.

A short time later, a volunteer approached Hap and tried to guide him toward the stairs. The toddler looked over at Will and bolted to him. Gripping his leg like a vice, Hap cried out. "No! Not go."

Mr. Clarke waved the volunteer away and placed Hap on his chair while talking to her. In a minute, Mr. Wakefield and the minister joined the conversation. After a time, Mr. Clarke returned to the boys as the others headed back upstairs. Soon, Hap had calmed down, but he was refusing to budge from Will's side. All the time, Will sat impassively.

A bit later, Wakefield and the minister returned with a couple from upstairs. After staring rather obviously at the boys, the couple spoke at length with the two men before they headed back up. Wakefield called Clarke over. What he heard angered him, and he made his feelings about it known but to no avail.

As Wakefield and the minister headed upstairs, an angry-looking Mr. Clarke returned to Will and Hap. Forcing a smile, he spoke softly and simply to both of them. "I'd like you two to come with me."

"No! No go! *Will Will Will!*" Hap protested.

"Oh, you'll be going together, Hap. Nobody will separate you." Clarke didn't know if what he'd just said was true, but his next words were, "I'll be right there with you both."

That seemed to appease the toddler, but Will remained indifferent. Clarke led the boys slowly upstairs. Much later, when it was time for those children not adopted to return to the train, Clarke came back to the basement with a sullen face. Pausing long enough to gather the belongings left behind, Clarke solemnly retraced his steps.

After leaving St. Vincent's, Jerome went directly to the office of the organization in New York that the mother superior had given him. It turned out they had coordinated all stops of the train that year and still had records. At that point, it seemed his luck ran out as he was informed the documents were not available to him under the current law.

After a great deal of effort and charm, a representative hesitantly agreed to a compromise that didn't violate the law. Jerome was given the first names assigned by St. Vincent's for those adopted at each stop. Since the mother superior had said there was only one Will and Hap on the train, he immediately knew where the boys had found their home.

The investigator had a location and names. Whether he could convince someone in Youngstown to part with the next critical pieces of the puzzle remained to be seen. Without it, however, he couldn't be sure of his theory and therefore not fulfill his promise to Henry. That would put the success of his entire assignment in jeopardy.

CHAPTER 23

Jerome arrived in Bedford Falls as dawn broke. He took the sidewalk next to the side of the station, thus avoiding Ernie Bishop's taxi at the station entrance. Walking briskly, he pulled his coat collar up, more to avoid being recognized than to stay warm.

Except for a paperboy on his bike, he passed no one as he made his way into the sleepy neighborhood just blocks from Main Street. In less than five minutes, he arrived at his destination. Striding quickly up to the front door, he knocked while glancing around furtively. When the door opened, he was greeted with a look of surprise and suspicion.

Jerome apologized for the early intrusion but asked if it would be possible to discuss a very important matter. The woman was less than eager, even after he promised to be brief. Reluctantly, she agreed but made him wait in the parlor while she dressed and made coffee.

When the two finally sat across from each other, the investigator began to tell her about his recent travels and what he had discovered. As he proceeded, the woman's anxiety noticeably grew. Seeing this, Jerome was convinced he was on the right track. When he shared about his last stop before returning to Bedford Falls, the woman's expression confirmed the story would soon be complete.

The investigator emerged from the conversation at midmorning and headed to the hotel. He no longer needed to remain incognito, so he was pleased to see Ernie's taxi idling as he approached. "Looks like my timing's good."

Peeking over the top of the cab from the running board, the cabby saw the investigator and smiled. "Why Mr. Jerome, I didn't know you were back in town."

"I guess I missed you at the station. Besides, the walk did me some good," Jerome said climbing into the cab. "I'm headed to the Potter estate."

That brought a raised eyebrow. "When you gonna see George?"

"Soon, Ernie, but I have things to discuss with Potter first."

They made the usual fifteen-minute trip with Ernie updating the investigator on all that had been going on in his absence. The cabbie's entertaining summary ended at the front steps of the estate.

"Can you wait? It could be a while."

Ernie gave him a thumbs-up. "Sure. It's been a slow day anyway."

As the investigator climbed the steps, Ernie drove to a sunny spot out of the wind and turned off the engine. Jerome rang the familiar bell and waited patiently. It wasn't long before Crosley opened the door. "Is Mr. Potter available?"

Indeed he was. Jerome was soon ushered into the study. He took a deep breath, preparing for what he expected to be a chilly reception. Potter sat in his usual place at the great desk with the only reliable friend he had, his wheelchair.

At first blush, the old man had changed little, which surprised Jerome. He had expected all the recent setbacks would have worn him down. Perhaps it was the fact that Potter had always looked old and pained. The investigator now knew all the reasons why. Still, it seemed something else had changed. Then it struck him. The man was nervous about what he was about to hear.

Jerome extended his hand. "Thank you for seeing me, Mr. Potter."

His words were received unenthusiastically. "I was wondering if you'd ever show again after what you suggested the last time we met. Remember?"

The investigator nodded and took a seat. "Indeed I do. And as promised, I'm here with news."

"Then get with it, man. Don't keep me waiting," Potter said impatiently. "It's all I have to look forward to with all that's happened since you left."

The investigator pursed his lips. "What I have to share doesn't help much in that regard I'm afraid. But as you requested, let me get started."

Jerome decided to skip the how part of the investigation since much of that did not deal with the critical questions of what had happened to Abigail and the boys. He got right to the point. "I'm convinced that the reason your wife was never found is that she went down on the *Titanic*."

Jerome saw the color drain from Potter's face as though he might have been having some kind of attack. But remarkably, the old man seemed to recover. He nodded. "That would explain a lot. It's not as though I was holding out hope that she—that any of them were still alive."

The investigator was a bit surprised at not being challenged. "I have a great deal of documentation to support this contention as well as evidence, perhaps circumstantial, as to how this fact went undiscovered for over thirty years."

"I'd like to hear that someday, but not now." Potter sounded exhausted. "Suffice it to say I've come to respect your detecting skills if not you."

Jerome heard more humor than malice in the comment.

"I've been envisioning Abby and the boys spending years in the wilderness only now to find they were dead practically from the day they disappeared."

Jerome shook his head. "That's not exactly true. Abigail did die on April fifteenth when the *Titanic* sank, but your boys survived."

Potter's head jerked up. His mouth moved, but no words came out. Once again, Jerome was concerned for his health. "I'm sorry to break it to you so abruptly, but I wasn't sure how else to do it."

Potter took a drink of water before trying to speak. After a false start, he croaked out a few words. "If this is some kind of a joke, sir, it is—"

"No, Henry, it's not a joke. It's the truth, and I have evidence, ironclad proof, of that." There was no doubt in the investigator's voice.

Potter still didn't look like he believed what he'd just heard. "But how—how could that be? If they were rescued, it should have been all over the papers."

"Under normal circumstances, that would have been the case. But these circumstances were anything but normal. Let me explain."

The investigator went over in detail what he had discovered—the hard evidence and logical extrapolations from what he'd collected. Potter challenged him several times, but Jerome handled the questions to the old man's satisfaction. In conclusion, the investigator told Henry he had irrefutable evidence supporting all his claims that he would present in the future.

"But why not now?"

"All in good time. I think I've provided enough already to support the contention."

Potter face reddened. "You're just counting on me buying your explanation because I want to believe it. And I was, but now I'm not so sure."

"Suit yourself," Jerome said with a shrug. "But I know your boys are alive and well. Doing well too, I might add. And I know where they are right now."

"So tell me!" the old man shouted. "Where are my boys?"

Jerome frowned. "The time's not right."

"What?" Potter nearly came out of his wheelchair. "The time's not right? Why ever not?"

The investigator stood. "Because that bit of news is the only leverage I have with you."

"Leverage?" Potter looked confused, then his anger returned. "So this is about money? Okay, Jerome, how much will it take?"

The investigator laughed. "It isn't about money. It's a lot more valuable than that."

"I don't understand." Potter softened. "All I want is to have my sons back."

"No, Henry, you *need* your sons back," Jerome said as he headed for the door. "But you've spent a lifetime learning how to hate and hurt others to ease your physical and mental pain. Such evil habits may be impossible to break even with such a worthwhile incentive, but I think it best for you to earn your sons back a little at a time."

"You think it's best? What gives you—"

Potter's angry retort was cut short by the closing of the door.

Ernie dropped Jerome at the hotel for lunch. An hour later, the investigator headed for the B&L. With uncertainly, he went up the stairs and entered the lobby. Eustace was at the teller window with a customer, so he waited patiently for him to finish before stepping up. "Hello, Eustace. Long time no see."

As Eustace looked up, his smile froze. "Oh, yes sir. What can I do for you?"

"Is George in?" Jerome asked, absentmindedly picking up a deposit slip from the counter.

Eustace looked around indecisively. "I, ahh, yes, I think he is. But I think he has an appointment shortly with one of the board members."

"Could you see if he'll see me?" Jerome asked cordially. "It won't take long."

As Eustace backed away from the counter, Jerome saw Tilly come out of the large, walk-in safe. Her cousin pointed surreptitiously toward him, and the woman almost dropped the wire baskets she was carrying.

Tilly mouthed the words, "He's back?"

"Yup," Eustace mouthed back. All this occurred in the investigator's field of vision and caused him to smile.

As Eustace headed to George's door, Tilly put the baskets on her desk and moved to Billy's office. She slowly pulled his door shut, unnoticed by her uncle. From a brief glimpse, the investigator thought Billy might have been napping.

It was several minutes before Eustace returned, giving the investigator a concerned look. "George said he can see you for a few minutes. Follow me."

George stepped out of his office as the investigator approached. "Well this is a surprise! I'd almost given up on you. Your last cable gave no indication of when you'd return."

"Some things took a bit longer than I expected," Jerome said. They shook hands vigorously. "I understand you have another appointment shortly, so I'll—"

George released his hand and waved him through the door. "Yes, it's with Potter." There was no enthusiasm in Bailey's voice. "Have a seat." He closed his door as the investigator took his coat off and sat it on his lap.

"So what's on your mind?" George asked.

Jerome cleared his throat. "Two things, George. First, I wanted to share my findings, and second, I'm asking for your help."

"Let me hear the first and then I'll let you know about the second," George replied with a smile.

Jerome hesitated. "I wasn't quite straight with Eustace. This could take a while, George. I at least wanted to let you know I was back. We can schedule another time."

"That's a problem. You see, Potter is still on the board in spite of everything. But he doesn't make most full board meetings. He prefers one-on-one sessions, actually one-on-two. I won't meet with him alone."

"Afraid he might try to use something you say against you?" Jerome asked perfunctorily.

"More like to prevent a homicide," George said irreverently, and they both chuckled.

Then George's intercom buzzed. When he picked it up, Jerome heard Tilly faintly in stereo. "Yes, Tilly ... Uh huh ... You told him what?" There was a garbled response. "And then he just hung up? Hmm, how interesting. Okay, Tilly. Thanks."

George hung up and gave Jerome a strange look. "We just gained some time. That was Tilly saying Potter just called to cancel."

"Did he give any reason?" Jerome wondered if it had had anything to do with his visit.

George spread his palms. "No, but Tilly said she did tell the old man you were in with me."

Knowing how he'd left the man that morning, he imagined that had ruffled his feathers. Not wanting to get distracted, the investigator asked, "Would you like to hear everything in detail or the *Reader's Digest* version?"

George thought for a moment. "The *Reader's Digest* version should suffice."

Jerome nodded and began. He got no further than the fact that Potter had once been a decent man with a wife and children before George reconsidered. From there on, the investigator provided the detail while answering a lot of questions. He stopped where he had with Potter, keeping further information about the boys from George as well.

"Why didn't you tell him?" George asked incredulously.

Jerome gave him the same response he'd given Henry. "All in good time, George. I intend to make him earn that information."

"How?"

"By proving he can once again become the man I described to you earlier, a hundred and eighty degrees from the man we know today."

George exhaled a grunt and a laugh. "Good luck with that. I've known only the hateful creature that tried to destroy the B&L and me. I can't see him changing his spots."

"I can't blame you." Jerome gave George a sly smile. "Tell you what. I won't share the information about the sons if he doesn't change enough to convince you. The secret will stay with me. Deal?"

"Deal." George slapped the table for emphasis. "Ah, such power over that old rascal," he said with a chuckle. He leaned in conspiratorially. "But you'll tell me, right?"

Jerome smiled. "All in good time, George." Bailey gave him a disappointed look. "It would be doubly cruel to tell you and not him. Let's wait and see what—"

Jerome was interrupted by angry voices coming from the main office.

"What the heck?" George was up and out his door in a flash with Jerome right behind. The sight of Uncle Billy in a heated argument with Potter stopped them in their tracks. Eustace and Tilly stood behind Billy while Crosley hid behind Potter's wheelchair. Two strong young men stood nearby breathing heavily and looking bemused.

"What on earth's going on here?" George moved forward with Jerome at his shoulder. Potter started to respond, but George stopped him. "You tell me first, Uncle Billy."

Billy spit out his version. "Those two men delivered Potter up here, and he started demanding to see you. I told him you were busy, George, but he insisted."

George turned to Potter. "You called not a quarter hour ago from the bank and canceled our meeting scheduled for *your* office. So why are you here making unreasonable demands?"

Jerome took pleasure in the flustered look on Potter's face as he attempted a reply. "I ... when I heard that you were meeting with him ..."

A bony finger pointed at Jerome. "I, well, I want to know why you two are meeting."

Jerome stepped forward. "You had your chance earlier, *Henry*. What we're talking about is none of your business. I suggest you stop making demands, go home, and stay miserable."

Everyone was shocked to hear the mild-mannered investigator raise his voice. George took up the slack. "Jerome's right, Mr. Potter. I want you to leave now."

For a moment, the old man seemed inclined to continue the argument then he slowly slumped into his chair. The investigator sensed something was amiss and rushed to his side. He grabbed the old man's wrist. The room fell silent.

A few seconds later, Jerome spoke urgently. "This is not good." Crosley hesitantly peeked around the chair, and Jerome snapped an order. "Go get the doctor."

"But I don't know where—"

Crosley didn't get a chance to finish before George took over. "Eustace, get Doc Roberts." Before the words were out, his cousin was off. "And call an ambulance, Tilly."

Meanwhile, George saw Uncle Billy collapse into Eustace's roller chair. His momentum propelled him across the room and against the wall. "Uncle Billy!"

George rushed to his uncle's side. Looking around desperately, he spotted the two young men frozen in place. "You two get over here!" Turning back to Tilly, who was speaking on the phone, he yelled, "Once you're off, get something to cover Billy."

The two young men arrived as George issued orders to the first of them. "Grab his legs and help me get him on the floor." As they gently moved Billy, George addressed Jerome. "You and Crosley take care of Potter."

The investigator turned to Crosley, who appeared about to join his boss. Deciding he would be no help, Jerome called to the second young man. "You there!" It took a few seconds to get his attention. "Get over here and help me get this man on the floor too."

Somehow, Tilly finished the call and found blankets from somewhere before either man was down. She got one beneath her uncle and covered him with another. She made a pillow out of a third.

George shook his head. "Put that under his knees—elevate his legs."

Tilly quickly made the change then moved to Jerome's side.

Soon, Potter was made comfortable joining Billy on the floor of the B&L. Both were unconscious. Checking the old man's pulse, Jerome frowned and looked at George. "How far is the doctor's office?"

Before he got an answer, they heard sirens in the distance. Very shortly, the room was filled will medical personnel. Doc Roberts, his nurse, and the ambulance attendants took over both patients without prejudice. Those pushed aside stood anxiously by as the two were taken gingerly down the stairs. While they were being placed in the ambulance, Ma Bailey and Mary arrived on foot, having been summoned by Tilly. They joined the others on the sidewalk as the vehicles pulled away.

The space vacated by the ambulances was quickly filled by Bert's patrol car and Ernie's cab. Soon, family members were in both vehicles on the way to the hospital. Eustace volunteered to stay behind and keep the B&L open. George glanced back as Bert drove away to see one lone figure standing on the curb. It was a sorrowful Mr. Crosley.

At the hospital, George watched as the patients entered the ER simultaneously and were wheeled into the high-risk unit.

Visiting two days later, he found Billy had been moved to a general medical room on the third floor. The next day, Potter arrived across the hall.

Days later, George asked a nurse how Potter had been treating her. He was surprised to hear that he was being cooperative and not making unreasonable demands. She added that that wasn't what the staff had expected. The nurse did voice a concern that Potter seemed depressed, perhaps because he had so few visitors.

One of those visitors had been Dalton Franks. He ran into George in the hall and shared that Potter's trial date had been extended due to his illness. Bailey begrudgingly understood and asked how the old man had reacted to the news. Franks said he was ambivalent. In fact, the man had hardly said a word during the attorney's visit.

While checking on Billy, Doctor Roberts let slip to George that he found Potter's heart mending nicely but that his head was another story. Though Potter was taken for physical therapy twice a day, his participation was halfhearted. In spite of the therapist's cajoling, he remained passive and disinterested.

Meanwhile, Uncle Billy seemed to be a new man. His health rebounded swiftly, and he'd made friends with the staff on all shifts. The stream of visitors to his room began to interfere with his care to the point that the doctor had to put tight restrictions in place.

As time passed, Billy appeared to shed years as well as pounds. His outlook was as upbeat as his progress was. His sense of humor was back and sharper than ever, and his mind too. As a result, Billy was scheduled for release while Potter languished in his room.

"Good morning, Uncle Billy. Ready to make your escape?" George asked, sweeping into the room on discharge day twirling his hat and wearing a smile.

Billy was already dressed and sitting on his bed. "I look like an escapee." He stood, showing his baggy wardrobe. "I had to put extra holes in my belt so I wouldn't embarrass any of the lovely nurses." He roared with laughter. "Boy oh boy, George, I feel like a million bucks, and I don't mean green and wrinkled."

"I'm beginning to think that run-in with Potter was one of the best things that ever happened to you," George said sincerely.

Billy moved to the window, taking a breath of fresh air on the gorgeous day. "Perhaps we should stop and thank the man." The two exchanged looks then started laughing just as the nurse brought a wheelchair through the door.

George followed his uncle and the nurse out. In the bed across the hall, he saw a man he hardly recognized. It was shocking to see how frail Potter was, and the expression he wore was one George had never seen. He couldn't decide if it was resignation or defeat. The label "old man" truly fit the pitiful figure lying in the hospital bed.

CHAPTER 24

After the incident at the B&L, Jerome had gone to his bosses seeking advice. They had been sympathetic but offered nothing more. They reminded him that it was his assignment to resolve without their help. Jerome cynically assumed the real reason was that they didn't have a clue about what he should do either.

Frustrated, Jerome returned to Bedford Falls in the same predicament that he'd left. His assignment had transitioned from investigation to a trial in which he'd rashly appointed himself the attorneys, judge, and jury. He'd started a fuzzy plan of his own design, but everything had gone a bit haywire. It was totally up to him to make it work.

He had not seen Potter since that dramatic day; he had purposely avoided visiting him during his lengthy hospital stay. George had shared bits and pieces of what he'd observed when visiting Billy at the hospital, but it had been hard for the investigator to determine much from that. He was relieved to hear that Potter had finally been released.

Calling ahead, for once, Jerome was a bit surprised and pleased to be granted an appointment with Potter. Upon arrival, he was ushered into the study where Potter, a shadow of his former self, sat in one of the leather chairs now facing the fire. In spite of the warm summer day, he was wrapped in a blanket. Potter waved Jerome to the other chair.

The investigator obliged as Crosley left the room. "Thank you for seeing me, Mr. Potter."

As his eyes adjusted, Potter's face slowly came into view. His expression was one of resignation. He still looked quite ill. It suddenly crossed Jerome's mind that Potter might truly be dying.

Clearing his throat, Potter responded in a voice stronger than Jerome expected. "I figured you would show up sooner or later. Thank you for waiting until I recovered."

The investigator found Potter's choice of words ironic. "Have you? I mean, speaking frankly, you don't look like you've recovered."

That brought a raspy laugh from the old man. "A reasonable observation, but it's still a little early to write my obit."

"I won't keep you long. I don't want to wear you out."

"Not to worry," Potter croaked. "I've not been busy. In fact, you're my first guest since being released," he said in a flat tone.

"I'm glad you're getting plenty of rest," Jerome said. "Still, I won't take up much of your time."

Potter nodded as he sat up, showing some interest for the first time. "Appreciated. Now why don't you tell me why you are here?"

"Very well." Jerome cleared his throat. "You've spent well over three decades without your family and worst of all not knowing what happened to them. The last time we talked, it didn't go well. Now I'm here to tell you a bit more."

"Like where my sons are?" Potter's question came without hostility.

"I'm still not prepared to share that." Jerome saw Potter start to bristle but then immediately settle down. "I need some things from you first."

"Some things from me?" Potter asked, his expression of resignation returning. It struck Jerome that the fight had gone out of the man. "Ask away then."

Jerome leaned in. "First, I need you to be patient, as I am not prepared to discuss anything more about your sons at this time. I don't know, at this point, when if ever I'll share that information."

"That's likely to be the hardest thing you'll ask of me." There was a touch of anger in Potter's voice. "At my age and in my condition, patience is a luxury. What else?"

"There are a few requests, perhaps I should say requirements, I'm afraid. And many won't be easy for you."

"As if asking me to be patient will be?" Potter asked with a wan smile.

Jerome ignored Potter's comment. "It's critical that you understand you must comply with *all* these requirements—no picking and choosing. It's all or nothing."

"That's a tall order especially when I don't know what all these so-called requirements are." Potter was clearly growing frustrated.

Jerome recognized that, but he had one more stipulation to make. "I'm sorry to drag this out, but there's one more overarching requirement before I get to the specifics."

"Oh good God, man! It seems this is already a test of my patience and I'm about to fail."

Jerome resisted a chuckle. "This is it, the last requirement—call it a rule. If you accept and accomplish all the requirements, I'll still consider you as having failed if you share any of this with anyone during the process. If you do tell or even hint to anyone, or someone guesses, you'll have failed no matter how well you meet the conditions, got it?"

Potter sat motionless and silent for what seemed a long time. He slowly nodded and uttered a lengthy sigh. "Let's hear the list."

Shortly after his visit to Potter, Jerome began making rounds of the town informing his acquaintances that he was leaving on a new assignment out of state. When asked if he would ever return, he explained that he wasn't sure.

No sooner had Jerome left than Potter's long limousine began pulling up regularly to the bank again as he'd done for so many years. Mrs. Taggart held the door open, and to the casual observer, things seemed to be back to normal.

Soon, the bank president had welcomed a long parade of lawyers, board members, business associates, and politicians to his office. They left behind an ever-growing collection of rumors and growing anxieties. It reached a fever pitch when news leaked that Potter's trial had been delayed yet again.

Almost every day, small clusters of the citizenry engaged in wild speculation. The consensus was that whatever he was up to was cause for concern. Guesses ranged from plotting revenge on the Baileys and their supporters to reestablishing his credibility and power. On the latter option, the townsfolk saw little chance of that happening.

Two weeks after Potter's return, Mrs. Taggart contacted George Bailey, attempting to schedule a meeting between Bailey and Potter. George initially refused the request, but eventually, curiosity won out. An uneasy George entered Potter's office early one Monday morning.

"Thank you for coming, George. Have a seat." The old man waved Bailey to the lone chair centered in front of the massive desk.

"I have to say I'm not excited to be here, Mr. Potter." George had not intended humor, and Potter knew that. "I guess the polite thing to do is to ask how you're doing."

Potter ignored the sarcasm. "Thank you for asking." His intentionally pleasant look seemed to disconcert his guest. "Though it was an eye-opener, I don't recommend having a heart attack to get attention."

"I'll make a note of that," George said snarkily. "With that behind us, why were you so insistent I meet with you?"

"Why, because I've missed you." Potter's attempt at humor fell far short. "I'm not mocking you, George. That was my attempt at a joke."

"I doubt anyone around here has ever heard you intentionally try to be funny."

"Good point. It's been a long time, a lifetime you might say." Potter's tone was casual. "But I understand that Mr. Jerome shared some of my ancient history with you."

"Yeah, interesting story," George said flatly. "But if you called me over here to get sympathy—"

Potter raised his hand. "No. Wouldn't expect any from you. Don't deserve it."

George nodded. "That's right. Over the last thirty years, I've known you only as, as ..." He searched for the right word.

"An evil, lonely, bitter old man?" Potter asked. "I believe you called me something like that once right in this office." His smile faded. "Can't deny that. Can't change it either." Potter settled back in his chair. "Anyway, so much for friendly small talk. I'll get to the point, or rather points."

"Please do." George was having a difficult time sustaining his anger.

"First, I hear there's a lot of gossip going around about what I'm up to these days."

George nodded. "For good reason. You've had a lot of powerful people in this office lately."

"Very true. So let me see what I can do to alleviate some of those concerns." Potter spread his gnarled hands on top of the desk with some difficulty. "Let's start with all the lawyers, shall we? They've been discussing my trial. Can't go into any detail though."

"Of course not."

Potter noticed that George had relaxed slightly.

"The bank's board members being here don't need any explanation. Investors and partners were here to discuss our relationships continuing, given my circumstances."

"And that's your private business," George said.

"True, but let me say this. Tell your friends that nothing I do related to these investments and partnerships will negatively impact anything or anyone in Bedford Falls."

George's eyes narrowed. "I'd like to believe that."

"You have my word." But Potter saw that remark hadn't convinced Bailey. He shrugged. "Okay, everyone will just have to wait and see. You decide what, if anything, about that you'll share."

"How long before we see evidence confirming what you just promised?"

"I can't give you a time line, I'm afraid," Potter said sincerely. "I'll be happy to discuss each significant change as it happens." Potter saw that George had missed his subtle suggestion of a future meeting.

"What about the politicians?" George asked. "Just about everyone holding an office has been in here."

"That's right," Potter said with a chuckle. "Some came with no more enthusiasm than you did. I trust they left more settled, but there's a natural tendency on others' parts to be leery of me. Why do you think that is, George?" He paused. "That was another joke, George."

"Very funny." Bailey stifled a smile. "Now, will you tell me why they were here?"

Potter sighed while remaining cordial. "Most paid respects because I donate to their campaigns. Some came to refuse future donations. And others came to offer support."

"In return for bribes or favors?"

"Some might have spoken in those terms, but I wasn't interested."

"Something else I'd like to believe."

Potter again ignored George's skepticism. "So I believe that covers all the visitors. Did I miss anything?"

"This is your agenda. I didn't come with anything specifically on my mind except surviving." This time, George was smiling, and Potter couldn't keep from laughing.

"Well you did. Would you like to go for double or nothing?" Potter asked.

George screwed up his face in confusion. "What do you mean?"

"I made a suggestion earlier about meeting again. You apparently missed it."

George shook his head. "No I didn't. I just didn't bite."

That disappointed Potter, but he decided to cast his line again. "I'm offering to meet with you again at your convenience. Given all that will be happening in the near term based on what we've just discussed, you and others might find ongoing communication valuable."

"You have a point, but I'm not sure I want people getting the wrong idea."

Potter smiled. "You mean that we're possibly getting along?"

George chuckled. "I doubt they would believe that, but you never know."

"Tell you what, George. Let's schedule one more meeting, say in a week, and go from there." Potter anxiously awaited George's response, which was some time in coming.

George finally nodded. "Okay, once more. But I'm not promising anything beyond that."

"Agreed," Potter said extending his hand. "Thanks for coming, George. Stop at Mrs. Taggart's desk and she'll schedule something convenient for us both."

George took Potter's hand somewhat tentatively. "The last time I shook hands with you, I felt like I was about to sell my soul to the devil." Letting go, George continued. "I may be crazy, but I don't feel quite that way this time. Don't let me be wrong about this."

With a feeling of satisfaction, Potter fixed George with an intense look. "You won't be wrong. It's more important that I be right for me more so than for you."

"Hello? Oh yes, Mr. Jerome." Potter had taken the call in his study. It was quite late on a hot, humid July evening. "What? Disappointed? I didn't mean to sound that way."

The old man was sipping a glass of brandy before heading to bed. It had been an uneventful Sunday—no business to conduct on the Sabbath. He had gone to church that morning and had gained some pleasure at the disbelieving looks he was still receiving after having regularly attended church for the last month. He would just give congregants a soft smile and sing loudly.

"I was wondering when you'd call again ... Hmm, seemed longer than that. What would you like to know?" was Potter's side of the conversation.

Distant thunder promised some welcome rain and a break in the weeklong heat wave withering most of Bedford Falls. Potter carried on his late-evening phone conversation, however, in air-conditioned comfort. "How am I doing? You mean with my assignments? ... You knew? How's that? ... Oh, I see, spies everywhere, eh? Then you know George and I have been meeting every week. It's still more difficult for him than me ... What's that? ... No, I haven't shared that yet. That comes next week." He finished his brandy. "So if you know so much already, why the call?"

The thunder grew louder, accompanied by flashes of lightning just above the treetops. "Couldn't hear that ... What? ... Oh, I feel better than I have in years ... Well of course I'm talking physically ... What? ... Oh, if it's not you it's Crosley after me about my brandy. I'm very disciplined. It's your questions that are driving me to drink."

The storm broke. A gust rattled the windows and brought a driving rain as lightning and thunder came almost nonstop. Static on the line signaled the possibility that the conversation might be cut short.

"Can we pick up the pace a bit?" Potter turned to watch the light show illuminating the grounds. "There's a heck of a storm here."

Whatever Jerome said next was lost in another roar just beyond the glass. "What was that? ... Oh, the other kind of feelings." Potter hesitated, knowing Jerome would not be pleased while hoping the line would go dead.

Potter turned to his desk. "Okay, I'll be totally honest … What? Oh, of course everything else was the truth as well. Now may I continue? Good. I'm still struggling." He sighed deeply. "I want so badly to move forward, find my sons, and shed the years of bitterness, but—" Thunder shaking the room caused him to pause. "I find my practical side, the one with all the baggage, creeping in, and, well, it's mentally exhausting. Too much head, not enough heart … Oh, I'm doing the assignments … What?" Potter turned back to the window. "I thought you knew all this stuff … No, I haven't told anybody anywhere about what I'm up to … No, I haven't sought sympathy. Wouldn't get any anyway."

The storm moved on toward Bedford Falls, leaving a steady rain in its wake. "I assure you, Mr. Jerome, I said nothing to George. I can't even get him to stop looking at me like a judge. Does that sound like I've given anything away to him? But the day after tomorrow is the next big day," Potter said with satisfaction. "After that, I'm hopeful there will be real movement in our relationship."

The rain had stopped; the sound of water rushing from the downspouts was its only legacy. The room had taken on a sudden chill with the air conditioner running full blast. "Look, Mr. Jerome, I need to finish this document. It has to be in early tomorrow. So if you'll excuse … What? Oh, that. I'm afraid it's still mostly a figure of speech to me. Okay, I'll keep trying. Is there an instruction manual for that, you know, the care and feeding of prayer? … Okay, not funny. Sorry. It's on my list. And please do the same for me. Good night."

Potter hung up and turned back to the latest version of his letter. The pile of rejected attempts at it littered the floor, reflecting his desire to get it right. He read over the few paragraphs again, making a few changes. Then after copying it again, he read it a final time aloud.

Bedford Falls Times
Monday, July 22, 1946
Opinions and Editorial
Coming Clean

Editor:

Since December 24th last, Bedford Falls has been under a dark cloud.

Though much of the suspense surrounding that day has been resolved, there remains a climate of doubt regarding many people and institutions in this fair city. I hope to remedy that situation with this editorial.

Effective this morning, I pled guilty on all charges stemming from the disappearance of the B&L's $8,000. I also exonerated my aide, Mr. Sterling Latimoore, whom I had coerced into assisting me. In return, I have received probation along with many hours of community service.

I declare unequivocally that the business and loan, the Baileys, and the entire staff are guiltless in this matter. Further, there was no error in judgment or action at any time by George Bailey. I and I alone perpetrated this crime.

Last, I apologize to this community not only for this recent mischief but also for my ongoing behavior that prolonged the fear and anxiety for so many for too long.

Only time will tell if I can truly make amends and positively influence this community. Your openness to that possibility will be welcomed.

Henry F. Potter

George was waiting early Tuesday hours before his regular appointment. He was outside the bank on Monday with the newspaper in hand when the old man arrived. He waited patiently as Crosley assisted Potter into his chair. George was struck by the two men's cheerfulness.

As the chair swung around, Potter raised a welcoming hand to Bailey. "Good morning, George. I thought you might be calling. Undoubtedly there will be others during the course of the day. I'm very glad you're the first."

Potter turned to his aide. "Why don't you let George roll me in, Crosley? I'll see you inside."

Without enthusiasm, Bailey complied, wheeling the chair through the door. Mrs. Taggart looked up from her desk wearing a pained expression. She stood stiffly and came forward. Her attempt to take over the wheelchair was rebuffed by Potter. "It's okay, Eloise. George and I need to talk. Hold all calls and visitors please."

Coolly, Mrs. Taggart moved to the office door and pushed it open. "Thank you, Eloise. Now could we get some coffee, please?"

Once the wheelchair was positioned behind the desk, George circled back and took a seat, pulling the paper out of his pocket. Holding it up, he started to speak, but the old man beat him to it. "I bet you choked on your toast when you saw that."

"If that was your goal, you darn near succeeded." George didn't know what look he should be wearing. His face was changing expressions like a chameleon changes colors. "Why'd you do it, Mr. Potter?"

Potter's soft smile remained. "I did it because it was the right thing to do." George's incredulous look made Potter chuckle. "I know, hard to believe. But last time I looked, the world didn't come to an end this morning."

After consulting the paper, Bailey's anger waned. "About this deal. You get off with probation and community service! That sounds pretty light."

"My team of lawyers probably would have gotten me even less time." The old man made the familiar church steeple with his hands. "I'm old, have no record, made restitution—the list goes on and on. But that would have cost time and a lot of money, not just mine. But I expect many, especially you, aren't happy with the agreement. I regret that, and I'll assume I'll continue filling the role of villain in this town until the day I die. I don't have time to dwell on that. I don't have a lot of time left for anything."

Mrs. Taggart tapped on the door, and George leaped up quickly to open it. She gave Bailey a curt nod of thanks and delivered the tray to the desk. She poured two cups and left the additives to them. She left not having said a word.

"What a woman. Cold as hell, but she's always looking out for me. She'd give St. Peter a run for the job of guarding the pearly gates." His church-steeple hands slid to the desk accompanied by a deep sigh. "I'm going to miss her."

That got George's attention. "Miss her? What do you mean?"

Potter reached for a folder on the desk and pulled a single sheet out. After a quick glance, he passed it across to Bailey, who read it once, glanced up in disbelief, and read it again. "That's right, George. I'm resigning as president and chairman of the bank board effective the end of this month."

While his guest groped for words, a second letter appeared in Potter's hand. "You'll probably find this one even more interesting."

Bailey grabbed the document from the old man and quickly read the two paragraphs. It informed George that Potter was resigning from the B&L's board. George stared at Potter in shock. "I can't believe it."

"You'll have to at some point. The resignation from these two places makes perfect sense. Continuing at the bank would jeopardize its credibility and future. And how could I stay on the board of a place I just pleaded guilty to robbing?"

"The only thing that doesn't make sense is your giving up all this power and control. You've held onto both tenaciously."

"Not any more it would seem." Ensuring the folder was empty, Potter shoved it into a drawer. "Perhaps you understand now why I've been circumspect at our meetings."

George showed sudden recognition. "Yes. Now I can. And this is a good start."

Potter threw up his hands. "A good start? You're a hard taskmaster, George Bailey." He shook his head then reconsidered. "Well if you mean a good start to moving on with my life, I guess you're right."

"I can tell you one thing for sure," George said. "Uncle Billy's life just got a whole new start."

At that moment, Mr. Crosley came in through the back entrance. "Do you want me to start boxing up your things, sir, or wait outside?"

"You can stay, Crosley. George and I have no secrets, do we George?" Turning to Bailey, Potter leaned on the great desk. "Is there anything else?"

"No, I think that's more than enough." George was suddenly filled with a sense of relief though he still was having a hard time believing what he'd just read.

Potter nodded. An exhausted look crossed his face. "Good, but we do have our regular meeting next week. Let's keep it, shall we?" The old man slowly leaned back. "I've gotten kind of used to seeing your charming face."

"I see no reason why not. I'll look forward to hearing about what happens the rest of this week. It should be very interesting," George said with conviction.

"I'm afraid we'll have to find a new place to meet after tomorrow's meeting, however."

George understood. "I'm sure you'll think of someplace. Just let me know where. Good day, Mr. Potter, and thanks for your time and, well, all this."

"You're welcome, George. Be sure to give Uncle Billy my best."

George smiled at the thought of his uncle's response to hearing that.

CHAPTER 25

Rain had been falling for more than a week as August came to an end. The hubbub created by Potter's July bombshells was still reverberating around the town. The news had been greeted mainly with pleasure and relief. There were those angry, however, that Potter would not be spending time behind bars. Still, the trade-offs seemed to mitigate most of this angst.

The B&L benefited immediately as did Uncle Billy, who was truly a new man. Free from alcohol and guilt, he was taking a stronger role in the business after more than forty years. Membership was growing nicely, and George was finally able to relax.

The bank was stable once more. George's replacement of Potter on the bank's board helped tremendously in solidifying its reputation. Mr. Robinson, the senior teller, had been promoted to president and was occupying Potter's old office. The board chairmanship was being rotated annually with Mr. Gower at the helm for the first year.

George and Henry continued to meet on a weekly basis at the hotel over lunch. Initially, seeing the former adversaries at the same table caused quite a stir. Though they treated each other respectfully, they did so also coolly.

Though no longer at the bank and B&L, Potter still wielded a great deal of influence. Many people were renting homes or space in office buildings he owned. There were also his companies in the area that generated jobs and much-needed tax revenue. So there were still plenty of things for the townsfolk to fret over when it came to Henry Potter.

Ironically, the person in the best position to know what might be coming was George Bailey, but he wasn't talking. So as the summer wore on, a welcomed calm settled over Bedford Falls along with the rains. The two most at ease during this period seemed to be Henry and George.

It was early one weekday morning on the cusp of September that the gothic doorbell rang at Potter's estate. Crosley opened the door and was surprised to see Mr. Jerome standing there illuminated by a rare ray of sunshine. "Good morning, sir," the aide said warily as he looked for Ernie Bishop's cab. It was nowhere to be seen.

Jerome smiled broadly as he delivered an enthusiastic response. "Good day to you too, Mr. Crosley. You're looking well. Can it be possible that working for Mr. Potter is beginning to agree with you?"

The aide ignored the question but managed a smile. "How may I help you, Mr. Jerome?"

"Would Mr. Potter be at home?" the investigator asked with a hopeful look.

Crosley considered the question for a moment before stepping aside. "Please come in. Mr. Potter is in residence, but I don't know his schedule." He led Jerome to the familiar wing-backed chairs in the entry hall. "Please wait here." The aide headed upstairs instead of to the study.

After waiting a few minutes, Jerome heard someone approaching across the main floor. When they came into view, the investigator's mouth fell open.

"Latimoore?"

"Mr. Jerome?" Latimoore replied in equal surprise and came to a halt.

For some time, the men were speechless. As they stood in silence, the door to the study opened; another figure entered the great hall and started toward them. The person was hidden by shadows initially as they approached. Emerging into the light, Jerome got his second shock of the day.

"Mrs. Taggart?" the investigator exclaimed, still reeling from seeing Latimoore.

In her usual fashion, the woman was unflappable. "Mr. Jerome." Her greeting was chilly.

The three stared at each other until Jerome's roar of laughter shattered the silence. Not unexpectedly, neither Latimoore nor Taggart joined in.

"Sorry. I'm not laughing at you, either of you." Jerome's head swiveled from one to the other. "It's just, well, I'm totally astonished to see the two of you here."

"As am I at the sight of you," said Mrs. Taggart; her stoic expression was all too familiar to George. Latimoore was less successful at remaining impassive. Only the investigator freely displayed his amazement, confusion, and delight.

"Frankly, I'm pleased to see anyone outside of a prison," Latimoore's dry reply coupled with the absurdly ill-fitting bib-overalls and flannel shirt the former aide wore caused the investigator to laugh aloud. Latimoore looked like a schoolboy wearing the previous year's hand-me-downs.

Seeing the investigator's reaction, Mrs. Taggart came to Latimoore's rescue. "Your new clothes are in at the mercantile." She turned to Jerome. "He's hard to fit."

"Obviously." Jerome felt out of touch for not having known that bit of news. "It's an unexpected pleasure seeing you both, but I'm here to see Mr. Potter."

As if on cue, Crosley came into view and descended the stairs. When he saw the others, his gait changed imperceptibly. For a moment, his expression reminded Jerome of the old Crosley. The investigator speculated that the return of the man he had replaced was unnerving. Mrs. Taggart was no less intimidating.

At the bottom of the stairs, Crosley addressed Jerome, his voice not betraying any anxiety. "Mr. Potter will see you upstairs."

He turned to the others. "I hope all is going well today, Latimoore."

He received a curt nod from the scarecrow-like figure. "No problem, Mr. Crosley." The former aide's reply carried no hostility. "I was just in to check on my new clothing."

"And it is in," Mrs. Taggart said.

Crosley gave them both a pleasant look then addressed Mrs. Taggart. "Very good, Eloise." This drew a frown from the woman as he turned to Latimoore. "Then why don't you go get them, Sterling? Also, check to see if Miss Pearl needs anything for the kitchen." He then spoke to Jerome. "If you will, please follow me."

As Taggart and Latimoore went about their business, Crosley

explained why they were headed upstairs. “Mr. Potter’s new office and library are up here, sir.” They turned left at the top and headed down a long hall.

Halfway down, Crosley opened a door and ushered Jerome into a large room. Henry sat on a couch covered with a blanket. Books lined three walls with windows on the forth. Matching couches faced each other with a low table between. There was no desk, but a new, modern wheelchair was parked in a corner near the windows.

“This is a surprise, Mr. Jerome.” Potter’s greeting sounded warm, but his face was hidden by shadows. “Does anyone else know you’re back?”

“I’m not really back,” the investigator replied.

“Bring us some coffee, please, Crosley,” Potter asked politely. The man bowed and left. Henry waved Jerome to the other couch. “Now, what brings you here so unexpectedly?”

“It wasn’t because of Latimoore and Taggart,” Jerome said. “But perhaps you’ll share that story first. I apparently am a bit out of the loop.”

Potter chuckled. “I see you ran into them. I’d be delighted to fill you in.”

For the next few minutes, Potter covered all the staff changes at the estate. As a reward for the job Crosley did running the place while the old man was recovering, he’d been promoted to butler and caregiver with a hefty raise. After several frank discussions, Latimoore, who had been released from jail based on Potter’s confession, returned as head mechanic and supervisor of the groundskeepers.

As for Eloise Taggart, she was too valuable for Potter to lose. She always handled his other ventures as well as helping him at the bank. The woman’s loyalty continued after he resigned as bank president, and she soon arrived to take over his business affairs as well as his study. That had led to his move upstairs.

“This is simply marvelous. I commend you,” Jerome said. “And I already have some of the information I came for today. But there are two parts to my visit. The first is an update on the assignments, the head part, and the second—”

“Is the heart part. You’re predictable, Mr. Jerome. But isn’t there a third reason?" He received a blank stare. "You know, the information about my boys?"

This was greeted with a frown. "Let's see where our conversation leads first."

"Very well, get on with it." There was disappointment and peevishness in Potter's voice.

Trying to ignore this, the investigator began. "We can skip the things you've done that have gone public, including your staff. What about the other things?"

"I'm honoring the requirement to keep quiet. That's most important. The citizenry seem to be a bit more accepting, skeptical but accepting, though I'll still never win man of the year, let alone win over George. Now as to what I've been up to, let me see."

For the next thirty minutes, Potter covered his wide-ranging activities from political to business, from organizations to individuals. Each interaction and the outcomes had remained as secret as possible to meet Jerome's requirements. Much had been done since the investigator's last update.

Potter closed his summary with information about the next steps. "I have Mrs. Taggart working on most of these things. She deserves all the credit. I have to say not being able to share with Eloise has been most difficult. Anyway, now, you're up to date."

"And?"

"And what?"

"You know what," the investigator said curtly. After a pause he added, "Look. There's no denying you're honoring our agreement."

"I know, you want to know about the impact all this is having on my ..." He searched for words unsuccessfully and settling for " ... outlook, my perspective on life. That's much more difficult to categorize I'm afraid."

Jerome had to marshal on. "I believe it's in First Corinthians that Paul talked about people doing all kinds of good deeds, but without love, the good deeds meant nothing."

Potter threw the investigator a quizzical look. It seemed Jerome always got surprised looks from people when he referenced the Bible. It was as if people thought one couldn't be a private investigator and be religious. That didn't say much for his profession.

Putting that aside, Jerome continued. "Let me put it to you simply. Are you still primarily motivated by the desire to find your boys?"

"And what's wrong with that? Is it not honorable to want to find my sons?" Henry sounded more hurt than angry.

Jerome shrugged. "Of course not, Henry. I was just hoping you were getting some joy, some sense of fulfillment from what you've done."

"I'm sorry if I'm disappointing you. I've done my best," Potter said apologetically.

Jerome sighed. "Tell me, would you suddenly stop what you've been doing, are doing, if the boys were no longer in the picture?"

"What are you saying?" Potter asked sharply. "Were you lying to me?"

"No, Henry, I didn't lie to you. But I can't tell you any more about them right now I'm afraid."

"But I've met all the requirements," Henry protested vehemently.

"Right to the letter. But there's still work to be done, and I didn't promise you when, if ever, I'd tell you. For certain, that time is not now."

"That is cruel considering what I've done in response to your request. Or should I say demand." Potter was growing angry; his old manner was returning. "I will ... I cannot ..." He never finished the sentence; he just glared at his guest.

"I'm sorry, Henry, truly I am." Jerome stood. "It seems I should be on my way. You have the choice of continuing with what has been started or not. That's up to you. It's easy to see why you might not. But if you do, I suggest you spend less time doing and more time seeing the impact of what you've done at a personal level."

George sat across from Potter in the old man's upstairs office sounding apologetic. "I wish I could stop doubting you, Mr. Potter. We've been meeting now for months, and you've done a lot of, well a lot of good things. Still, I struggle to let go of the past."

"This isn't about winning you over, George. Oh, it would be nice if that happened, but it's not critical from my perspective." He took a sip of coffee. "The coffee's cold. I guess that means the meeting's over."

"Yes indeed." George put down his cup and stood looking out the large windows at the brilliant colors of fall. "Where did the time go? Some of the trees have already lost most of their leaves. Won't be long before the first snow."

"That is a *pleasant* thought," Potter said sarcastically then blew out a long breath. "I don't look forward to being trapped in here for four or five months."

George collected his hat and coat as he responded. "Well, I have to say these meetings have been quite pleasant and enlightening for the most part. But bringing them to an end is long overdue."

"They have become rather a habit," Potter said with amusement. "They certainly kept me on my toes. You never cut me any slack no matter what the news."

"You never cut me any slack over the years either, Mr. Potter."

"Touché." Potter raised his arms in mock surrender. "But feel free to call and discuss anything even if it's about what I'm up to, good or bad."

"Count on it especially if that other shoe ever falls."

Potter laughed heartily. "At least you said if and not when." Then he became serious. "Honestly, I will miss the business discussions we've had. Your mind confirmed I was smart in trying to hire you long ago. Still I believe my style works best in some situations and yours in others. We might have made a good team if—"

"You weren't such an ass?" George said without malice. "Truth be told, I've also enjoyed our mental jousting though I could never see us as a *team*. Goodbye, Mr. Potter. I wish you good health, and more important, a good heart."

The meaning of these words was not lost on Potter. "From your lips to God's ears, George." He gave the younger man a warm smile and waved goodbye.

Before George reached the door, however, there came a soft knock followed by Crosley entering. "I beg your pardon, sirs, but there is someone waiting downstairs to see you."

"I don't have another appointment," Potter said. "Who is it?"

Crosley seemed hesitant to reply. "It's Mr. Jerome, sir. He wishes to see you both."

“Both?” they said in unison.

George asked, “How did he even know I was here?”

Crosley’s expression was blank. “No idea, Mr. Bailey, But he was most particular about that point. He also said it was important, his word, sir. What would you like me to do?”

Henry turned to George. “Do you have the time to meet with him?”

“Yes, if it doesn’t take too long I’d be able to stay.”

“Very well, Crosley, get me in my chair then send him up.”

Shortly, after another soft knock, Crosley entered with Jerome on his heels. “Mr. Jerome, sirs.” The investigator dropped his briefcase near the couches and extended his hand to George.

“Hello, George.” They shook as Jerome turned to Potter. “Henry, gracious of you to meet with me unscheduled yet again.”

Releasing the investigator’s hand, George spoke for Henry. “You have us both more than a little curious as to why you’re here.”

“May I sit?” Asked Jerome. Potter waved at the couch across from George. Once settled, the investigator spoke. “Gentlemen, I’m here for two reasons. The first relates mainly to Henry. For reasons you aren’t privy to, George, Henry has been working on some very challenging assignments over many months.”

“Are you talking about his plea bargain?” George asked.

“No, this is totally different. As I said, you’re not privy to exactly what was involved. But I’ll be sharing the results with Henry today, and if it’s okay with him, do so while you’re present.” He looked to Potter for permission.

Potter looked doubtful. “I don’t think I’m open to that.”

“What if I tell you that the news is good?” Jerome asked with a smile.

Receiving a tentative nod, Jerome rushed ahead. “Thank you, Henry. I’ll be direct. I’m now authorized to share all the information I gathered about your boys.”

CHAPTER 26

"That is wonderful news, Mr. Jerome." Henry could hardly contain himself. "But you want to share this information in front of George?"

"I'd like to, but it's up to you. George knows the story of your family right up to the point you know. It will all come out shortly, and George learning now, given his place in the community, would be a good thing in my opinion."

Potter contemplated this for a long moment. His impatience won out. "I want to know where my sons are. Who else knows and when is irrelevant right this moment. Please go on."

To Potter's continued frustration, Jerome didn't just go on. He started by telling them about the part of his investigation that led to discovering the boys' brief stay at St. Vincent's and their trip on the orphan train. That phase of the story ended with both boys being adopted by the same couple in Youngstown, Ohio.

"So they live in Youngstown?" Henry asked impatiently.

"No. They didn't stay there. In fact, the couple moved the boys from Youngstown within weeks of the adoption. The parents were well known and respected in the community, however, so it was relatively easy for me to find out where they had gone. It helped that the couple moved only once.

"I was able to speak to the adoptive mother, the father being deceased. Though she had no idea who the boys were at the time of the adoption, we were able to confirm conclusively that her boys were indeed William and Charles," Jerome said with assurance. "Of course, they don't go by those names now."

“You sound awfully certain about that. How can you be so sure?” Henry sounded unconvinced.

Jerome smiled and reached for his briefcase. After a short search, he emerged with a loose collection of papers. “Because of these. They are the birth certificates and medical histories of the boys I brought back from England. You can confirm all this for yourself. I invited the adoptive mother to join us if you don’t mind,” the investigator said as he stood.

Both Potter and George looked shocked. Potter asked the obvious question. “She lives nearby?”

“Fortunately, yes.”

Potter gave that fact consideration. “Do the boys live around here too?”

“Let’s not get ahead of ourselves,” Jerome replied as he went to the window. Tapping the glass lightly, he waved his hand. “She’s been waiting down in Ernie’s cab. Crosley will have her up here in a minute I’m sure.”

Jerome calmly moved from the window to the door and waited. While Potter fidgeted, George’s face showed a mixture of confusion and embarrassment at still being in the room. Then there was another tap on the door.

The air left Potter at the sight of Jerome’s guest. He sat open mouthed in shock and disbelief. Before he could muster a voice to challenge the investigator, George leaped to his feet.

“Mother? Jerome? Is this some kind of sick practical joke?” George asked in a rage. “What kind of man would perpetrate such an outrage? I’ll tell you, a hateful one, an evil one!” He turned to Henry. “If you don’t throw him out, I will.”

Henry remained speechless; he hardly heard George’s outburst. The color had drained from the old man’s face causing Jerome to grab for the water pitcher and glass. “Get over here, Mr. Crosley.”

As the butler rushed over and took the glass from Jerome, George continued his tirade, this time directly at Ma Bailey. “Mother, how did you get roped into this little charade? What possible reason could you have for doing something like this to me?”

“Because what you’ve just heard is true.” Velma Bailey’s reply was so soft that George had to ask for her to repeat her answer.

Henry began to recover as George turned on Jerome again. "What kind of foolish ideas did you put in my mother's head?"

"The only thing I shared with Velma that she didn't already know was who the biological parents of you and Harry were." Jerome left Henry's side and stepped to Mrs. Bailey. "Here, Velma, have a seat." He faced George again. "Look, I had no idea when this started where it would lead. I certainly didn't expect this. How could I?"

Ignoring the investigator, George turned on Henry displaying a snarling smile. "You put him up to this, didn't you? This is that other shoe I've been expecting to fall."

Potter was still stunned but managed to say, "Don't be ridiculous, George."

George scoffed. "What's ridiculous is this whole preposterous fairytale. It has your fingerprints all over it."

"Listen to what you're saying." Henry's recovery was now fueled by anger. "Why on earth would I help fabricate a story that would end with me being your father? Get a grip, man." Potter slumped back exhausted from the effort.

George headed for the door. "I can't deal with this, this insanity! I'm leaving."

Velma Bailey stood catching his sleeve as he passed. "Please, Son, don't go. Let me explain."

"No, Mother. I don't want you to try to explain how this could possibly be true," George said harshly then pulled away and started to leave again.

At hearing and seeing this, Velma's tone took on that of a mother talking to a petulant child. "Stop right there, George Peter Bailey. You have to listen. Everyone needs to listen. Running away won't change the truth. The sooner we get this out, the sooner we can move on."

"Move on? Now that sounds like a good idea. I'll just move on out of here if you don't mind," George said sarcastically but didn't move.

Velma's voice softened. "Come on, George, sit with me. We need to talk this out. The story isn't just yours; it's mine, your father's, and surely Mr. Potter's."

After a glance toward his escape route, George slowly and reluctantly moved to his mother's side. She gave him a loving look and guided him to the couch where they sat while she unsuccessfully tried to take his hand.

Jerome attempted to provide background in support of Ma Bailey. "I met with Velma some time back to confirm my suspicions. At the end of our conversation, I swore her to secrecy until now. During the intervening period, she has been coming to grips with this herself. Hearing the true identity of her adopted sons' birth father devastated her as well. Velma needs to share this story. You need to show the respect she has earned and deserves from you, George. Will you do that?"

George mustered only a slow, pitiful nod as he sank deeper into the leather. Jerome turned to Potter. "And I expect the same from you, Henry."

"You'll have no trouble from me."

"Good." Jerome sat next to Potter. "Please, Velma, tell your story."

The wet spring of 1912 found Velma and Peter Bailey living in a small but well-kept house in Youngstown as they approached their tenth anniversary. They had met in the upstate college town where Peter had been studying, and Velma was just finishing high school. They married after his graduation and started life together in Pittsburgh, where he'd found an entry-level position.

The firm moved Peter around a great deal to small offices in Ohio and Pennsylvania. They were seldom in one location more than a year. When possible during this time, Velma had worked part-time at florist shops while running the household.

They weren't getting rich, but they felt quite happy. Each Friday, Peter brought home his pay in cash and handed it to Velma. She would pull out her meticulously maintained accounts book and divvy up the money. They had envelopes for everything—expenses, savings, a major buys fund, a rainy-day fund, and a "fun" fund.

While saving money for big purchases such as furniture, they would clip pictures and put them in their dream drawer. Then each Friday after dividing Peter's pay, they would pull the pictures out to remind them why they were sacrificing. More often than not, there was nothing to go into the fun fund, but they didn't mind. They were young and in love.

Nearly from day one, the two wanted children. Unfortunately, Velma had miscarried three times in their first decade together. With each failure, they took solace in saving for and then purchasing homes, the last of these in Youngstown. Still, they longed for a family.

A deep recession hit during the Baileys' second year in Youngstown. When it lingered, the Youngstown office was closed, throwing Peter out of work. In the midst of this crisis, Velma became pregnant again only to miscarry in less than three months. Worse yet, the doctor told them that she could not get pregnant again.

Peter was able to find an entry-level position, but his pay was far less than before, so Velma went back to work at a florist shop. They were barely making ends meet. Adding to their difficulties was Velma's depression over not being able to have a child and Peter's resistance to adoption.

This was the backdrop entering the dismal spring of 1912. Then two things happened that changed their lives forever. In many respects, each event argued against the logic of the other. One created the potential for children. The second development was a business proposition that, if pursued, made expanding the family at that time imprudent.

At dinner one night, Velma shared an advertisement about an orphan train coming to Youngstown that fall. These trains had started in the mid-1800s and once came regularly to their town. Back then, the train stopped in Youngstown three times a year. More than two hundred children had found homes there. The trains had not stopped there, however, since the mid-1890s.

Recent local interest had been rekindled. Representatives of the town had succeeded in getting the Children's Aid Society's agreement to stop in Youngstown again that fall. The article in the local paper was the first request for applicants wishing to adopt.

After learning she could no longer get pregnant, Velma immediately wanted to adopt. Peter was opposed at first because of wanting his own child. But with each passing year, she argued that their age would soon work against qualifying to adopt. By the time of the orphan train article, Peter had relented, and they were among the first to apply.

The next July, Peter arrived home to find Velma holding two letters for him to read. The first informed them that they had been approved to participate in the orphan train process. The second came from Peter's older brother, Billy, who lived in a place called Bedford Falls.

The letter outlined the ominous situation at the Bailey B&L. Billy and his wife, Laura, had opened the business some ten years earlier. It had been a struggle from the beginning. Then Laura had died, and Billy found the bottle. When the recession hit, the business suffered greatly. Billy's letter said he was on the verge of declaring bankruptcy.

After much soul searching, the two agreed that a move to Bedford Falls made sense. Peter was underemployed, and Billy needed help. Together, the brothers might just salvage the B&L. His brother's house had lots of room for them to stay. And if successful in adopting, they could raise the child in a new town as their own, making it easier for whomever they adopted. So with much trepidation, they began planning for big changes.

Peter and Velma had been on the platform for hours on an unusually sweltering October day when they finally saw the train approaching. What had started out as a nearly empty station in the predawn had expanded to an overflow crowd. They were oblivious to the others, however; their wait was nearly over.

After the decision to help Billy, Peter made several weekend visits to Bedford Falls and immersed himself in the affairs of the B&L. With his involvement and an improving economy, things began to look up. Seeing improvement in the business had been a huge relief, allowing Velma and Peter to focus on the arrival of the orphan train.

The couple along with other hopefuls trailed along behind the children as they left the train and headed for the church. Almost immediately, Velma was drawn to a toddler of around two who clung firmly to an older boy of five or six. Once in the basement, Peter scanned the room while Velma remained focused on the two boys.

When the prospective parents were taken upstairs, Velma asked about the two boys. The representative told them that the older one was under the weather. He had been brought along to get him out of the heat and to encourage the younger boy to participate.

Velma and Peter had come hoping for one child, preferably younger. They were rightly concerned they were biting off more than they could chew already with the pending move to Bedford Falls. Peter reminded his wife of this and suggested they focus on the towheaded boy, which Velma agreed to reluctantly.

This plan immediately faltered when the toddler loudly refused to be separated from the older boy, throwing the basement into chaos. The representative in charge urged them to make another choice. Instead, Velma suggested that both children be brought up together. Given time, she was confident the younger one would succumb to her motherly charms.

To the surprise of the representative, the boys came quietly upstairs. While getting to know the toddler, Velma kept glancing toward the older boy. Soon, Peter was doing the same. Remarkably, the older boy slowly became more interested in the proceedings. By the end of the day, Hap was laughing, Will was talking a bit, and the Baileys were smitten with them both.

"The next morning, after the excitement and euphoria wore off, reality set in," Ma Bailey said. "We had two children, not one, sleeping in the small bedroom down the hall. We spent that morning giving them names, George after my father and Harry after Peter's." She looked to her son, hoping for some kind of reaction.

George's only response was to stare glumly at the door. With a sigh, she marshaled on. "The wisdom of our decision was tested early on when George here nearly died."

"Died?" George swung around to face his mother.

Jerome spoke up. "I told you about the head injury you received on the boat."

"And we were told the day of the adoption that the reason you were so lethargic was that you had relapsed during the journey, actually been unconscious for a time. Then there was the amnesia."

"I had amnesia?"

"That's what we were told." Velma frowned at the memory. "We almost didn't take you because of all those reasons. But then Harry would have been devastated. Anyway, we soon confirmed you didn't recall anything before that day. Still don't obviously."

The investigator pulled Ma Bailey back to her earlier comment. "Tell us about what happened with George."

Velma nodded and launched into the events of that first week with the boys. George had been easy to deal with as he spent most of his time sleeping. Harry was another story. He made it very difficult on the couple as they tried to pack for the move to Bedford Falls. The toddler spent a good deal of his time in the boxes they were trying to fill.

By the third day, Velma and Peter became worried about George's lack of improvement. She took him to their doctor, who checked him over, but he recommended only castor oil and more rest. In spite of their concern, the couple had to be out of the house and headed for Bedford Falls at the end of that first week.

Their old jalopy got the family to Uncle Billy's house barely, and they settled in for the first night in the new town. In the early hours, George began to convulse. They took him to the tiny new hospital. The diagnosis was a slow bleed in the brain. Surgery was in order, and the place for that was in Albany at the medical college.

"My Lord!" Henry's exclamation brought Ma Bailey up short. "That's the same place I was treated when I came back to Albany after the attack in New York."

George came out of his daze. "Attack? What attack?"

Henry tossed the younger man a dismissive wave but seemed to change his mind. "I was attacked the day I was to sail for England to bring my wife and sons back to America. I believe my wife's father, the earl, had other ideas and tried to have me murdered."

Ma Bailey's hand flew to her mouth while George looked incredulous.

"He sent a man to arrange the deed. I was kidnapped and taken to a warehouse, where some men tried to make it look like a robbery gone wrong. Before I was knocked out, I discovered their real motive. By luck, and I'm not sure if it was good or bad, I survived, but I was sentenced to spend the rest of my life in this chair without the possibility of parole."

"How awful, Mr. Potter," Velma said on the verge of tears. "I had no idea."

Potter gave a dismissive shake of the head. "No one knew, at least no one in Bedford Falls ever did. At that time, I lived near Albany."

"You mean you were only a few miles away when we brought George, your William, to the medical college?" Velma asked.

"No, not by then. I contracted pneumonia followed by tuberculosis after my initial recovery from injuries I received in the attack. I was whisked away to a sanatorium in northern Maine, where I spent nearly a year."

"You left for the sanatorium around the time the *Titanic* went down," Jerome added.

Potter pondered that for a moment. "That's right. Once I got out of the sanatorium without a family and in such physical and mental distress, I made the decision to make a change. That was when I relocated to Bedford Falls and finished this place."

"That was a dramatic decision," Jerome said.

A strange smile appeared on Henry's face. "It was only slightly less dramatic than what I originally planned to do."

"What was that, Mr. Potter?" Velma asked naively.

As the old man shifted uneasily, Jerome came to his rescue. "Let's not get too far afield, shall we? Tell us about George's surgery in Albany, Velma."

With a shrug, Mrs. Bailey shared what she understood. The doctor had drilled a small hole in George's skull that relieved the pressure. They waited, as he was kept in a semi-coma for several weeks while the bleeding slowly stopped. From then on, he improved quickly.

"The only symptoms you ever had from the experience were occasional headaches and nightmares early on. And you do have a small scar hidden under all that hair."

George reflexively put his hand to his head then dropped it. "I recall the headaches. They went away for good by the time I was in my teens. But as to nightmares, I don't ..." He suddenly paused as a strange expression crossed his face. Then he continued hesitantly. "I don't *think* I recall any nightmares."

"Like I said, they stopped shortly after we adopted you. The headaches left you shortly after you rescued Harry from that hole in the ice," Velma clarified. "And I think everyone knows the story from that point." Velma looked around to confirm that all agreed. With a pleased nod, she started to settle back on the couch when she suddenly sat up straight again. "Oh! I forgot the most important aftermath of George's surgery. When he came out of the induced coma, he couldn't remember anything."

Jerome asked, "Are you saying he remembered nothing about the incident?"

"Nothing at all. He might as well have been a newborn. He had to relearn who we were—Peter, Harry, and me. But in a way, that worked out well for us all."

"How so?"

"With Harry too young to remember his past and George forgetting his, they never saw us as other than their biological parents. And the town never knew any different, up until now that is." Velma fixed Jerome with a benign stare and forgiving smile.

"I was just as surprised as you all are today when Mr. Jerome arrived at my door knowing my secret and more." Tears filled Velma's eyes. "I cried buckets after hearing about how you and Harry became orphans and about Mr. Potter's losses."

After a brief break at the investigator's suggestion, they reassembled. Henry was surprised that George had not taken the opportunity to escape. The younger man would not make eye contact with him, but he did return to his seat on the couch. Potter had to admit that he understood why. The thought of George being his son was nearly inconceivable.

Henry had found Velma's emotional conclusion had gotten to him. Memories of his wife and sons—young, vibrant, and hopeful—filled his thoughts as he stared at George. It was almost unbearable. He spoke up. "On second thought, this is too much for me to deal with anymore today. Can we end this for now at least?"

"Ending this forever would suit me," George said, looking pleased at Potter's suggestion. "I still don't believe what I've heard. And even if it were true, it would not change my feelings about *that* man." He didn't look at Henry as he said that.

Potter bristled. "I a*ssume* you are referring to me?" He suddenly felt reenergized by the insult. He turned to Jerome with a humorless smile. "The evidence at this point seems overwhelming, but in spite of this, my *friend* here still seems unconvinced. So I've changed my mind again. Is there more evidence to share with this stubborn cuss?"

George threw up his hands and sat back. Jerome took up the challenge. "We'll try, but it will require me to ask a few more questions."

Potter held up his hand to stop a renewed protest from George. "If you must. But please be brief."

George leaped to his feet. "I won't stay here one more minute. Listen if you want, Potter, but I'm out of here."

"Suit yourself," Henry replied without missing a beat. "Would you rather have Jerome or your mother call to share what is to come? I'm sure Mary will want to know." That stopped George in his tracks. "You *are* going to share this with her, aren't you?"

Henry and the others waited for an answer. It didn't come. Potter continued. "Another five minutes won't kill either of us, and then we'll all have the same information. If what I hear or don't hear changes my opinion, I'll fully support your contention."

"Gee, *Dad,* that's generous of you, but I think not."

Henry's voice rose to a shout. "How dare you! What gives you the idea that I would even want to have you call me—"

"Hold it! Stop right now!" Velma cried out. "You two are acting like children, worse than children. You sit down, George, and both of you stop slinging insults. Why, we could have been done with this by now if you two could act like adults."

The room fell silent as the two men glared at each other but complied. "That's better. Now I believe you had a question or two, Mr. Jerome?"

"Thank you, Velma." The investigator gave her a broad smile. "One of the best ways to identify people is from birthmarks and scars. Does Harry or George have any?"

"Why yes, hey, but you already know that," she said then blushed. "Oh, right. Anyway, Harry has a birthmark on his lower back."

Jerome turned to Henry. "Please find Charles's birth certificate." After shuffling through several sheets, Potter pulled one out. "Is there a reference to a birthmark?"

Checking, Potter looked and nodded. "Yes. It says he has one on his lower back."

The investigator turned to Velma. "Can you be more specific about the location?"

She blushed before replying. “If you look at him from behind, it’s just above his right buttock.”

“Does the mark have a distinct shape?” Jerome asked.

“Oh yes. It looks like a doughnut, a near perfect circle with a hole in the middle.”

Potter checked the paper and looked up. “It says that here. The word *perfect* isn’t noted.”

“You don’t remember seeing that on Charles when he was a baby?” the investigator asked Henry.

“I’m afraid not. In those days, we men didn’t provide much care for the children. I don’t think I ever changed a diaper.”

Jerome let that drop and asked Henry, “Do you know if William had a birthmark?”

“No, but let me check the certificate.”

Velma interjected. “You won’t find any. He doesn’t.”

Potter looked up from William’s certificate and nodded.

“Did he have any marks on his body you can recall?” Jerome asked him.

After a long pause, he shook his head. “Nothing comes to mind.”

“What about you, Velma?”

“Oh yes. It wasn’t a birthmark, but it was quite evident. It had to have been from some kind of accident when he was quite young because it was well healed by the time he came to us.”

As she spoke, something was triggered in Henry’s memory. “The burn!” he nearly shouted.

“The burn? What burn?” Jerome asked.

“The scar from the burn. How could I have forgotten that?”

“Tell us about it.”

Henry shared the memory from one of his last times with his oldest. He arrived home from work to find that William had pulled a hot iron off the ironing board on to his bare leg. “He—” Henry looked at George. “You were screaming bloody murder and rightly so. It was a nasty looking burn that was still healing when I left for America the last time.”

“How old was he at the time?” the investigator asked.

“Let’s see, he had to be just five. That was shortly after his birthday.”

“Can you describe the scar? Which leg? The size? Shape?”

Henry scratched his chin, desperately trying to visualize his son lying on the floor of the bedroom that night. With eyes closed, he moved his arm as if lifting something. When his eyes opened, he spoke confidently. "It was on the outside of his left leg below the knee. It was easy to tell what had made it. The shape was a triangle like the end of an iron."

Velma turned to her son. "George, why don't you show your father that scar."

CHAPTER 27

The weather forecast for Christmas Eve was the same as the previous year—cold with lots of snow. At that moment, however, George stood in the place where the miracle had started twelve months earlier. It was noon, and a warm front lingered. He could see storm clouds gathering, however, above Bedford Mountain. Things would be changing soon.

He was there contemplating all that had happened since *the* crime. Since then, he had experienced life-changing events at an alarming rate. As the year closed, the B&L was growing, his reputation was intact, and life had settled back into a comfortable routine. The only cloud was his conflicted relationship with Henry Potter.

His half hour on the bridge had resolved nothing, so George headed back to the office content with the broad truth that his life was more or less wonderful again. As he buttoned his suit coat against a chill breeze, he realized it was the same one he had worn to the bridge the year before. With a laugh, he realized that at least a few things hadn't changed.

Turning onto Main Street just below the police station, George saw Bert pulling out in his cruiser. Retracing his steps a few yards, Bailey waved his friend to a stop. Officer Riley reached over and rolled the passenger window down smiling broadly.

George stuck his own smiling face in. "You have the look of a happy man on the way home early, Bert."

"One advantage of seniority. The missus called to say her sister—" The cop's smile waned "—and her gang just got in. That means we have a full house and they're cooking up a storm." He patted his generous tummy. "I guess I can put up with the brothers-in-law for a few days in trade for prime rib and Yorkshire pudding."

The officer glanced in his mirror, eying a car going a bit too fast for the slushy street. With a wave of his hand out the window, the driver slowed quickly. Satisfied, Riley turned back to George while he put the car in first. "Got to get goin'. Wish Mary and everyone a merry from the Riley clan." He pulled away, nearly taking his friend with him.

"Same to you." George threw a wasted wave at the rear of the cruiser still smiling. It was hard not to smile these days.

Once on Main, George passed the bank and hotel where Ernie Bishop's taxi sat. Seeing George, the cabby put his flag down and jumped out. The two men converged on the sidewalk. "Headin' home, George? I'll give you a free ride, an early Christmas present."

"Afraid not, Ernie," George said wishing he could take his friend up on the offer. "I promised Tilly and Eustace they could go home early to get ready for the party tonight. Say, Mr. Tightwad, why so generous all of a sudden?"

"Actually, I just dropped a mutual friend of ours at the train station." Ernie held up a ten-dollar bill. "He's a big tipper."

"Who has that kind of money to spare this time of year?" Bailey asked.

"You mean other than Henry Potter?" the cabbie asked ironically. "Actually, it was Mr. Jerome."

"Mr. Jerome!" George was shocked. "He's in town?"

Ernie glanced at his watch as they heard a train whistle. "Was."

"But I didn't even know—" George slid his hat up and scratched his head distractedly. "Well I'll be. How long was he here?"

The cabbie shrugged. "Have no idea. Picked him up here at the hotel this morning."

"I don't get it. First, he just disappeared at Thanksgiving without an explanation. I haven't heard anything from him since. Now you say he was here?"

"Sure enough." Ernie shivered in his thin leather jacket as a sudden burst of a cold wind invaded the afternoon's warmth.

"I'd like to hear more, but I need to get back." George moved off in the direction of the B&L then paused. "Say, if your offer of a ride extends to going home tonight, stop by early and you can fill me in on Jerome. Might be snowing by then."

Ernie opened the cab door and climbed in. "That's a deal. How about four thirty?"

"Any time after four. I'm sure it'll be just Billy and me there closing things up," George shouted over his shoulder as he crossed the street dodging traffic.

Racing up the stairs, George burst in, voicing an apology. "Sorry to keep you all waiting."

Eustace looked up from the cash drawer at the window and glanced to the clock. "Oh, didn't notice." His sly smile said something different.

"I was about to send out the cavalry," Tilly said less pleasantly. "But all's well that—"

The phone rang. Tilly answered. "Bailey Building and Loan, Merry Christmas. How may I— ... Oh, hello, Mary. Yes. George *finally* got back. George, it's Mary, her third call in the last hour."

George waved that he'd take it in his office. He rushed in and grabbed the receiver. "Hello, dear. Oh yes. Tilly and Eustace will be leaving soon. Billy and I will ... by five at the latest. The sign is already on the door, and Ernie's giving me a ride home." A worried look crossed his face. "Are you all right, Mary?" His expression changed to confusion. "Who? ... What for? ... That's curious. What does it say?" George noticed the time. "Look, Mary, it's getting late. Let's discuss this when I get home, okay? ... Good. See you shortly ... What? ... Oh yeah, the wreath. Don't worry. I'll get one. Goodbye."

As he hung up, there was a knock at the door. "Come in."

It was Uncle Billy. "Just wanted to tell you our friend the bank examiner got here while you were gone," he said with a confident smile. "He should be done soon."

"What? No missing money this year?" George asked wryly.

Billy laughed heartily. "Boy oh boy. What a difference a year makes."

"Indeed. Have him stop in before he leaves, will ya?"

"For sure. By the way, I was going to send Tilly and Eustace home now."

"Great. I'll be done clearing this mess soon. Then we can lock up if no customers show."

Billy nodded. "I'm for that. Already getting hungry. One interesting thing with the bank examiner though."

"What's that?"

"When I asked after Mr. Jerome, he didn't seem to know the man."

George looked surprised, but he shrugged. "Lots of folks at the bank examiner's office in Albany, different divisions too. That's probably all there is to it. Anyway, let me get back to this mess."

"Right." Billy closed the door, and George returned to the stacks before him.

The next time George looked at the clock, it read 4:05. He heard a soft rap on his office door. Ernie Bishop stuck his head in. "Anyone left here? I could have cleaned out the cash drawer and nobody would have known."

"Not really. Billy is counting it in his office. We haven't had a *real* customer since two," George replied waving his friend in. "I'm just a few minutes away from being done myself. Can you hang around?"

Ernie took off his wet jacket and hat. "No problem. I'm not ready to face a houseful of over-sugared kids just yet. Your chariot awaits. Oh, and the snow is really coming down now."

George glanced out the window. "Huh. I hadn't noticed. Well, take a seat and fill me in about Jerome's visit, and I know one place you took him. I talked to Mary briefly."

"Did she give you any details?" Ernie frowned at George's shake of his head. "Dang. I was hoping for more. All I did was drop the man off."

Settling into the chair, he rubbed his hands to warm them while describing his time with the elusive Mr. Jerome. He had been surprised to see the man on the street, not sure where he'd come from. The investigator had greeted him saying he was just the person he wanted to see. He had climbed in the back of the cab, and they were off.

The first stop was at the Potter estate. Ernie was prepared for a long wait, but within ten minutes, Jerome was back in the cab shaking his head. The cabbie had asked if Potter had treated him badly, but he said no. It was just sad to see the man alone on Christmas Eve with no plans.

Then they headed to Ma Bailey's, where he spent longer and came out with Christmas cookies for Ernie. Jerome seemed pleased with how the conversation had gone there. His smile dimmed when he said his next stop was to see Mary. Apparently, Jerome hadn't seen her since dropping the bombshell about George's past. He wondered how she'd taken it.

Then it was back to the train station. The entire time making the rounds, Jerome had engaged in mundane conversation but gave no clue regarding what he was about. When Ernie pressed him, he just smiled and said he was delivering messages of the season then changed the subject.

"I got him to the station with time to spare, and he paid the fare plus that more-than-generous tip." Ernie concluded his summary then got a queer look on his face. "Strange, but the last thing he said was congratulations on the new baby."

"Why was that strange?"

Ernie's expression remained confused. "'Cause I don't recall telling him about her."

"Hmm, interesting." George looked at the clock. "Say, time's a movin'. I better get this done." George began to sort through the last of the papers.

"While you're at that, I've been wondering how everyone is doing after the news. It seems like that was just yesterday, but it's been well over a month."

George didn't feel like answering just then. "I don't think there's time for all that now, and I still have to get a wreath for the front door."

"By that clock, we have time if you quit stalling and keep it short," Ernie said.

Seeing there was no putting the man off, George sighed and shoved the stack aside. "Okay, I'll just leave this for the moment and give you what you want in return for that free ride home. But you have to take Billy too."

Ernie laughed. "Gee, I don't know. He's such a troublesome sort. But since you *are* about to answer my question ... aren't you?"

With a nod, George proceeded with a brief update on the principal players. He had not seen Potter since the awkward dinner his mother had held when Harry and Ruth came. It seemed to George that Potter spent the whole night lobbying his brother. He apparently continued the effort during several meetings with Harry over his brief visit. Since the dinner, there had been no contact between the two major antagonists.

Being the analytical type, Harry more easily accepted the facts of his parentage. Since Harry hadn't had the same experiences with Potter over the years, his feelings were more ambivalent, less hostile. He and George spent hours in debate over the remainder of Harry's visit, George being obstinately rigid and Harry more malleable, about what the future might bring. They agreed to continue discussing the matter at Christmas.

Uncle Billy and Velma had been the easiest converts. After all, Billy's life changed overnight with Potter's editorial in the *Gazette*. He was a new man and was not shy about giving Potter a piece of the credit. And Ma Bailey felt great compassion for what the old man had been through mentally and physically. Neither could sway George, however.

Tilly and Eustace had a harder time. They were inclined toward forgiveness in light of Billy's transformation, but they also wanted to support George. They knew they would have little influence on their cousin, so they kept their opinions to themselves.

Then there was Mary, who had been in shock for days after he came home with the news. She was as skeptical of the claim as George was. After a long session with Velma, however, she accepted the reality. Then her attention turned to whether the revelation changed her feelings toward the old man. In support of George, her first reaction was no.

It took another couple of visits by Ma Bailey coupled with Potter's continued good deeds for her perspective to mellow. At that point, Mary began trying to convince George to accept the truth and move on but without success. She claimed his negative behavior was changing him and slowly driving a wedge between his friends, family, and wife.

"That's one opinion," George said. "I on the other hand think it a worthy effort working to ensure the man doesn't insinuate his way into my family's lives."

"You mean the lives of his daughter-in-law and grandchildren?" Ernie said ironically.

"Absolutely. Look, he's already got my uncle and mother on his side." George was growing a bit heated. "For God's sake, my brother might be next. I can't do anything about them, but my family's another story. I don't like how he's acting toward them, toward everybody."

"Oh, right, George, Potter ought to be careful behaving the way he is. Good deeds are a sure sign that his villainous ways continue."

George pointed a finger at his friend. "Not you too, Ernie. He even has you campaigning for him."

"I'm certainly not campaigning for him, I'm just trying to talk logic to the guy who used to be, well, the good guy. Now it's almost like the shoe is on the other foot."

"Meaning?"

"Meaning, with all the things Potter's done, from relinquishing positions of power to all the stuff he's given away, well, he's been behaving like you, the regular you," Ernie said with a weak smile.

"Do you really think I've become the bad guy in this?"

"I'm not good with words like you and Potter," Ernie said, "but I'm good at seeing what is. And where you're headed is not good. I'll leave it at that."

"Please do." George was glad to end the conversation. "Let's not ruin the holiday spirit." He glanced at the clock, which read 4:25. "I'll be ready in twenty minutes. Got it?"

"Got it," the cabbie said as he stood. He grabbed his coat and hat heading to the door. "I'll be waitin' out front." He turned back in the doorway. "I know I said I was leavin' it at that, but I just got to say it seems to me you're the only one still strugglin'. You should take a hint from the others and move on."

"By moving on, do you mean accepting Potter as my real father?"

"I'm just sayin' you're missin' a lot of good stuff while you're down in the pit you've dug for yourself. This Christmas Eve is very different from last year. It was a tough road to get here, but everything seems to be turning out pretty fine."

"Pretty fine is it?" Intensity returned to George's voice. "Is it fine that a man I despised, who nearly destroyed me and helped kill my *true* dad turned out to be my biological father? I don't think so." The passion left him as quickly as it had come.

Ernie grabbed the door handle. "You're right, George. I'm not in your shoes, so I should just keep my mouth shut. After all, I'm just your dumb old cab driver friend."

George cringed. "I'm sorry, Ernie. I'm taking out my frustration on you, and I apologize." He forced a smile. "Why don't you just head home? No need to wait for me. I'll walk. The fresh air might do me some good."

"You want Billy to walk too?" Ernie asked casually.

"Oh, right," George said sheepishly.

"And if you're going to get home by five, you'll need me."

Ernie moved out the door just as Uncle Billy and another man arrived on the other side. "See you two downstairs." Ernie patted Billy on the shoulder and was gone.

After exchanging holiday pleasantries, the bank examiner was off to Elmira as Billy shut the door. He turned with a concerned expression and several envelopes in his hand. "Is everything all right, George? You were getting kind a loud in here just now."

"Yeah yeah, just fine, Uncle Billy." His nephew's tone said otherwise. "'Bout time for us to get out of here." George redirected the conversation. "We're running short of time."

"I'm ready to go if you are. I hope what I heard didn't mean a new problem."

It was immediately clear to George that his uncle was thinking back to the previous year. It was no wonder the older man looked concerned. "No, Uncle Billy. Everything is fine this Christmas Eve. You and I know that we've never been in better financial shape."

"That's what I thought." A look of relief crossed Billy's face. "But what were you yellin' at Ernie about?"

George suddenly realized the absurdity of his outburst. He forced a smile. "It was nothing really."

"Didn't sound like nothin' to me."

George changed the subject. "It looks like you got something there I need to see. Can it wait?" He glanced out the window. "The snow is really coming down."

Billy stepped further into George's office and handed over the envelopes. "There's one you might want to read now, and the others are a bit of a mystery."

"Mystery? Let me see." George glanced at the envelopes. "These are the letters I sent to Mr. Jerome at the bank examiner's office in Albany. They're all returned unopened?"

"Yup."

George looked at each more closely. "They're all marked addressee unknown?"

"A mystery."

George was incredulous. "How can that be? Did we, I, have the wrong address?"

"I thought the same thing." Billy's eyes flicked nervously from George to the clock. "So I called Albany and talked to several people there who confirmed the address was correct. But no one I talked to had ever heard of a Mr. Jerome."

George gazed at his uncle. "What?"

"No one. I was transferred from office to office finally ending up with the head of personnel." George listened with his mouth agape. "That gentleman confirmed what everyone else had said and told me to stop badgering the staff."

"Well if that don't beat all." George placed the envelopes on his desk. "It truly is a mystery."

"If you think that's mysterious, check the one addressed to you," Billy said. "But make it fast, George. It's almost five."

George looked over the face of the letter, the addressee first:

Mr. George P. Bailey
President and CEO
The Bailey Building and Loan
1934B Main Street
Bedford Falls, New York

Then he looked for the return address. He found the handwritten name Mark Jerome but nothing else. "There's no return address, just Jerome's name."

Billy nodded. "I noticed that right off. No stamp or postmark either."

His nephew looked down at the front of the letter then turned it over. "Right."

"But I'm sure it came in with the rest of the mail. We had a lot today. I was at the counter when the postman came in complaining about the load. I went through it once and didn't find that letter the first time through. But back at my desk, there it was sticking out of the stack like it was calling to me."

"Could Mr. Jerome have dropped it off personally?"

"Jerome was in town today?" It was Billy's turn to be surprised.

George nodded. "Apparently so. I didn't see him, but Ernie and some others did."

"Well even if he was, there was no way he got past us. The three of us were here all day, even ate lunch in so we could close early."

George pondered that for a minute. "But somehow Jerome got it in the post." A thought struck him. "What time did the mail come?"

"At the usual time, one on the dot. We're the first stop on the postman's route."

"I just wonder what with all that holiday mail they might have been running late." While George was speaking, the sound of a horn came from below. He was shocked into action by the sound as well as the clock, which read five. He jumped up, putting the unopened letter from Jerome on the desk. Leaving his coat on the hook near the door, he headed out of his office.

"Hey, aren't you going to take the letter? What about your coat?" Billy shouted after his nephew, who rushed by him.

"I'm not leaving just yet. I have to ask Ernie something." In an instant, George was out the double doors, leaving his uncle in confusion.

Nearly as quickly, George was back covered in a light layer of fresh snow. Billy didn't understand what had just happened. "What'd ya ask Ernie?"

"I asked him when he picked Jerome up today and if they'd gone by the post office."

"And?"

"They connected about eleven, and Ernie dropped him at the station at one forty-five. They never went near the post office."

His uncle scratched his head, thinking hard without results. "I don't get it. How did the letter get here without postage or a postmark?"

"A very good question. Maybe the letter will give us a clue. But first ..."

Pulling open his desk drawer, George rummaged around before emerging with a business card.

"What's that?"

"The business card Jerome gave me the first day he arrived." He handed it to Billy. "Does that look like the same number you just called?"

"Can't say. I'll check." As he rose to leave, George continued. "If it isn't, call the number and see if anyone answers."

With a nod, Billy headed to his office. Meanwhile, George pulled Jerome's letter from his pocket just as the phone rang. He picked up his extension knowing who it had to be. "Hello Mary. Yes, I see the time. But a kind of an emergency came up. It relates to what we talked about earlier ... Yes, Jerome. Look, Ernie's cab is waiting, so I'm on my way."

George hung up and began to tear the letter open carelessly. When it finally came free, he was suddenly hesitant to read it. Why that was, he wasn't sure.

As he stared at the letter, Billy came back. "There was no answer. Well, that's not exactly true. I tried more than once and each time got a different message from a machine."

"A machine?" George said in disbelief.

"It must have been. The voice wouldn't respond to me." Billy saw his nephew's confused look. "Some places have what they call answering machines now. Maybe Jerome's office is equipped with one. I tried the number three times."

The doubtful look remained on George's face. "So what did this machine say?"

"You call and hear for yourself."

"Read me the number." Billy did. George dialed. The line rang three times before being answered by a stilted voice: "Your party can no longer be reached in this manner." The line went dead. George looked to his uncle. "Strange. A voice said Jerome could no longer be reached in this manner, not at this number."

Billy nodded.

George dialed again. After three rings, the line was answered again: "This line no longer can connect with your party."

George slammed the receiver down, picked it up, and dialed a third time. That time, it didn't ring. There was no busy signal. It was dead. He slowly hung up.

"Incredible," George said as his uncle nodded.

"But how do you explain that after me getting two messages and then the line went dead on my third try you called and got through?" Billy asked uneasily.

"A good question." George fell silent as the two men stared at each other.

George grabbed the letter from Jerome and swept up his coat. "This is too weird, Uncle Billy."

George pushed his uncle out his office door. "This kind of stuff on Christmas Eve is getting a little too habit forming for my liking. Grab your coat. We're out of here."

CHAPTER 28

"You can sure stretch a man's generosity," Ernie said with a grin as the two men dove into the backseat. "This is a free ride home, remember? And we're all late."

George hardly listened as he turned on the cab's tiny dome light. "Huh? Oh, sorry, Ernie. Something else came up."

"I know that experience. In fact, it's going to take longer to get you home because—"

George's head jerked up. "What?"

Ernie looked distressed. "I was trying to say that while you kept me waiting, I called Trixie. She said I needed to stop by Gower's for some medicine for my oldest."

George's concern shifted to Ernie. "What happened? Is it serious?"

"If you call a six-year-old eating too many sweets at the school Christmas party an emergency, then yes. I'll just grab some bicarbonate. You'll be home in no time."

"That better be right or I'll have to haul you up to my front door to explain the delay to Mary. And you don't want to face that, do you?"

"Are you threatening me?" Ernie asked with a smile as he slid into the near empty street. "For that, I shouldn't remind you about getting that Christmas wreath."

"Oh, great! Thanks, Ernie." George dug in his pocket and pulled out a few dollars. "Uncle Billy, when Ernie stops at Gower's, jump out and buy a door wreath while I read this."

"Okay, George," Billy replied. "Any particular one?"

"One that amount will cover, that's all. Now let me concentrate. This light is abysmal."

Ernie slowly covered the two blocks to Gower's through half a foot of snow. The cab slid to a stop under the streetlight in front of the drugstore. Ernie and Billy quickly exited the cab, leaving George to read in silence.

Dear George,

I am sorry for leaving you so often without explanation. Part of the reason was time spent visiting with the many people who contributed to my successful efforts along the way. Unlike you, some had fond memories of a young Henry Potter and his wife. Others had interest in finding out about lost loved ones. Still others had a burning need to know the solution to the mystery. To fill them all required a great deal of correspondence and a significant amount of travel.

I prayed my intentional absence from Bedford Falls would allow time for all to accept, reflect, and heal. Of course, that is an ongoing process taking much time if it happens at all. The goal was for that healing to get a good start. So I chose to first communicate with others who had an interest in the outcome.

With that now behind me, I feel it is time to come clean, give you a full explanation starting from the first day we met and ending with this letter. I will explain a few last things that may help you understand all that has happened.

I chose not to be totally honest with you at our first meeting regarding why I had come to Bedford Falls. The unsolved mystery of the money was an excuse for my presence and secondary to my true purpose. That was part of the plan, but the twist and turns that followed were often as surprising to me as they were to you.

Back on December 24, 1945, someone helped you

to see things more clearly. From your perspective at that moment, there was nothing left to be resolved. Of course, that didn't prove to be the case. Unfortunately, you were left with the mistaken belief that your experience was the end of something. In fact, it was the prologue to what was to come. That was when I entered the picture.

I arrived as a rookie who happened to have skills that seemed well suited for the assignment. It wasn't long, however, before my bosses and mentor began to feel I was doing my best to prove their confidence in me was wrong.

The front and back doors of the cab flew open simultaneously as Ernie and Billy climbed back in, snow covered and breathing heavily. "I got the medicine." Ernie held up a bag.

"And here's the wreath, George," Billy said displaying a snow-fringed evergreen.

Ernie started the cab and slid the car into gear. "Then let's get you two home."

"Wait!" George shouted as he opened to car door. "I'll be back shortly."

"But George!" Ernie yelled as George disappeared into the pharmacy.

Seeing Mr. Gower through the back pharmacy window, George headed his way. Passing through the familiar curtain, he approached his friend. "Mr. Gower, could I steal a little privacy back here before I head home?"

"We were due to close a few minutes ago, George, but go ahead." Mr. Gower moved toward the main part of the store. "I'll just finish closing up."

"Thanks, friend," George said as he sat down in the old stuffed chair Gower used. He quickly found his place and continued with Jerome's letter.

Thankfully, the powers that be stuck with me, and I muddled through at least with the detective part. Then the hard work began. Finding a strategy to deal with Henry Potter and a recalcitrant fellow named George

Bailey was new and difficult territory for me. Both are still works in progress it would seem.

Thanks to my second chance and the success it brought, I was promoted. That made new resources available to me. With help from an old friend of yours, I used these tools to keep an eye on Bedford Falls from afar. I've been pleased to see many accepting the profound revelations of a short time ago.

That brings me to this letter delivered via one of the new tools at my disposal. I'm writing because though many are on the verge of breaking free from the burdens of the past, things have stalled. And you are to blame for that. You see everyone is waiting for you to join him or her in taking the plunge. They need you to give your blessing through word and deed to take the next step.

I want to remind you that everyone's life has twists and turns, decisions, and choices. No one can know for sure whether his or her life ended better or worse because of one event or decision. All anyone can say with certainty is that his or her life was different because of those events and especially the choices made.

What's important now is how you live tomorrow. You are already blessed but have a chance for new blessing in unexpected ways. Peter Bailey cannot be replaced, but he's gone. Now, you've been given a new gift. Henry Potter may not seem like a gift, but trust me, there is much good that could be exchanged if given the chance. And there are few things more tragic than a wasted gift.

I came back to Bedford Falls today to personally deliver three letters—to Velma, Mary, and Henry. I did not deliver yours in person, choosing a bit more dramatic method hoping to ensure you recognize the ultimate source of this message. Then when you share it with Mary, you can explain and she'll believe.

I have our mutual friend to thank for the idea. Clever, hey?

I expect by the time you read this, I will know where the other three stand on their own incredible journeys. I already know they are doing much better than you. Listen to them if you can, George.

The choice is yours, and you have free will to make it. I pray that you don't wait too long. I urge you to stop being stuck in the past. I implore you to again live the wonderful life that is your present and start building an even brighter future this very night.

I'll close by loosely paraphrasing what our mutual friend once said: Remember, no man is a failure who has friends and family.

Blessings,
Mark Jerome

Trying to make up for lost time, Ernie swerved carelessly off Elm and onto Sycamore. As a result, his passengers slid across the seat and into the passenger side door. Thankfully, it held. Billy's protest was met by a dismissive wave from their driver and a wobble from the cab still seeking traction on the snow. In response, the older man offered a short prayer for deliverance.

Through all this, George was oblivious. He now stared at the letter unreadable in the dark and bouncy vehicle, but still vivid in his mind. He folded it purposefully and placed it in his pocket. As he mumbled something to himself, 320 Sycamore came into view.

"What's that ya say, George?" Ernie managed as he just missed the Waverings' old Plymouth parked haphazardly on the snow-clogged street.

"Huh? Oh, I was just remembering what an old friend of mine told me once, actually about this time last year." A wistful smile spread across George's face.

Before he could ask for more information, Ernie reached George's house, managing a gentle stop in the middle of the snow-covered street.

Vehicles lined both sides, signaling that everyone had already arrived for the party. As George and Billy exited the cab, they heard happy voices from inside. The event was off to a lively start.

"If this snow keeps up, Santa's gonna have a hard time getting around tonight," said the cabbie through the open back door. "Now get in there and start celebratin'. Merry Christmas!"

George stepped back as the cab moved off. Billy yelled a reply and waved while George remained preoccupied. Through the swirling snow, the two men made their way gingerly between parked cars and up to the gate. Swinging it wide for his uncle, who carried the wreath, George followed him up to the door.

They burst in to find a warm room and a cold wife. Mary's dark stare contrasted dramatically with the bright and noisy atmosphere. Knowing what was good for him, Billy handed the wreath to George, gave Mary a quick hug and greeting, then escaped to the kitchen.

George delivered the wreath with an awkward smile, which did nothing to change his wife's mood. "I'm so sorry, Mary, but I have a very good reason. You see ... ahh, wait. Let me get this on the door before more guests arrive." He opened it to a rush of snow and found the year-round hook while Mary chastised him.

"Since you and Billy are the *last* to arrive, I guess the wreath will have to last until next Christmas Eve." Her voice matched the severity of her look.

The wreath in place, George shut the door against the cold and replied still smiling. "Perhaps Santa will enjoy it later tonight. Besides, next year, we won't be hosting."

"That is truly a lame effort to win me over."

"But Mary, you need to ... we have to talk ... you see, Jerome ..."

Mary struggled not to laugh as he twisted in the wind. "Yes, I know. We need to talk about Jerome but not now. We have guests."

"No, no! They can wait!"

Mary's eyes narrowed. "Wait? They've been waiting for you for nearly an hour."

"But Mary, I need you to read Jerome's letter to me." Her husband groped in his topcoat pocket pulling out the neatly folded pages.

"You got one too? Did you see him?" Mary's focus had changed from concern for her guests to what George held. "If it's anything like mine, it has to be a doozy."

After failing to find a space for his coat on the overflowing rack, he dropped it on the floor. "No I didn't, but Mary, oh Mary, wait till you find out who Jerome really was."

"Really was? I don't understand."

He handed her the letter. "Read this, then you will."

Mary shook her head. "First, go in and greet everyone, especially your children, who are about to burst with excitement. Even Pete is caught up in it. I guess he's not too old to still believe."

"Ahh, but Mary," George pleaded.

She remained resolute. "In the kitchen George Bailey." As they entered the dining room, Mary stopped him. "By the way, did you know your mother got a visit and a letter too?"

"Yup, and Henry Potter as well. That's all explained in my letter. You sure you don't want to look at this first?"

After a moment's hesitation, Mary grabbed the letter and shoved it into her apron pocket. "No. We'll make the rounds then sneak away. Five minutes max. Now go."

As the two started to enter the kitchen, a crowd came streaming out like a herd of circus clowns exiting a tiny car. Everyone joyously greeted George then scattered throughout the first floor. Loud conversations drowned out the Christmas carols on the radio. The children scurrying about the tree hooting and hollering completed the chaotic scene.

Ten minutes, many hugs, and several brief conversations later, George and Mary made their first attempt to escape. As they reached the stairs, Velma grabbed them. She wanted to talk about her letter and visit from Jerome. They agreed to do that after dinner then left her. Once upstairs with the door shut, they exchanged letters.

Mary's letter was short and sweet. The words made George more thankful than ever that she was his wife. He read her letter a second time while Mary worked her way through the three packed pages of his. They exchanged letters and read their own again.

The reading was both exhilarating and exhausting. At last, they looked at each other searching for words but found none. They sat on the edge of the bed in silence watching the snow come down. A roar of laughter from downstairs brought them out of their reflections.

Shaking her head, Mary glanced at the long letter in her hand. "First, there was that Clarence fellow you told me about last year. Now there's Jerome."

"Do you believe in Clarence now?" George asked sliding his free hand over to squeeze hers.

She looked dazed. "I would have to be a bit crazy if I said yes."

"I guess that means I'm already crazy," he said, smiling broadly.

"You've had more experience with crazy, unbelievable things. I need to think on it some more." She touched his face. "It's nice to see you smiling again, George." Then she kissed his cheek.

"What was that for?"

"For all you've been through this past year and still being pretty much the wonderful man I married." She kissed him again, this time on the lips.

"Pretty much?"

"As Jerome said, you're still struggling." Mary nodded to the letter she held. "By the way, what did you think of what Jerome had to say?"

"In your letter or mine?"

"Let's stick with yours for now." Mary placed hers on the nightstand. "It certainly gives one a lot to think about."

"I had to rush through it the first time. These two additional reads helped. Still, I haven't had much time to think about what I think."

"I can certainly understand that. So do you want to leave it at that for tonight?" Mary eased George's letter out of his hand as if giving him permission. When he didn't resist, she turned and placed it with hers on the nightstand.

George's shoulder rose and settled before he started to answer. "I guess that might be a good idea, but ..."

"But what? Come on, George, out with it."

"I just had an idea but not a very good one." He moved to the window. Flickering shadows from the heavy snow illuminated by the streetlight played across his face.

Mary spoke from the darkness behind him. "Tell you what, George. Don't think about it. Just get it out. What are you thinking?"

George hesitated. He shook his head and mumbled something.

"What, George?"

He remained silent then started to smile. His smile became a laugh. Though she had no clue what was going on in his head, Mary soon found herself smiling too. "I give up, George. What's so funny?"

"More freeing than funny." George moved quickly to the bed and grabbed Mary's hand. "Follow me."

Caught off guard, Mary stumbled out the door behind her fast-moving husband. "Where are we going?" she asked as they bounded down the stairs.

They reached the bottom tread, knocking the infamous newel ball across the entryway. This commotion halted all conversation. Tommy and Zuzu raced after the wooden sphere as George headed for the coat rack.

As he searched through the coats, he spoke to his mother. "Ma, I need you and Ruth to hold dinner for say another hour, please. There ought to be plenty of hors d'oeuvres and drinks to tide everyone over, except maybe Uncle Billy."

While everyone else laughed at his comment, Velma asked incredulously, "But why?"

He found Mary's coat and scarf and tossed them her way, then replied while picking his own coat up off the floor, "You'll see, I hope." He winked at his mother. "Where's Harry?" He looked around frantically. "Anyone seen Harry?"

"He went upstairs to put little Mary down," Ruth said, a quizzical look on her face. It was the same look everyone in the room had.

"Never mind him. Where are your car keys?" This question only added to his sister-in-law's bewilderment. After a brief pause, however, she pointed to the mass of coats on the rack. "They should be in his coat, the black one there. That one at the top of that mess."

After a quick search, George emerged triumphantly with the shiny new keys. "Ta-da! Ruth, tell him thanks and I'll take good care of it. We'll be back within the hour. I'll fill him in then." Turning back to Mary, he frowned. "Come on dear, get a move on."

"But George, you're not suggesting we go out in this storm. And where *are* we going?" Though Mary's voice sounded upset, she looked excited as she eagerly put on her coat and hat.

With an assured smile and confident air, George reached for the front door. "I'll explain in the car, Mary. If we don't go now, it might never happen, and this needs to happen."

"What needs to happen, George? Where are we going?"

Flinging open the door, George waved his wife out into the storm. "For a short ride to end a long journey. With luck, we'll be starting a new adventure. Are you game?"

EPILOGUE

The headstones in the graveyard stood stark against a steel-gray sky. The leafless trees rattled in a strong, chilly north wind that promised snow. The view reminded George of earlier Christmas Eves when such skies had been the portent of incredible things to come, events that ultimately led him to where he stood that day.

Small groups of mourners made haste to the gravel parking lot, weaving through the ancient stones as they pulled their collars tighter against the growing cold. Many had already left for the wake or headed to the warmth of their homes, wishing to beat the coming darkness and the approaching storm.

The young Bailey clan, however, lingered at the graveside. As he watched, George could hardly believe Pete, now taller than he, was a college man. Janie, the spitting image of Mary and just as smart, was also home from college. Zuzu, Bedford Falls High School's homecoming queen, and Tommy, the quarterback, still kept their home lively but would be gone all too soon as well.

The four gazed at the fresh earth and talked softly. George wished he could hear what they were saying. He was pretty sure each had a different perspective on the Henry Potter who had entered their lives in such a big way ten years earlier. Zuzu and Tommy had come to call him Grandpa. Pete and Janie, being older and having some bad memories of the man, never got beyond calling him Henry.

A strong gust of wind brought their conversation to an end. The four turned and, seeing George at the gate, waved. Linking arms, they made their way slowly toward him, seemingly oblivious to the cold. At the same time, Mary appeared at George's side.

Becoming aware of her presence, George spoke loudly into the growing wind. "This certainly closes a major chapter in my—our lives. Who would have thought Henry Potter with all his afflictions would be the last of his generation to go? And look at the timing. It's ironic how often important events have happened around Christmas Eve." As he finished, George turned Mary toward the car idling nearby.

Mary frowned. "That's stretching things, don't you think? The last funeral in December was Uncle Billy five years ago. Velma's was in late summer, and"—she paused as he opened the passenger door—"what else would you classify as important events?"

"Give me a chance to think. I'll come up with more," George said and closed the door. He moved around to the driver's side door and got in.

"Well?" Mary asked impatiently as he settled on the seat.

George sighed. "Never mind, dear. I guess I was just consumed by my emotions."

"I'll agree a lot of important things have happened over the last decade, some even in December." Mary attempted a compromise. "And the two most incredible events happened on Christmas Eves. But collectively, George, I believe everything else fell in the broad category called life and death."

George sighed again, still feeling weighed down by his thoughts. "You're right as usual, Mary." His gloominess became a weak chuckle. "It's just that when I see weather like this, I can't help but look around expecting one of *them* to show up."

Mary smiled. "I think those visits are reserved for real problems, not life's realities. Since we saw them last, we've been truly blessed even with the losses. And we got to watch Henry leave this world a happy, generous, and respected citizen and grandfather."

"Father too," George said, suddenly realizing how much he meant the word. "Say, maybe those two sent this weather as a reminder of what you just said so eloquently, Mary. We have been truly blessed." George looked skyward and raised his voice. "Okay, guys. I get it. You can stop with the blizzards already." The comment had them laughing.

Just then, the back door opened and their sons and daughters climbed in noisily. Pete spoke for his siblings. "Who you yelling at, Pops?"

"Oh? Was I yelling?" George feigned ignorance. "I was just complaining about the weather."

"You're good at that," Zuzu said and blew on her hands. "But it does look ominous out there."

Tommy changed to his favorite subject. "So we better get to the estate for the wake."

"You mean for the food," Pete corrected, giving his younger brother a poke.

"We're all hungry," Tommy and Zuzu protested in unison.

"Nothing like a funeral to build an—" Realizing what he was saying, Tommy stopped then and put his hands on his parents' shoulders. "Sorry, Mom, Dad."

"Apology accepted," George said without turning.

Mary leaned toward her husband. "It's okay to feel badly."

"I know, but my feelings go beyond a funeral." George struggled for words. "I knew Henry Potter practically all my life. Most of those memories were bad. When Dad died, I took over battling him every day, and it was ugly. Then one day, I awoke to find he's my biological father. Even now, I struggle with that undeniable and unbelievable truth."

Mary turned to him. "I thought you started getting past that on the Christmas Eve we went out in that raging storm and brought him back for dinner."

George nodded. "And the last ten years with him in my life have been very good."

Janie spoke up from the backseat. "That's kind of what we were talking about at the grave just a few minutes ago."

"He was sure a wonderful grandfather to us," Zuzu said, and Tommy grunted his agreement.

Pete put in his two cents. "I can remember the bad, but, ah, well, he was sure good to us and the town in the end."

George remained conflicted. "All true, but I guess I've continued to carry around those old wounds and resentment for the man without realizing it."

"Oh, George," Mary said sadly. "That must be a heavy burden."

He turned to her, frowning. "It is."

"Then perhaps it's the time to lay it down," Mary said with a soft smile.

There was a long silence in the car as everyone thought of something to say but said nothing. With a nod, George opened the car door. "I might as well give it a try. I'll be back soon, I hope." He shut the door and headed back to the graveyard.

Mary and the children watched him head to Henry's grave. The fresh earth was already coated with snow and beginning to freeze. He stood there with hat in hand. Mary told the children to stay warm in the car and headed out to join her husband.

Stopping on a knoll, Mary was shielded from the wind by an oak tree some ten yards from the gravesite. For a long time, she watched George motionless, head bowed, his coat whipping around in a near gale. Snow had already covered his shoulders before George realized the growing intensity of the storm.

Covering the short distance to his side, Mary stepped in front of him. "Any luck?"

"Maybe. At least it feels like a start." He sighed and wrapped his arms around her. "If you'd told me ten years ago I'd be standing here today sorting through all these emotions in the middle of a blizzard, I'd have called you crazy."

"Do you want some more alone time?" Mary broke away to emphasize her willingness.

"No, I'm ready to go." But he made no attempt to move. "You know, every time something major happens in our lives now, I find myself going back to one paragraph in my letter from Mark Jerome."

"Which one?" Mary asked as she looped her arm though his and drew him closer.

George looked skyward briefly and then into Mary's loving eyes. "The one that said something like, you can't know with certainty if one event or decision will cause a life to be better or worse. The only certainty is that life will be different."

"Like if you and Henry had never learned the truth, we wouldn't be here right now?"

"Good analogy," George said beginning to feel lighter. "This time, however, I also recalled something implied in the letter that I'd lost sight of. Each change, each ending, is a new beginning, and we all have the choice of where that new beginning will take us.

"I believe my dad—Peter Bailey, that is—understood that lesson early on and gave in great measure his whole life making the best of each change and challenge to create good. What I accepted just now is that Henry, my father, learned this lesson late but gave back much during the time he had left in return for the new beginning he was granted."

Stepping off with Mary toward the car, George continued. "So I was just giving an 'attaboy' to the old man, to Henry F. Potter, to my father." He paused and smiled at Mary. "And let him know that at last he had truly become the richest man in town."

As they walked down the gentle slope, the wind grew even more intense and the snow began to blow in earnest. The feeling was exhilarating to George, who laughed out loud. At Mary's curious look, he explained himself. "If I didn't know better, I'd say we were getting a familiar message from our friends on high."

Mary stopped. "You mean from Clarence and Mark?"

George nodded.

"Okay, I'll bite. What familiar message?"

"The one about Christmas Eve plus a big event equaling the need for a blizzard heralding angelic works to come."

Mary laughed as she jerked him through the cemetery gate.

"Seriously, Mary. Can't you just feel there's an angel out there somewhere ready to help someone write a new beginning to their life?" He grabbed Mary and gave her a playful kiss, which brought jeers from the car.

Ignoring the children, George suddenly felt giddy. "And if that earthly soul has our luck in guardian angels, they're about to meet a bumbling, well-intended, tenacious rookie on their first assignment."

"Any advice for them, George?" Mary asked.

"Patience and faith—that's all. Patience and faith."

ABOUT THE AUTHOR

G. L. Gooding's corporate career and family life restricted his creative-writing side to unpublished works and accumulated ideas. With retirement, however, came one of those ideas that has become his first novel, *Fresh Snow on Bedford Falls,* a tribute to Frank Capra's epic *It's a Wonderful life.* He and wife, Sarah, live in Santa Rosa, California.